SCREAMING
IN THE
NIGHT

THE SINISTER SUPERNATURAL SERIES VOLUME I

SCREAMING
IN THE
NIGHT

THE SINISTER SUPERNATURAL SERIES VOLUME 1

PRESENTED BY SINISTER SMILE PRESS

Screaming In The Night
The Sinister Supernatural Series Volume 1

Presented by Sinister Smile Press
Edited by R.E. Sargent & Steven Pajak

Published by Sinister Smile Press, LLC
P.O. Box 637
Newberg, OR 97132

Trade Hardcover ISBN – 978-1-953112-23-1

www.sinistersmilepress.com

"The oldest and strongest emotion of mankind is fear, and the oldest and strongest kind of fear is fear of the unknown."

-H.P. Lovecraft

FOREWORD

William Malmborg

ONE NIGHT SIX YEARS AGO, I let out a scream. It wasn't a playful "oh my god, you got me good" scream, but a horrifying "oh my god, I'm about to die" scream. I was in the kitchen at the time, getting a bowl of Frosted Flakes. It was around midnight. Both cats were sleeping, longwise, across my bed, so I had every reason to assume I was all alone while downstairs in the dimly lit room, bowl of freshly poured cereal in hand...

They say that everyone laughs in the same language. The same is true of screaming. One doesn't need a translation to understand the sound coming out of a person's mouth when they scream. It's built into our DNA, something that likely dates back to the days when our ancestors climbed out of the primordial ooze (or if you are a History Channel fan, something our alien overlords programed into us when upgrading our basic design).

I've heard quite a few screams during my lifetime, but two specific ones will always come to the forefront of my mind when thinking about such things.

The first still puzzles me. My family was at a restaurant eating breakfast when a young lady at the table next to us let out the most chilling, bloodcurdling scream anyone could ever make. This thing was so intense that a few people actually fell out of their chairs. Others knocked plates to the floor. Juices were spilled, coffee was splashed, bacon thrown...all because the young lady saw a friend who she hadn't seen in a while.

Um...

Now, if that friend had been a serial killer holding a bloody kitchen knife, then maybe I could understand the scream, but that was not the case. This simply was two people who hadn't seen each other in a while, one of whom decided to scream at the top of her lungs while the other stood in total shock.

The second scream was—in my not-so-humble opinion—far more warranted. It occurred during my high school gymnastics days. A fellow gymnast was learning how to do a double backflip with a twist. He was in a spotting belt for this, but when one is attempting acts that seem to spit in the face of gravity, things still have the potential to go wrong. In this case, that "wrong" involved landing before his body had finished rotating, which meant that while his legs seemed to plant themselves firmly upon the padded surface, his kneecaps didn't.

I still get chills thinking about the gut-wrenching scream that echoed from his lungs moments before he went unconscious. The sight of his backwards-looking legs also imprinted themselves upon my mind.

Of course, hearing a scream and being the one that is screaming are two different things. When hearing a scream, one potentially has the chance to take action (run away from it, run toward it, pull out a phone to capture a video for social media fame). When making a scream...not so much. Sure, one might still be able to make a move or two while in the midst of screaming, but chances are those moves won't amount to much.

For me, while in the kitchen, that move involved throwing my freshly poured bowl of Frosted Flakes straight up into the air, an act that was not all that different than one my grandmother apparently made with a bag of popcorn when she saw *Jaws* for the first time. One big difference: my grandmother was in a safe theater environment where screams were expected; I was in my—supposedly—empty kitchen.

Then again, maybe screams of terror should be expected within the various rooms of my house given the age and creepiness of the place. I mean, okay, all old houses are a bit creepy, but not all old houses have a history like mine.

Deaths have occurred within these walls.

Horrible deaths.

Or so I've been told.

The first mention of these deaths was from a complete stranger who randomly walked up to me one summer day while I was cutting the grass and casually started talking about the poor children that burned to death up on the second floor several decades earlier.

Wait? What?

Burned to death?

I don't remember hearing anything about that when purchasing the house!

Not much more was said about it, the guy simply snapping a few pictures of the house and walking away. A search of various newspaper stories about the house and neighborhood also yielded nothing.

Maybe he had the wrong house...

I was on the path toward this simple conclusion when a few weeks later, a pizza delivery guy decided to mention that he doesn't like bringing pizzas to my house, because of all the strange deaths that have unfolded within.

Whoa! Whoa! Whoa!

Again with the deaths?

What's next? Is someone going to tell me the house is built atop an ancient burial...

Oh no...

That "someone" turned out to be the history page on the city's official website. It doesn't specially say ancient burial ground, but it does mention how this particular area west of the river was sacred land that was taken during the Blackhawk Wars.

Sacred land, horrible deaths, an odd room in the old coal cellar with stains on the floor...a room that can be padlocked from the outside...

If I had actually been trying to find a potentially haunted house to live in, I probably would have been hard-pressed to find such a perfect combination of haunted house cliches, and yet I somehow did it without even thinking about it.

So yeah, screams of terror should probably be expected to occur within the various rooms of this house, and honestly, I should have been prepared for something like a voice speaking to me without warning in the middle of the night, but I wasn't, which is why a bowl of Frosted Flakes ended up all over the ceiling, walls, and floor. And as for that voice that spoke to me that night...why in the world would someone install smoke alarms that literally say "low battery" in a sultry female voice when needing to be changed out?

Many bloodcurdling screams echo in the stories that follow, and while I hold firm that a sultry female voice speaking from a smoke alarm in the middle of the night is by far the scariest event to ever befall a person in all of human history, the terrors and screams that unfold within these stories will be sure to give you quite a few chills. Maybe even a sleepless night or two. And if this is the case, and if you find yourself down in a dimly lit kitchen getting a bowl of Frosted Flakes, I wish you luck, for one never knows what might be waiting within the shadows.

And now if you'll excuse me, I'm going to, once again, try to tackle all those odd stains that mark the floor of the old coal room in the cellar. Wish me luck.

SALLY UNDER THE BED

Nick Roberts

T ASHA BROWN HAD NOTHING, AND she knew it. The pressure
of contributing a monthly—sometimes weekly—article to her online
publisher was as terrifying at times as it was motivating. She normally thrived
on deadlines. With years of experience cranking out quality work during
crunch time, she learned how to trust her instincts and produce like the professional she was.

Not this time, however. This time, the white page on her computer
screen seemed determined to stay blank, taunting her with every wink of the
cursor.

She specialized in darkness. Any "true" supernatural story was fair game,
though she tended to stay away from legends that had been reported to death:
mainstreamers like Bigfoot, Area 51, Chupacabra, etc. Her investigative nose
was drawn more toward the obscure. After her husband and daughter would
go to sleep, she would put on a pot of coffee and scour the infinite recesses of
the internet, reading one ghoulish tale after another, each more disturbing
than the last.

The first story she sold nearly twenty years ago (back when the sales of
physical publications began their downward trajectory) was to a local quar-
terly magazine called *The West Virginia Review*. They were running a contest
for new insights into known Appalachian cryptids. At first, she thought about

researching the Mothman of Point Pleasant, or the Braxton County Monster, but figured everyone would try to cover one of those. She even briefly considered Bat Boy from the glory days of the *Weekly World News* tabloid, knowing full well that it was a completely fabricated story.

Ultimately, she landed on the "Hill People" of West Virginia—the supposed inspiration for the then-newly released film *Wrong Turn*, which depicted a group of stranded teens getting picked off by a family of inbred cannibals residing in the Appalachian hills. This portrayal of West Virginia hillbillies was not well received by the locals, so Tasha knew she was writing an uphill battle. It was her skillful approach of addressing the stereotype from the movie, as well as tracing the film's true inspiration back to the sixteenth-century account of the Sawney Bean clan of Scotland, that won her the cash prize and publication, and her momentum never slowed.

All that meant dogshit right now. She had four days to produce a two thousand–word profile of a relatively unknown "true" account of some spooky occurrence, and she had nothing. There was always the option of going on scary story websites and trying to track down anything that claimed to be based in reality, but that was the easy way out. She prided herself on discovering something new to bring to the world.

After sitting in her office/basement scrolling through decades' worth of old, digitized newspaper articles while her family slept peacefully upstairs, she was tempted to call it quits for the night. She let her eyes drift away from the screen and land on the 5" x 7" picture of her mother and father on the corner of her desk. They were in their early thirties, smiling, and had their arms wrapped around each other. Her mom had since passed from breast cancer at age sixty, and her father had a fatal heart attack not more than a year after. Tasha realized that she was around the same age now that they had been in that happy moment.

"Help me out here, guys," she said to the framed photo. Her parents' fixed faces only smiled back. "Got any paranormal encounters you want to tell me about?"

She let out a deep sigh and rubbed her temples. The clock on her computer read 2:32 a.m. She looked at the empty coffee cup and was beginning to accept defeat when a long-forgotten memory surfaced. It was her mother, young, like she was in the picture, reading a newspaper while Tasha ate breakfast at the kitchen table in their old home in Mingo County.

Her father walked in, and her mom showed him something in the paper.

His eyes widened, and he took the newspaper into the living room with her in tow. Tasha listened as they too loudly discussed the article about a local man shooting himself.

She remembered bits of what they said. Stuff about how the man's daughter had disappeared long ago, and he never got over it—how the mystery drove him insane. But the one thing they said that stood out was a chilling phrase.

"Sally under the bed," she muttered to the empty room.

Her heart beat faster. She grabbed the wireless mouse and clicked the search bar on the screen. She typed in "Sally under the bed," but nothing about any crime appeared. Page after page she clicked. The links varied from furniture stores to makeup shops to song lyrics with the name Sally in them. There was nothing about a missing girl or a suicide.

She exited out of the search and went to an online newspaper database. If the man in the article shot himself approximately thirty years ago because his daughter vanished approximately twenty years before that, then that should place the girl's disappearance in the late sixties or early seventies. And the disappearance must have occurred in Mingo County, if not in Williamson itself, the city where they used to live. She typed: "Girl disappears, Mingo County, West Virginia, 1968–1971, Sally under the bed" and clicked the search button.

Three articles resulted from the search, all from *The Williamson Daily News*. The first one was dated October 17, 1968, with the title "Local girl missing from her home." Tasha clicked it and read about how ten-year-old Margaret Means was having a sleepover with her cousin and another friend at her parents' home in Williamson. The father, Amos Means, heard screaming from the girl's bedroom and ran inside to discover that Margaret was missing. There was no sign of foul play.

The second article, written a few months later (January 18, 1969), was titled "Case of missing girl remains unsolved." It detailed how the authorities had made no progress on Margaret's mysterious disappearance and that the incident was ruled a missing persons' case. There was one additional fact printed in the last paragraph of the story. Tasha's heart pounded again when she read, "The only lead investigators had to work with was that of ten-year-old Suzanne Davies, who, when prompted about the case, could only say, 'Sally under the bed.'"

"Sally under the bed," Tasha echoed with glee.

7

The final article must have been the one her parents read that morning in the kitchen. This one was written twenty years after Margaret's disappearance and was titled "Father of long-lost missing girl takes own life." It summed up the original case from a twenty-year perspective and mentioned that the two other girls involved in the infamous sleepover—both of whom were now in their thirties—had each had traumatic lives since the event, stating that they had several run-ins with the law, resulting in Margaret's cousin, Wendy Means, moving out of town and Suzanne Davies, the giver of the "Sally under the bed" clue, becoming something of a town recluse.

Tasha pounced on that lead, opening her people-finding software and typing "Suzanne Davies, Williamson, West Virginia." The name and address popped up, and she fell back into her rolling chair, extending both fists up in triumph. She knew that Williamson was only an hour and a half from where she lived in Charleston, and she planned to be there by tomorrow afternoon.

TASHA CAUGHT A quick glimpse of the faded Williamson city limit sign as she pulled into town. She drove past one historic building after another, remembering times she would stroll the downtown sidewalks holding her father's hand.

A gaunt, bearded man in a sleeveless shirt smiled at her from an alley, his mouth fitting for an anti-meth poster. Like many Appalachian regions, Williamson was fighting a growing addiction problem. *That's the real monster,* she thought and continued forward.

So much had changed since she had last been here, yet enough of the past lingered to give her that swirl of nostalgia in her belly. She passed the Coal House and the new Hatfield and McCoy museum and briefly saw some obvious out-of-towners walking in for some local history. Almost as quickly as she entered the main drag, she was off it, driving parallel to the Tug Fork River, which separated her state from South Williamson, Kentucky.

A few miles later, her phone's GPS told her to turn right onto a gravel road that disappeared into the woods. She obeyed the directions and steered her Honda Civic onto the crunchy new path. Again, she looked at her phone screen. The robotic voice said, "Your destination is in two miles on the right."

The road dead-ended into a small clearing on a dirt-covered hillside.

Tasha came to a stop and stared at a double-wide trailer sitting off-kilter on an uneven terrain. A rusty, green Chevy was parked out front. Two windows blacked out by heavy curtains were on either side of the front door. One of them slightly moved.

Tasha shut her car off and stepped outside. The cool mountain breeze blew her hair across her face as she folded her arms and quickened her pace. She kept her eyes on both windows, which now appeared motionless. Three wooden steps led to the bottom of the front door, but there was a six-inch gap between the two. The flimsy staircase creaked and wobbled as soon as she put her weight on it. She balled up her fist and extended her arm to knock when the door jerked open before her knuckles made contact.

A skeleton of a woman, middle-aged but looking well-beyond her years, stood wide-eyed inside the dark trailer. "Yeah?" she asked with bulging eyes.

"Hi, my name is Tasha Brown…"

"What'dya want?"

Tasha couldn't help but notice the needle marks on her arms and meth scars on her face. She glanced at the mess behind the woman: dirty plates and cups were strewn about, empty vodka bottles were piled near one side of the stained couch, a full ashtray and what looked like a syringe sat openly on the coffee table. She averted her eyes.

"I'm trying to locate Suzanne Davies."

"What for?"

"I'm a writer…"

"Ain't interested," she said, taking a step back and closing the door.

"I'll pay!"

It opened back up.

"Pay for what?"

"If you're Suzanne Davies, I'll pay you to answer some questions about what happened the night Margaret Means went missing. And I'd really like to know about Sally under the bed."

A look of fear swept over the woman's already paranoid gaze. She took a quick step forward and shoved her finger in Tasha's face.

"Don't you dare say that fuckin' name!"

"I'm sorry," Tasha stammered and took a step back. The two women stood in a silent showdown.

"I'm not here to cause harm. I just want to hear your story. *Your* story. The truth."

Suzanne lowered her finger.

"How much you gonna pay?"

Tasha fumbled in her jacket pocket and withdrew two fifties. "A hundred now and two hundred more after you give me a story worth writing."

"What kind of news are you?"

"I write for a website about supernatural stuff. It's not like this will air on the evening news."

Suzanne hadn't taken her eyes off the cash since Tasha had pulled it out. She scratched the back of her neck, thinking about the dope she could buy. She snatched the bills out of her hand, took a step back, and pulled the door wide open. "Come on in, I reckon."

"Thank you."

Tasha walked inside and tried not to gag at the putrid smell of body odor, booze, and rotten food.

"Have a seat over there."

She sidestepped all the debris on the carpet as she made her way to a broken recliner in the corner of the room and sat with as little of herself on the chair as possible. The two rooms down the hall were empty from what she could tell: no bed, no other furniture. The kitchen was just as barren except for the gnats hovering over a sink full of crusty dishes.

She watched Suzanne sit on the couch, which had a pillow and a blanket on it. It also sat flat on the floor because the legs had been unscrewed, which she thought was odd. The woman glared at the stranger in her living room.

"What'dya wanna know?"

Tasha pulled her cellphone out.

"Do you mind if I record this conversation?"

"Hang on before you do that," Suzanne said as she hopped back up and walked to the kitchen on the other side of the room. "I was gonna save this for tomorrow, but now that I got a little bitta cash, I guess I don't need to." Tasha watched her grab a small plate with some white powder from the top of the refrigerator and place it on the cluttered counter. She picked up a piece of a straw and looked over at Tasha.

"Do whatever you need to do," Tasha said, averting her eyes as the sickly woman snorted a line of methamphetamine. She walked back to the couch, clearing her nose. After she sat down, she reached for the ashtray and grabbed a cigarette butt with a little bit left to smoke on it. She lit it, fell back into the couch, and looked at Tasha.

"You can start recording now."

"Perfect."

Tasha pressed record and leaned forward.

"Suzanne Davies, take me back to October 16, 1968—the night Margaret Means disappeared from her home here in Williamson, West Virginia."

Suzanne took a long drag, which brought the cherry down to the filter. She jammed it back into the porcupine of butts in the ashtray.

"I was ten back then. All three of us was. Wendy was my best friend. We did all kindsa shit together. She got invited to her cousin's house for a birthday sleepover. Margaret was her cousin. I never met Margaret before that night. Wendy told me that she didn't really like her, but her mom was makin' her go to her sleepover 'cause they was cousins. I guess Wendy told her mom the only way she was goin' was if she could bring me with her. I wish I woulda said, 'No.'"

Tasha forced an understanding look, making sure Suzanne knew that she had her undivided attention.

"Anyway, we get to Margaret's house, and it was awkward right from the get-go. Me and Wendy was just playin' with each other mostly. Wendy didn't want nothin' to do with Margaret because she was chubby and talked too much. I didn't think she was too annoyin', but I didn't know her like Wendy. I know that she musta asked us to play Twister at least a dozen times—ya know that fuckin' game where you bend 'round each other and shit?"

Tasha nodded with a smile. She could tell the meth was beginning to fuel her storytelling abilities. She no longer seemed as scared.

"Well, we never did play it, but she kept on askin'. She was dead set on playin' somethin'. She asked so many times that Wendy finally snapped. Wendy said, 'Fine, Margaret! If you wanna play a game, I got one for ya!' That's what got her to break out the rhyme game. I guess it's more of a challenge really..."

"What rhyme?"

"Sally Under the Bed," Suzanne said with confusion. "Ain't that what you're here for?"

"Yeah, but how is that a game, though?" she asked.

Suzanne raised her eyebrows and took a deep breath.

"You really don't know, do ya?"

"I just know about what I read in the paper: your quote about Sally

Under the Bed."

"That game fucked me up for good. I used to wonder about where that rhyme come from, but there's no use. Ain't gonna change nothin'.

"I guess I should start by sayin' that Margaret's daddy's name was Means, but her mama's maiden name was Hatfield."

"The good old Hatfields and McCoys," Tasha began. "I can't tell you how many Hatfields I went to school with here. I actually grew up in Williamson."

Suzanne, completely uninterested in the reporter's upbringing, reached for something beside the couch. She brought up a fifth of vodka that was some brand Tasha had never heard of, and poured some in one of the dirty glasses on the table.

"Want some?"

"No, thank you," Tasha replied, feeling sorry for the woman. "I have to drive home."

Suzanne smiled at her guest's concern for following the law and brought the glass to her lips.

"Where was I?"

"The game and where it came from."

"Oh yeah. So, the rhyme supposedly come from a Hatfield a couple branches down her family tree. I'll tell ya how I heard it from Wendy that night. See, right after she said she had a game for Margaret to play, she started tellin' us the history of it. She made us shut off the lights and sit in a circle, and we was all three sittin' in Margaret's livin' room like Wendy wanted. We was supposed to be goin' to bed, but ya know how those sleepovers go."

Tasha nodded her head and glanced down at her phone to make sure it was still recording.

"Wendy told us that her daddy's, daddy's, daddy's cousin or some shit was a Hatfield. Huck was his name. I ain't never found no record of a Huck Hatfield, but that's what she said. Supposedly, ol' Huck had a crush on a girl named Sally, but Sally wasn't interested in him. He got drunk on 'shine one night and asked her to marry him in front of his friends. She shot him down...embarrassed the shit out of him. Huck went blind with rage. He waited until Sally was all alone and then he took her. Dragged her screamin' through the woods to his cabin on the hill. He threw her on the floor, lit his lantern, and beat the tar out of her. When Margaret told us this part, she made sure to do these slow, dramatic punches...ya know how kids tellin' ghost stories is."

Tasha forced a smile and continued to listen, already making a mental note to fact-check all of this when she got home.

"Anyway, Huck beat her to death, plain and simple. Margaret made sure we knew that the girl's head looked like a smashed watermelon...said her eyes was busted in so bad they was nothin' but black holes. She was really layin' it on for us.

"You'd think most people would feel bad when they realized they just killed the woman they love, but not Huck. Huck ripped off her clothes and did God knows what with her. And then he shoved her naked body under his bed and went to sleep! Didn't even bother to clean up the mess. I don't know why he done that other than maybe if he couldn't sleep with her, then nobody could.

"Now, when Margaret got to this part in tellin' the story, we was hooked already, but then her voice got real low. She said somehow the lantern in that cabin mysteriously fell over. Everything went up in flames, includin' both of them bodies. People around town started spreadin' rumors 'bout what happened, and it became this little ghost story: somethin' the kids would tell to scare each other.

"Somewhere down the line, somebody came up with a game involvin' this rhyme. The game was that you say this rhyme about Sally, and she would appear under your bed at night, all bloodied and busted like she was just freshly killed.

"Needless to say, we was scared shitless by this point, but Wendy wasn't done. Just to make sure we *really* believed her, she told us about how she found the rhyme. *The actual rhyme!* That evil little bitch said she was noseyin' around her attic one day just lookin' through boxes of shit and she come upon a trunk that had been passed down from her mama's side—the Hatfield side. She opened it and found this old journal with some Hatfield's name that was too smudged to read, but she flipped through the pages and found this rhyme...poem...song... whatever the fuck it is. She read it in her head over and over. The page opposite the rhyme told the game: say the rhyme if you dare but just know that you are disturbin' the rest of a vengeful spirit, and she probably ain't gonna be too happy about it.

"Wendy said she knew the rhyme by heart but never said it. She got up and walked over to Margaret's daddy's office supplies in the corner and scribbled somethin' down on a piece of paper for a minute. She came back with it and put it in the middle of our little circle. The top of the paper said 'Sally Under the Bed,' and the rest was the rhyme."

"What was the rhyme?" Tasha interrupted.

"Hell no," Suzanne said as she downed the rest of her vodka. "Ain't you been listenin'? You can't say it."

"Are you saying that you believe in this?"

Suzanne looked at her with disbelief.

"I saw it. I saw what happened. You wasn't there, and the rest of them fuckers wasn't there neither! Everybody thinks I'm crazy, but I saw what I fuckin' saw!"

"Okay, okay, Suzanne. I'm sorry. I didn't mean to offend you. Please, tell me the rest of the story."

The agitated woman went from rage to utter sadness in seconds.

"What Wendy wrote on that paper was twelve lines long…three sections with four lines each."

"Stanzas."

"Yeah, stanzas, whatever. Three of 'em. Well, I read the poem first in my head and then handed it to Margaret. It was one of the creepiest things I'd ever read. While Margaret was readin' the poem, Wendy whispered to me, 'Don't say the last line.' I thought that was weird at first but then realized that she was wantin' us to trick Margaret into sayin' the full thing by herself. Margaret finished the poem and put it back in the middle of our circle. Wendy said, 'We're all gonna say it, and whoever doesn't is a chicken,' but she gave me a little wink that Margaret didn't see.

"I agreed without really thinkin' about it. We both looked at Margaret, and it was obvious she didn't wanna say it. Wendy had to ask her if she was a chicken a few times and make those 'BAWK' sounds to finally get her to do it, but she did.

"We all sat there starin' at that paper on the floor. Wendy said, 'Well, let's get on with it,' and we did. We said it line-by-line in that sing-songy way it was written. When we got to the last line, Wendy and I looked at each other, and we both stopped. Margaret said the last line by herself just like Wendy wanted. Margaret freaked right out. I remember Wendy sayin', 'Looks like Sally is just comin' for you tonight, Margaret!' Man, it was so fucked. Kids are fucked up, ya know?"

Tasha gave a slight nod. Wendy poured herself another drink. She took a big gulp and sat there staring at the table in front of her for a moment before continuing.

"After Margaret yelled at us a good bit for trickin' her, we all settled down and went to bed. We was in Margaret's room. She was on her bed, and me and Wendy were on the floor in sleepin' bags. Margaret was tryin' to go to sleep, but Wendy wasn't done with her yet. She whispered to me that we should crawl on the floor and make scratchy sounds and *really* scare Margaret. I agreed to it, but I felt rotten about it. I never picked on no one before, but I didn't want Wendy to look at me like she looked at Margaret.

"So Margaret was fallin' asleep, and she heard the scratchin' beside her bed. I heard her up there start to breathe a little faster like she was scared. I looked up and saw that she had the covers pulled over her head. Wendy held her hand up to me and used her fingers to count down from three. I knew what that meant: when she got to zero, we were gonna give Margaret the final scare, and we did. We both sprung up from the floor. I yanked the covers off her just as Wendy made a loud, growling sound and pounced on her. Margaret screamed, but Wendy covered her mouth real quick so she didn't wake her dad up.

"Once Margaret realized what was goin' on, Wendy let go of her and fell to the floor laughin'. She said, 'We got you good, Margaret.' I saw that Margaret was cryin', and that made me feel real bad. Wendy kept laughin', though. The last thing Margaret ever said was, 'I hate you guys.'"

Tears were welling up in Suzanne's eyes as she stared off into space like she was afraid to keep going.

"What happened next, Suzanne?" After a long pause, she continued.

"Wendy and I got back in our sleepin' bags, and she was asleep in two minutes. I don't know how she did that. I was starin' at the ceiling feelin' like a real asshole. I musta stared up there for a half hour. Margaret fell asleep before me, too. I could tell, because she stopped sobbin' and wimperin' and started to snore a little bit. It's always the worst when you're the last one to fall asleep at a sleepover, but when ya add the guilt I was feelin', it took me extra long.

"I guess it was just a little after that when I finally started to doze off. I was in that place when you're not quite sure if you're awake or dreamin' when I heard the sounds comin' from Margaret's side of the room."

"What sounds?"

Suzanne closed her eyes, and a tear rolled down one cheek.

"I looked over there, and there was a dark figure layin' flat on her back under her bed. She was the size of a grownup and had no clothes on. I was frozen. I've never been so scared in my life. The dark woman's head slowly turned her face toward me until she was starin' straight at me. My stomach got all knotted, but I couldn't look away. Her left arm shot out first, and then she kinda pulled herself toward me real slow. I pissed myself when she got completely out from under there and gave me a good look at her.

"She was pale like a corpse that's been dead long. She had this dark hair that hung down around her face. Her face…the middle of her face was caved in and bloody. Her jaw hung sideways, too. It almost looked like she was smilin'. Once she stood up, the moonlight gave me an even better view: there were two blackened sockets where her eyes shoulda been. One eyeball dangled by a nerve. She was facing me for a moment, but then she turned back to Margaret. I wish I had the guts to scream right then, but ya know what? I was just glad she wasn't interested in me anymore. Ain't that horrible?

"She climbed her naked body on top of Margaret. I heard her wake up and try to scream, but I guess that thing was coverin' her mouth. I closed my eyes and put my hands on my ears. I just couldn't take it anymore. I felt the thud of something hittin' the floor and peeked through one eyelid just enough to see Margaret on the floor starin' at me with those terrified eyes and that thing's hand around her mouth. The rest of it was back under the bed. It squeezed the bottom of Margaret's face and snapped her head completely around and then sucked her under the bed. They was both gone after that.

"I finally found it in me to scream. Wendy woke up and Margaret's daddy came runnin' in to see what was goin' on. He obviously didn't find Margaret. He looked everywhere. He grabbed me by the shoulders and shook me, wantin' to know where she went. All I could do was point to the place she last was and say, 'Sally under the bed'."

Tasha was speechless. She felt for the woman. She felt how tortured and traumatized she was. Worst of all, she felt how badly she believed that that was what actually happened.

Suzanne started to whimper and then stood up and wobbled a bit.

"I ain't slept in a bed since. I even took the legs off that couch. I ain't takin' any chances, and I'll definitely never talk about this shit again. I can't do it," she said as she stumbled back into the kitchen and took a snort of whatever was left on that plate.

Tasha hit the pause button on her phone.

"Thank you for sharing that with me, Suzanne. I know that wasn't easy."

"You don't know shit about it."

"You're right. I don't." Tasha got up and walked over to Suzanne. She pulled out two one hundred dollar bills as promised and placed them on the counter. "But I feel like I know so much more thanks to you." She put her hand back in her pocket and withdrew two more hundreds. "And this is yours, too…" Suzanne looked at her in confusion. "…if you can remember that poem."

The drugged-out woman was shocked.

"Are you fuckin' nuts? Did you not listen to anything I just said?"

"I did. *Of course, I did.* But if I'm really going to tell this story, I have to know what it is."

Suzanne didn't know what to think.

"Fine," Tasha said as she pulled out the last of her cash and dropped it all on the counter. "There you go. All you have to do it write it down. I promise I won't print it. If you say that's off the record, then it's off the record."

Suzanne scooped up the cash and walked to one of the back rooms. She came back with a pen and a torn piece of paper. Tasha watched as she struggled to write one word after another, her hands shaking uncontrollably. When she finished, she held out the paper.

"Here. Take it and go."

Tasha looked down and saw three stanzas of scribbled lines.

"Don't you dare say it," Suzanne warned. "Don't show it to no one neither. Just read it and burn it. Promise me that."

Tasha smiled at her and said, "I promise."

IT WAS NEARLY dinner time when Tasha walked through her front door. Mike was in the kitchen cooking. Their five-year-old daughter was playing on the iPad in the living room.

"Hi, Mommy," Leah said without looking up from the screen.

"Hey, honey," Wendy replied. She patted the little girl's head as she walked by. Mike turned from the vat of boiling pasta.

"Hey, babe. Was it productive?"

17

"You have no idea." Tasha beamed with excitement. "Wait until I tell you. No, never mind. I want you to read it when I'm finished."

"Okay…"

"I'm so excited, Mike. This is going to be the best story I've ever published. If I do this right, it could blow up." She took off her coat and set her purse on the counter. Her phone was still in her pocket. "I've got to get started right now."

"Now? Don't you at least want to eat first?"

"I have to do it while it's still fresh in my mind," she said as she kissed him on the cheek and scurried back through the living room toward the basement stairs. "You know how these things go!"

"Mommy, where are you going?"

"Down to my office, honey. I'll be back up in a little bit."

AS USUAL, TASHA lost all track of time while she was writing. She had spent the first two hours looking into the three girls' lives but not finding much that would enhance the story. Mike brought a plate of spaghetti down to her and set it on her desk, but she never touched it. She went down several rabbit holes of any record she could find on different members of the Hatfield clan. There was no mention of a Huck Hatfield anywhere. After coming up short on that front, she decided to continue that research tomorrow. Worst-case scenario: she'd issue a disclaimer before that part of the piece noting it as unsubstantiated backstory.

Once she started to play the recording, she never stopped transcribing. She got everything down in just ninety minutes. She spent the next few hours building a narrative. Rather than just report Suzanne's testimony as fact, she inserted herself into the story, which was something that she'd never done before. Writing in the first person just opened the article up in a way that she knew would draw in the reader. She would end on an ambiguous note, the way all good unsolved mysteries should. The one thing she didn't put in the article was the poem itself. Even though it would up the creep factor to include it, she knew that once someone tried the game and it didn't work, the story would lose its punch.

Satisfied with what she had produced, she saved her document and checked the time. It was just a little after eleven p.m. She knew Mike had probably just put Leah down, so she booked it upstairs to tell her goodnight before her daughter fell asleep. She reached the top of the stairs and saw that her bedroom door was already shut. Mike was in their bed, shirtless, reading a book. Tasha entered their room.

"How long ago did you put her down?"

"About thirty minutes. I tried to keep her up, but she conked out on me. Sorry, babe."

"It's okay. I'm the one who worked…"

She stopped when she saw the paper that Suzanne had given her on the nightstand.

"Why is this here?"

"Oh, that, yeah. Leah pulled that creepy-ass thing out of your purse and wanted me to read it to her."

"Did you?"

"Yeah. I said it, and then she wanted me to sing it like a song, so I did that until she knew the words and started singing along with me. What is it anyway?"

Before Tasha could answer, a faint scream came from their daughter's bedroom, but it was quickly silenced.

"What the hell was that?" Mike said, setting his book aside.

Tasha sprinted down the hall and burst into the room.

"Leah! Leah!" she screamed as she scanned the empty room. She dropped to the floor and looked under the bed but saw nothing. "Leah!"

She heard her husband getting up, now realizing that something was seriously wrong. Tasha pushed herself off the ground and ran to meet Mike in the hallway.

"What is it?" he asked.

Tasha's eyes widened with abject terror when she saw the woman crawling across the floor behind her husband. Mike whipped around just as Sally grabbed him by both ankles and pulled his legs out from under him. His body hit the ground, causing the back of his head to crack the tile floor.

"No!"

Tasha desperately tried to get to her husband as he was being dragged under the bed. She dove for his hand and missed by inches. They both screamed as he disappeared into the darkness below. She wailed until her throat hurt. She kicked the nightstand and slammed her fist repeatedly against the floor. She didn't even notice that she had knocked Suzanne's note off until it drifted down and landed in front of her.

The cursed words taunted her bloodshot eyes, but she now knew what she had to do. She grabbed the paper and rolled on her side letting her cheek rest in the puddle of Mike's blood. There was no other way for her to be with her family. She spoke the title, "Sally Under the Bed," and then, in a hoarse whisper, she read what was in front of her.

> *They said, they said*
> *Keep it in your head.*
> *If you say it out loud*
> *Then you'll be dead.*
>
> *I said it, I said it*
> *And now I regret it.*
> *I sang this song and*
> *I wish I could forget it.*
>
> *They said, they said*
> *Keep it in your head.*
> *But it's too late 'cause*
> *Sally's under the bed.*

I DO THEE WOE

Matthew R. Davis

BLACK BLINDS FLAPPED UP LIKE opening eyelids, allowing the pupils in the classroom to look out upon the bright world once more, and Dragan flinched at the incursion of reality. Watching a film, even in a group, had always felt like an escape into a better place, and there were few things he dreaded more than the credit roll. For him, that meant the dream was over, and his life had always been a poor substitute.

With reality restored, Peter Lamb stopped the movie and stood in its place, framed by the large TV screen as he invited his class to discuss what they'd seen. They'd just watched Tarantino's *Pulp Fiction*, and today's subject was the magpie tendencies of directors and the relative worth of what they liked to call *homage*. Dragan would have loved to sink his teeth into meatier examples of that subject—the debt De Palma and Argento owed to Hitchcock, for example, or the way Italian directors such as Margheriti and Cozzi had blatantly riffed on whatever Hollywood film had made money that year—but it was clear that no one else in the class was steeped as deeply in film lore as he. His fellow adult students ranged from enthusiastic school-leavers used to viewing hyper-cut movies on portable devices to loose-end retirees who thought true quality in film had gone out when digital came in.

And somewhere in the middle, adrift on a tepid sea, was Dragan.

His eyes drifted from their lecturer to the white screen behind him, a blank sheet of paper that only reminded him of the scripts he wasn't writing. Dragan's dearest dream was to make his own film, and while he had no idea how he might achieve such a thing, this course was his first step toward that ultimate end. He'd thought he might meet like-minded people here, hardcore movie geeks with whom he might form a collective and set about the serious business of birthing an independent feature, but once again he found himself slipping through the cracks thanks to his niche tastes and social incompatibility. It was like his time at Magellan Video all over again.

At three o'clock, Peter Lamb wrapped up the discussion and announced the end of class, leaning back against his desk with arms folded as his students stuffed books and laptops into bags and shuffled their chairs back. Dragan looked across the room to where Chloe kept her habitual seat, and as always, she was packed and heading for the door before anyone else had even risen to their feet. She seemed to enjoy the lessons, so why was she in such a hurry to leave? Maybe she had another class, a part-time job, or a demanding boyfriend. Dragan sighed at yet another missed opportunity to walk her out. With her sea-green eyes and chocolate curls, she reminded him of the Final Girl from a slasher film, the shy straight-arrow who contained enough inner strength to survive the bloody cull.

Chloe was long gone by the time Dragan left the transportable that housed his screen and media course. Along with other adult education classes, it was held on the premises of a high school, which had always made him a little uncomfortable—not least because it recalled his own awkward and miserable teenage experience. And there were other reasons, as he was reminded when his path crossed that of a trio of uniformed girls.

He paid as little attention to these young women as possible lest they suspect he was harboring inappropriate thoughts, or worse, in case he began to do so—some of the seniors were far too developed to be seen as children. Take the one closest to him now: no more than seventeen, yet she carried herself like a full-fledged woman, sultry and jaded and wise to the ways of the world. Her eyes flicked to him briefly as they passed in the yard, her full lips wrapped around the striped paper straw of a takeaway juice, and Dragan felt the less mature of the two even though he had more than ten years on her. She'd be familiar with the foibles of boys and men both, had no doubt experienced more attention and attraction than he—a very low bar, to be certain, but still. The world was at her feet. The unspoken promise of those lips, those curves, those eyes would be enough to get her anything, anyone she wanted.

How wonderful that must be.

Her gaze held his for only a second, empty of any interest—she might as well have been looking at a lamppost. Then her friend cried, "Layla!" and those eyes slid away, and as the girls walked on, Dragan heard them laughing at some private joke. He tried to believe it wasn't him, and that was probably true, but the response had long been ingrained.

He walked to the bus stop surrounded by a dozen high schoolers who ignored him as they exchanged slang-warped banter that he found harder to understand every year. He found himself glad to be beneath their notice; if their attention should be called to him, it would be only to jeer and mock. And even he could understand that, because when he looked in a mirror, he saw the same thing as they: not so much a man as an inflated boy, incapable of cultivating more than a thin pubertal wisp of a moustache, his lumpy figure thrown out of proportion by broad hips. Add his flabby chest to the equation and he cut more of a womanly figure than many of the stripling girls around him at the bus stop, not to mention less of a manly one than the strapping boys who already looked like they needed to shave every morning.

"You inherited your mother's hips," his father had said, more than once, with the unspoken implication that Dragan had taken on other characteristics deemed unsuitable for a man. He'd always been clumsy and uncoordinated, bad at sports, soft-spoken and insular. Little wonder *Tata* had long since stopped asking when he was going to bring a girl home. On the few occasions Dragan had done just that, inviting Bessie or Alita from work over in the days when he'd still lived with his family, his father hadn't bothered with the conspiratorial winks he parcelled out to his other sons. He'd been convinced that nothing more than talk and movie-watching was going to happen behind that closed bedroom door—and what really burned was that he'd been right, every single time.

Dragan boarded the bus and slipped in a pair of earbuds like at least half the high schoolers around him, though he chose to listen to synth-heavy horror soundtracks rather than blandly lascivious modern R&B. He disembarked at the shopping center near his apartment building and trudged inside, too much time on his hands and too little inspiration to use it well. He wandered the modest mall for as long as he could, lingering in an entertainment outlet and flicking through movies he couldn't afford, and then he sat alone in the food court and picked at some noodles like an alternate-universe George Lucas who'd never struck upon the idea that would carve his name into history.

Dusk was shading into night when he left the mall. He passed a graffiti-scarred video kiosk and paused before it, wondering how a world of Block-busters had ever come to this. Once rental stores had graced every major road, and now they'd been replaced by vending machines that stocked only the most popular new releases as if they were cans of soft drink—and for all their bubbly insipidity and lack of substance, they might as well have been.

He was reminded of his years at Magellan Video, a perfect job that had come to an end when declining business had seen its owners lay off most of their staff. He'd hoped that seniority and loyalty might preserve his position, but even there, where his knowledge and experience should have counted for something, he'd been regarded as dispensable. Worse, that job had shown him how little the general populace cared for innovation or engagement in movies—he'd had to bite his tongue every time he'd checked out another lamebrained dudebro comedy or homogenous PG-13 horror, and that was precisely the kind of crap kept in these kiosks. Why didn't the general public want more from their films? A life so artless and prosaic scarcely seemed worth living.

Dragan turned away from the treasonous kiosk and spotted a pale face and hands hovering in the shadows nearby. He assumed it was an advertisement hung in a darkened window, then started as he realized its true dimensions—a young woman, wrapped in a black kaftan that matched her hair so perfectly she seemed to disappear into the fabric just as her clothing bled into the shadows around it. She might have been dressed in the sleek fur of a panther, camouflaged by the falling night as she waited for prey. Her face was a beautiful mask, achingly familiar and completely foreign at the same time. Her long fingers clutched a thin stack of flyers.

Dragan hoped the woman would speak to him, but his heart sank a little at the thought of what she might say. Her unusual dress and fistful of propaganda led him to assume her purpose was religious in nature, and such people always seemed to zero in on him as if sensing a soul susceptible to their dogma. Sure enough, a smile broke across her face like she'd recognized a perfect mark as she glided out of the deeper shade and extended a flyer toward him.

He took it out of weary obligation, for at least a woman was showing him some little attention, no matter the reason. Expecting cult mysticism or fringe politics, Dragan was pleasantly surprised to find that the flyer advertised an arthouse film called *I Do Thee Woe* and that it doubled as a free pass for the following night's screening at the Viceroy.

Despite his love of cinema, theatrical excursions were a rare and expensive indulgence for Dragan, and he missed the experience. Going out to catch a movie was what regular people did at night, instead of praying for oblivion to bring back the dawn or just swallow them entirely. And they took dates.

A reckless notion occurred to him then, and he grabbed at this rare chance to be bold.

"Could I have two? I might bring someone along."

The young woman smiled again—had he really not seen her somewhere before?—and he told himself there hadn't been a condescending edge to it. She handed him another flyer in any case, her cool fingertip touching his for one long second, and then nodded in encouragement before slipping away as if a long day's work was finally done. Dragan idly imagined she'd been waiting there in the shadows just for him, then dismissed the fancy with a shiver. No one would linger for him, not for any reason that bade well.

He wondered if the flyer lady would be there at the screening tomorrow night, if she'd smile at him again, and thought the odds of both were quite good. That hardly mattered, though, since he'd set himself on a separate and equally hapless course by asking for a second ticket. He wasn't sure what kind of movies Chloe liked, but it was a stretch to hope she'd be into something as obscure as this, a further stretch to assume there was any chance she'd agree to accompany him. Still, he didn't have to actually *ask* her. He'd been bold enough to obtain two passes and give himself that option, and to his way of thinking, that was bravery enough for one day.

Dragan walked home and let himself into the drab apartment he'd tried to lighten with framed posters of *Zombie Flesh Eaters*, *It Follows*, and *The Hunt for Candy Parker*. He grabbed a two-liter bottle of Coke from the fridge and sat down to start an essay on the scripts of Pegg and Wright that Peter Lamb wanted turned in Monday of next week. But beyond that distraction, the evening stretched out before him like an endless empty shadow, and those dark hours hung around him and rotted. He watched a Flanagan film. He opened the IDEAS folder on his laptop and wracked his brain in vain before closing it an hour later. He watched another Flanagan film. He was glad when sleep beckoned him to bed, closing the curtains on another lackluster day.

Dragan regarded dream sequences as a bit of a cheat, as movie dreams were usually too linear and plot-relevant to be believable and were often used merely as an excuse to cram in a cheap jump scare. Real life wasn't so neatly plotted; his own dreams were nonsensical, impenetrable, unspectacular. To-night's mental movie, then, was remarkable for its thematic consistency.

He was sitting in a cinema auditorium, somewhere toward the middle, and the rest of the seats were packed with people he knew and people he didn't—a full house tonight. The lights dimmed to darkness, and the curtain flapped up like a black blind to reveal a blank white screen that faded to its opposing shade. One line of credits came up in a sober font: *A Film by Dragan Stojanović.*

He settled back in his seat, surprised and pleased. Finally! He wasn't a failure anymore. He'd made it. He'd made *this*.

The black screen cut to a plain and shabby bathroom—grubby mirror, dirty tiles, very much like the one in his apartment. The shot was uninspired and poorly set up, angled at an accidental Dutch tilt, and Dragan wriggled uncomfortably in his seat. A simple pseudo-spooky synth score kicked in, sounding less like John Carpenter than a ham-fisted child hammering away at a cheap Casio. The audience was dead silent as the bathroom door opened and an actor edged into the fringe of the shot. He stepped to his mark in the middle of the room, glancing briefly at the camera like the rankest of amateurs. The actor was Dragan himself.

A couple of pre-emptory titters could be heard rising from the audience, and he came to a dreadful understanding: this was not a triumphant dream of self-realization but an excruciating nightmare just beginning to unfold. He wanted to leave before things got any worse, but the crowd hemmed him into his narrow seat. He could do nothing but watch as the screen-Dragan took off his shirt and dropped it to one side in a poor attempt at casual sultriness.

A laugh rang out from the row behind him, female and raucous. He sank into his seat in horror as his doppelgänger then stepped out of his pants and stood there on the screen completely naked, running his hands through his hair in a self-conscious attempt to seduce the camera. The clumsy angle made his dimensions look even worse than a mirror did, emphasising the bulge of his broad hips and the sag of his breasts whilst diminishing his genitalia to proportions usually associated with Michelangelo's *David.*

The crowd erupted into gales of laughter. They hooted like mocking monkeys. They threw handfuls of popcorn at the screen as if its occupant deserved to be stoned. Dragan looked away, excoriated by his own work, and saw that the young girl in the seat beside him was Layla. She watched the film with a cruel grin, her full wet lips teasing the tip of a striped paper straw, dressed in a tube top and jean shorts so skimpy that she showed almost as much skin as the hapless actor up on the screen. She seemed to feel his eyes upon her and turned, her vicious grin growing wider as she recognized him.

"He's here!" she cried, and of course, her voice somehow cut through the pandemonium all around them. She pointed at Dragan and laughed, laughed. "It's HIM! He's HERE!"

Everyone turned to look. Everyone pointed. Everyone laughed. Dragan tried to stand and push his way along the aisle, but Chloe was sitting on the other side of him, and she pushed him back into his seat, snapping handcuffs closed around his wrist to secure him to the armrest. She sneered at his pleas for release, her usual modest blouse and jeans swapped for a revealing stars and stripes bikini, and one hand was reaching into the seat next to her to pleasure a grinning Peter Lamb while the other held up an ancient film camera to record Dragan's humiliation. Somewhere behind the jeering crowd stood a woman in a black kaftan who smiled and licked her lips and brought curtains of deep pitch down over the whole wretched scene.

Dragan burst back into consciousness, inexplicably aroused and utterly mortified. He tried to take revenge on dream-Chloe by thinking of her figure in that scanty bikini as he attempted to relieve himself, but in the end, her mocking eyes and cruel laugh drove his readiness away. A half-hour passed before he managed to return to sleep, and if he dreamed anything else that night, he chose not to remember it.

WHEN THREE O'CLOCK came around the next day and brought film class to an end, Dragan was already packed up and ready to go. He was second to leave after Chloe, and as he followed her out onto the asphalt, he summoned every reserve of courage he could muster. *Be bold and breathe fire, Dragan*, he told himself, though it didn't help that he knew his name had nothing to do with dragons and in fact meant *beloved*. Well, he'd never end up that way unless he did something about it.

"Hey, Chloe."

She turned and shifted her bag on her shoulder, flicking brown curls out of her face with a toss of her head. Her sea-green eyes showed no particular interest, but at least no boredom or contempt, either. Here in daylit consciousness, he found it hard to imagine her ever being so cruel or blatantly sexual as she had been in his dream, and he cringed at the humiliated arousal that vision had provoked in him.

"Hey, Dragan."

"Did you like the film?" They'd just sat through another of Peter Lamb's keynote movies, a Jim Jarmusch flick that Dragan had drifted in and out of as he'd prepared for this moment. "I mean, are you into arty stuff like that?"

She shrugged. "It was okay. I'm into all sorts, really. What about you?"

"It was all right. I like a lot of things, too. Arthouse stuff can be pretty cool."

"Yeah."

He was never going to become a screenwriter if he produced dialogue as flat as this. Listening to himself force out these clumsy words was almost as excruciating as his dream from the night before. Dragan paused a moment, hoping his classmates would disperse quickly and give them privacy but knowing he couldn't wait any longer.

"So, I hope this doesn't sound weird or anything, but I got given a couple of free passes to a film tonight." He could already see the shutters coming down behind her eyes as she realized where he was headed, but he flailed on regardless. "Did you have any plans? I mean, would you be interested in going?"

"Yeah, I've got things to be doing. Sorry."

"No problem. Have a nice night."

Chloe flexed her lips into a polite parting smile, and then she was off, head down and moving fast. Dragan told himself she wasn't walking any more swiftly than usual, that he hadn't just embarrassed them both. Well, at least he'd tried—even that poor effort had to be worth celebrating.

His father wouldn't have said so. Letting out a breath redolent with the rotting remnants of his anxiety, Dragan took his usual path toward the street and the bus stop. On the way, he saw a schoolgirl sitting alone on a bench attached to another transportable and slowed for a moment. It was Layla.

She didn't look anywhere near as salacious as she had in his dream, nor as womanly as she had yesterday afternoon. She was staring glumly down at her phone, feet crossed and swaying absently beneath her, and she looked more like a lost child than a confident young adult. Dragan felt a pang of guilt for subconsciously sexualizing her, for assuming she had it so much easier than him. Sure, young women seemed like they had the world at their feet, but often that world was snapping at their toes. Layla could look forward to being marginalized, manipulated, objectified, and hated merely for being who and what she was. Some people—men like *him*, whether he intended it or not—saw her only as a thing to be equally craved and feared, coveted and loathed. She might strive and succeed or fail and fall by her own standards, but as far as the world was concerned, she was just more meat for the machine.

For a moment, Dragan considered offering her the spare movie ticket as a peace offering and nothing more, a consolation for the contempt she had already faced and would go on enduring the rest of her life. But he knew how *that* would look, and he was bitterly amused as he imagined her response. If asking Chloe out had been a bad idea, this fleeting one—no matter how well-intentioned—was so much worse.

Dragan found he couldn't face his apartment today; the last thing he needed was to be alone in that rancid cell. Since he had plans for the night, he avoided his usual stop and headed down the road to catch a different bus. This one took him to a mall he'd never visited before, where he browsed Blu-ray re-releases of classic horror films that his student's income would not stretch to afford. How lucky he was that tonight's entertainment had been offered *gratis*.

I Do Thee Woe was about as obscure a film as he'd ever come across. It was not listed on IMDb or Wikipedia, and any references were limited to reproductions of the flyer on indie websites that hadn't seen the flick themselves and could offer no other details about it. He couldn't tell if it was supposed to be horror, arthouse, or both. An enigma, then, and hopefully a pleasant surprise.

He loitered around the mall until it was time for dinner, then bought something cheap and packed with carbohydrates that would do his figure no favors at all. But what did it matter, in the end? He was born to this body and it would never bend to his will, so he might as well get used to it. He looked up the Viceroy's location and caught the bus he needed to get him in the general vicinity. By the time he had disembarked and walked the rest of the way to the cinema, the free film's eight o'clock start was just a quarter-hour off.

The Viceroy was an old Art Deco theater tucked away down a side street in a quiet suburb, its former grandeur much reduced by its long-standing state of disrepair. The fading posters that sagged behind its smeared windows advertised the kind of mild melodramas he assumed only pensioners would want to watch, and its cream façade was chipped and shabby from lack of care. Still, Dragan found it a thing of beauty and was glad for this shake-up of his routine as he pushed through its glass doors and stepped into the foyer.

The paisley-patterned carpet retained too much color to be the original, and modern soft-drink signage marred the bar's old-school charm, but otherwise the place was a time capsule. A central pillar dominated the room, girt by a ring of cushioned seating; neon tube lighting above the auditorium declared IN SESSION but was currently dull and lifeless. One wall was affixed with old photographs of the Viceroy in better days, of its sister theater the Black Regent before its decline into dereliction, and another held a period-accurate ticket booth that was closed for the night. There was little need of it, as the Viceroy appeared to be empty of any other custom. He thought that was a shame for the clearly ailing cinema, but it suited his mood just fine.

Dragan crossed to the mirror-backed bar and bought a large cup of Coke, savoring the wonderful scent of hot popcorn but skipping snacks for reasons both nutritional and financial. The man who served him was a skeletal relic in a burgundy vest who might well have worked here his whole life, who might have died years before but carried on in his role regardless for all the animation and vigor he displayed, and Dragan amused himself by imagining the man collecting dust and cobwebs in a broom closet between shifts. Refreshment procured, he walked over to the black velvet curtains that marked the entrance to the theater proper, and the drapes parted to reveal the young woman who'd given him his free pass.

She was wearing the same kaftan from the day before and it shaded into the darkness beyond her, leaving her foreign/familiar face and pale hands to hover in the air like a puppeteer's tools. Again, her finger touched his when he handed the flyer back to her, and she smiled as if his presence was in response to a personal invitation and very welcome. He thought he knew why when she gestured down the aisle, for he wandered in to find the auditorium almost empty.

Of the red vinyl seats that sloped down toward the veiled screen in twenty rows, only two were occupied. The first filmgoer was a tubby young fellow in a *Call of Duty* T-shirt who was already halfway through a tub of popcorn and wiping greasy fingers on his trackpants like someone who had long given up on the attention of others, and the second was twice Dragan's age, gray hair straggling from a high forehead down onto the shoulders of his battered leather jacket. Dragan chose a spot near the center of the auditorium and made himself comfortable, gazing up at the Art Deco rosettes around each embedded ceiling light and listening to the quiet piano music that filtered in through hidden speakers.

Shoes trod the carpeted aisle behind him, and he turned in his seat to see a bespectacled woman whose psychedelic tie-dye shirt might have been intended to distract from her drab face and flyaway hair. She took a seat on the other side of the aisle, a few rows back from him. Four patrons—hardly a bumper turnout. No wonder the woman in black had been so glad to see him.

At eight o'clock, the lights grew dim and winked out as drapes squeaked apart on their tracks to reveal the glowing screen. Dragan looked back and glimpsed the hovering face of the flyer lady before she closed the foyer curtain and the auditorium fell into darkness. Thankfully, the feature was not preceded with adverts and previews and admonitions to turn off one's phone. The projector cast its storied beam upon the screen, and the movie began at once.

As the flyer had led him to believe, the film was in black and white. He didn't mind that, but the first shot dragged on for at least a minute, and the ones that followed were scarcely shorter. Combined with the camera's focus on a young woman drifting through desolate cityscapes, this put him in mind of Amirpour's *A Girl Walks Home Alone at Night*, which he'd liked but thought could do with a judicious trim. A man appeared, exuding ennui as he gazed profoundly into the empty distance, and eventually his path crossed with that of the mysterious woman. What happened next was not clear, but the man was no longer to be seen and the woman returned to her aimless wandering.

Dragan heard someone entering through the foyer curtain and shuffling along the seats a few rows back—a late arrival. By their position, they must have been joining the tubby young man, who muttered something and then fell silent. Good; Dragan hated chatter during films. But soon he heard worse: soft, wet sounds came from the couple, the dude's dubious hygiene apparently no barrier to public affection. The intimacy only reminded him of everything he was missing in life—all the things he had always gone without and was terrified to think he would never know.

Onscreen, another lonely man travelled a hollow world. Dragan might have thought his solitary despondence a suitable reflection of the people in the meager audience tonight, but despite their apparent diffidence, it seemed

SCREAMING IN THE NIGHT

they were better off than he. The discreet sounds behind him carried on un-abated, and Dragan turned in his seat to glare back at the offending couple. The young man had been joined by a woman made anonymous by the shad-ows, and they were sitting close, their faces pushed together as if feeding on each other. His greasy hands were wrapped in her dark hair, and as Dragan watched, the man's neglected popcorn tumbled to the floor unnoticed.

He faced front, determined to enjoy his free film. If that couple was going to make out the whole time and miss it, that was their call, and he couldn't let it distract him. He slurped his Coke and lost himself in the long, drawn-out scenes projected before him.

Perhaps ten minutes later, he allowed himself a sigh of relief as the inti-mate sounds ended and one of the pair—the woman, he assumed—slipped back along the row to the aisle. Had she really come in here only to swap spit with that dude? The guy hardly seemed to give off the magnetism required for such devotion. Dragan imagined for a moment that his companion had been the strangely familiar beauty from the foyer, but that was ridiculous. The flash of a face he'd seen in the screen's light hadn't been enough to con-firm or deny it, but the flyer lady was well out of the young man's league—or, indeed, his own lowly reach.

Another sad-eyed loner encountered the enigmatic woman on the screen, another wordless confrontation ended with him disappearing from the narrative and her drifting on through windswept streets. Was she preying on these men? Perhaps this was a subtle vampire flick that ignored all the standard tropes of such, or maybe it was something like Glazer's *Under the Skin*, a movie whose celebrity nudity had garnered more attention than the truly disturbing fates met by its male characters. Whatever the case, the other filmgoers must have had more on their minds than what was occurring on-screen, for now Dragan heard another couple making out across the aisle.

The sounds were coming from behind him, back where the old dude in the leather jacket had been sitting. Jesus, even *he* was getting more play than Dragan? The world must be as cruel as his dreams sometimes made it out to be. Dragan tried to console himself by imagining the superannuated rocker's partner was just as old and liver-spotted, but it didn't help. After all, they'd probably been together for decades and notched up thousands of experiences together, and now here they were necking in a movie theater like a couple of excitable teenagers while Dragan sat alone as he had ever been, untouched, unwanted.

He told himself he wasn't going to look. When he did, he saw very little across the dim auditorium—just two dark shapes with their pale faces pressed together. The bespectacled woman in the tie-dye shirt was sitting three rows ahead of the couple, her brow furrowed in annoyance as she slurped her soft drink, as put out by these public displays of affection as Dragan. For a moment he entertained the notion of crossing the aisle to sit alongside her, to reach out and share the connection everyone else seemed to be flaunting tonight—but that was laughable. Plain as she was, she probably felt she could do better than him, or maybe she had a partner at home. She would be insulted and reject him out of hand, and rightfully so. Feeling a little sick, he turned back to the screen.

Soon the old rocker and his partner must have bored of their fun, for Dragan heard one of them swishing along their row toward the aisle. Did everyone here tonight have a lover to sneak in and suck their face? Perhaps so, for now someone made their way down the center of the auditorium and slipped into a seat alongside the bespectacled woman. Dragan told himself it was a friend, another arthouse nerd who was running late, but it wasn't long before the wet smacking sounds began again. He twisted around in disbelief and saw the woman's bright shirt obscured by the darker shade of her partner's clothing. She must have been too lost in the clinch to notice that her hand was squeezing the soft drink cup, crushing it until ice cubes spilled into her lap.

Dragan folded his arms, glaring at the screen, and listened as the world drove its merciless point home once again. He'd been born an outsider, foreign to his family, misshapen and maladjusted. He was a man of almost thirty whose body was ill-made for love, whose womanly hips and chest inspired laughter rather than lust, whose intelligence and enthusiasm counted for nothing. He had no skills, no features that would redeem him in the eyes of the world at large. His mother was the only woman who'd ever seen him naked, and that was out of parental obligation—no one had ever *chosen* to see him, touch him, know him.

He was barely paying attention to the film now. What solace could it be when his life was such a farce? No woman was going to sneak in here and make out with *him*. He thought bitterly of such a thing happening, imagined the woman in the black kaftan slipping into the seat alongside his and raising her lips to his lips. He imagined that it had been her sitting alongside the other three, a promiscuous film freak or a professional lover working a specialized pitch, moving from one patron to the next when she'd had her fill. He opened his mouth to laugh and found that he could not. That line of thought led him to finally understand what he'd been hearing and seeing tonight.

Twisting around, Dragan looked for the tubby young man and saw that his seat was empty. He stared across the aisle to see that the old rocker was also gone—and yet he'd only heard one person leaving their places after each make-out session. Looking to where the current necking couple sat, Dragan could no longer see the lighter shades of the woman's tie-dye shirt. Her dark companion was facing away from him, hunched over the seat where the woman had been as if looking for something, but still the wet sounds continued.

No latecomers had been admitted to share their affections. None of his fellow filmgoers had struck it lucky tonight. With a belated chill, Dragan understood that even someone as inexperienced as he should have known the difference between the sounds of kissing and those of eating.

He faced front again, his mouth dry. Onscreen, that mysterious woman was wandering off into the sunrise with a sated smile, the streets empty of life around her. Maybe if he'd paid more attention to the film, he'd have understood what was going on around him. Even the title was a warning.

The wet sounds across the aisle abated, and now the only noise above the film's soundtrack came from his heaving lungs. Dragan made a cursory attempt to stand up, but his hips had wedged themselves into the armrests, his feet were tired of carrying his dead weight around, his heart was heavy and sick and sore. He was a coward, but that could be a good thing. All he had to do now was give up and let it happen.

The credits had started rolling, each name and role a nonsensical string of random letters, when the flyer lady slipped into the seat alongside him. Her hand rested atop his, and by its touch he understood that she was not wearing a kaftan after all. His earlier idle impression had been correct: her face and hands were the costume. The black matter he had assumed to be her hair and kaftan was the truth of her, and now strands of it slipped swift and soft around his wrist to lash it to the armrest. Her deep eyes ate him up, hypnotic screens reflecting his final scene, and he realized why she looked familiar to him and how that served her purpose: she roughly resembled Chloe, if his classmate had lingered in dark depths all her life, and she looked a little like Layla, too, if that schoolgirl had been swollen with sated appetites and yet still yearned for more. He wondered how she'd appeared to the other filmgoers tonight, if they'd seen unrequited crushes or former lovers or dead wives, but that didn't matter now. Nothing did. His tale had reached its final-act twist and now that sorry story was over. It had not been a success, and there would be no sequel.

The credits ended and the screen cut to black, but the theatre lights did not come on. Dragan sat in the darkness and let it happen, watching on like an impartial camera as she leaned her face into his, her mouth opening impossibly wide to deliver his first and final kiss.

AT THE WINDOW

Alexandr Bond

I YAWN, THEN SHAKE MY HEAD. The weariness tugs on my eyes, and like some poor imitation of King Midas, its touch turns them to lead. Throughout my vigil, I try to resist that pull. It reminds me of the time my family and I went to Jones Beach last summer. I had gotten caught in a riptide and though my father had been there to pull me out, I still remember that damn pull. I might only be twelve, but I am afraid I will never forget it. And now, here, I feel it again, only there is no water around me.

Just the cabin, my family, and the woods.

I yawn again and my head droops. The gaping darkness of sleep smiles up at me.

"Come," it says warmly. "Rest. You have done enough."

The clatter of the poker on the wooden floor pushes the welcoming voice away.

Blinking quickly, I pick up the iron poker, the grip a bit too large for my hand. I am a little small for my age, shorter than the rest of my classmates, and naturally thin. My father promises I will grow. He told me that he too was small growing up. I hope my father is right. I have grown tired of the teasing. Father said that goes away, too. Of course, my stature is the least of my worries presently.

I peer around, partly to keep up my self-appointed duty and partly to push away the weight of sleep. My bedroom in the cabin is old-fashioned. Wooden walls, wooden floors, a wide dresser sitting opposite my twin bed. The furniture looks right out of some old western, the sheets and comforter handwoven and just as itchy. I lay a finger against the powder blue material but pull away quickly. The mere feel of it speaks of sleep and dreams.

I need to stay awake, I think as my lids drift over my eyes.

"Scotty." My father's familiar voice draws my attention toward the window. I keep the curtains drawn, hoping that would mean something. "Scotty," my father says again. "Can you let me in?"

Taking a deep breath, I get to my feet and move carefully to the window. Pushing aside one of the drapes, I look out. My father stands three inches from the glass. The light from my room spills on his face, his russet-colored beard seemingly absorbing it like some strange sponge. He smiles at me. Warm, caring, a smile I see every day. I can't help it. I smile back. He glances down at the window's latch. My father is tall but lanky. He could easily climb in through the window.

"Can you open it, Scotty? It's getting a bit chilly out." He is dressed for bed and autumn is in full swing in the Vermont country. He rubs his hands together and breathes into them, his eyes never leaving my face. "When I get in, we can have some hot chocolate, just the two of us. I can make it with the nutmeg. There is some in the cabinet." The thought of the warm drink draws my free hand toward the latch. My father nods, his nose reddening in the cold night air.

My fingers, inches from the latch, stop.

"Scotty, come on. It's getting even colder out here. What are you doing?"

When I don't move, his smile fades into a scowl.

"This isn't funny, Scotty. Open the window."

I don't move.

"Open the window!" He bangs on the glass, hard enough for the window frame to shudder.

"Scotty, I will not tell you again, open the window and let me in!"

My hand moves even closer to the latch, until I am touching it. I shake my head.

My father's anger falls away. "Please, son. Please. It's so cold." He places a hand on the glass, his eyes pleading.

I want to open the window. I can feel the cold metal of the latch. All it would take is a slight pull and the window would be unbound. He begs me, his voice creeping in until there is nearly no reason not to.

He's cold, freezing. I have to. I start to pull on the latch.

No, wait. I stop, finally remembering something.

I look at my father, his lips just starting to turn blue.

"My father's asleep. I checked on him after he went to bed to make sure." I lift up the poker, and the man who looks like my father frowns. He cocks his head, then shrugs. His eyes darken and move like something slithers beneath them.

"Goodnight, Scotty. There's always tomorrow." With that he backs away from the window, his gaze never leaving me, until he disappears into the woods near the cabin.

Just as he had two nights ago.

I had promised myself I wouldn't hesitate this time, but still I came too close to opening the window. I don't know why, but I know he wants in. I can't let him.

I finally lower the poker and take a breath. My heart pounds in my ears. Now I can't sleep. I know it. Despite that, I move to my bed, replace the poker beneath the mattress where I have been keeping it, and turn out the light.

To my surprise, I fall asleep in minutes.

"DID YOU SLEEP well last night?" my mother asks at breakfast.

I nod and yawn. My father rolls his eyes but smiles. "Stayed up reading again..." He lets the next part of his question trail off, but it is finished by my mother.

"Did you see him again?"

I told them about the—I am not sure what to call him. The imposter? The other father? I don't know. But I told them the next day after it happened the first time, over a week ago. They were sympathetic. They said all the things. It's not real; it's just an imaginary friend. Of course it is normal to think you see things in the woods at night. My father shared a story from when he was young, about a monster in the basement of his house. Shelley, my seven-year-old sister, nearly bawled as he told the story. I knew he was putting it on for her sake. Still, I tried to convince them that my "boogeyman" was real. I asked them to stay up with me, to prove it. Of course, he did not come that night.

Now it is a joke, a child's tale.

I shake my head as I eat my oatmeal. My mother caresses my brown hair before sitting down to her own bowl. The conversation quickly turns away from my night visitor to Father's plans for the day. We are on vacation, a family tradition. We usually stay in town, but Father decided this year would be different. I suppose he was right in more ways than one. Had I known, I would have stayed at home, even if it meant going to school.

"So, there is a really neat hiking trail near here. I think we should check it out today."

"Is there?" my mother asks and gives me a look. She is not one to go on a hike, not like Father who fancies himself "an outdoorsman," as Mother says. I smirk, then frown. The thought of the woods is a stone in my stomach.

"Can we see more of the pretty leaves?" Shelley asks.

"Of course, sweetie," my father says and grins.

Shelley squeals with delight and claps her hands. She has been having a ton of fun since we got here. I'm glad for her but...

"Aren't you excited, too?"

"Yeah," I reply, glancing up at my father. For a moment, his lips look blue, his nose red, and something slithers behind his eyes. I jerk, nearly toppling over my glass of apple juice.

"Honey, are you all right?"

"I'm okay," I say, looking back at my father. The only expression on his face is one of concern. "I'm okay," I say again. My parents share a glance, and I can already see another therapy session in my future. The rest of the meal, I am quiet while my sister sings about leaves.

By noon, we are walking the trail, a sea of black trees covered in orange, yellow, and red leaves spreading out around us, broken up by stubborn green bushes unwilling to accept the change of season. My shoes crunch as I walk, and I zip my red jacket up just a bit more. The mid-October day is cool, a sharp breeze slicing through the path toward us. Mother takes a few pictures as we go, pointing out interesting sights: a fallen tree, small, flat orange mushrooms, a lone shoe, and a gray rabbit. Shelley wants to go after it, but Father holds her back.

He grins and takes a big whiff of the air. "Isn't this great, Scotty?"

I nod, silently wishing to be anywhere else.

As the day wears on, I start to feel better. Mother declares it is time for a rest, mostly due to Shelley complaining that she is going to starve to death. The spot we pick is peaceful, almost as if it was made to rest in. Wide-cut stumps pepper the clearing, a carpet of leaves act as a perimeter while browning grass fills the center. Staring up, I can see the cloudy sky. A few birds flitter here and there.

My thoughts drift away from the previous evening as I eat my turkey sandwich. Our picnic reminds me of one of the books left in our cabin from a previous visitor. I might try to read it before we leave. Soon my father begins to sing, and without thinking, I join my mother and sister as they add their voices to my father's. The clearing fills with song and the muffled quiet of the woods falls away before us. Laughter fills the echo of our singing, and for a time, it is like it has always been when we take these vacations. Just us, having fun. I throw leaves at Shelley and she chases me out of anger.

"Stop that, you two," Mother says, laughing and shaking her head. Father picks up a lone branch and charges at us.

"Avast, ye heathens! Stop I say!" he roars and joins in the chase.

Shelley darts past me and breaks through the tree line, shrieking and laughing.

"Stay in the clearing!" Mother calls, but it is too late. Father and I run after her, Father threatening to make her "walk the plank" and "feed her to the Kraken" if she does not stop. I catch glimpses of her ahead of me, giggling. I finally catch up with her, accidentally slamming into her back. I clasp her by the arm before she falls.

"Ow, watch it, you big meanie!"

"Hey, you stopped," I say back. She pouts and steps away from me, then points to my right.

"There you guys are," my father says, a bit out of breath.

I ignore him, my eyes on the dilapidated cabin about twenty feet away. It looks like ours, only weather-worn and hollowed out, a skeletal face with windows like glassless gaping eyes, sunken in beside a lopsided mouth of a door. The porch sags in places and many of the boards are missing. A nearby tree seemingly grows from the roof, or into the roof. From where I stand, I can't say. All I know is I am certain it is a haunted place. I can already see it now, monsters under the floorboards, shadows in the closets, voices from beneath the beds, and scratches at the windows.

"Will you look at that!" Father steps past us, surveying the looming carcass.

"Where are you guys?" Mother calls loudly from somewhere behind us.

"Over here, Katie!" Father calls back, still admiring the cabin. "Come see this."

Within a few moments, Mother joins us. "Shelley," she starts, stepping in front of my sister, "you know better than to run off like that. What if you got lost?"

Shelley frowns and shakes her head.

"It's all right," Father says. "Look what she found."

"Oh my, that is a mess," she says, finally looking at the wrecked cabin.

"I know. Who wants to check it out?" My father grins and starts walking slowly toward the cabin.

"Archie, no."

"Come on, one quick look." He peers at Shelley, who buries her head in Mother's side. Father turns to me. "It's up to us then?"

I shake my head.

"Oh, come on, Scotty. There's nothing to be scared of. You're with your old man. I'll protect you." He grins again and gestures at me to follow.

Dejectedly, I join him.

"Don't stay in there too long. We should be starting back soon," Mother says as we reach the rotted porch.

Father moves carefully, showing me where to set my foot as to not fall through any slats. The door is barely hanging by a hinge, and Father pushes it aside with ease. The creak of our feet on the wooden planks sounds like cracking bones. Father leads the way into the darkened building. I follow closely.

"What is that?" I ask as I cover my nose. A sickly sweet smell fills the room. Dark stains, old leaves, spider webs, and dust blanket everything.

"I think some…animals went at it in here." Father glances at the stains.

"I don't like this place," I say and start backing up. "Let's just go."

Father looks around. "Go back out with your mom. I'll just be a few minutes."

"I think we should both go…" My father just smiles at me reassuringly, then gestures for me to go. Still covering my nose and trying not to gag, I quickly dash out of the cabin and join my mother and sister.

To his word, a few minutes pass and my father exits the cabin, moving quickly over to us.

"Satisfied?" Mother asks, and he nods. "Good, it's starting to get cold." She takes Shelley's hand and leads her toward a side path that curves back the way we started. Father falls in step with me as the others move ahead. My father sets a hand on my shoulder and smiles at me.

"Nothing to be ashamed of, Scotty. There are some places children shouldn't go. I forget that sometimes."

I frown. I am not a child. I am almost a teenager. As if he knows what I'm thinking, he squeezes my shoulder. The distance between us and Mother and Shelley widens as they quicken their pace. He looks around, taking in the scenery as we walk. I catch something in the distance, a sound behind us. I just want to get back now, but I pause. The sound comes again, a bit louder but still undecipherable. I try to move toward it, but Father is still holding on to me. I don't think he notices the sound. I am about to tell him to let go when I hear the sound once again, louder.

"Scotty!" It is my father's voice, far away, muffled by distance. I peer in its direction.

It has to be the other one. Father has to believe me now.

I look up at my father beside me, hope filling my chest. He peers toward the sound of his voice, a frown on his face. He hears it.

He will believe me now.

The voice sounds closer, and I can hear the sound of leaves crunching, a steady march toward us. I meet my father's gaze. He looks down at me, cocks his head, then shrugs as something slithers behind his eyes.

"See you later, Scotty," he says, then walks quickly backwards into the woods, disappearing from sight.

I am almost hyperventilating by the time my real father reaches me.

"Why did you guys leave?" my father asks, panting. "Did your mom get cold?"

"Did you see him?" I ask. The questioning look on my father's face answers me. "Never mind," I say softly.

"Let's catch up with the girls." He ushers me forward to rejoin my mother and sister. The entire time it takes us to walk back, I am watching for any sign of the other one.

I SPEND THE night with the poker in my hand, the small lamp near my bed on, and my attention drawn to the slightest sound. I wake up the next morning still gripping the poker and have to hide it quickly before anyone else sees it. They have been looking for it since I took it on our fourth night here. Slipping it back under the mattress, I move over to the window.

There was no sign of the other one at my window last night.

Looking now, all I see are the trees and falling leaves. Before, the nights scared me, but now, I peer at the woods, looking for any sign, any shadow. Nothing moves except for two crows hopping along the earthen floor before taking off.

Still, I am uneasy.

The next two days drift by with no sign of the other father. On the second day, we head to town. Halloween is nearly upon us, and people are already decorating. Mother wants to go thrift-store shopping while Father's interest lies with Worthington's Antiques. I am not a fan of such places, but I don't dare let him out of my sight, not after the other day. What if the other one is not confined to the woods? What if he can appear anywhere? So I follow my father into the smelly old store, a step behind him as he admires ancient clocks and lumpy-looking chairs. Father greets the shop owner, a small man in a large suit. The owner smiles, and the two quickly begin a conversation. Father enjoys speaking to everyone.

Still keeping them in view, I pass by busts of old men and polished wooden chests, until I find myself at a bulletin board. On it are dozens of faded fliers, all held up by different-colored push pins. Some are old newspaper clippings about the shop, some are open posts about concerts from bands that were together thirty years ago, and some are old advertisements. But what draws my attention are the eyes that stare back. At least a dozen faces, yellowed and worn, look at me from old fliers. Boys and girls, some with braces, some with freckles, all of them are smiling, unmoving. I read the names of a handful of them: Martin Dempsey, Edith Hughes, Mary O'Brien, Terrence Warren, and Logan Peter Rory. There are more hidden beneath other, newer bulletins. They all seem different, their ages, the looks in their eyes, but what they all have in common is a single word: Missing. I stare at them until their flattened gazes start to feel real, and then I turn away.

I hurry back to my father, still keenly aware that they are watching me. The conversation between my father and the shop owner has turned toward the old cabin we had found.

"Oh, there are numerous cabins like that in those woods." The owner chuckles. "Spooky place," he adds when he notices me.

"Beautiful place to walk. My wife has taken so many pictures of the leaves, I'm worried she'll become a tree." My father laughs loudly.

"Yes, it is a popular draw. Many of us locals don't bother with them. There are…better places to hike. Have you tried Lake Dunmore?" The owner's face looks stretched, his smile tight as he tells my father about the lake. He keeps glancing at me from the corner of his eye. My heart skips a beat, and I peer at him intently.

Did his eyes slither? His clothes look too big, like they weren't meant for him. I peer around quickly, looking for some sign that my suspicions are right, proof that the owner isn't who he says he is. All that I see is old furniture. I look back at the owner; he is still eyeing me. I pull on my father's shirt twice before finally getting his attention.

"Can we go?"

"In a minute," he says before returning his attention to the owner.

My skin itches with all the attention the man is giving me. I think of the fliers of the missing children and pull on my father's shirt harder.

"What?"

"I have to go to the bathroom." It is the best thing I can come up with.

Father smiles apologetically at the owner. "I don't suppose you have a bathroom?"

I didn't think of that. I glance up at the owner. He eyes me once again, then smiles.

"Unfortunately, it is out of order, but there is one at the gas station at the end of the block." He gestures to the left.

"I see. All right, well, thank you."

"Of course. Check out the lake. It is much better than the woods," he calls as we leave.

For the rest of the day, my semblance of ease is gone. Every face we pass, I look for slithering behind their eyes, while every reflection in shop windows holds a face from a missing kid. I barely touch my hamburger at dinner. I don't like the way the waitress is looking at me.

By the time we get home, I am exhausted. Shelley wants to play a board game, and I play along. She is ecstatic when she beats me. I am not paying attention. I still see those flat eyes from the flyers and feel the stare of the shop owner. All I can do is count the minutes until my family is asleep. A restlessness fills me like Christmas Eve but for all the wrong reasons. My friend Jakob told me when I still believed in Santa that there was another Claus, one with horns and a sack, who took the naughty kids away. No one believed him, of course. But if it is true, then this other Claus would be whom I am waiting for.

Thinking of Jakob only worsens my mood.

As the lights in my parents' room finally go out, I take the poker from its hiding place and begin my vigil. Every hour, I slip out of my room and sit next to my parents' door. The heavy breathing of my father is unmistakable. It relaxes me and urges me to keep up my watch.

As the clock nears three in the morning, I creep through the cabin, looking out the windows. We are surrounded by trees on three sides. Near the front door, I glance out at the station wagon. Beyond it lies the driveway and the side road that leads to the highway. My gaze lingers, focusing on the driveway. I don't notice the shadow until I hear the creak of wood from the porch.

The figure passes the front door until he is standing at the window, looking down at me. I grip my poker tighter. My father, this time, is dressed like the shop owner from earlier. He eyes the poker in my hand, then focuses on me. He seems so tall. The bulky suit makes him look so wide. I steal a glance at the front door. *Could he break through it?* When I look back, his attention is no longer on me, but on something behind me. Before I can turn, he moves quickly toward the kitchen, out of my sight.

I sigh and relax my grip. I finally turn to peer at what caught his attention, hoping it is something I might use in the future, like garlic for a vampire. When I finally realize what he was looking at, my blood freezes. The window near the northern side of the cabin is open about an inch. I dart forward and reach it just as he comes into view. I shut the window, almost on top of his fingers, and lock it. He scowls at me, then grins. Gesturing behind me, I quickly turn to see the hall light on and my mother in her bathrobe stepping into the room.

Yawning, she says, "Honey, what are you doing up? It's very late."

"Look," I start and turn back to the window, but the other father is gone.

"Honey, where did you find that?" Mother asks as she walks over and takes the poker from my hand. "We've been looking everywhere for it." She yawns again as she sets the poker in the rack by the fireplace. "Did your boogeyman come again?"

I don't say anything. She smiles and pulls me close to her.

"Come on, let's go back to bed." She leads me back to my room.

Once she is asleep, I retrieve the poker and go back to bed.

AS OUR TRIP draws to a close, I feel like I need a vacation. The last twelve days have weighed on me. I am quiet all day, just waiting for the night to fall.

One more vigil, that is all. Then we leave in the morning.

I long for my small room in our little apartment overlooking 51st Avenue in the city, without these dark trees where shadows linger. I think of my friends, but every time I see their faces, they look yellowed and flat. I am tired of looking at my father's face and wondering if he is the one staring back at me. And even if it is my father, the looks he gives me now when he thinks I'm not paying attention are filled with worry. Mother's too. I know they have discussed me; I can practically hear the conversation.

"I'm worried, Katie. This other father business is not normal," I imagine him saying.

"Archie, it's only natural to have a boogeyman," Mother would reply.

"But Katie, this is a bit much. He keeps a poker under his mattress." My father would pinch the bridge of his nose.

"I know, Archie. But it makes him feel safe." She would try to reassure him even if her voice catches a bit.

"Now Katie, he is nearly thirteen. I think he should speak to the doctor again. He helped him before after that Jakob boy incident," Father would say, a shake of his head as he spoke.

Mother would pause, thinking before finally saying, "Perhaps you are right, Archie. It certainly can't hurt. Dr. Rosenbaum fixed him before."

I shake my head as the scenario plays out in my mind. I don't want to see Dr. Rosenbaum. I don't like how he coughs into his closed fist when he talks, or how he writes in his notepad whenever I answer his questions, or how, because of him, I can't see my friend Jakob anymore.

I don't care if he was a "bad influence."

It will get better once we are back home, I tell myself as the sun starts to set. We had dinner in town, a little Italian place we always eat at when we come up here. The drive back to our cabin is mostly quiet, with Mother and Father listening to Sinatra or what they called "decent music." I keep my gaze on the woods as we drive by, the fuchsia sky darkening to purple then navy blue. The trees stand black and tall, shadows spread between them like a secret shared amongst friends. Shelley is beside me, drawing with her crayons. Her pictures are filled with trees, an autumnal display. Her tongue pokes out the edge of her lips and her brow furrows as she works. She takes her coloring very seriously. Any other time, I would have snatched the page from her to see exactly what she was drawing, but I just don't feel like it right now.

As we turn down the driveway to our cabin, the headlights illuminate the porch, and I blink. For a second, it reminds me of the cabin we found, a darkened monster, a skeleton of a building. But it has to be a trick of the headlights…

Right?

Once we are inside, Shelley heads to the coffee table to finish her coloring while Mother and Father put on the radio to listen to the news. I try to read one of the books that I had found on my second day here, but my attention keeps drifting toward the woods. *Will he come tonight?* In my gut, I know he will. It is his last chance. I am tempted to simply ignore him.

I push the thoughts away and return to the book. It is a level above what I usually read and set in exotic Australia. It talks about a picnic and a girl's boarding school. To be honest, I have read the same sentence four times. I am only a couple of pages in.

Sighing, I set the book down. Between the sound of the news anchor talking about a new federal holiday in January, and my parents' conversation regarding what to do for Thanksgiving this year, I can't focus. The drone of the anchor is grating, and even from where I am sitting near the fireplace, I can hear my sister's crayons on the paper.

"Aren't you done yet?" I say, and she peers up at me, her surprise turning to a pout.

"No."

"Honey, let her draw. She isn't bothering anyone," Mother says.

Their eyes are on me now, that same worry that has deepened ever since we came here. I clench my fist, and without realizing it, I move over to the coffee table and swat at the collection of drawings. Pages scatter like leaves, falling to the floor. Shelley lets out a shriek and runs to Mother, who, along with Father, is already hurrying over.

"To your room!" my mother commands.

"That's not my room," I say to myself as I leave the living room and my sister's tears.

I didn't mean to do that. I feel a bit bad, but at least I am away from all the noise.

By the time my official bedtime rolls around, my father opens my door to tell me to get ready for bed. There is a stern look in his eye, different than the other ones, and I am almost happy to have earned such an expression, even if I know a conversation is in my future. He waits for me to finish getting ready. He is on my bed when I come back into the room, his gaze on the window.

Does he see something? Could he? Or is that just for me?

Father pats the comforter, and I sit beside him. "Your mother and I have been talking."

Here it comes, I think.

"And we think that it wouldn't hurt to see Dr. Rosenbaum."

"I don't want to," I say as I look at the floor. "He's weird."

My father pats my back. "Now that isn't fair. He is a fine therapist, and he helped you before. He can help you again with this acting out and boogeyman business."

"But..."

"It is for the best, Scotty," he says, his tone final.

All I can do is nod.

He gets to his feet and walks to my door. "Also, you owe your sister an apology tomorrow at breakfast." There is no anger in his voice, just certainty.

Again, I nod.

"Good night, Scotty."

"Good night."

He turns off the light as he exits the room, leaving the door ajar.

My parents stay awake for a long time. I can hear the radio in their room, the shuffle of movement behind the door, and the sharp yellow glow of a lamp that seeps into the hall. I wait in my room, the poker hidden under the covers with me. I can't wait for this night to end, but I also don't want to go home. The other father scares me. Dr. Rosenbaum scares me.

Maybe Father will relent? It is possible, if I can capture the other father, prove he is real.

"Then they have to believe me," I whisper to the pillow. *But how?* I stew over ideas, of things I have read, of cartoons I have watched. The longer I mull over it, the less certain I feel. I should have planned for this. I could have set something up in the daylight. Frowning, I sit up and peer at the window in the gloom.

The first night, I thought I was dreaming. The scratching sound had been soft, almost hesitant, until it wasn't. I had woken up with a start in darkness. Yawning, I laid back down when I heard it again, more clearly. I had called out for Shelley, thinking she was trying to mess with me. It wasn't Shelley who had answered. Like the other times to follow, he started by calling my name. Soft at first, then more insistent. The voice belonged to my father. I had gotten out of bed and went to the door at first but quickly realized where the voice was coming from. It was strange to see my father out there. I nearly opened the window immediately. He asked, then demanded, then pleaded, and like many of the times after, I found myself about to unlatch the window. Something about him frightened me the first night, and before he could persuade me, or stop me, I ran to get Mother. Seeing my father in bed was quite a shock. Mother and Father called it a nightmare, then a boogeyman.

Now I am sitting up, waiting for this boogeyman, still uncertain how I can trap him. The radio in my parents' room is silent, no more movement from behind their door, and I have only the darkness of night around me. I turn on my lamp, hurry up and prepare. I carefully pull down the drapes and begin tying knots. I envision this tightly woven net. I make a thick rope, barely three feet long. Committed, I hurry into the living room and, as quietly as I can, pull down the drapes there. By the time I am done, the thick rope is longer now, enough for me to mimic the snare I saw in a cartoon. I set it down next to the window and wait. For this to work, I need to let him in a bit. Halfway through, I will throw the snare around him and trap him. Then I will call for my parents. They will see him and finally believe me.

Gripping the poker, I stand near the window, waiting.

The minutes tick by until an hour passes. I begin to fidget. Where is he? I know he will come. Out of everything, I know that. He will come. He *will* come. I shift from one foot to the other as I wipe my palms on my pajama bottoms. Every sound is a boom. I listen for the scratches, the creak of wood, or the crunch of a foot on the grass outside my window.

Nothing.

One hour becomes two, and I am pacing. I imagine if I continue, I will wear a trench into the wooden floor. More importantly, the more I think about it, the less certain I am about my plan. He can't come in. He can't. It is what he wants. I will not let him. His eyes, they stand out, even now. A slither beneath the white almost as if his eyes are made up of hundreds of worms or maggots. My skin crawls, gooseflesh blanketing me. I kick the makeshift snare away.

Dr. Rosenbaum is better than him.

Still... I glance at the window. I was so sure he would come. Biting my lip, I creep closer, looking out into the night. Nothing moves. Maybe I am wrong? My glimmer of hope grays as I remember the other night. Hurrying into the living room, I start looking at all the windows. Is one open? Did he get in? I move quickly. No. That one is closed. Kitchen? Closed. Back door? He never tried any of the doors. Still, I check the knob. Locked. I hurry over to the back windows. Shut.

Panting, I sink to the floor.

Am I wrong? He's not coming? Relief floods me. Tomorrow I am free of him. I lay on my back on the wooden floor. Home. Away from this place. It is all I can picture. I want to laugh. Instead, I punch the air before letting my arms fall back down. My left hand grazes something thin. It makes a crinkling sound when I touch it again. Rolling over toward it, I pick it up. It is a piece of paper. Getting up, I try to look it over, but the room is too dark.

I head toward my room. A soft glow stops me in my tracks. Are Mother and Father awake? I can picture the door opening and them, in their bathrobes, with sleep in their eyes and scowls on their faces, looking at me. Another line to add to Dr. Rosenbaum's notepad. But my thoughts get ahead of me. The light is coming from Shelley's room. I shake my head and let out a breath.

What is she doing up? I am about to push open the door when my hand stops in midair. She is probably still mad at me. She is like that. And besides, I don't want her waking up Mother and Father. Turning away, I hurry into my room.

I move to the window. No sign of him. I let out a laugh. He gave up. I win. I want to shout, but I know better. Setting the poker beside my bed, I finally peer down at the piece of paper I am holding. It is one of Shelley's drawings. Her precise lines and careful strokes are immediately apparent. I was more of a color-outside-the-lines type. Shelley would be mortified if even a line was out of place. Looking over the picture, it is easy to figure out. A girl with light brown hair lies atop a yellow bed with a chocolate brown head-board. The floor is a tan line bleeding into a peach-colored wall. In the center of the wall is a window showing a midnight blue sky. It is her room here. I am about to set it on the nightstand by the bed when I notice something in her drawing. Looking closer at the picture, there is another person in it. In the window.

My heart pounds.

"Shelley!"

I drop the paper and hurry to her room. Flinging the door open, I step in and stop. Shelley turns to look at me, surprise mixed with sleep. She stands by her window. Her open window. Beside her, slowly getting to his feet, dressed in familiar light blue, pinstripe pajamas, is my father.

"Daddy was cold," she says, but I am not listening. My eyes are glued to him.

He gets to his feet and stretches his back. He looks around as if taking in the room for the first time. His eyes finally settle back on me, his moving, slithering eyes. He isn't even trying to hide them now. He smiles deeply, the corners of his lips growing wider and wider. He sets a hand on Shelley's shoulder, drawing her close while still staring at me.

"Father," I try to call out, but my voice is a wheeze.

The other father cocks his head before finally speaking.

"I'm inside, Scotty. I'm inside."

In an instant he is beside me, looming over me. I can't move. He seems so large now, so close. All I see is him, his face, those eyes. Shelley is behind him, still addled by sleep. He reaches up and grabs the edge of the door. His eyes never leave me.

"It's all right, Scotty. Everything will be all right." He grins wider. "I can't wait for you to meet the others."

He pulls me forward and shuts the door.

GHOUL KING

Scott Harper

F LAYER OBSERVED FROM UNDER A canopy of thick oak trees as
the human tribe prepared for battle. The men with war-painted faces
armed themselves with swords and axes and donned leather cuirasses, intent
on raiding a neighboring village for supplies and slaves. Flayer grinned, exposing his sharp teeth—he knew these warriors were dead men walking.

A waxing gibbous moon lit the flatland as Flayer rose and signaled his
second-in-command. Liverbelch was stout for a ghoul, with a bull neck and
thick upper torso covered in battle scars. He sounded the cry, his shrill voice
echoing in the night like the clarion call of a hunting horn. The assembled
ghouls under Flayer's command responded, surging from their hiding spots
and descending on the startled villagers like a dark tidal wave.

The lithe flesh-eaters loped across the clearing with unnatural speed and
grace, more animal than human, deftly avoiding the warriors' weapons. Their
claws easily tore through leather and skin, ripping muscle and scraping bone.
The village men screamed as they died, their blood and entrails splashing on
the uncaring ground.

Flayer strode into the battle, a look of contentment on his hawkish face.
He sidestepped a thrust from a warrior's blade and slashed the man's throat
with his sharp claws. Flayer followed the man to the ground, latching his
black maw onto the ruptured neck and gulping down a fast meal of blood

and muscle. The sweet flesh filled him with renewed energy and strength.

The ghoul leader's attention was abruptly drawn from his prey to the panicked cries of his people. He watched the human chieftain and his captains enter the fray. The man was much taller and broader than his kinsman, his large frame filled with corded muscle and covered in protective metal. A gold crown inlaid with rubies sat atop his raven-maned head. Confidence beamed from the chieftain's blue eyes as he wielded a massive war hammer. The destructive weapon boasted a heavy flat iron head on one side wedded to a sharp spike on the other. The ground seemed to shake under his strides. He batted the attacking ghouls away, smashing the bones of some and puncturing the skulls of others, leaving a trail of ruptured corpses in his wake. His captains flared out, striking down ghouls with expert precision, their swords pinioning the flesh-eaters' hearts.

Liverbelch tossed aside his most recent kill and moved to intercept the chieftain, but Flayer growled menacingly, calling Liverbelch off. The second-in-command dipped his head, acknowledged the will of his leader, and moved to help the other flesh-eaters counter the captains' offensive.

Flayer sprinted across the clearing and leaped high in the air, his long arms outstretched to tear the human apart. The chieftain stood his ground and punched the ghoul leader in the jaw, a resounding blow that broke a tooth and sent him staggering back. Flayer regrouped, only to have the chieftain strike him in the chest with the blunt end of the war hammer, splintering bone with a sickening crack. Flayer fell to the ground and lay still, his arms splayed out to his sides.

The chieftain cautiously approached, his weapon raised spike-side-forward above his head to deliver the final blow. Flayer felt the broken bones in his chest realign and heal. He was not a common flesh-eater—having drunk from the dark veins of Lord Marrowthirst, he possessed the strength of many of his kind.

The chieftain stopped dead in his tracks, a look of astonishment on his face as Flayer rose with inhuman dexterity to his feet. The ghoul leader gestured with his claws, eyes bright with anticipation, encouraging the human to attack. The chieftain accepted, bellowing as he brought the war hammer down with tremendous force toward Flayer's head.

But Flayer caught the iron head in his claws and stopped its momentum. His strength far outstripped the human's as he tore the weapon from the man's grip. Flayer seized the astonished chieftain by the throat and lifted him high in the air. He held him there, the man's hands and legs futilely flailing, as if making an example of him for the others to see. The ghoul brought the warrior down across his outstretched knee, breaking his back with a sickening cracking sound.

Flayer tore away the protective metal cuirass from the chieftain's torso and ripped into the exposed stomach. As the paralyzed man screamed in agony, Flayer dug his claws deep and ripped out the stringy intestines in a spray of gore. He stepped aside as his people descended upon the chieftain's twitching body and tore it to shreds.

Flayer surveyed the battle as it drew to a conclusion. The captains had effectively been dealt with, their broken forms spread out across the field. The final one fell to his knees, battered to the point of unconsciousness by Liverbelch. Flayer's second-in-command quickly ended the contest, smashing in the captain's head with a bone club. The man's brains leaked out of his ears and nose onto the ground.

While his ghouls feasted on their enemies' corpses, Flayer looked to a nearby wooden hut in the slave quarters, his keen senses detecting warm human flesh within. A young slave woman looked out from the entrance. She showed no fear as Flayer approached her.

The woman was attractive, with sapphire eyes framed by flowing black hair. Her features were symmetrical, the nose thin and lips heart-shaped. The cloth tunic she wore emphasized her wiry muscularity, her belly taut below her sculptured breasts. Numerous welt marks discolored her skin, signs of ongoing abuse from her master. Despite her circumstance, she carried herself proudly. Flayer felt a tinge of lust swell in his loins, a faded memory of his discarded human life. He instinctively reached out to her.

The woman did not flinch as he took her small hand in his bloody claw, nor did she shy away from the cool touch of his sallow skin.

"Amala," the woman said, pointing to her chest.

Flayer nodded his head in acknowledgment, impressed by her boldness: few were the humans (let alone a woman at that) who did not immediately turn and flee from his presence.

But then a thin hand wrapped itself in Amala's hair and pulled her back through the portal. Flayer raced in to find an older, pot-bellied man in a red robe repeatedly striking the woman about the face and shoulders. Amala countered the slave owner's offensive, biting the hand that struck her, drawing blood, and causing the man to scream in agony.

Flayer had seen enough. He seized the slave owner and broke his neck with a brutal economy of movement. Amala crouched in the corner of the hut, sniffling, humiliated by what had just occurred.

Flayer paid it no mind. He grasped Amala by her forearms and pulled her gently into his embrace. Her eyes silently thanked him as he led her away from the hut to his people.

The ghouls looked upon her in awe as she walked unafraid among them. One of the younger ghouls, a flesh-eater named Gizzard, tried to touch the woman's hand. Flayer clawed the youngling's face, leaving oozing furrows on his cheek. The young ghoul cried out in pain and darted away. The other ghouls kept their distance.

Flayer screeched at Liverbelch, instructing him to pilfer the chieftain's ornate hut. Liverbelch complied, darting into the large domicile at the center of the village. The remaining villagers, a mix of young and old with women outnumbering men, lingered on the outskirts, hoping for the invaders to soon depart. A few former slaves discovered that they were now free and hid amongst the survivors. Flayer made sure enough young men remained alive that the village could eventually repopulate and provide a food source for his people.

A young boy approached the bloody mess that had been the chieftain, tears in his eyes as he reached down and held the fallen man's bloody hand. The image caught Flayer off-guard, causing long-suppressed memories to flood his brain.

Flayer saw himself as a child in a simple hut, sitting in front of a warm fireplace, his eyes captivated by the dancing flames. "Flayer" had not been his name then, though he could no longer recall his birth name. Mother was setting the small dinner table, the sweet aroma of scented meat, vegetables, and fresh bread brimming in the air. He knew his father was absent, on a mission with the other men to end the scourge of death that had recently visited the town. A mysterious creature preyed on the village, claiming a victim nightly and leaving bloodless corpses in its wake.

Father returned that night, smashing in the front door and letting in the freezing wind that blew down from the mountains. A chill ran down Flayer's back as he regarded the imposing figure standing before him. This person was not the same man who had left them two days earlier; instead, it was an alien creature masquerading in his father's form. Father's green eyes were now bloodshot and feral, beaming wickedly from black sockets; saliva dripped from sharp yellowed teeth. Father's skin was fish-white and lined with pale lacerations, as if he had been clawed many times by a fierce animal. Most of his ample hair had fallen out. His big hands, the hands with which he cradled Flayer and rocked him to sleep at night, were now claws, the long fingers ending in sharp nails. Father had become a creature of nightmare—a monstrous ghoul.

He lunged at Mother as she screamed in horror. The monster threw her to the ground and bit into her throat, ripping out chunks of bloody meat. Flayer picked up a blade Mother had been using to prepare dinner and attacked the creature, but it slapped the knife from his hands, clawing his forearms in the process. At that moment, the ghoul transferred its strange curse to Flayer, the poison of its claws seeping into his veins and changing him. He felt a peculiar hunger come over him as Father signaled to him with gory nails, bidding him partake from mother's corpse.

The lust for flesh was suddenly overwhelming. Saliva pooled hot in his mouth as his teeth became tiny daggers. Flayer dug his newly sharp claws into her stomach, through skin and muscle, tearing out trails of viscera and stuffing them in his drooling mouth. The taste was beyond anything he had ever experienced up until that point in his young life, far sweeter than any dish Mother had ever prepared. He savored each and every morsel as they devoured Mother, and the flesh-eater curse was forever sealed.

Flayer's attention was brought back to matters at hand as Liverbelch soon returned with a heavy wooden chest filled with gold coins. Flayer screeched at the young boy, scaring it away from the chieftain's corpse and back into the protective arms of its mother. The boy regarded him with aggrieved eyes as he was led away.

At Flayer's behest, Liverbelch also retrieved the defeated chieftain's crown from his scalp. Some of the village women cast looks of derision toward Amala, but the young woman ignored them. Flayer led her and his crew of fiends away from the shattered town, through the dense forest to the desolate cave they called home. Wolves and other night predators approached the group as they traveled but quickly fled back into the woods, steering clear of the greater predators.

The ghoul leader's mind was conflicted as they walked: he knew from past experience that Lord Marrowthirst would immediately claim Amala for his own, as the vampire routinely did with anything of value the hunting party returned with. Perhaps he should take his chances and make off with her now? But where would they go, and how would they live? He had been a flesh-eater for many years now and could barely recall the day-to-day needs of human beings. And, despite his many victories as their leader, he doubted the other ghouls would follow him in defiance of the dark lord.

They marched into the dark cave opening, which jutted like an open maw from the base of a barren mountain, the peak of which was hidden in swirling black clouds. Darkness surrounded them as they descended into the earth, the air becoming hot and stagnant. Human skeletons littered the ground, evidence of past ghoul meals. Amala walked by his side, firmly gripping his hand.

The tunnel opened into a large, dank cavern lit by dozens of tallow candles. Stalactites hung from the cave ceiling, surrounded by crowded swarms of bats. In one corner stood the weathered skeleton of an enormous bear posed on its hind legs, its vast jaws open in a soundless snarl, held together by strips of human ligament and tendon.

In the center of the cave, atop a massive throne of articulated bone, sat Lord Marrowthirst.

The ancient vampire was more beast than man. His long canine teeth hung over his thin bottom lip, the tips shining in the ambient light. Marrowthirst's ears were long and pointed, resting on either side of his large bald head. The vampire's nose was short and blunt like a bat's, set beneath black eye sockets framing smoldering crimson eyes. His elongated claws clutched the skull armrests of the throne in a regal posture. A creature of the dead, Marrowthirst's chest did not rise and fall with the passage of breath; he sat with a preternatural stillness, silently observing like a stone gargoyle from his perch on high.

The vampire was quite insane. Where the source of the madness sprang from was an unsettled matter. Perhaps it was a quirk of the creature's bloodline passed down from his sire, or possibly lunacy engendered by centuries of endless killing and bloodshed. Whatever the source, the results were clear. Where others would see a motley assortment of wretched, pale-skinned flesh-eaters, Marrowthirst beheld a regiment of loyal, splendidly armored knights carrying brilliant-colored banners. He effusively welcomed the triumphant return of his victorious warriors.

"My battalion returns in glory," Marrowthirst said, rising from the throne, a tattered lavender cape spotted with bloodstains trailing behind him. A large bat perched atop the vampire's naked shoulder. "Regale me with the stories of your triumphs, Lord Flayer."

Flayer cleared his throat. He was used to speaking in the growls and screeches that passed for language among the ghouls. Conversing in the long-forgotten tongue of Marrowthirst's native land took great effort and concentration.

"It was as you said, great Marrowthirst, ruler of the living and the dead. The humans made ready to attack their rivals and were unprepared for our lightning assault."

The vampire smiled. "Gregor is a most wonderful spy," he said, indicating the bat. "Gregor surveilled their activities from the forest for over a week, paving the way for our success. Here, now, Gregor is your reward."

Marrowthirst drew a long black claw across the side of his neck, opening up a black vein. The bat latched its maw to the viscous liquid that dribbled forth. After a few sips, the creature screeched and flew off into the ceiling to join its brethren. The wound in the vampire's neck healed with supernatural celerity.

"Your troops fed abundantly after the victory and will be sated for weeks," Flayer continued. "And we bring you the fruits of battle, Lord Marrowthirst, to honor your greatness."

Flayer screeched at Liverbelch, who brought forth the gold chest and the defeated chieftain's crown. Marrowthirst bellowed in joy as he dug his talons in the coins and flipped them in the air. The vampire seized the ruby crown from Liverbelch and placed it atop his enormous head. Though the headdress appeared comically out of proportion on Marrowthirst's oversized cranium, the vampire paraded around the cavern for all his retinue to see, striking dramatic poses as if he were a thespian.

Amid his ostentatious revels, the vampire's red eyes suddenly fixed on Amala. Marrowthirst smiled in anticipation as he dropped the coins and moved with inhuman speed to her side, sending several ghouls sprawling in his wake.

"What have we here?" the vampire asked, seizing Amala's chin. He moved her head from side to side, inspecting her. Amala's eyes teared at the rough treatment. She sought to pull away but was no match for Marrowthirst's enormous strength.

"A queen you shall be, my love," the vampire said. "I will dress you in the finest silks and feed you meals of pure ambrosia. You shall rule by my side, loving and loyal to my every command."

Flayer felt his stomach sink as he listened to Marrowthirst's delusional rantings, dreading the impending need to confront him. He tried to appease the vampire.

"My lord, I beg you to allow the woman to be with me," Flayer said, moving to interpose himself between Amala and the vampire.

Marrowthirst looked shocked at Flayer's impudence, his lips curling in scorn.

"What?" the vampire asked.

"Surely I deserve her after achieving so many glorious victories for you. Have I not brought you other women in the past?" Flayer inwardly flinched as he recalled the sad fates of those women, their yellowed bones lying unforgotten somewhere on the floor of a branching tunnel.

Marrowthirst gave Flayer a perplexed look.

Flayer persevered. "Would it not show proof of your great benevolence and set an example for the others, the time you chose to gift your man-at-arms with a most simple request?"

"Bah!" the old vampire scoffed. He swatted Flayer aside, smacking him open-faced across the jaw. The blow would have taken a human's head off. As it was, Flayer was knocked off his feet, sailing across the cavern and striking a nearby stalagmite. The mineral stone exploded as the ghoul crashed through it.

For a moment, Flayer wondered if his back was broken. He ignored the pain shooting through his body and steadily rose to his feet.

Amala was screaming as Marrowthirst licked her cheek with a long black tongue and cooed in her ear.

The look of triumph in the vampire's crimson eyes reminded Flayer of the first time he had seen those twin burning orbs up close so soon after his mother's murder.

His father had spoken to him as they made their way from the village to their new home at the base of the barren mountain, shrieking and growling in a guttural language he intuitively understood. Father claimed to have been gifted by Lord Marrowthirst, elevated by claws of the vampire's ghoul retainers, and inducted into the brotherhood of flesh. The ghoul retinue served their lord, protecting him during the day when he was vulnerable and hunting at night to provide him with the blood of fresh victims. In return, the vampire bestowed his sacred blood on a select few of the brotherhood, strengthening and elevating them far beyond simple ghouldom.

When they reached the cave, the other ghouls had parted like a sea before them. He saw Marrowthirst feeding on a woman he recognized from the village, a woman who had disappeared from her hut just the other night. The vampire sucked greedily at her neck, holding her upright with a bat-like arm. The woman's eyes rolled up gruesomely in her head as she was exsanguinated.

When Marrowthirst was finished, he shoved the bloodless corpse aside with enormous vigor. The woman's body flew across the cavern and broke against the stone wall. Then the vampire gestured at them to approach.

His father spoke in the squealing ghoul language. "Lord Marrowthirst, this is my son. I have gifted him with the flesh hunger. He will now serve you in all things."

Marrowthirst looked the young ghoul up and down as if inspecting him.

"He does appear to be a fine, strong lad. The future may well look kindly upon him. But if he is to prosper, his traitorous lineage must be expunged."

A look of horror crossed Father's feral face as the vampire's intent was made manifest.

"Little ghoul, did you think I would so quickly forget that it was you who led the village uprising against me, that it was you drove a wooden stake into my chest as I slept in the daytime?" the vampire asked, pushing aside his tattered clothing to reveal a bloody puncture wound in the chest. "A little closer, and my heart would have been pierced."

Marrowthirst reached out and surrounded his father's head in his long claws. The vampire effortlessly tore off the head with a brutal twist. As the headless body collapsed to the floor, Flayer sank to his knees with it. Grief socked him in the gut, leaving him breathless.

"Forget your old life, child," Marrowthirst said. "Where your father was weak, you shall be strong. I christen you Flayer of the flesh-eaters—embrace your new existence and serve your king well."

The vampire sliced open his wrist and offered his black blood to the young ghoul. The smell of the vitae was overwhelming—Flayer bit into the undead flesh and gulped down the cold fluid. A new strength flooded his body as the vampire's will invaded the ragged remnants of his soul. He became Marrowthirst's creature in both body and mind.

Flayer fought against the vampire's domination as he brought both of his fists down on Marrowthirst's neck, the cavern echoing with the smack of flesh. Marrowthirst ignored the blow and pushed Amala away. He seized Flayer by the neck in a viselike grip. The vampire's long fingers squeezed together as he lifted Flayer into the air, closing off the ghoul's windpipe and threatening to break his neck.

Flayer panicked as he gasped for air, his hands scrabbling uselessly against Marrowthirst's iron grasp. He looked to his fellow ghouls for aid and saw only fear and helplessness in their bright eyes; they knew it was impossible to oppose the will of the dark lord.

Marrowthirst's eyes blazed in triumph as he shook Flayer like a child in his grip. The ghoul felt the vampire's will clamp down on his mind.

"Traitor!" the raving vampire bellowed. "Just like your father! The punishment for treason is death!"

Darkness descended on Flayer's vision as he was strangled. His hands dropped limply to his sides.

A vision unfolded before his mind's eye. He saw himself at the edge of a swirling dark pit, being sucked inexorably toward the vortex. Inside the roiling pit, Father and Mother called to him, beckoning him to rejoin his family. He found himself stepping forward, ready to launch himself from the edge.

As abruptly as it had begun, the vision ended, and Flayer was thrust back into his body. Marrowthirst stumbled forward, loosening his clutch. Flayer fell to the ground. He saw a large spike of broken stalagmite protruding from the vampire's back, the undead creature's black ichor pooling from the wound.

Marrowthirst turned slowly to face his attacker.

Amala shrunk back from the vampire, her hands in front of her to ward off his attack.

"He has infected you with his treasonous ways, my queen," Marrowthirst said. "I will rectify that immediately."

Flayer seized upon the moment, rushing Marrowthirst as the vampire reached for Amala and knocking him to the ground. Rage fueled the ghoul, bitter hatred for the living dead creature as he rained blow after blow upon the vampire's face, breaking bone. Still, despite the damage he inflicted, Flayer could feel the ancient undead regrouping, gathering his strength and preparing to thrust Flayer off.

Then the other ghouls unexpectedly descended like a wolf pack on Marrowthirst. Freed from the paralysis of fear and spurred by the courage of Flayer and Amala, they grappled the vampire's limbs in an attempt to pin him to the ground. The undead monster did not go down easily. A swipe of his claws relieved a ghoul named Viscera of his head. Marrowthirst tore another ghoul's arm from its socket in a bloody spray. His long fangs punctured the forehead of a third ghoul who foolishly tried to bite the vampire's neck.

Yet, where one ghoul fell, two more took its place. Despite his ferocious strength and the aura of dread he projected, Marrowthirst was forced to the ground, each limb covered in writhing flesh eaters. The vampire bellowed, his rage echoing in the cavern.

Flayer bestrode Marrowthirst and smashed his claws through the vampire's chest, digging through muscle and bone until his fingers encircled the cold black heart. The ghoul leader tore the organ free and held it high, black blood spraying in the air.

Simultaneously, Liverbelch buried his claws deep into Marrowthirst's neck. He dug down until he reached the spine, then pulled with all his feral strength, wrenching the vampire's head from his shoulders. The dark lord's body immediately ceased its struggle, though its eyes still batted back and forth in their black sockets, conscious of what was occurring.

Flayer bit deep into the vampire's pulsing heart, draining black ichor from it. The ghoul felt icy tendrils shoot throughout his body, driving out any remnants of the man he had once been. Great strength flooded his limbs as his heart stopped beating, and he ceased breathing. Two ancient curses collided and jostled for supremacy within him, birthing a new and unique eldritch entity.

With the vampire's blood also came his memories—Marrowthirst's unlife unfurled before Flayer.

He saw the dark lord as a newly born vampire freshly risen from the grave, tearing aside dirt and stone as he burst from his thin wooden coffin in a grim parody of birth. This Marrowthirst was youthful in appearance, with flowing brown hair framing the handsome features of his face.

His maker, a dark woman dressed in a black grave shroud, awaited him, exuding eldritch power as she welcomed him into her cold arms. Together they ruled a kingdom from atop a great castle, feeding on the helpless mortals whenever they saw fit. Humans betrayed humans, offering their brothers and sisters up to the vampires in the hopes of one day being chosen to join the undead in eternal life.

But humans were a varied lot; while many willingly groveled before the immortals, some had steel spines and rose to throw off their vampire oppressors. Flayer watched as a sea of mortals armed with swords and stakes descended on the castle, murdering the human servants and stringing up their disemboweled bodies from the palisades to warn others. He saw the vampires fight back in all their glory, moving amongst the fragile humans with the force of a hurricane. The undead shattered spines and severed throats, their regal clothing dripping in blood as they killed and fed, ignoring wounds that would have slain living men a dozen times over.

Marrowthirst and his maker created a mountain of the human dead, a river of blood flowing from the shattered corpses. Still, in the end, it was not enough. The human forces continued to surge in numbers. And while their metal swords and blades left the vampires unscathed, the mortals' wooden stakes drew brackish black blood and caused the undead pain.

Flayer looked on as the war reached the stone battlement. Marrowthirst was pushed toward a crenellation by a roiling sea of humanity, his claws tearing bloody furrows in the faces of his attackers as he dug his feet into the stone floor. The sun was cresting on the horizon as he reached out to his sire, feeling his night powers dissipate. The vampire woman fell beneath the human wave, each of her hands throttling an attacker as she was borne to the ground. Marrowthirst saw a stake descend as a silver ax flashed down, and the connection with his maker was severed.

The young vampire knew grief as he was pushed back, his strength ebbing as his spirit waned. They threw him through the crenellation, hoping the hundred-meter fall to the ground would end him. Marrowthirst stifled his emotions and concentrated, transforming as his late maker had shown him. His arms and fingers lengthened as leather membrane expanded between the digits. He sailed into the air in the form of a great vampire bat, flying away from the castle and avoiding the rising sun.

Marrowthirst took shelter from the day in an abandoned graveyard. In the nights that came, he hid from the roving bands of humans that sought to end his existence. The vampire soon discovered he was not the only occupant of the graveyard: a score of ghouls called the cemetery home, feeding on the bodies inside the tombs and crypts. These flesh-eaters were quickly overcome by Marrowthirst's supernatural charm and fell to his command.

Prey in the cemetery area was scarce. Human blood was hard to come by as mortals patrolled the highways and warned off unwary travelers. Over time, the vampire's attractive looks faded as he was forced to feed on the dead blood of cemetery corpses and the cursed ichor running in the ghouls' veins. His mind slowly became unhinged as the quality of his food deteriorated.

Eventually, the vampire and his flesh-eater retinue fled the cemetery and sought refuge in the great cave.

Control of the cave did not come easily. Marrowthirst's ghoul scouts had inconveniently overlooked the presence of a great Kodiak bear that made the tunnels its home. The beast resisted the vampire's efforts to compel it, and Marrowthirst had been forced to engage the great bruin in a physical conflict of tooth and claw. The bear put up a tremendous battle, at one point latching its massive jaws around the vampire's neck and threatening to sever his throat. Marrowthirst had been forced to call upon the full extent of his undead powers, his body swelling to great size as he summoned the cave's shadows to him. Brimming with dark energy, the vampire buried his fangs into the bear's neck, tapping a thick vein and drinking the titan dry. Marrowthirst added the bear's strength to his own, the victory making him appear invincible to his cadre of flesh-eaters.

Flayer realized that there was now a dark cohort inside him, that more than mere memories had accompanied the vampire's cursed blood. He sifted through the slew of Marrowthirst's recollections, hoping to pinpoint one in particular.

It was shortly after Marrowthirst's rebirth. The young vampire climbed the sheer walls of the castle like a giant spider, side by side with his maker, returning to their sheltered coffins after a night of feeding. Marrowthirst reveled in his new abilities.

"Strength, speed, supernatural resilience, even shape-changing…is there no limit to the extent of our powers?" he asked.

"You forget our greatest strength, young one," the dark woman counseled. "Our memories are transferred with our blood in the blood kiss. When we create a fledgling, as I did with you, we pass on all our knowledge, the accumulated wisdom of centuries. Each newborn vampire is superior to the one who created it, ensuring the vampire race will continue on forever and never become extinct."

The dark woman's words uttered millennia ago now had an impact on Flayer's existence. He looked upon Amala with the eyes of an apex predator, hearing the deep thunder of blood pulsing through her veins. He seized her mind with his new powers, overwhelming her will and dragging her into his cold embrace. At his command, she exposed her neck.

The bat Gregor flew down and perched on his shoulder, acknowledging the new leader of the cave. Flayer buried his long fangs into Amala's neck while the other ghouls looked on. He would elevate her to vampire status and make her his queen. Starting with Liverbelch, he would bestow his potent hybrid blood upon select members of his cadre. Empowered by his blood, his minions would go on to achieve even greater victories in his name.

The world would not soon forget the name Marrowthirst.

STAYED AWAKE ALL NIGHT

R.E. Sargent

S OAKED IN SWEAT, SHANE WALSH peeled the damp cotton sheet and the down comforter away from his clammy skin. He grunted, wondering if the heater was not turning off automatically like it should. God knows he shouldn't be sweating when outside looked like pictures he had seen of a frigid Russian winter. Last time he had checked, before bed, there were several inches of wet snow on the ground, and it was only going to get worse.

A chill shook him as a cold draft hit his already glistening body, and he pulled the covers back up. The room wasn't too warm after all.

What the hell?

Rolling onto his left side, Shane slipped one eye open and looked at the clock. Only eleven p.m. He had gone to bed early to get some much needed rest for a job interview in the morning. He had been unemployed for weeks, and the bills weren't paying themselves, so getting this job was paramount for his continued survival.

Falling back into slumber, his mind went back to the dream he had been deeply immersed in when his extreme body temperature had woken him up, only it wasn't a lucid dream and he hadn't remembered it upon waking.

Now, back inside the dream—or what was quickly becoming a nightmare—Shane fidgeted as he was deeply immersed in REM sleep, something that never happened to him so early during his slumber.

He suddenly became aware. Aware that he had just been awake. Aware that he had been profusely sweating and soaking the bed. Aware that something bad—really fucking bad—had pulled him deep down again into a nightmare he had just woken up from. And then he remembered: The hands. The claws.

The atmosphere in the dream was similar to his bedroom. He was lying in bed. The room was eerie, shadows and swirls of black and gray shifting through the air. An orange glow added ambience to the creepiness, but the location of the source was impossible to identify, and although the glow was bright, it did nothing to disperse the shadows.

Shane tried to wake up, sit up, or do anything to pull himself out of this dreamscape he did not want to be a part of, but nothing worked.

A guttural growl and a hiss came from everywhere and nowhere. Shane tried to get out of bed, but his body felt like he was being held down—was this sleep paralysis he had read about? He was confused by the dream, the lighting, the fog and shadows, and the white din that seemed to grow louder as he struggled. Suddenly he was unsure if he was trying to get out of his real bed, or his dream bed. Reality and the world he was now immersed in became one.

He jumped as a hand—at least he thought it was a hand—grabbed his face. Another covered his mouth. He tried to claw them off him, but his arms wouldn't move. More hands grabbed his arms, his torso, his legs, and his feet. He struggled, but his efforts resulted in no more than a body spasm. Pain shot through his side as sharp fingernails pierced his flesh. He tried to scream, but the hand over his mouth clamped down tighter. Suddenly he felt himself being pulled down—into the mattress. As if the mattress was not a solid substance, his body began to press through the material, the springs, the filling. A spring pierced his back and he let out a cry behind the hand—the one clamped down in a death-grip.

Tears leaked out of the corner of his eyes and splotched on the already soaked sheets; dream bed or real bed, or maybe both.

Shane found it hard to breathe as his mouth was covered and his chest was being compressed. He tried to struggle again, to scream again. He continued to be pulled down into the bed, deeper, through the mattress, partially through the box spring. Was the floor next? Would he be yanked into the dark depths of the earth?

The pain in his side increased as the fingernails penetrated deeper. His breath caught in his throat, and he coughed violently. His resolve dissipated as hopelessness took over. He stopped trying to move, hoping to either wake up or never wake up—either option would be better than this.

He coughed again, and his mouth forcefully opened as spittle flew out. A finger pressed inside his mouth. Without thinking, he bit down as hard as he could, severing the digit. A chorus of screams rose up through the room as his throat flooded with the sweet-tasting ichor. As if the hands were all connected to the same being, they all retracted at once, and Shane felt himself spring back up to the top of the mattress, as if he'd been held below the surface of a pool and released only to buoy back to the top.

His sleep paralysis was gone, and in the same instance, the hands were retracted. He tried to get out of bed, got his foot tangled in the covers, and fell headfirst on his face. The breath was knocked from his lungs, and he gasped for air as he tried to get his fill of the sweet oxygen that he had been deprived of.

Minutes later, he started to breathe more freely, and he opened his eyes, not realizing they had been clenched tightly. The room was dark, except for the glow from the red numbers on the alarm clock beside his bed. He was in his room, no longer stuck in the terrifying situation that had seemed all too real. It had only been a nightmare after all.

Hoping to rid himself of the layer of perspiration that had coated his body—not to mention the musky smell—Shane started the shower, stripped out of his shorts, and got in. He would change the bedsheets as soon as he was done and try to get back to sleep. Already, he was anxious about his interview and how this sequence of events was throwing a monkey wrench into his carefully laid-out plans to be properly prepared.

Squirting shampoo into his hand, he washed his newly cut sandy-blond hair and then rinsed it. The nightmare had affected him, and he was still reeling from it, but the magical hot water of the shower was slowly eating away at the negative effects of the experience. Shane always felt that a hot shower had healing powers, and he breathed easier as he stood under the hotter-than-normal stream of the showerhead.

He followed up with a handful of bodywash, then started washing his slightly muscular arms, shoulders, and torso. Already feeling better, he was looking forward to getting back to sleep. A sting of pain stripped away his relief. Grimacing with a slight shake of his head, Shane looked down at his side, where the pain had erupted from. There was an open wound, and blood was dripping onto the bottom of the shower stall, diluting with the water and swirling its way down the drain. Shane touched the wound and winced. It was tender.

"What the fuck?"

This was the exact spot the nails had punctured his flesh in the horrendous nightmare that had paralyzed him. His eyes bulged and his mouth fell open as he leaned his body against the tile walls of the shower and slid down it, his butt landing on the wet shower floor. He watched in disbelief as a small but steady stream of his own blood flowed down the drain.

Shane shook his head, unable to connect all the pieces. "No, no, NOOOO!" His voice boomed in the tiny bathroom as his mind whirled. He was not safe and he knew it.

Frantically, he pulled himself up to a standing position, turned off the water, and got out, grabbing the nearest towel. He patted off some of the water, quickly dried the spot on his side that had been punctured, taped some gauze to it, and grabbed the clothes that he had left on the chair the night before, slipping into them before yanking on his shoes. Grabbing his wallet, phone, and keys, he rushed to the door of his small two-bedroom home before coming to his senses and grabbing a jacket. He pulled it on and grabbed a beanie as well, pulling it over his damp hair. As he was about to exit his room again for the second time, he spotted something on the floor beside the bed. Puzzled, he bent down and picked it up, then screamed and dropped it before running out the front door, slamming it shut behind him.

A finger—it was a fucking finger.

His Toyota RAV4 was covered with at least six inches of snow, but he was grateful that it was all-wheel drive. Unlocking it using his keyfob, he yanked the door open as a cascade of snow slipped off the side above the door and covered his seat and the floorboard. Wiping it off the seat the best he could with the sleeve of his jacket, Shane jumped in, started it, turned the defroster to high, grabbed the snow scraper he had in the back seat, and got back out, scraping the snow off the windows as quickly as he could. He was freaking out about the finger, but he knew he could not drive blind.

When the glass was clear enough to see through, Shane climbed into the driver's seat again, threw the snow scraper behind him into the dark abyss, closed the door, and shifted into reverse. The headlights barely cut through the flurries pelting the windshield, and he had no idea where he was going, but he knew he could not stay home. Something bad had transpired, and he wasn't going to wait around for it to happen again. Next time, he may not be so lucky. Shane hit the gas, and the SUV slid sideways as it rocketed out of the driveway. Shifting into drive, Shane hit the gas and the back of the RAV4 fishtailed as he blasted down the otherwise quiet street, destination unknown.

SHANE DROVE AIMLESSLY for a couple of hours. This late at night, he didn't really know where to go. He considered pulling into some parking lot, but he was scared he would fall asleep. Sleep was not something he felt comfortable doing at the moment. He thought about restaurants that might be open all night, but none came to mind. With no other options, he decided to wake Becca up. She would know what to do.

His mind drifted and he thought about her short, thin frame, her dark—almost goth—hair. She was really quite beautiful—and sexy. Shane enjoyed spending time with her—in and out of the bedroom—but she was always pushing him to get married and he wasn't ready for that level of commitment. He was still trying to get his own shit together.

Becca had to be up early for work, so he hated to wake her, but desperate times called for desperate measures. He would be happy to see her and have someone to share his experience with. She wouldn't judge him or make him think he was crazy. She wasn't like that. She was a good girl. A much better person than him.

Shane turned right and headed toward her apartment. The streets were empty, and not only had he seen no other vehicles moving about on the road, his seemed to be the only tire tracks. Luckily, the Rav4 handled the snow well, but he drove slowly out of caution. He didn't want to end up sliding into something and messing up his vehicle. The night was already bad enough. A blanket of quiet enveloped him and the streets, the snow creating an effect like he was the only person alive in this little town. He felt like a night wolf, stalking through the streets as if he were looking for prey, but it was quite the opposite. He was trying to *avoid* being the prey.

As if on cue, the wound to his side throbbed, and he winced. He reached under his jacket with his left hand and touched it through his shirt. His hand came away sticky. The blood seeped through the gauze and the material of his T-shirt. He wiped his hand on his pants, reminding himself to ask Becca to look at it.

Her apartment complex was small and no one seemed to be awake. The complex was older and consisted of four buildings with four single-story apartments in each. As he entered the parking lot, he saw the two units on the left and the two on the right. Her apartment was in the building to the right, at the rear of the complex. Apartment number sixteen.

He parked, then approached her door quietly and listened. No sounds wafted to him from the building, and no light leaked out from behind the blinds. He paused a moment longer, then tapped softly on the door. He waited, but she didn't answer. He pulled out his phone and texted her.

Are you up?

He waited a minute with no response. Finally, he knocked. A minute later, he knocked again, harder this time. Eventually, a light popped on in the apartment. He sensed someone at the peephole, trying to determine what asshat was at her door in the wee hours of the morning. Finally, she must have recognized that the asshat was him and she cracked the door open. Shane could make her out through the slit in the door, glasses on (she normally wore contacts), robe held closed at the neckline with her free hand.

"Shane? Is everything okay?"

"Can I come in?"

"Oh, yeah, sorry." Becca opened the door and let him in, abruptly closing it after him to keep the cold out.

"You okay?" she asked. "What time is it?"

"Late. I...uh, need your help."

Concern crossed Becca's face. "What's going on? It's not like you to come by here in the middle of the night."

Shane took off his jacket.

"Is that blood?"

"Yes. Could you look at it for me?"

"Shane? Are you okay?" she repeated. "What happened? Maybe we should take you to the hospital."

"Not sure what I would tell them."

"The truth? But maybe you can start by telling me."

"Okay. While you clean this up for me?"

"Deal."

Becca took Shane into the bathroom and made him sit on the closed toilet. She gingerly pulled his shirt over his head. The blood-soaked gauze hung partially off his skin.

"Look over there," Becca told him, pointing. When he looked, she ripped the gauze and tape off in one quick motion.

"OW!"

"Would you have preferred the slow tear? Jesus! That looks terrible. Now tell me how this happened. What's going on with you?"

While Becca cleaned up the wound and rebandaged it, Shane recounted his nightmare and the strange happenings surrounding it.

Becca squinted her eyes and wrinkled her forehead. "Wow. That's a lot to take in. Are you sure it just wasn't *all* a nightmare?"

"Have you seen my side?"

"Yeah, you definitely got hurt, but maybe you did it while you were sleeping."

"That doesn't explain the finger on my floor."

"I forgot about the finger."

"I wish I could."

"Any idea what this is all about?" Becca asked, concern etched across her forehead.

"Not a clue."

"Have you been having other bad dreams recently?"

"No. This was the first."

"So what are you gonna do?"

"No clue. I don't suppose *not* sleeping is an option."

"Probably not. In fact, don't you have that interview this morning?"

"Yeah."

"Are you still going to it?"

"I kinda need to. Getting a job is a necessity."

"So why don't you crash here?"

"Um…"

"I know, but you can't stay awake all night. At least get a little rest. I'll stay up and keep an eye on you. I have some vacation days due me, and I really don't want to go in anyway, so I don't mind staying up."

"I don't know…"

"C'mon, Shane, don't be so stubborn. You're safer here then back at your house."

"I don't disagree with you. It's just—"

"Scary?"

"Yeah."

"I can only imagine. I'm sorry, babe."

"Thanks."

"So really…please. Go lay down on my bed. I got you."

"Will you come with me?"

"Not a chance. Someone has to keep watch."

"Okay, but please leave the door open—and if you hear me fussing in my sleep, come wake my ass up."

"Deal."

Shane went to Becca and pulled her against his chest. She hugged him tight, grabbed his face with her hands, stood on her tippy-toes, and kissed his forehead.

"It'll be okay," she told him. "Go." She pointed toward the bedroom.

Shane slipped into the dark room and turned on the bedside light. He sat down on his side of the bed—the side he slept on when he stayed over. Apprehension crept through him as he pulled off his shoes and laid on the pillowtop mattress, pulling the covers over him as he settled in.

He laid awake and thought about going to sleep. He was exhausted. Then he caught himself *actually* falling asleep, and now he thought it might be better to stay awake. Conflicted, he hoped that the rays of the morning sun would shed some light on the situation. His mind raced as he poured over the events from earlier. He felt himself slipping behind the dark veil of sleep that was overcoming him.

His eyes shot open in the dark room as he was yanked forcefully down into the mattress. A scream tried to leave his throat, but it was stifled as he struggled to free himself. The elements of the mattress started closing in on him as he was forcefully pulled down. He felt sharp claws digging in to both his wrists and ankles.

As Shane tried to pull himself free, he felt himself being pulled down farther, more aggressively. The room glowed, eerie shades of grays, reds, and blacks. He tried to call out to Becca for help, but his voice was a mere whisper. A croak escaped his lips.

Knowing he would not survive this attack if he didn't think of something quickly, he tried to remember how he had gotten free earlier. The finger…of course. He had bit it off. But this *thing* was being more careful, keeping its claws off his face. He had no way to get leverage on it—no way to pull himself free.

A thought penetrated his brain, and as a last-ditch effort, he started throwing his weight to the right, instead of trying to pull himself upward and out of the mattress that was eating him alive. He felt the mattress shift a little off the box spring. Hope flitted through his senses as he flung his weight right again and again. Each time, he felt the mattress shift a little more. The edge started bowing down toward the floor, and he took the opportunity to shift his weight one last time. The mattress finally slipped over the edge, landed on its end, then flipped completely over on top of him as his body thudded on the hard floor.

Shane tried to gulp air into his lungs after the fall knocked the air out of him for the second time that night. The heavy mattress on top of him wasn't helping, either. Finally, he could breathe, and his feet found purchase on the carpet, allowing him to slip out from under the mattress, a half-running, half-crawling maneuver that most likely looked ridiculous had anyone been watching, but he didn't care. His only thought was he had to get the hell out of there.

A bright flash of light filled the room, and it took him a second to realize Becca had heard the racket and had come in, flipping on the overhead light in the process.

"Shane? What's going on?"

Shane grabbed his shoes off the floor and ran out of the bedroom door, into the living room.

"Shane? What's going on? What happened?"

He slid on his shirt and picked his jacket up off the chair and shrugged it on, making sure his keys and phone were still in the pocket.

"SHANE! Talk to me!"

Shane paused. "I have to go."

"Why?"

"That thing."

"Here? No way."

"Yes. Here. Didn't you hear it?"

"Well...no. I just heard a thump and found you and the mattress on the floor."

"Sorry, Becca, I should have known better. I have to go. I'm not safe here, and you aren't safe with me here, either."

"But where will you go?"

"I have no idea."

With that, he leaned in, gave Becca a peck on the lips, and ran out the door.

"Shane? Come back!" she called after him.

Shane climbed into his SUV, started it, backed out of the parking spot, and exited the parking lot, his tires crunching on the frozen snow. In his rearview mirror, he saw her standing at the door, her hands clutching clumps of her hair. Feeling guilty for leaving her alone, he turned his attention to the road and started driving.

SHANE STARED OUT over the frigid-looking lake, the instrument panel lights casting a glow across the front seats of the RAV4. He had run out of ideas on where to go. He had considered a motel, but the thought of being near another bed was unthinkable. The cozy air from the heater kept him warm, but he shivered anyway when he thought about the events of the evening. The dashboard proudly displayed that it was two thirty-one a.m. Daylight was several hours away—not that it mattered. He held no expectations that the sun would burn away his problem. He still had to sleep eventually. Daytime or nighttime, he was vulnerable, but at least in the day, it was easier to identify the evil that was coming for him.

Although the vehicle was running, the silence of the winter wonderland was absolute. The hood of the SUV was clear of snow, a result of the heat generated by the engine, but beyond that, nothing was left untouched by the beautiful and serene winter gift. Any other time, the landscape would have had a calming effect on him, but not under the current circumstances.

The snow continued to come down steadily, wiping away any tracks he had created when he had driven to the lake. On this side of the water, there was no sign of people—people typically launched boats or fished from the shore of this side of the lake. It was the other side where the lakeside houses—the "rich fuckers" as him and his friends referred to them—sat, overlooking the water. He could make out some of the lights from behind the foggy glass winking in and out, dancing in between snowflakes.

A pressure in his bladder pulled him from his trance. He didn't remember the last time he had gone.

Time to make yellow snow.

Shane opened the door to the RAV4 and got out, pulling his jacket closed around his neck. There was no wind, but the cold jabbed at his skin, like tiny little needles. Finding a bush nearby, he unzipped his fly and pulled himself free, the stream intense and immediate. He hadn't realized how badly he needed to go. He made a game of trying to melt as much snow off the branches of the bush as possible. He closed his eyes and continued to pee, the relief slow to come, but slowly the burn subsided and he felt liberated—dick hanging in the wind, peeing freely out in the middle of nature during a snow-storm. He opened his eyes when he smelled smoke.

Twirling around toward his vehicle, his mouth fell open, and it took him a minute to realize he was peeing on his shoe. He hurriedly tucked him-self back in his pants and zipped up, unable to believe what he was seeing. The SUV was gone. In its place was a huge fire, long lengths of timber burn-ing beneath a large cauldron-like pot. A shape stood nearby—it appeared to be a man, with his hands in the air. Savages surrounded the man, spears at the ready.

"No! Please!" the man sobbed.

The spears were thrust forward and upward, and blood spilled from the wounds, changing the pure-white snow to a crimson mess. The man toppled face-first into the snow, and the savages were on him in seconds. They tore at him, yanking at his limbs. An arm tore free, and the savage held it up in the air in celebration before putting it on a spit over the fire. Within minutes, the body was dismantled, a head simply tilting at an angle from a torso. That was until one of the savages pulled out a machete and severed the head from the torso with one whack. The head rolled a few feet away, leaving a patterned trail of blood across the stark white. Two savages picked up the torso and took it over to the massive fire, the headless, armless, legless hunk of bone, muscle, and flesh, ready to burn. Shane watched in horror as another savage grabbed a sharp stick, impaled the head on it, and walked around the fire, holding the head-on-a-stick high in the air, the other savages cheering, waving their spears in the air.

Shane felt his stomach lurch, and he tried to hold back, but the contents surged up his throat before he could stop them. Any hopes of having a quiet, discreet puke session were immediately squashed as he violently heaved any-thing that was possibly left over in his stomach. All celebration stopped and all eyes turned toward him—eyes that were penetrating, hungry, rabid.

Petrified, Shane did the only thing he could. He turned and ran as fast as he could over the slippery terrain. As he turned, he heard whoops and the sound of many feet coming after him. He dodged left, then right, anticipating the sharp steel of a spearhead bursting through his body any second.

He ran toward the water, blindly, and he knew he was in trouble, but there was nowhere else to run, nowhere to hide. The screams behind him were still in pursuit, but he felt like he had gained on them as the sound seemed a little farther away. Still, he ran as fast as he could, slipping and occasionally falling but pulling himself back to his feet and scrambling across the rugged landscape. Here, there was no trail. Just a hillside that would eventually lead to the lake.

His foot caught on the base of the brush, and Shane fell on a bush, rolled off it, and slid down an embankment before splashing into the water. The intense cold caused instant pain, and he immediately felt it impossible to breathe. Numb, he scrambled out of the icy water and slipped and slid as he tried to gain traction on the snowy bank. Finally on solid ground, he tried to inhale gulps of air as quickly as he could, his hands on his knees as he tried get his breathing under control.

He shivered, beyond cold, his entire body like a paint shaker, his blood the paint. He needed to get in the RAV4 and crank the heat.

The RAV4. It's gone.

How was that even possible? He remembered when he had turned around from taking a piss and the fire that the savages surrounded was right where his vehicle had been. Had he imagined everything? Shane listened intently and tried to peer through the fat flakes that continued to fall from the sky. He concentrated on *turning up* all his senses—up to ten. He looked, he listened. He saw nothing and heard nothing.

The fire. The smell of the fire caused me to turn around.

Shane inhaled the night air. He could not detect smoke in the air. How could that be with the fire directly up the hill from him? Where was the fire's glow?

Apprehensively, Shane started working his way back up the embankment. If he stayed where he was, he'd get hypothermia—maybe even freeze to death. But if the savages were there, he'd probably be ripped into shreds or burned to death. Either way, his chances were slim.

As he crested the hill, he stopped and reevaluated the situation. All was quiet. He poked his head up to look. No fire. No savages. Only his RAV4, running, and exactly where he had left it.

I'm fucking losing my mind.

Shane apprehensively approached his vehicle and looked around. Everything was as he had left it. There were no savages. There was no dismembered body. There was no head on a stick. Was it all in his mind? What about the incidents at his house and in Becca's apartment? Did they even really happen? He thought about the stress he had recently been under and started to second guess himself.

Teeth chattering, he opened the door to the Toyota and climbed inside, closing the door quickly and turning the heat to the max setting. He reached down and clicked the heated seat to the max setting as well. Although the climate of the interior was much warmer than outside, the conditions out there had been extreme. He peeled off his sopping wet jacket, hoping he would warm up faster.

It was almost twenty minutes before he stopped shivering. Another twenty passed before he felt fairly normal again, even though his clothes were still soaked. He'd have to figure out where to get some dry ones.

Shane shifted the vehicle into reverse and backed away from the edge of the embankment that overlooked the lake. Twenty feet back, his eyes caught something off about the snow. He threw the transmission into park and, grabbing his phone, turned on the flashlight, getting out to investigate.

He approached the area where his truck had been parked, his eyes squinting as he tried to process what he was looking at. He shone his light on the area and bent down to get a closer look. His mouth fell open, and he bolted upright, scrambling backward toward the RAV4. Climbing back inside, he yanked the shifter into reverse and the wheels spun as he backed up enough to turn and tear out of the parking area. The vehicle fishtailed erratically, but Shane did not slow down. All he could think about was getting the hell out of there.

"I'VE BEEN WORRIED about you." Becca's voice was laced with concern.

"I'm worried about me, too."

"Where are you?"

"I'm surprised you are still up. Sorry to call so late."

"It's not like I can sleep after…well…after everything."

"You and me both."

"Where are you?" she repeated.

"Driving."

"You've been driving this entire time? Since you ran out of here?"

"No. I went to the lake."

"The lake? Why?"

"It felt like it would be safe. Peaceful. Becca, am I fucking crazy?"

"Crazy?"

"Yeah, do you think this is all in my mind?"

"I'm not sure what to think."

"Maybe if I tell you what happened at the lake…"

"Something happened?" Her voice raised an octave as she asked.

"Yeah. Something even weirder than before."

"Why don't you start with my apartment. What happened here? Why did you take off?"

Shane recounted the events with the bed, the claws, his escape.

"Damn," was all Becca could say. Then, "Okay, I understand why you took off. Seems like no place is safe. So what happened at the lake?"

"You aren't gonna believe me."

"Try me."

"Fucking headhunters."

"What?"

"Headhunters," Shane repeated.

"Like the people that find employees for their company?"

"No, like the savages that tear people apart, eat them, and keep their heads as souvenirs."

"Okay, I have *got* to hear this story."

Shane recounted his time at the lake, him stepping out of the vehicle to pee, the smell of smoke, his discovery of the savages, the dismembered body, and the fact that they came after him.

"Wait," Becca interrupted. "So these…headhunters… were coming after you?"

"Yes."

"What were their intentions?"

"I think they wanted to invite me to dinner. I was the main course."

"You think they would have eaten you?"

"I have no doubt."

79

"Don't headhunters only eat the rich? Like that Michael Rockefeller dude?"

"I don't think they discriminate. They definitely didn't ask to see a bank statement."

Becca was silent for a moment, taking it all in.

"How did you get away?"

"I ran. Ended up falling into the lake. Oh my god, it was fucking cold."

"Are you okay?"

"I'm finally warm, but my clothes are still soaked."

"How did you get away from them? Where did you find your car?"

"Me falling into the lake somehow returned things to normal. Another reason I wonder if I'm insane. The RAV4 was where I had left it, still running. But—"

"But?"

"That doesn't explain the blood and the ashes."

"Huh?"

"As I was backing out, I spotted something. I got out of my car to find out what it was. Under where I was parked, there was a puddle of blood in the snow, surrounded by ash and coal. Like you would get from a fire."

The line was quiet.

"Becca? You still there?"

"Sorry. Yeah. I'm just trying to digest all of this."

"It doesn't get any easier."

"Now what?"

"I have no clue. I'm fucked. There's nowhere I can go where I feel safe. I wasn't even asleep this time. I'm beginning to feel like my only two options are a bullet or a padded cell."

"Shane, stop."

"Easy for you to say."

"Come back to the apartment."

"Not a chance."

"Just to get some dry clothes. I washed the ones you left here last week...you could change, I'll pack you some food for the road, make you some coffee, pump you full of NoDoz, and you can be in and out of here in five minutes. I won't leave you alone and whatever forces are coming at you won't come near you."

Shane paused. "I don't know..."

"It's not like I'm asking you to go back to bed. Come in. Change. Grab goodies. Leave. That simple."

Shane sighed. "Fine. I'll be there in about twenty minutes."

"Be safe."

THE DOOR TO the apartment opened before Shane could even knock on it. Becca grabbed his hand and pulled him inside before quickly shutting the door.

"I really need to make this quick," he told her.

"The clothes you have here are in the bottom drawer of the dresser."

Shane grabbed her face with his hands and kissed her forehead.

"Thanks, babe."

Shane went into Becca's bedroom, flicking on the lights in the hallway and in the room as he went. He side-eyed the bed, which he assumed Becca had put back together after his hasty departure. There didn't seem to be anything out of place, and if the incident hadn't been burned in his memory, he wouldn't be able to tell that anything had happened here. Still, evidence or not, he knew he wasn't crazy. Everything that had happened in the last several hours was real. He had the throbbing wound in his side—which he had almost forgotten about due to all the other chaos going on—and the finger was real as well. He was certain if he went back to his house, he would find the finger and the associated blood on the carpet of his bedroom.

He rushed over to the dresser, yanked the bottom drawer open, and took out a pair of jeans and a T-shirt, as well as a pair of socks and underwear. He peeled off his wet clothes and dropped them on the floor, grabbed a towel off the bed that Becca had left for him, dried off, and slipped on the clean, dry garments. He looked at his wet shoes, not wanting to put them back on now that his feet were dry. Unfortunately, he did not have an extra pair of shoes at Becca's house.

Scooping his wet clothes up in one hand and picking up the shoes with the other, he left the lights on and joined Becca back in the living room.

"My shoes are soaked."

"Oh, shit. I forgot about those."

"I really want to go, but I need to dry these things a bit first. Can I use your dryer?"

"Yeah. Why don't you dump your wet clothes in the washing machine while you're there? I'll wash them later."

"'Kay."

Shane went into the hallway and opened the folding doors that concealed the washer and dryer. He dumped the wet clothes in the washer and left the lid open. Then he put his shoes in the dryer, closed the door, and turned it to high heat. The *thump-thump-thump* of the shoes bouncing against the stainless walls was immediate and loud, so he closed the accordion doors to block some of the sound.

Back in the living room, he sat on the couch next to Becca.

"Bec, do you—" He was cut off by the sound of the toilet flushing behind the closed bathroom door. Shane's eyes went wide.

"Who's here?"

"Oh crap, I forgot to tell you. My girl, Amanda, came over a little bit ago. I didn't want to be alone. Not with everything going on."

Shane relaxed a little bit. "I don't blame you. Amanda? I don't remember you having a friend named Amanda."

"It's a fairly new friendship."

"Oh."

Shane heard the bathroom door open from the hallway behind him and sensed a presence out of his peripheral vision.

"Oh, Amanda! Good! I want you to finally meet Shane..."

Shane turned toward the figure that was approaching on his left. His first thought was that she was extremely attractive. His second thought was that she looked familiar.

"Hi, Shane! Nice to meet you!" Amanda held out her hand.

Shane's mouth dropped open, and he was at a loss for words. His third thought was that he was fucked.

Becca touched his shoulder. "Hello? Earth to Shane. Are you going to say hi to my friend?"

Shane turned toward Becca to gage her expression, then turned toward Amanda, reached out, and shook her hand, and tried to return the greeting.

"Uh...hi there...uh...Amanda. I'm...uh...pleased to meet you."

"The pleasure is *all* mine, trust me," Amanda said.

Is she going to keep my secret? Why the FUCK is she here?

Shane brushed his hand through his damp hair, then covered his mouth with his hand. Finally, he spoke, afraid of the answer to his question.

"So where did you guys meet?"

Becca smiled. Shane couldn't help but feel there was something hidden behind the grin.

"We have a friend in common."

"Small world," Shane said.

"Isn't it?" Amanda asked. "Anyway, when Becca told me that she needed me, I came rushing. I don't care what time it is. No one screws with my girl."

Shane let out a nervous laugh.

"Amanda, I thought you were bringing your boyfriend," Becca said.

"I wouldn't really classify him as my boyfriend. Just some guy I'm fucking."

Shane gulped, looking at the carpet.

"I bet he and Shane would get along great," Becca said. "Shane, when all of this is over, you guys should hang out."

"Yeah, Shane. You guys should hang out."

Shane held up his hand. "Just stop, Amanda."

Becca feigned shock. "What's gotten into you, Shane? That was rude. You don't even know Amanda. Do you?"

"No. I don't." Shane gave Amanda a stern look.

Becca looked back and forth between the two of them. "You sure?"

"Positive."

"Not even when you were giving it to her from behind last week?"

Shane's mouth fell open, and he tried to speak, but he only stuttered incoherently.

Amanda smiled. "You sure knew me then, didn't you, Shane? When you were screaming my name over and over?"

"This is bullshit. I'm leaving." Shane got up and headed toward the door.

"I wouldn't do that if I were you, sweetie," Becca said in a saccharine tone.

Shane stopped, looked from Becca to Amanda, grabbed the doorknob, twisted, and opened the door fully, letting a blast of cold air in. It was then that the floor buckled underneath him as his legs were ensnared in the clasp of four brownish-red claws. The claws yanked him down to the ground and tore their way through the flooring to the center of the living room, dragging him through the destruction, the floor repairing itself in the wake of the creature's travels. Wood chunks fell into place and carpet magically repaired itself, leaving no trace of the damage.

Once Shane was yanked back to the center of the living room, in front of the couch where the girls were sitting, the grisly talons held him down to the ground.

Shane's eyes were wide as he struggled to get free.

"What the fuck is this? What's going on?" He looked from his restrained arms to his restrained legs, the claws dug in so deep, five wounds wept crimson from each of his appendages.

"Oh, poor Shane," Becca said, mockingly. "Haven't figured it out yet? Are you that slow?"

"Apparently," Amanda said.

Becca flashed a sinister smile he had never seen before. "You didn't think we would find out about each other, did you?"

"I...I didn't..."

"You didn't what?"

"I didn't want to hurt anybody."

"It's a little too late for that."

"I'm...I'm sor...sorry."

"That you got caught?"

"How did—?"

"Last week when you came over, you smelled like her. I found out later that you had a two-hour marathon fuck-fest with her before coming to my bed. You couldn't even bother to take a shower first. Talk about cocky. Did you know that face recognition passwords on your phone work when your eyes are closed? You really should delete your incriminating texts if you are going to fuck around."

Shane grimaced as the claws dug in deeper. "Becca, you and I weren't exclusive...we never discussed it. For all I know, you were seeing other people, too."

"Uh, no. I'm not a dirtbag, and I would never do anything to hurt you. Wouldn't have before, anyway."

Shane looked defeated, but in a sudden fit, he tried to pull free. The claws ripped deeper into his skin and pulled him back down. He screamed. Between gasping breaths, he said, "What is all of this?" He nodded at his feet.

Amanda spoke finally. "It's anything we want it to be. Mattress monsters, hell creatures, and my favorite, motherfucking headhunters. I'm quite proud of myself for that one, I must admit."

"Y…You did this?"

"And me," Becca piped in, raising her hand like a timid kid in school. "I have a lot to learn, but Amanda has taught me a few things. You got the better of me, though, when you flipped the mattress off the bed."

Shane's eyes grew wide and his face turned red. "What the hell are you, you bitch?" he yelled at Amanda.

"I prefer witch over bitch, but both work. Did I forget to mention I'm Wiccan?"

In an instant, Shane's expression turned from one of rage to one of fear. Slobber started to drip out of his mouth, and he fumbled over his words. Finally, he mumbled, "Please. I'm sorry. I'm so sorry. Please…get this fucking thing off me and let me up. I'll explain. I was completely wrong, but I'd like to explain. Please?" His eyes pleaded with them both.

Amanda turned to Becca. "Well, Becca? Let's take a vote. Do we want to let him up and listen to his bullshit excuses? Stand and be counted—cast your ballot…if it's a tie, we'll let the creatures decide."

Becca made a show of rubbing her chin as she thought about it.

"Fine. Let the asshole up. Let's hear what he has to say."

Amanda nodded, and the claws disintegrated, a small puff of smoke escaping from each of the disappearing limbs. The floor immediately repaired itself.

Shane sat up, holding one wrist and one ankle. The blood continued to trickle down his limbs and drip onto the carpet.

"So what do you have to say for yourself, asshole?" Becca yelled. "I trusted you. I gave you the best of me. You didn't give two shits about me."

"That's not true. I did."

"Then why did you fuck Amanda?"

Shane shrugged.

"Why?"

"Well…"

"WHY?"

"It's just…"

"YEAH?"

"You're kind of boring in bed. Amanda is like a caged animal. She keeps it interesting."

"You bastard!" Becca yelled as she flew off the couch, her hands wrapping around his throat before she could think about it.

"Becca, STOP!" he grunted, his vocal cords restricted. "I don't care about her...she was just a piece of ass!"

"You piece of shit," Amanda screamed, diving off the couch and going for his eyes. Without even thinking about it, Shane reached for her hair and yanked forcefully, slamming her forehead into Becca's, the sound a loud crack, like that of a baseball being hit out of the park. The girls collapsed into a heap on the floor, and after a couple of twitches, they both fell silent and still.

SHANE PEERED DOWN at the two bodies in the cargo area of his RAV4. His breathing was ragged, and he tried massaging his temples, but it did nothing to alleviate the cloudiness that pulsed through his head. He hadn't meant to kill them—actually, he had imagined they would wake the hell up eventually, but they hadn't, and he could not seem to locate a pulse on either of them.

A smart person would probably have called the police and told them about the terrible accident that had transpired, but obviously, Shane wasn't that smart. Plus he was at a loss for what the hell he would have told the police.

You gotta believe me, officer...it was self-defense. These girls are witches, and they summoned demons to snatch me and pull me down into the bowels of hell. I barely escaped.

Yeah, that'd work out well for him.

It seemed like much of his life was one big fucking mistake. Being disowned by his parents. Not having the willpower to ignore her when Amanda had flirted with him in the bar, leaning forward enough to expose plenty of cleavage—a move that was extremely intentional. Screwing up at work and losing his job. But this...THIS! This was the biggest mess he had ever created. If he could just cover it up, maybe he could get his shit together. That's what he needed...a fresh start. Maybe he'd move somewhere and start over, away from this place. Away from the memories. Away from the guilt.

Shane reached in the cargo area and lifted Amanda out, flinging her over his shoulder like a sack of potatoes. He looked around. He could not believe that he had come back *here*, but he didn't know what else to do with the bodies, and with all the snow, it would be several weeks at the minimum before they were found. He would be long gone by then.

The snow crunched under Shane's feet as he carried Amanda's body down to the side of the lake. He laid her down gingerly and brushed the hair out of her eyes. She was definitely a beautiful girl, but Shane had never really had feelings for her—at least feelings of the heart. It was a relationship built on lust alone. She hadn't known about Becca. He was a fool to think he would get away with cheating. But in his mind, he assumed the worst that could happen if he got caught would be for Becca to leave him. What had actually happened seemed surreal. Impossible. Like the bad dream he almost thought it was.

Sadly, this was all his fault—all his doing. He couldn't blame anyone else, and he couldn't rely on anyone else to get him out of this jam. He was on his own.

Shivering, Shane started the trek back up the hillside to the RAV4. All reminders of the previous incident there had vanished—whether entirely, or just hidden underneath a new layer of snow, he did not know.

He approached the cargo area again, glad that the early hour of the day was conducive to him not being seen—the sun was a couple of hours from rising and the snow made visibility poor. Even if someone on the other side of the lake had binoculars, or a telescope, they'd never be able to make out anything transpiring on this wicked side of the lake.

At the hatch door, he reached in and then stopped. His mouth dropped open, and he froze. Spinning around on his heels, he looked behind him as well as left and right. He was certain that he was mistaken, and so he ran to the driver's door of the SUV and opened it, flooding the interior of the vehicle with light. Back around the back side, he looked once again. The back was not only void of shadows now, but there was no longer a body there. Becca was gone.

"What the actual fuck..."

Shane looked down and saw another set of footprints on the ground. They were smaller, like a woman's. They were headed down toward the lake. Was Becca alive? That would be great news. Maybe he could get her to the hospital and everything would be okay. He could simply say Amanda left town out of embarrassment.

But the footprints were leading toward the lake. How was that possible when she would have had to pass him as he came back up the trail? It didn't make sense, and so he studied the tracks in the snow a little harder. Confused, he pulled out his phone—which he had changed to airplane mode before coming out to the lake—and turned on the flashlight, studying the prints. They followed the same path that he had been on, but how? And then realization smashed into him like a blast of heavy wind, and his stomach lurched.

"Nononononono!"

How could it be possible? The prints weren't leading *down* to the lake after all. The prints were coming *from* the lake.

They'd have to be Amanda's prints then. So where was she? And what the hell happened to Becca? Could they both still be alive?

A whisper reached him through the wind, which had just started blowing, as if on cue.

"Shaaaaaaaane."

He spun around. "Who is it? Stop fucking around."

"Thanks for bringing us to the lake."

It sounded like a chorus of multiple voices—definitely more than two.

"Becca? Amanda? Where are you? Stop fucking around and let's go home and talk this out."

"Shaaaaaaaane…why are we here?"

The voices came from everywhere and nowhere.

Shane edged his way to the fringe of the parking area, looking down the incline to see if they were hiding somewhere among the shrubbery.

"Where are you guys?" he asked.

"Shaaaaaaaane."

"WHAT?" His nerves caused him to snap back at the voices.

"What were you going to do?"

"Not…nothing!"

It was then that Shane noticed the drums, the volume building like it would have had someone been twisting the volume knob on a radio. Rhythmic. Almost tribal. Shane spun around toward the RAV4, fully intending to get the hell out of there before something really bad happened. He blinked twice, mouth agape. It was too late…something bad was already happening.

The RAV4 was gone once again. In its place was a large fire, a huge black pot cooking over it. The flames were orange and red and danced ten feet in the air. The drums reached a crescendo, and before Shane could take off running, he noticed from his peripheral vision a shadowy figure emerging from the tree line to his right. And then in front of him. And then from the left. The shadowy figures crept closer and then multiplied. Three became six. Six became eighteen. Eighteen became a hundred, and as they crept closer, the light from the fire lit up their faces, their bodies—loincloths, tribal tattoos, bone piercings, and wicked fucking spears held at the ready, waiting to ventilate his body, waiting to create a blood fountain out of his flesh.

Shane froze as they approached, the headhunter directly in front of him clearly in charge, time etching his face in such a way that he looked like a mummy—a mummy that was very much alive. Alive and dangerous.

The savage spoke—a language Shane had never heard before, gibberish. Shane stared at him, shaking, frozen. The headhunter repeated himself, this time more forcefully. Shane gulped, shrugging.

The leader raised his spear in the air, shook it, threw his head back, and yelled another phrase that Shane had never heard. It must have been a command, because savages moved in, surrounding him from all sides. Two of them took Shane by the arms. The touch released him from his frozen state, and his fight-or-flight responses took over. He brought his foot up and kicked the savage to his left right in the kneecap and the man went down screaming. Before the one on this right could react, Shane brought his left knee around and smashed it right into the headhunter's balls, collapsing the man on the spot. Free of the hands holding him in captivity, Shane knew this would be his only chance. He knew he had to take it, or he would never survive. He had stayed awake all night—fought to be aware, fought to be alive. There was no way he was going down like this.

Shane ducked between a gap in the savages and ran toward the tree line. Angry shouts rang out behind him. They would have to be disappointed— he wasn't going to be anyone's dinner.

The distance between him and them multiplied. He was ten feet beyond them. Then twenty. Then forty. The trees were fifteen feet away. Once he got beyond the first of them, he would be able to lose them, hide, escape.

Five feet from the edge of the trees, Shane stopped in his tracks, falling to his knees. He tried to scream, but only a gurgle came out. Pain shot through his body, and he felt blood run from his mouth. Looking down, he saw a foot of metal and wood protruding from his chest.

There's no coming back from that.

Two savages grabbed him by the arms, threw him face down on the ground, and put their feet on his back. His chest didn't touch the ground, the spear holding him a few inches above it. He then felt someone grab the back of the spear, pulling on it, twisting it. The wood snapped, and he was tossed on his back, the head of the spear still protruding. He then found himself being pulled through the snow by his feet, his back being scraped and cut by craggy rocks along the way.

He watched as he was being pulled along, unable to move much, wondering if his spine had been damaged. They drug him back past the fire, back to the leader, who made a motion, causing them to pull Shane back to his feet, supporting his weight for him as he could not.

The leader made hand motions and yelled something to the men surrounding Shane, and before he could understand what was happening, four men grabbed him while another three grabbed his left arm. The pain ripped through Shane's body, and he screamed, as the arm was first dislocated, then yanked free from his torso. The savages held the severed arm in the air while they whooped and hollered, and Shane almost passed out from the pain. He knew he had mere minutes left in this world—or less.

"Help! Becca?" he tried to scream, but it merely came out as a whisper. His eyes grew heavy, and he stopped fighting them, the lure of death becoming more appealing as each miserable second ticked by.

"Shane?"

Shane opened his eyes, trying to focus, wondering if he was hallucinating.

"Becca? Amanda?" His voice was merely a whisper.

"We're here," Amanda said.

"Pl...please..." he whispered.

"Please what, Shane?" Becca said, fire lacing her words.

"H...help me."

"Sadly, no one can help you, Shane."

"I'm...I'm sor...sorry."

"That's the most truthful thing you've ever told us," Amanda said. "You are indeed sorry...a sorry sack of shit. I don't need you. I have someone better."

Shane looked away from Amanda to Becca.

"Becca, pl...please. I'm sorry. You can fix this. You can save me. I need you."

Becca paused, tried to say something, but then stopped. Finally, she spoke. "Sorry, Shane. It's too late for that. Way too fucking late. And I don't need you, either. I also have someone better."

Defeated, Shane let the pain take over...It pulled him down, down toward the edge of consciousness.

In a last moment of lucidity, he watched as Amanda took Becca's face into hers, as their lips touched, as their tongues snaked in and out of each other's mouths.

"Someone so much better!" they said in unison.

That vision seared itself into his brain, so much so that Shane wasn't even aware as the machete took his head clean off, nor was he aware when the head was secured to a stick, a trophy to be treasured by the tribe for eternity.

REMEMBER ME?

Richard Clive

C OLIN FINCH ARRIVED AT WORK early, as always. It was Monday, his favorite day of the week. *Usually.*

September sunbeams sliced through the half-open blinds, basking his office in golden autumnal light. Disturbed dust motes floated in galactic orbits above his desktop monitor, though the wet streaks on the screen proved the place *had* been cleaned.

"Morning, Mr. Finch."

He jumped. Maggie, the cleaner, appeared from beneath his desk, holding a wet cloth and a can of air freshener.

"Indeed," he replied curtly, his heart hammering. *Stupid woman.* "You could've turned on the lights. You scared the hell out of—never mind." He flicked the light switch.

"Sorry," she said sheepishly.

Still, his office *looked* clean this morning. More importantly, it smelled clean. If anything, the citrus scent of air freshener was too sharp, a little overpowering. But he hadn't forgotten, nor forgiven, the disgusting mess he'd discovered the previous week. But the disciplinary hearing had, apparently, worked. *Good.* Colin Finch didn't do second warnings.

"No need to lock your office this morning, then?" she asked.

"No, why? Were you planning on locking me in?"

She laughed nervously.

"As we discussed, Maggie, if I'm here, there's no need to lock up. Evenings, you make sure you lock the door."

She nodded.

"*Right?*"

"Right," she agreed, still sitting under his desk and looking up at him with a confused expression.

She had sworn she'd locked up and had left the room spotless. But on *that* morning, he'd discovered a mess so unforgivably bad that someone had to be held accountable. Someone had been in his office. Someone had kicked over his trash bin and spilt something disgusting on his desk and keyboard. Maggie was the only other person who had a key. His desk had been sticky, the smell like a pig farm.

"Well, all clean today," she said, wiping a bead of sweat from her brow.

He stood over her as she got to her feet, picked up her plastic bucket, and hurried out of the office.

As he turned back toward his desk, a deeper voice rumbled from the door that Maggie had vacated a second before.

"Morning, Mr. Finch," said Brian Hughes, peeking around the doorframe, like an anxious meerkat. "How's your day?"

Colin grunted and said, "Oh, you've returned. Feeling better, then?"

"*Much*, thank you. Deirdre hooked me up with her chiropractor. Worked wonders."

"*Deirdre?*"

"My wife."

"Come in here."

Brian looked baffled but did.

"Shut the door."

He closed the door behind him. Concern was etched into the brow beneath his bald and now lightly perspiring head.

"Everything all right?"

"You left us in a…predicament."

"Beg your pardon?"

"Tax discrepancy."

Brian shook his head. "No—I always…"

"How could you go off and leave this company in that state?"

"I don't know what—"

"The numbers don't add up. Kelly looked at the accounts in your absence. The returns are wrong. We're not talking a few omissions here. When you've omitted a contract with the damn council, a contract worth tens of thousands of dollars—"

"It's on a separate—"

"I've told you a million times, *Brian*. You're an accountant, for crying out loud. If we were audited today, *right now*, it's *my ass* on the line."

"I can explain."

"Did you not see the emails I sent you?"

"I was off sick."

"I left three voice messages."

"I was away. My phone—"

"*Away?* While out sick?"

"The chiropractor, he's a family friend, in Washington."

A vacation.

Brian refused to make eye contact. "Come back here in one hour with those accounts. And bring Kelly with you," Colin growled.

"I'm sorry. I can fix this. If you'd only listen…"

Colin said nothing more and let the moment descend into an uncomfortable silence. It was a tactic he knew unnerved staff—that, and his unwavering stare—but he didn't look up for fear of exploding with incandescent rage. He knew what they called him—*Dracula*. He didn't care.

"You'll see. It's fine," said Brian, smiling awkwardly. He opened the door, backed away, and retreated into the corridor.

In the silence of his office, Colin sighed deeply, took a moment, and got back to it. With clockwork efficiency, he laid his briefcase on the desk, removed his laptop, and connected it to the portal that allowed him to work from the full-sized desktop. He wouldn't work all day on that cramped little laptop. Health and safety were paramount. The last thing he wanted to develop was some musculoskeletal repetitive strain disorder, like Brian. He swatted away the thought of Brian Hughes and instead looked at the framed poem on his desk.

"And—which is more—you'll be a Man, my son!"

If was his favorite. Usually, he didn't go for namby-pamby poetry. But Kipling's parable evoked in him a true sense of self. "You'll be a Man, my son!" *Unless*, he thought, *your name is Brian Hughes. Or Tom Griffiths in finance.* Depression was even worse than back pain, as far as he was concerned. He could barely tolerate a member of his staff not handling their workload due to physical pain, but mental health problems were in a league of their own.

Once those accounts are sorted, I can get on with some real work. That's the problem with being a chief executive—always firefighting, always sorting out everybody else's mess.

The computer screen blipped on. He waited while the PC installed Microsoft's latest round of updates. A full minute went by, and he felt his edging impatience, his anger spike. He resisted the urge to pound his fist against his desk. *More lost time!* Sometimes, he wondered if it had been better the old way, with typewriters and fax machines.

To calm himself, he looked at the only other decorative indulgence he afforded his office, apart from the framed poem. He was a believer in efficient workspaces, and he had no time for employees who distracted themselves with desktop clutter, including photos of children and families. But this single elegant painting on the wall opposite his desk enriched the room.

The painting depicted a lonely looking track that wound through a dense wood, the trees bustling with leaves of red and gold. The path was deep with fallen leaves, but the trees were still thick, and their intertwining boughs on either side of the path formed a canopy, resembling a tunnel. The painting was magical. He had stared at it for hours over the years, especially when his ponderous computer was acting up, as it did now. But the artist's sense of perspective was so refined that, when you looked hard enough, the tunnel appeared not as a painting, but almost as a three-dimensional portal. It drew your eyes into the forest, deeper and deeper. Today, lit in the beautiful autumn sunshine, the painting looked even more entrancing than usual, like a window to Narnia or some enchanted kingdom.

Finally, his computer finished its business and beeped, waking him from his daydream.

He opened his email.

Five messages had arrived since the night before, and he'd not logged off till nearly ten p.m. As usual, he'd worked late from home the previous evening.

First job: calendar. Colin already knew what his day entailed. He'd had Angela, his receptionist, recite his crammed schedule of meetings twice before he'd let her leave the previous evening, but he always checked the next morning, anyway, and since Angela was still at home shoveling Corn Flakes down her throat, he would do it himself. He was about to minimize his email and open his electronic Outlook calendar when he spotted an odd-looking arrival.

eden.crow1973@hotmail.com

The emails he received were mainly from corporate email addresses. Businesses. Suppliers. Staff. He rarely received personal mail. The word "Hotmail" was true to its name because nothing made his blood boil more. Hotmail, Gmail, or Yahoo meant one thing: staff calling in sick or late and not adhering to the company policy of using the telephone. The difference here, though, was Eden Crow didn't work at Bush Home Windows—not anymore. And not for a long time.

The email had arrived at 2:25 a.m.

Eden Crow's beaky features appeared in his mind, his pale face lost in a tangle of hair that jutted out of his narrow head like black straw.

Mildly intrigued, Colin clicked on the email. It opened. There was no message, only an attached file. He considered deleting it immediately. IT had briefed staff about the threat of viruses and malicious malware. But this wasn't anonymous. This was from a known person. A former employee.

Perhaps this was something he needed to see?

He'd let Crow go five years ago, and good riddance! He'd disliked the skinny creep the second he'd set eyes on him. How had his predecessor tolerated him? Colin refused to tolerate unpunctual, scruffy-looking freaks, especially those who drank to excess, and often. He might've only been a caretaker, but the man was a liability.

Curiosity, though, nagged at him to click on the file. He considered the scenario of some trojan computer bug shutting his PC down and infecting the whole network. But he doubted the drunk had the capacity for setting his alarm clock, never mind cooking up some malevolent cyber-attack. And the company systems were good. Very good. If this was malicious, Crow better look out. The police would be involved. And with that thought in mind— Crow being handcuffed and led out of whatever grubby hovel he occupied— he shut his office door, returned to his desk, sat down, and clicked on the link.

The video played.

Colin flinched when he realized the empty office on the video was his own. The light was gloomy, the hour late, but it was his orderly desk. His chair. His working space. The camera was positioned from the far side of the desk.

A lank-haired man walked into shot and sloped into Colin's chair.

"Remember me?"

How could he forget? The camera angle was far enough away that it showed the man's profile in full, head to toe, although Crow had aged terribly. His ravaged face reminded him of one of those five-years-on-crystal-meth mug shots. His once jet-black, shoulder-length hair was striped with gray. His skin looked sallow and jaundiced. The bone structure of his face was altered, perhaps by tooth loss.

On the screen, Crow swept a long, thin arm across the expanse of his desk, knocking over his tubular desk organizer and spilling pencils, pens, and stationary onto the floor. Slouched in the chair and smiling, his thin body was wrapped in a too-tight, black but dirty-looking trench coat with the collar turned up. His black jeans were painted on. Oversized buckled boots completed the look. He resembled a cartoonish scarecrow. A cliché, and a middle-aged one at that. Still, he looked more ghoul than man.

So, Maggie *had* told the truth—it wasn't her who had made the mess. At the time he'd wondered if she'd done it out of spite or revenge, perhaps for him taking issue with her cleaning standards. But how had Crow got hold of a key? The locks had been changed since he'd left, as part of an office refurbishment.

He felt anger seethe through him.

On screen, Crow drank from a hipflask. After a long silence, he jangled a large ring with three keys and a tattered-looking ticket attached. "These are for you," he said, his effeminate voice breaking the video's undercurrent of white noise. He opened the desk drawer, tossed in the keys, and slammed the drawer shut. "You'll need those, soon enough." He leaned forward, his hair tumbling over his narrow eyes, and said, "You do remember me, don't cha? I'm the poor fucker you sacked five years ago." He coughed, took a hand-rolled cigarette from his coat pocket, and lit it with a cheap plastic lighter, the flame revealing a pinched-looking face. "I say *sacked*—you chose not to renew my contract. Amounts to the same thing." He exhaled a long stream of blue smoke and flicked ash on the floor.

Silence.

Crow worked his jaw, and Colin could almost hear the man's few remaining teeth grind, as if they were a mechanism that drove the gears of a sick mind left to fester. For *five* years.

Finally, Crow held up his hands, exposing his white palms to the camera, as if in protest. "Fuck's sake, I was a caretaker—nothing to you. You knew nothing about me, not anything. I was an artist, you know. You should've left me alone. So, a man likes a little drink…I was late a couple of times." He was still grinding his jaw, shaking his head in disapproval. He sank back in the chair, his face obscured by a mass of shadows.

Colin stared at the screen, as horrified as he was captivated. It was then Crow sprang forward, back into the camera's light, quick as a viper, teeth bared, his face feral, a contorted mask of hate. "You should have let it go," he growled, spit hitting the camera lens.

Colin recoiled.

Again, Crow sank back in the chair, his flaring anger abating. And at once, his expression became vacant and hopeless. "You see, Colin, I didn't *just* lose my job." He coughed, snorted a ball of thick phlegm, and spat it into the air. "I lost my wife. She *died*."

Colin had heard rumors, office gossip, although Crow was not part of the social circle of staff who enjoyed drinks together after hours or who got together for hoops or racketball. Instead, he was a peripheral figure who was only seen by those who came in early or worked late—if he bothered to turn up at all. But what had the death of this man's wife got to do with him? Nothing, of course.

Crow said, "Financial strain's a terrible thing. I tried to keep the plates spinning. Art was everything to me, but it never did take off, and when you took my job, you took everything. My life fell apart." An angry glint flared in his eyes. "Alison died of a heart attack. Thirty-seven. Such a young age. She'd have been an older first-time mom—I'll give you that. But thirty-seven…nobody deserves that. Our unborn kid went with her, to the grave." He took another drag from his cigarette, the little fire at its end reddening as he drew in its smoke. "After I lost my home, I lived in my car for six months. Six fucking months in that barrel of rust. Didn't care by then, but I couldn't afford the repairs, so I lost the car too.

"They did do an autopsy, though. Coroner explained Alison had a heart condition, *undiagnosed*. Could've been treated if they'd known, but her body was under strain—pregnancy and my…my…unemployment." He spoke the word through gritted teeth. "We were destitute. She didn't eat. Stress, that's what the coroner said. He didn't blame me, but I know. *It* finished her off."

For a fleeting second, Crow stared directly at the camera. *"You* finished her off."

Composing himself, Crow stiffened in the chair. "I could go on with this, tell you all the sordid details, get those violins going, tell you about the time when a policewoman caught me shitting in an alley or when I stopped breathing after a seizure. Some off-duty paramedic saved me, you know. Excuse me if I forgot to thank the interfering twat.

"So, in the interests of brevity, I'll get to the fucking point." Crow's expression was now deadpan. When he spoke, his voice settled on a monotone pitch of irrelevance. "I hate you. You've taken everything. My job. My wife. My child." He motioned downward with a sweeping hand, sarcastically presenting his addled body. "My *health.*"

Crow smiled again, revealing his few remaining teeth, tombstones that, even in the dusky light, Colin could see protruded from red and prematurely receded gums. "I know what you're thinking: *Police.* Go ahead, call 'em, Colin. I know what a straight shooter you are."

That alligator grin again.

"But I've had a look at your email. Password was predictable, to say the least. Took a few goes, but I got it—*Kipling.*" He winked. "*If* only you'd better set your security. I saw the email, to Brian, about the accounts, the ones you warned could be considered tax evasion." Crow raised his eyebrows knowingly.

Colin's stomach acid was rising, threatening to evict his breakfast of wholemeal toast and coffee.

Crow shook his head. "I'm no expert. Probably not a police matter, not initially, I'm sure, but one for the tax man to run his eye over. What do you think?"

So, it was blackmail. That's what this was all about. Panic started to set in. He was in this up to his neck. What was the saying? *Up shit creek without a paddle?* And none of it was his fault. *Fucking Brian fucking Hughes.* But *he'd* condemned himself by acknowledging the discrepancy in an email. He'd done nothing about it since Brian had returned that morning after a month off work. He could see the headlines in the local press: CHIEF EXEC IS TAX EVASION CHEAT.

How much does the bastard want?

As if in psychic response, Crow raised his eyebrows in mockery, his timing as impeccable as the most seasoned stage actor. "Oh, no, Colin. I don't want your money. There's an address in your drawer, together with the keys. I want to see you, in person. We're going to straighten all this out. I've been busy. There's something I've been working on I know you'll appreciate."

Still grinning at the camera, Crow hocked another ball of spit and gobbed it onto the computer before proceeding to wipe it across his rattling keyboard. The man stood, unzipped his skin-tight jeans, produced his long, thin uncircumcised penis, and proceeded to piss a fountain of orange-looking urine onto the desk, splashing everywhere, leering at the camera as he did. When he finished, Crow pulled a handful of tissues out from the box on Colin's desk and wiped up.

"Can't leave it sopping wet," he said, smirking. "Don't want to give the game away. I like to think of you sitting in this—in my piss. After all the shit you've put me through, fair's fair."

Colin stifled vomit. He felt dizzy, felt his body trembling with fury and disgust. To think, even after Maggie had cleaned up, he had sat there; it made him shudder.

Crow leaned forward and spoke quickly. "You better come here. *Today. Right now. Alone.* Take the keys with the address and meet me. Tell the police, and I'll get breaking and entering. You'll get tax evasion, not a criminal offense, unless of course they deem it fraud. I think you'll be all right, but it might be the end of your career." He smiled again. "Your move, *boss.*"

Crow waved, reached toward the invisible camera, and the screen turned to black.

CHECKMATE.

The weaselly little shit had him. Colin sat in his office for what seemed like forever, listening to his colleagues arrive for work, chatting, laughing, discussing normal things like Saturday cinema, nights out, and kids' ballet. All the while, he felt trapped, terrified to open his office door.

He contemplated every foreseeable outcome. And he couldn't get the grotesque image of Crow holding his flaccid cock out of his mind. It played on repeat, Crow pissing all over his desk like an alley cat marking his territory.

He looked at the drawer where Crow had chucked the keys. He didn't use that drawer. How could Crow have left those keys there a whole week, knowing that he wouldn't find them? And how had he got into his office?

And if he went to this mysterious address, who knew what Crow had planned? The man was a depraved lunatic, an alcoholic, and judging by the state of his ravaged body, likely on crack cocaine or heroin. He was capable of anything, ambushing him, attacking him, stabbing him with a dirty needle.

And he knew about the *discrepancy*.

His career was at serious risk.

Slowly, tentatively, he opened the desk drawer. Sure enough, the keys were there, waiting. And so was the address. It was spiked through by the steel ring that held the keys. He picked up the keys with his thumb and forefinger, as if they might be infected with some terrible disease.

In spidery, black letters the address read:

Aluminium Works, Old Mill Road

He knew the site, vaguely. The factory was derelict, a forgotten relic of an industrial age. It was out in the sticks, too, ten or fifteen miles from the office, where there was nothing but farmland, grazing fields, and a small, now-abandoned village built for factory staff.

Shit.

Colin entered the business name into Google Maps and came up with nothing. He typed "Old Mill Road" and switched to street view, navigating the country lanes on screen. Not a building in sight, only a sign directing traffic to the now-abandoned village of prefabricated houses built to serve the works. And then he saw it, in the distance, a gray, ominous, hulking structure, poking over treetops.

He'd found the old factory, and an hour later, he was on the road, fearing his career was ruined.

AS HE DROVE his head echoed with the lies he'd fed his colleagues. *Queasy stomach. Got to leave. Ate something bad.* They all knew. Colin Finch would have had to be dying before he'd leave sick—leave work like the rest of the shirkers. Why he'd said he was sick, he did not know. Maybe it was closest to the truth. It would have made more sense to invent some meeting appointment—after all, he was the chief exec. But he'd ran to his car. He'd ripped his phone from the wall where it was charging and staggered out into the parking lot, his eyes busy in their sockets. And he'd seen his own reflection. Even in the dull mirrors of the car windows, he could see he looked ill. He'd never looked so pale. He had simply wanted to get out of that office.

Colin had never been more terrified. He feared for his career, his empire, his professional reputation. Marriage, kids, they'd held little appeal. Instead, he'd invested his energies and climbed the corporate ladder and destroyed anyone who'd stood in the way of his ambition. It was dog-eat-dog—jungle law. And he'd done what he needed to do to get where he was going. And he'd gotten there, all right. And now, this drunken pissant threatened it all.

The bright morning sky was clear, and the sun blazed, dazzling his eyes. He'd long left the town and its urban streets behind, and his Mercedes accelerated, passing green fields bordered by wild hedgerow. A gentle wind rustled the trees, occasionally freeing a scatter of leaves that blew across the sleek hood of his car. Autumn was pretty much here, and the chilling breeze whistled through his open window, whispering in his ear that winter was not far behind.

This wouldn't end well. What could they possibly straighten out? The best way this could end was blackmail. The worst, violence. Who knew what Crow wanted—*really* wanted? Colin had propped his five-iron against the passenger seat. It'd be useless if Crow came at him with a gun, but he doubted that. A knife, maybe.

Ahead, he could see the gray roofs of the old buildings protruding from above the treetops—the same as he'd seen on Google Maps. A minute's drive separated him from the madman who had invaded his office. Soon he'd know, one way or the other, how this would play out.

He turned off the main road and onto a pot-holed track that shook his car like an old washing machine. He cursed as branches scratched the paintwork. Ahead, the aluminium works loomed. The old factory consisted of three ugly square brick buildings, whose chimneys had once spewed pollution into the surrounding countryside. Even from this distance, he could see the boarded-up windows. It saddened him to think of what had become of this place of men and work.

The road's condition worsened, and the suspension now rattled even more violently. He thought about walking the rest of the way, but the decision was made for him. An old, rusted gate blocked his path. A weather-beaten sign read NO ENTRY. Beyond the gate, a path wound between a wood of densely packed trees.

Colin pulled over, got out of his car, removed his jacket, and took the golf club from the passenger seat.

He stood before the gate. The hulking aluminium works towered above him, three ugly sisters, each a colossus of neglect, casting their long shadows over the woods beneath.

He climbed the gate and walked the path toward the buildings where Eden Crow waited.

AS HE APPROACHED, even the tallest of the three main buildings sank below the level of the trees through which he walked, and the pot-holed road became a disused dirt track that soon was hardly even a path at all. The surrounding forest was thick. He had a deep sense of déjà vu. He stopped, taking in the mulchy aroma of dead leaves, looking around between the many tree trunks. He was aware that Crow could ambush him at any point. He was glad he'd brought the club. The light was dull here and the land quiet. The main road was only five hundred yards behind him, but the silence was unnerving. He was so alone. Somewhere, a bird chirped, and another fluttered its small wings, darting between the branches of one tree and then another. Too small to be a crow.

The trees stood tall, their branches joining hands above and suffocating the light. He had seen this place before—the painting, on his office wall.

How could that be?

A chain of irrepressible thoughts went off like fireworks, and he felt claustrophobia begin to choke his confidence. He gripped the golf club harder, his eyes scanning the trees around him.

Where had he got that painting? It had been on his wall as long as he could remember. He wanted out of this eerie woods, and so he marched quickly along the trail. He walked through the tunnel of trees, listening for signs of civilization. There were none, not even the distant hum of traffic. The deeper he walked into the woods, the more he felt he left the real world behind. He thought of all the times he'd spent admiring the painting on his office wall, imagining what enchanted land the wooded passage led to. Never did he daydream the path led to a derelict factory.

He reached a wire fence, eight feet high and topped with barbed wire. A large wooden sign read DANGER! KEEP OUT. TRESPASSERS WILL BE PROSECUTED. On the other side of the fence, the woods were sparser, although the area was still covered with smaller trees, overgrown weeds, and shrubs that had long claimed back the land from the now-crumbling concrete.

Another heavy gate blocked his way. It was too high and difficult to climb. But there was an old, rusted padlock, sealing the gate shut. He took the keys—which Crow had hurled into his desk drawer—from his pants pocket and tried the lock. The second key was stiff, but the lock popped, and the gates squealed open.

In he walked.

Ahead an old brick shed with flaking gray paint revealed itself through the foliage. The building's windows were smashed, splinters of glass scattered on the ground. Nearby, a burnt-out car, an oil drum, and broken wooden crates with rusted nails exposed to the elements gave the ground the look of an abandoned rubbish dump.

The early autumn sun strobed between the trees as he walked. Now and then, leaves gently fell around him. Farther ahead, an old, military-style, semi-circular hut was boarded up. It was so covered with ivy and vines, the building appeared like a tunnel burrowing into the thicker woods surrounding the land. A section of the building's corrugated roof lay on the ground, gathering moss.

Somewhere, a bird fluttered its wings. Another squawked. His heart beating hard, he walked onward, kicking dust and gravel, his polished shoes scuffing as he went.

He reached a larger clearing. Now he could see the three towering factory buildings before him. Colin despised fiction, but he was reminded of a book he'd read as a child. The gray factories stood like dark towers in Mordor. Even from two hundred yards away, it was obvious the buildings were little more than shells. The industry had long left, and the buildings remained a haunting testament to a bygone age.

Tied between two trees, a banner hung before him, blowing gently in the breeze. The banner was homemade from white frayed cloth and crudely painted with red letters: Welcome to the Eden Crow Festival of Art. An arrow pointed to the middle factory building, the largest of the three. He shivered.

He looked around at the waste-covered ground, at the thick forest behind, and finally to the hulking, dilapidated factories and their towering chimneys.

He studied the banner and the arrow pointing to the building. He knew this was a trap, but he'd come this far. Eden Crow watched him. Of that, he was certain. He could feel the other man's narrow eyes on him, observing him like a sniper from one of those towering monstrosities. He could turn away and run, get back to his car, but he'd be running away from one trap and falling into another. The taxman would be waiting and possibly the police. His career would end, everything he'd worked for—twenty-five years down the drain.

No!

The words of Kipling's poem flashed in his mind.

If you can keep your head when all about you…are losing theirs and blaming it on you…

…You'll be a Man, my son.

With the guiding light of these words engraved in his thoughts, Colin Finch marched toward the old factory.

AFTER WALKING BACK and forth around the perimeter of the building, he found a loose board blocking a doorway. The rackety board lifted easily, and he discovered a dusky passage leading to a second heavy-set door. It was metal and rusted with age and locked with another padlock.

If Crow was in here, how had these locks been secured?

He stepped over a pile of rubble, tripping over a coil of discarded wire, and tried the lock. The keys were distinctly shaped, and so he picked a key at random from the remaining two, ignoring the key which had opened the first padlock at the gate.

The padlock opened with ease, as if it had been oiled.

The door, though, refused to budge. He pushed, aware of his palms scraping against the coarse, rusted surface of the cold metal. The discomfort reminded him he was no longer a young man; soft hands, withered muscle, and slumped shoulders were the legacy of a career spent behind a desk. Crow looked older than his years, and he was in poor health, but he was a younger man with the calloused hands and sinewy strength of a manual worker.

I've got the club, thought Colin.

He squatted and pressed his shoulder to the door, and finally something gave. The door scraped against the uneven ground, and the creaking echo became a metallic wail that travelled deep within the factory's gutted shell. As the door opened and the old hinges protested, he felt the damp air escape, brushing his cheek like a cold, shallow gasp.

If Crow had missed his approach, he had warning now.

Inside, darkness enveloped him. High above, he could see the narrowest traces of sunlight at the edges of the boarded windows, but the shaft of gray light surrounding his entry did nothing to disperse the gloom. He was blindly aware of the vast expanse of space around him, the hollow, pressing darkness.

Colin stood on the fringes of the vast black space before him, and for the first time, he checked his mobile phone. No signal. Was there ever? He'd seen films like these before. He was miles out, and the nearby abandoned village that had once served this factory had no need of modern amenities, like internet. But what he feared most was the taxman. The police. His job. Tangible fears. Unlike Crow, he was not a coward. He would meet this head on. He wasn't a child, and a dark room didn't frighten him.

He pressed the flashlight app on his mobile phone. Twelve percent charge left on the battery. He had meant to charge it. Shadows scattered in the white light. He discovered an old mattress, a filthy blanket, and a pile of cans of super-strength lager. Then the beam of light revealed the room in pieces. Piles of bricks. The littered floor. The graffiti. The rusted piping on the walls. Finally, the gargantuan metal platforms and stairwells that had collapsed beneath the cathedral-high ceiling. Dust swam in the light, like plankton at the bottom of the deep. The flashlight swept through the layers of gloom, casting shadows and illuminating pockets of detail until the light lit up a face in the black sea of murk.

The face was pale, the eyes hideously fixed black points.

He lurched back toward the door, his heart thudding, his sweaty left hand gripping the club.

The face had disappeared. He'd been startled and had let the face out of his sight.

He held up his phone, scanning the black space, and called out, "I know you're there." His voice boomed in the cavernous tomb between the high factory walls.

Silence.

"Come out, you bastard."

The sound of his own voice spooked him; it was an intrusive presence.

His flashlight beam again found the pale face. His heart quickened until he realized the face was still. He was looking at a painting. He walked toward it. The painting was huge, four feet in height, in portrait orientation. It was of Crow, a ghastly self-portrait propped against a collapsed iron stairwell. In the painting, Crow sat staring into oblivion, his hands folded over his thin knees, his eyes fixed. Crow's lips were pressed tight in a grimace that hinted at some secret satisfaction.

His foot kicked something that toppled over with a flat-sounding clap. He shone the light at his feet and discovered another framed painting. Bending to pick it up, he realized the picture depicted the wooded path that had led him here, the same scene he'd admired on his office wall for years. If he got out of this alive, he'd throw the damn painting away, he decided.

The light cut through the gloom, and he discovered more of them—paintings hung, quite literally, from the highest rafters. On the walls. Propped up against sleeping, rusted, cobwebbed mechanical beasts of industry. Propped against bare-bricked walls and hiding the profane graffiti behind. Hundreds of paintings. Hundreds and hundreds.

Every painting was unique. Some depicted the surrounding grounds, others that wooded path, others the gloom of the disused factory, each arranged erratically and one overlapping the next, every canvas covered in dust.

On a back wall he found a painting of a naked and heavily pregnant woman lying flat on a table. She was obviously pregnant because of the globular protrusion of her swollen stomach, and she was obviously dead, too, because her eyes were flat and staring into eternity. But it was the stitched Y-shaped incision on her chest that really gave it away. A second wound under her belly had been similarly repaired with thread.

Next to the painting of the dead woman was a painting of an aborted, red fetus. It, too, had obviously perished.

He looked away, disgusted, but the light from his phone fell on a picture he found more horrifying than anything he'd seen before.

Hanging on the bare wall, on a rusted nail hammered through a wooden beam, the painting depicted his little, modern-furnished office. He could see it all. His desk. His computer. His coffee mug branded with the word THE BOSS in bold capital letters. He squinted at the painting in disbelief.

Again his foot kicked something on the littered floor. He pointed his phone and the light revealed a small steel box. It was a security box, one you might use to lock away something important or dangerous, like a gun. He bent lower, picked up the box, and saw it was locked. He used the third key, and the box opened.

Inside was a rolled piece of parchment paper tied neatly with a red ribbon.

Colin shone the light around, in case Crow had sneaked up on him. The white light swept across the black room and revealed he had not. With unsteady hands, he untied the ribbon and flattened the parchment.

"Welcome to the prison of my mind," it read.

He huffed. Was that it? Crow wanted him to look at these sick and twisted paintings, to give him a taste of the pain and suffering he'd endured, because of him. He scrunched the paper into a ball and threw the box, which tumbled across the hard floor with a metallic prang.

"You brought it on yourself," Colin bellowed. "All of it."

His words echoed, booming in the vast space of dilapidation.

He shone the flashlight around again, a trick of the light revealing the dead woman's eyes moving in the painting. He squinted, dismissing the optical illusion. Dead women's eyes didn't move. Anyway, it was a painting.

As he continued to scan the light around the room, throwing shadows that scattered like fleeing phantoms, in the peripheries of the light, in a fleeting moment of insanity, he saw—thought he saw—imagined—Maggie, his cleaner, walking across and out of frame in the painting of his office, as if he gazed upon a video and not a dusty canvas.

Impossible.

He had to get out of here. This place, it was creepy. His mind was playing tricks.

As he rushed back toward the door, the shaft of light at the entrance narrowed. The door wailed on its hinges and closed.

He ran, reaching the door too late.

Oh God, please don't do this.

"Let me out, you fucking maniac."

There was no response, only silence as the echoes of his screams dispersed.

He checked his phone. The flashlight was draining the battery fast.

Three percent.

He flashed the light around the room, looking for a way out. There was none. The room was huge, but six windows had once provided the light. Those windows were too high to reach and boarded. Once the stairwell would have provided access to the iron walkways above. But not now. The remnants of those second and third floors were a collapsed pile of wrought iron, rusting in this forgotten ruin.

Welcome to the prison of my mind.

"Let me out, please."

On the other side of the door, he heard the key turning, securing the padlock with a hollow click.

Colin tried to stay calm, but his heart pounded, and he dreaded the impending, total darkness that would soon arrive.

Two percent.

He shone the light around him. The painting of the dead woman had changed. She sat up now, smiling, her breasts sagging beneath the sewed-up incision. The painting of the fetus was now an empty canvas. He hammered the door with his fists. His mind was playing stupid tricks—stupid, childish tricks!

Something darted in the corner of his vision. A rat. If it was, it was a big one.

He breathed deeply and attempted to steady his mind. He was Colin Finch, Chief Executive. *If...* he thought. But the words that had been his mantra felt pathetic and useless.

His lip quivered. He lost his footing and staggered, his hand finding a nearby canvas, pawing at it like Braille. The picture was of the woods. He could have sworn, for a split second, the canvas puddled like water to his fumbling touch.

One percent.

Colin Finch waited for the arriving dark. When it came, he felt the air solidifying, like paint drying, his fate setting. But in the black room, he sensed nothing was still, the room abounding with pictures he could not see.

PROVIDE

Renee M.P.T. Kray

KEN SPUN THE STEERING WHEEL of the Tesla in his sweat-slicked palms as he stood on the brake, swerving onto the shoulder just before his car almost slammed into the back of the white minivan that had rattled into his lane.

"Fuck it, Granny!" Ken screamed as he roared past the old woman whose nose barely poked above her steering wheel. In his defense, it was a fifty-five-mile-per-hour zone and the minivan was barely pulling thirty. In *her* defense, it was a fifty-five-mile-per-hour zone and Ken was edging toward seventy-five. He barely cleared her front bumper before swinging back into the lane and switching his foot from the brake to the accelerator, urging his vehicle forward with all the muster of Charlton Heston at the reins of Ben-Hur's chariot team. Ken glanced in the rearview mirror and saw only what was to be expected: the asphalt and yellow dotted lines steadily rolling away from him, taking along with it the trimmed trees by the sides of the road and the minivan that probably didn't even have another two years of life in it. It was exactly as it should be, completely normal, and yet the sight did nothing to calm his nerves.

Because even if Ken couldn't see him, he knew that Francisco was still out there somewhere.

Ken dropped back into his seat with a sigh that shot out of his throat as more of a gasp. He worked in marketing, and a big part of his job was to make sure that his clients had the (best? ideal? perfect?) most concise description for any given situation, but he had no words for the hell that this day had become. He swerved again as he came up close behind another car, then eased up on the accelerator as he drew near the school zone. He'd definitely already pushed his luck in the mad dash from the hospital to this point, but the cops were always hiding near the school zone, waiting for speeders who didn't pay attention to the flashing yellow lights. Ken couldn't afford to be stopped right now. There was no way he was going to be able to explain to an officer that a ghost was following him, one who'd been coming closer and closer every time he saw it, and that he couldn't let it catch up to him before he'd gotten what it needed.

Not to mention the fact that the ghost was his own son, who had died less than four hours ago.

The uninspired brown frame of the school loomed up on the left side of the road, and the sudden urge to vomit, an acid twist deep in Ken's guts, came on out of nowhere.

Doesn't matter, he thought. *Got nothing left.* He'd already (barfed? up-chucked? blown chunks?) regurgitated his breakfast into the hospital bathroom about an hour ago, just after the grief counselor had presented him with photographs of his son's body so that he could confirm that, yes, it was indeed Francisco who was lying cold under a sheet somewhere in the morgue. The little blond woman had been sitting prim and composed as she gestured to the two small white squares on the table between them, cautioning Ken to take his time and only flip them over when he felt he was ready. What a load of bullshit; it wasn't like he'd ever be ready. So Ken had ripped the Band-Aid off, turning over the photographs quickly, one in each hand…and then he'd suddenly been unable to move.

On the other side of those unassuming white sheets of paper were images that Ken would never forget. It was undoubtedly Francisco's face printed there in full color, but it was all wrong. Francisco's normally tousled black hair was lying sticky and limp against the giant gash on his forehead, exposing a rash of raw meat underneath that would never have the ability to heal. The eyes that Ken had looked into a thousand times and seen cloaked in every possible emotion were now closed, enfolded in skin so lifelessly gray that it almost matched the lilac of the grief counselor's shirt. There was no noose, thank high heaven for that, but the massive slash of dark purple and blue skin where it had done its damage drew Ken's eye in with viciousness, sagging inwards across Francisco's throat to illustrate where his windpipe had collapsed under the weight of his body and everything had come to an end.

Twelve years. That was all that his boy had gotten.

It was too much. Ken had rushed into the adjoining bathroom and barely made it to the toilet before the sausage-and-egg-white breakfast sandwich he'd bought on the way to work that morning made a frothy appearance. As half-digested pieces of his breakfast reappeared one by one into the toilet bowl, Ken's head had replayed—for his viewing enjoyment—the scene at the breakfast table that morning, the last time he'd seen Francisco alive.

"Hi, Dad."

"Hey, Big F. We got any milk left?"

"It's spoiled. What time are you gonna be home from work today?"

"Dunno, man. Got a lot of meetings and it might not be till late. Why? Do you need something?"

"No, I was just wondering. No big deal if you're busy."

"Well, I'll try to get home as quick as I can, but it's been madness at the office the past few weeks."

"You mean the past few months?"

"Ha! Yeah, I guess so. Hey, I need to scram or I'll be late for my eight o'clock. And the bus should be here soon. I'll try to get out as early as I can, okay?"

"Yeah, okay. Bye, Dad."

"See you later."

Ken blinked and was suddenly back to the present: not at his kitchen table with Francisco or in the stark white office of the hospital counselor, but in his car, slowed to almost a standstill outside the school where it had all gone down. The big brown building was exactly the same as it had been when he himself had attended as a child, with the same playground in the front and big oak tree that was probably too tall to be so close to the front doors. But when Ken had gone to school, the tree hadn't been surrounded by caution tape and orange-painted construction horses like a damn maypole; hell, those hadn't been there that morning. Ken's throat grew dry and hard as he looked at the tree, and he tried to convince himself to look anywhere, anywhere at all except the big branch where Francisco had died, but his eyes traveled along it of their own accord. There was the gnarled skin that his child must have grasped with clutching fingers as he struggled to escape, and here was the smaller crisscross of branches growing off the main one, where the rope attached to Francisco's school tie had caught and then doomed him when he slipped and fell in his rush. Somewhere right around *there* must have been where he bashed his forehead against the big branch on the way down, which meant that right under the middle of said branch was where Francisco must have landed, hovering halfway between earth and sky, already dead before the teachers came running to cut him down. But Ken didn't have to imagine what it must have looked like four hours ago when Francisco had exhaled his last breath and his schoolmates had scattered, because Francisco was there.

Ken slammed on the brakes, eliciting irritated honks from drivers behind him, but he barely noticed as they passed him, yelling and flipping birds his way. Even if he had noticed, he wouldn't have given a shit about them, anyway. Ken blinked hard, expecting the vision to vanish in the sunlight, but when he looked again, the figure was still there. It was the exact same Francisco that he had first seen in the hospital lobby from probably thirty feet away, and then again in the parking lot only slightly closer, and now Ken was sure that the distance between himself and the apparition was shrinking, with maybe only twenty feet or so between them.

Francisco was (flying? floating? levitating?) hovering underneath the big oak branch with his toes pointed downward in a perfect ballerina form. His chin lay against his neck, obscuring most of his face, but Ken didn't need to see him head-on to know that this was his child. He recognized the outline of that slightly Roman nose they both shared, the black hair that Francisco had inherited from Janet's father, and the shape and size of his body. But his skin was the same watercolor purple of death that had saturated the postmortem pictures, while his arms hung limp from his sides like a doll that had come unstrung. There had been no noose in the pictures but there certainly was one now, a makeshift creation that had been hobbled together when bullies tied a length of white rope to Francisco's red and blue school tie. Ken had taught his son how to fasten that tie, and now it was pulled back so far into his skin that it was practically lost to sight, eaten up by the lips of bruised flesh on the top and bottom. Behind Francisco, the white rope stretched straight upwards before disappearing into thin air. As Ken watched, Francisco suddenly shuddered, and the shimmying motion jumped up his body and bounced through the white rope behind his body like electricity in an old time cartoon. It should have been impossible with the window closed, but somehow Ken heard the sound of the rope groaning under its burden as it moved.

Creakek.

Francisco's right arm (jerked? spasmed? quivered?) twitched erratically, then rolled upwards sloppily, hands flopping over on their wrists as the arm reached his chest and then dropped toward Ken. Ken's skin prickled as he looked at his child with hand outstretched, the symbol of supplication. Ken's own hand went to the door handle and hovered there for a moment, half contemplating opening the door and rushing over to the shade that was left of his son, embracing—or trying to embrace—the last bit of Francisco he would ever see.

But that wouldn't do anything for Francisco.

I promised. And I failed.

An adrenaline rush of fight or flight overwhelmed Ken for the second time that day, and he jerked the car back onto the road. He watched in the rearview mirror as the ghost of Francisco beneath the tree grew smaller and smaller until it was finally cut off by a turn in the road.

"Shit," Ken gasped. He hated himself for feeling so relieved when he could no longer see the specter of his son, because after all, this was all his fault. Ken took another look in the mirror, but it was only his reflection there now, his own gray-peppered hair and brown eyes bloodshot from the tears and then the terror. He'd spent what felt like his whole life looking down into a set of eyes just like his, and during that entire time he'd only had one goal in life:

Provide.

The day Francisco had been born was the happiest of Ken's life. Francisco had been unplanned, and Ken suspected that that was the first tip of a wedge between himself and Janet. She didn't want kids, but he was overjoyed to have a baby; whatever, they would make it work. She'd been a good sport about it for a long time, and Ken had made sure to make adjustments to his life to ensure that Janet's world didn't have to change too drastically. So it was Ken who'd dropped down to part-time hours and spent many happy afternoons playing make-believe with a toddler, building forts and shooting pretend guns at imaginary mountain lions, reveling in the sound of the sharp, high laughter that Francisco would squeal whenever Ken lifted him up in the air. Meanwhile Janet spent most of her time pursuing her airline stewardess jet-setting dreams, and while it seemed like a good arrangement for both of them at first, somewhere along the line, Ken and Janet had simply grown

apart. By the time their marriage had reached its seventh year, Janet was looking for something more, something Ken and Francisco couldn't seem to give
her.

Francisco had been five that year. He was a bundle of knobby knees and
curiosity during the day but a timid cuddler at night, when he would run
down the hallway to his parents' room and snuggle between them. But finally
there had come the night when Francisco had run into the room and it was
only Ken in bed, wide awake as he tried to figure out what he would do to
make ends meet and how he would explain to Francisco what D-I-V-O-R-
C-E spelled. Ken remembered clearly the moment that the bedroom door
had creaked open to reveal the outline of little Francisco in the doorway. He'd
wasted no time in pattering across the carpeted floor and then pulling himself
up into the bed, while Ken desperately tried to prepare himself for whatever
was to come. Would Francisco ask where his mommy was? Cry? Go back to
his own bed? But instead, Francisco had curled right up beside his father and
promptly fallen asleep without a care in the world.

As if Ken were enough for him.

In the deep hours of that night, Ken had watched his child sleep and
had made a solemn promise: that no matter what it took, Francisco would
never know anything but happiness. Those two tiny fists curled against Ken's
chest had been the motivation that stuck with him through the years as he
pursued and finally achieved a better job, then struggled to rise to the top,
and then stuck with the long hours so that he could make sure his son not
only had everything he needed but everything he wanted. As Francisco entered his double digits, Ken made sure that he had absolutely every bauble
and electronic toy that any kid could have ever dreamed of, enough so that
any school friend who walked in the door wouldn't have a minute to think,
Oh, you're the kid whose mom ran out on him, because they'd be too busy
soaking up the stacks of latest consoles and games with jealous eyes. Sure, that
meant taking on extra assignments at work and adopting a schedule so wild
that he and Francisco sometimes went long periods without seeing each other
until the weekends, but Ken had counted it all worth it. Francisco wanted for
nothing, which meant that he was happy. Or at least, so Ken had thought.

"*What time are you gonna be home from work today?*"

"*Dunno, man. Got a lot of meetings and might not be till late. Why?
Do you need something?*"

"Maybe that's why he was asking," Ken said aloud as he twisted the steering wheel again, pulling into his own driveway and up into the garage. "Maybe he was going to tell you today." But it didn't make sense for Francisco to have kept his condition at school a secret at all. He knew that his dad took care of everything and always made sure to get him whatever he needed. That was their understanding. So Francisco should have known that if he'd told his father about the bullies at school, Ken would have made sure those turkey-shit bastards rued the day they ever turned their eyes on his son.

Ken put the car in park and opened the door. Typically he had a ritual for whenever he arrived home: after finishing whatever energy drink he'd gotten to keep him awake during the ride home, he would toss the empty can like a basketball into the recycling bin that was stationed beside the door for exactly that purpose, then he would give himself a long moment to stretch his arms and back as the butterfly doors folded shut behind him. In years past, before he'd gotten so high up on the ladder in his company and committed to so many late nights, Francisco would have been awake and waiting for him and they would swap notes at the kitchen counter, comparing their school and work days and having good-natured debates about whose situation was harder and why.

Today was the first day that Ken could remember in years that the ritual was broken. Before the doors were even shut, he bolted up the two wooden steps to the door to the house and grabbed the knob, which rolled fruitlessly between his soggy hands like a ship caught between waves.

"Come on," Ken groaned. He looked behind himself, but there was nothing in the garage except himself and the car.

I still have time. He hasn't caught up to me yet. He wiped his hands against his dress pants and simultaneously tried to push down the awful thought that he was trying to put distance between himself and his own son. What kind of father did that make him?

The kind who gets things done, he reminded himself harshly. There was no time to think or indulge in self-pity. There was only time to act. Ken pressed down on the knob and finally his palm gripped the metal, forcing the handle to turn and the door to open.

The basics of what Ken saw as he stepped over the threshold and headed straight for his office were business as usual. The minimalistic white walls, tan furniture, and Joanna Gaines-esque decor had essentially remained the same as it had been when Janet had put it all together, but the smaller details were unnervingly normal, too: the pot that Francisco had used to make his dinner of ramen noodles at six last night was still in the sink, along with the plate on which Ken had reheated pizza when he'd come home at ten. Francisco's collective jackets, cups, socks, and electronics were still scattered about like they almost always were, which Ken didn't clean up both because of his busy schedule and because it was a subtle middle finger to the hyperactively clean environment Janet had insisted upon back when she'd lived here. But as Ken rushed past each familiar item, he sensed an invisible fog of strangeness woven between them that hadn't existed that morning, a quiet so tense that each snap of the clock above the mantle landed with the atrocity of a gunshot in a no-fire zone. In the few hours that had passed since he'd left for work, his home had somehow become just a house with all his—their—things in it.

I could've stopped them, Ken reminded himself for probably the fifth time that day, not daring to look too closely at the game controller on the couch that Francisco had been holding last night. *I could've made them stop.* But even as he reassured himself that he would have done something about the situation if Francisco had only told him about the school bullies who had apparently tormented him every day, Ken felt the presence of a far uglier question bubbling up, one that he'd been trying to suppress all day.

Why didn't I see it?

Ken had been so busy this year after his most recent promotion that he hadn't been able to tell his ass from a hole in the ground half the time, but when he'd been able to see Francisco on weekends he'd seemed...well...normal enough. Now that Ken was thinking about the situation with the clarity that only comes after incredibly stupid decisions, uncomfortable scenes were floating through his head as he entered his office and pulled a small gray safe from the top of his bookshelf. In his mind's eye, Ken saw Francisco talking less over the past year, spending more time in his room, getting even more involved in video games and online chatting than he ever had before.

But isn't that also a sign of teen hormones? Isn't that normal? Ken didn't know. It struck him that he'd never thought to outright ask Francisco if he had any troubles at school, because Francisco had never brought anything up or seemed particularly unhappy.

"We believe the leader of this incident was James Ellison, a boy one grade ahead of Francisco. Apparently James has a bit of...a bit of a bullying issue, and this wasn't the first confrontation between the two of them. James and his friends were teasing Francisco about something, and it escalated, and

James tied the rope to Francisco's tie to be…well, some sort of a dog leash joke. From what other students have told us, Francisco bolted, and they were chasing him so he tried to get away by climbing the tree. The bottom of the rope caught, and he slipped somewhere on the way up and fell. Completely accidental; in fact James is the one who alerted the teachers. Death would have been instant from that great of a height. Francisco probably didn't even realize what had happened. Absolutely no pain."

The police had circled around that point over and over again like scum swirling down a drain, as if the horror of Francisco's death could somehow be made okay if it were painless. As if it were an avoidable thing, no one's fault, a horrible accident that Ken shouldn't beat himself up over. But how could he not beat himself up over it? Ken had made a promise that he would provide whatever Francisco needed, and despite working himself to the bone, he had managed to completely fail, because Francisco had died terrified, and horribly. No wonder he wasn't able to move on.

And as if the thought had been a cue, Ken heard a noise from behind him.

Creakek.

Icey cold shot up Ken's spine at the sound of the rope, straightening him as quickly as if he'd been kicked in the back. He spun on his heel and faced the door, clutching the safe in both hands like a sacred totem that could save him from the ungodly horror that his own failure had brought down upon him.

Francisco was in the living room, his downcast head facing toward the spot on the couch that had been his favorite when he'd been alive. The distance between them was barely fifteen feet now, and at this close vantage point, Ken observed that Francisco's fingers were curled up into his palms like the paws of an old arthritic cat, and his blue-tinged skin glistened with a fine layer of sweat that had probably cooled on his actual body the moment he died.

The edges of Ken's sight grew bright and wavered a little, and Ken tried to take a deep breath to steady himself, but it only sputtered unevenly through his nose and mouth. He didn't know for sure what Francisco wanted, but he did know that ghosts only came back if they had unfinished business or died unhappily, both of which checked out in this case. And as the person who'd sworn that Francisco would be happy, Ken was clearly the one responsible for his current state, and the one who had to fix it.

The soft carpet of the office absorbed the sound as Ken slowly pressed his right foot backward, but at the motion, Francisco's body jerked as if Ken had stepped on raw gravel. Ken's eyes widened and started to go dry as he watched the specter of his son turn—*Creakekek*—ever so slowly to face the office door, then stopped. Francisco's head rolled back and forth above the noose, while behind their closed lids his eyes started to rove feverishly in their sockets with the fury of a dreamer trying to escape a nightmare.

"No." The word escaped Ken's throat in a soft mewl. Ken had spent his entire life looking down into those eyes that were the same sharp brown as his own. He'd watched them cry as a child, go dull over boring homework, and—his favorite—sparkle with excitement whenever Ken brought home some new gift. But now Ken was sure that if those purpled lids were to crank back, what looked at him from underneath would be (bloody? mottled? pustulated?) not the eyes of his son, and if he were to see that, Ken knew for certain that he would go mad.

At the sound of Ken's voice, Francisco suddenly went still. His head lolled slowly onto his right shoulder in a sluggish imitation of a dog cocking its head at a strange noise. Ken saw that the acne on Francisco's chin, which had appeared earlier in the week, a sign of oncoming puberty stamped across a twelve-year-old face, was still there. An army of tiny pink pustules blossomed horribly bright against the dead skin.

"I'm sorry," Ken whispered. "But I'm making it right. You have to believe me. Give me some time. I'll make it right." Francisco made no further motion. Ken licked his lips, then he looked down at the safe in his hands. It was small but heavy, a case that he hadn't opened in years but which he always kept in a safe place and close at hand. He entered in the six-digit code—081709, Francisco's birthdate—and the safe beeped as the lid popped open. Ken looked down at the silver Glock that he'd bought as a young man, one which he never had to use but which he'd always had nearby, simply as a precaution. More importantly, it was the final tool he had at his disposal if he wanted to be able to provide for Francisco. Ken hadn't seen that Francisco was unhappy at school in time to make a difference, but he could at least bring justice to the situation.

He would make sure the bully who took Francisco's life didn't live to tell the tale.

Ken didn't dare test his luck sneaking past Francisco. When he and Janet had selected this house back when they were trying to save their marriage and had thought a slight change of scenery could do it, Ken had insisted that they choose a home with a lot of exit points in case there were ever a fire, meaning that almost every room had a window. The office was no exception, and Ken started to back toward the large window beside his desk, never once taking his eyes off the ghost of his son. But before he'd made more than a few steps, Francisco seemed to sense Ken pulling away, and his body suddenly spasmed like a ragdoll being whipped in the hand of a toddler, a horrible sight to see at such close proximity, while the noose tightened against his windpipe so harshly that Ken felt his own throat ache.

Creakekekekek!

Ken turned and leapt toward the window, slamming the lid of the safe shut and tucking it under his left arm before snapping back the locks and pushing the panel of glass upward.

"Dad!"

The voice was like the echo of a whisper, something so quiet it might as well have been carried in on the wind, but it still stopped Ken cold. He stopped and looked back toward the office door, unable to resist the sound of the voice he hadn't ever expected to hear again. It was so normal, so perfectly Francisco, that for a moment Ken was convinced that he would see his son standing with his feet on the ground, staring at his father going out the window as if that were the most insane thing happening in the world...but no. Whether it had been a trick of his ears or just a memory that had leapt to the surface, it was clear that Francisco hadn't said anything, because Francisco was still dead.

Only now he was directly in the entryway of the study.

"Just hold on," Ken promised. "I'll fix this and then you'll be at peace. I swear. I'll take care of it." He turned and ducked under the windowpane, pulling himself out of the house and tumbling into the grass a short distance below. Ken had barely touched the ground before he stood up and ran from his house, merging onto the nature trail that snaked along behind and would, eventually, twist along behind the house of James Ellison.

The most fucked-up thing about the entire day should have been that Francisco was dead, or maybe even the way that he'd died, but Ken thought the fact that the little shit the cops had named as the chief instigator of the fatal bullying incident used to actually be friends with Francisco was the most (surprising? unexpected? ironic?) mordant shock of the day. He hadn't seen James in years, but how quickly his mind was able to pull up a memory of the little traitor: blond, with watery green eyes and big ears that stuck out the sides of his head. Never the type of kid that you'd expect to grow up to become a bully or, even worse, a murderer. The memories of ten-year-old James and nine-year-old Francisco riding their bikes together along this very trail were so pristine and present in Ken's mind that what had happened between them today seemed impossible. Ken slowed down as, in his mind's eye, he watched the two boys whipping past, James on his big hand-me-down bike and Francisco on the sleek black bicycle that Ken had upgraded him to, hollering as they flew over the discarded McDonald's bag that was blowing in the wind on Ken's left and scaring the squirrel that was chittering up ahead.

Is that why you didn't tell me? Ken wanted to ask. *Were you afraid of getting him in trouble for bullying, because you used to be friends?* But the time for questions was past; all too quickly the (daydream? hallucination? vision?) wishful thinking faded, and instead of Francisco's excited laughter, which always jumped as high and clear as it had when he'd been a child, Ken was left with the sound of a stretching rope groaning from somewhere behind him.

Creakek.

Ultimately it didn't matter why Francisco hadn't said anything. What mattered now was providing what Francisco needed. Ken picked the pace back up and started jogging down the path. Forget the fact that James and Francisco used to be friends. James had clearly found a new crowd to run with at Francisco's expense, and Ken had promised that *nothing* would ever be done at Francisco's expense. It was unfortunate that it would require such a cost, and deep inside, Ken's guts squirmed uncomfortably at the thought of putting a bullet into a child, but there was surprisingly little resistance otherwise. If this was what had to be done, it would be done. Ken wouldn't, couldn't, go through life with each memory of his child's smiling face replaced by the image of what Francisco had become: a tortured specter of pain and death, always roaming and never satisfied.

Ken reached a garbage can set to the side of the path, one of those massive buckets made of crisscrossing metal silver and sheathed with a thick plastic bag big enough to fit a small person inside. Ken looked around to make sure no one was coming, then he pulled the gun safe out from underneath his arm and quickly opened it. The handgun was still inside, and as the sun hit it, it seemed to grin up at Ken with a dull metal sheen. In spite of himself, Ken grinned back down at the weapon. He was surprised that the horror he'd felt just a little earlier at what he had to do was already fading away. This was nothing more than a tool to get Francisco what he needed, the same as the spoons that he'd used to feed his child mashed-up fruits as an infant, or the thermometer that checked his temperature when he felt under the weather. Ken took the box of ammunition from the bottom of the safe and loaded the weapon, then slipped the box and the gun into his pants pocket. He tossed the safe into the trash can where it landed with a loud clang, then with a shrug of his shoulders, he removed his suit jacket and added it, along with his tie, into the can. Nothing was more conspicuous than a man in business attire out jogging with a safe under his arm, and he didn't want to draw any extra attention to himself in case someone came along. It was only a few minutes to the Ellisons' house, and Ken couldn't risk anything getting in the way of what Francisco needed. He set off again at a quick pace, arms pumping at his sides, sweat beading the sides of his neck and pooling under his arms, his mind nipping at his heels by replaying the last words Francisco had said that morning on a loop.

"Hi, Dad. *It's spoiled. What time are you gonna be home from work today? No, I was just wondering. No big deal if you're busy. You mean the past few months? Yeah, okay. Bye, Dad.*

Bye, Dad.

Bye, Dad.

Bye, Dad."

Creakek. The sound of the rope whined again from somewhere behind Ken as Francisco came closer, taking up the rear. Ken pushed his legs to go faster. He'd failed Francisco once by not seeing what was going on and putting a stop to it. He wouldn't fail again. Francisco would be happy, no matter the cost, and then Ken could face his son again.

KEN HAD TO go back and forth a couple of times before he figured out which house belonged to the Ellisons. Back when James and Francisco had been friends, Ken had known where all of his friends and acquaintances were so that he would know exactly whose house he would need to go to in case of an emergency. But that had been years ago, and from the back, all these subdivision houses looked the same. He finally recognized it from the big porch that had been added on to the back, which he vaguely remembered James' prick of a father bragging about the last time they'd seen each other. He allowed himself a second of rest, doubling over and breathing deeply as his heart raced.

This was it. This was the (finale? showstopper? culmination?) resolution to Francisco's final problem, the justice that he surely needed to move on to the other side. Ken took the safety off the gun, then abandoned the path. As soon as he set his bright black shadow in the matte grass of their yard, the situation seemed to solidify, as if the gun in his jacket had been nothing more than a cardboard prop before, but now that he was on their property, it was real. And there was absolutely no going back.

Premeditated murder of a minor. The legal definition swam through his mind so clearly he could almost hear a judge saying it in front of him. *They're going to lock you up and throw away the key.* Ken froze as he suddenly imagined himself on the front page of every newspaper, some unflattering picture that matched the description as the articles screamed about child killers. His name would forever be looped in with psychos like Bundy or Gacy, and he would be remembered by the world as—

No, he interrupted himself. *It doesn't matter what they think of you.* He had one job, and that was to make Francisco happy. And he made Francisco happy by providing him what he needed. So it didn't matter what the rest of the world painted him as, or what the costs were, or whether or not he himself lived with the guilt for the rest of his days. He forced his other foot forward and the next step came easier, while the next after that followed automatically. Ken walked quickly up the inclined side of the property, praying that no one inside the house would look out at exactly the wrong time and see him. His heartbeat switched from an over-exerted pitter-patter to a pounding drum solo so intense it could have been the work of Ringo Starr or Bonzo Bonham, and the sound of it filled Ken's ears so fully that it was almost inconceivable that no one else could hear it.

Puh-pwack. Puh-pwack.

Wait. That wasn't the sound of his heart, that was the sound of a basketball. Ken stood still for a moment, concentrating on the rhythmic slap of synthetic rubber against concrete, then hurried toward the front of the house. It was unnervingly like Ken's own: two stories with a black roof, white siding exterior, and an ornate glass storm door, the type that let passersby see into the house if the front door behind it was left open. But there was one major difference between this house and Ken's own, of course: at least the little boy who lived here had been given a chance to come home, to see it one more time, to die on his own turf. He wouldn't spend his last moments in terror as former friends laughed and chased him up a tree, calling him a dog and tugging on a leash until he died publicly in front of everyone he knew like an executed criminal.

Ken reached the front of the house and carefully approached the driveway where, sure enough, a kid was playing basketball. But it wasn't a sibling, or even the frustrated father trying to work out some nerves over what his child had done. No. Ken recognized the blond moppy hair and little rodent nose that hadn't changed much at all in the past few years, but he also knew him in a different way, maybe one that only parents could pick up on. An ugly yellow aura that screamed, "THIS ONE RIGHT HERE, THIS IS THE PERSON WHO HURT YOUR CHILD, HURT YOUR CHILD, HURT YOUR CHILD."

It was James Ellison himself, the murderer who had bullied Francisco to death, shooting hoops with his back to Ken as if this were just a normal fucking day after school.

Puh-pwack. Puh-pwack. James threw the ball, and it swished through the net. *Puh-pwack. Puh-pwack.*

And from behind: *creakek.*

Ken looked over his shoulder at the stretch of decorative trees lining the walking path. Francisco emerged slowly from the green boughs, following his father with the smooth consistency of a lifeboat being pulled along behind a main vessel.

He's coming, Ken thought, and the realization was an equal mixture of terror at the thought of the dead Francisco finally coming so close that they could touch again—if that was still possible—and adrenaline, as he reflected that Francisco was arriving to get something that his father had provided. This was the culmination of every Christmas morning that Francisco had run down the stairs or after-school birthday when he would walk into the house and see the kitchen counter piled high with sweets and gifts. Francisco might not have died happily, but Ken would damn well make sure that his (ghost? soul? spirit?) essence left this world with everything it wanted.

Puh-pwack. The basketball hit the pavement, and James caught it, spun on the ball of his foot, and tried to do a layup against the backboard. The move failed miserably, and James turned to chase the ball. He stopped as he registered the sight of Ken standing behind him, blinking stupidly with his mouth hinged wide open. The kid certainly wouldn't be winning any scholarships or pulling A-grades, not like Francisco, who had been a good student and probably would have gone on to attend a good college. Ken could practically see that future that had been stolen from both Francisco and himself: helping his boy get a first job, choosing a college, dating, breakups, marriage, grandkids, the whole beautiful and crazy cycle of life all snuffed out in one stupid instant by this ridiculous bully. Ken's anger flared white-hot behind his eyes, and he pulled the gun out of his pocket.

James saw it coming and his eyes widened, but he did not run. Maybe he was rooted to the spot in fear, or maybe he was just too incredibly idiotic to know what to do.

"Muh-muh-Mister…" Ken saw the recognition dim slowly in James' eyes as his mouth blubbered pointless sounds. He knew that this was Francisco's father, but he still stood rooted to the spot. Ken pointed the gun toward James' chest; at this close of range there was no way to miss and no way to…

"Bye, Dad."

…not kill…

Creakek.

…the little fucker. Ken stared into that uncomprehending bovine face that was somehow so shocked, as if James hadn't expected this at all. The kid's eyes were wide and watery as they stared up at the gun, drowning in complete fear exactly as Francisco's eyes must have been. Ken willed himself to pull the trigger and make things right, to give Francisco what he surely wanted. To close those eyes that had been the last that Francisco had ever looked into.

It should have been me, he somehow had time to think. *If someone had to be looking into Francisco's eyes before he died, it should have been me.*

But where had he been? Where was he always?

"Well, I'll try to get home as quick as I can, but it's been madness at the office the past few weeks."

"You mean the past few months?"

Ken's hands were shaking, but he would still be able to make the shot. All he had to do was pull the trigger and justice would be delivered. But his fingers were unable to squeeze, as if the neural pathway between his hand and his brain had been severed. He heard, rather than felt, the gasp come out of himself, and tears stung at his eyes.

Shoot him. Do it. Do it for Francisco.

But shooting James wouldn't bring Francisco back.

James had apparently stared up at Ken long enough that his spell of fear, or stupidity, began to dissipate, because he suddenly turned tail and bolted toward his front door, shrieking for his parents. Ken tracked James with the gun as James ran, curling his finger around the trigger.

You can still get him. You have to do this. It's your job. To Provide.

But his finger refused to pull the trigger, and James disappeared into the house.

KEN DID NOT feel the sun on his face or the tears pouring out of his own eyes as he walked away from James' house in an empty daze. For the first time in his life, he had failed to get something for Francisco, and he didn't know how to fix it. But maybe shooting James wouldn't have fixed anything, anyway. Time had passed him by, and regardless of how hard he worked or what he did or bought, it wouldn't buy him more time with Francisco. Memories that he hadn't thought about for years started pouring through Ken's mind as he walked, one after the other, a nonstop parade of what he could never go back to.

Francisco's first lost tooth. He'd cried and wanted to put it back in.

Francisco's first day at little league. The helmet had been outlandishly huge against his tiny head, making him look like a cartoon baby with a giant melon skull.

Francisco's first completed video game. He'd leaned back and looked at Ken with an accomplished smirk as if to say, "*Beat that score, you old fart,*" and Ken had nearly shit himself with pride.

Francisco's last day of sixth grade. He'd been so relieved to have the summer to look forward to and Ken had taken him out to a pizza joint to celebrate.

Ken started shivering and realized he was cold. He looked down at his feet and noticed that he was no longer walking; he was sitting on the ground in a patch of shade and the sweat on his body was beginning to cool. He looked up and saw a thick tree branch stretching overhead like a stairway to

Heaven, disappearing in the late afternoon sun as if it went on forever.

He had walked all the way back to the school, to the very place where Francisco had died.

Ken lay his head back against the tree and let the rough bark gnaw against his scalp. He had nothing more to give his son, and he felt as empty and pointless as a corn-husk doll, just a hollow space crudely wrapped in the form of a human. He looked down at his hands and saw that he was no longer holding the gun; he must've dropped it during the walk here. His fingers were red and there were small crescent bruises on his palms from where the tips of his nails had burrowed into the meat.

I hope a kid doesn't find that gun, he thought incoherently, but he had no real desire to get up and re-trace his steps. He had failed, and in fact, he had failed before he ever faced James Ellison. Long before he'd ever gotten this crazy idea to shoot a child to please a ghost...hell, before Francisco had even died. Ken had sworn that Francisco would be happy, and he hadn't been happy, and Ken should have seen it. The fact that Francisco was stuck here in a tortured state was on his shoulders and his alone, and he would have to accept those consequences.

Creakek. Ken looked up from his hands. Francisco was right in front of him, the noose stretching up to the tree branch the way it had earlier that day, Francisco's feet hovering above the green lawn where hundreds of kids had played jump rope or tea party or soccer over the years. His body swayed slightly in a breeze that was not there, and with a low creak of stiff bones—or was it the boughs of the tree above them?—he reached out his hand toward his father just as he had earlier.

But for the first time, Ken had nothing to give.

"I'm sorry," Ken said. His voice was flat and lifeless, and the apology sounded fake to his own ears, but he had no more energy to be emphatic. "I couldn't do it. I'm sorry." Francisco was still for a moment, then he tilted his head back on his ruined neck, his eyes roving underneath the eyelids that were sealed with dried blood and tears. It was the moment that Ken had feared back in the house, the consequence of his actions. He would see Francisco's eyes open and they would be horrible, ghostly, disturbing, and worst of all, disappointed. Ken tried to brace himself for what he knew was coming, pressing his palms against the cool grass and stiffening against the tree. Francisco's eyelids separated a little at the center of his eyes, fighting against the crust of dried fluid, and then they peeled open.

Ken's breath caught in his throat as he looked into the dead eyes of his child, and Francisco looked back. For a second, the pupils contracted and dilated while the irises shifted from milky white to silver, but then they focused in on Ken and suddenly became clear, and Ken found himself looking into the shining brown eyes that he'd know anywhere.

Francisco's eyes.

"Dad." Francisco's mouth didn't move but Ken heard his voice anyway. And it wasn't the croak of a vengeful ghost, but the exhausted and relieved exhale of a child that had lost their parent in a mall, then found them again. Francisco smiled, and as he did so, the signs of death on his face seemed to melt away. He didn't explain, but Ken suddenly understood as clearly as if it had been spelled out.

His unfinished business was to say goodbye.

"I wish I'd had more time with you," Francisco's voice whispered in Ken's ear. Ken got to his knees and held out a hand toward Francisco's outstretched fingers, but Francisco was already fading in the sunlight, like a dream that recesses deep into the mind upon waking.

"Wait! Francisco!" Ken yelled, suddenly wide awake and desperate, but there was nothing he could do. The last thing to disappear were Francisco's eyes, watching Ken until the end, the eyes he'd spent the day running from.

Then Francisco was gone.

"No! Wait!" Ken roared as he staggered to his feet. He looked around anxiously, but there was neither sight nor sound of his son. "Come back!" The absolute idiocy of Ken's own actions came back to him with the fury of a tidal wave crashing down and dragging him out to sea. He'd made Francisco chase him down all afternoon, the same way he'd made him practically beg for Ken to come home from work early for once. Ken had been so focused on trying to give Francisco things that he'd forgotten to give him time.

"I wish I'd had more time with you."

Ken rested his forehead against the tree, Francisco's final goodbye playing through his head like the theme song to Ken's stupidity.

Of course, he wouldn't have wanted revenge. That's not who he ever was. All he wanted was some of my time. My time! That's fucking free! And now I'll never get to give it.

Or would he?

Ken smiled as the idea hatched fully formed in his mind. For a moment, another sheen of sweat broke across his skin, a chemical reaction to what he was contemplating, but there was no real resistance. What else did he have to lose? He patted down his pockets and felt a bulge in the right one—apparently he hadn't dropped the gun after all. He pulled it out, and it winked at him again in the sunlight, like it was happy with him for figuring out what he needed to do. Ken sat back down against the tree trunk, looked up into the branches that Francisco had died in, and set the gun under his chin.

If Francisco wanted more time together, then Ken would make it happen. After all, it was his job to provide.

A THING OF BEAUTY

Warren Benedetto

THE BODY HANGING FROM THE ceiling began to writhe, straining against the inside of the translucent, teardrop-shaped sac in which it was encased. The sac stretched and distended, pressing outward in all directions as the figure inside struggled to break free. A soft white glow emanated from within.

Anastasia Dao entered the room through a doorway covered by a heavy black curtain. She was a tall, slim Asian woman in her early thirties. A knee-length rubber apron covered her faded jeans and her gray V-neck shirt. Matching rubber gloves stretched up to her elbows. Her hair was pulled back in a tight ponytail. A clear plastic shield protected her face.

She drew a utility knife from the front pocket of the apron, found an area of the sac that wasn't too close to the body inside, then carefully slit it open. Grayish-white fluid spilled out, sloshing into the tiled drain on the floor underneath. Slowly, the gash widened and tore, revealing a curve of dark flesh underneath.

Anastasia knelt and cradled her gloved arms under the body as it slipped soundlessly from the membrane. She lowered it gently to the floor.

As it unfolded, the body revealed itself to be a woman, long and lean, with skin the color of roasted chestnuts. The woman gasped, drawing in a sharp breath as if surfacing from a near-drowning. Her eyes opened. They were unfocused at first: scared, confused, searching. She groped blindly at Anastasia, clutching at her shirt, a panicked sound rising in her throat. Finally, her gaze settled on Anastasia's face. The woman relaxed. The sound tapered off. She touched Anastasia's cheek. Anastasia smiled.

"Hi, Juliet," she said. "Welcome back."

IT WAS ALL a game to them.

They came into the grocery store every day after baseball practice, sweat soaking through their grass-stained jerseys, their cleats dropping clumps of dirt on the floor as they stampeded to the coolers to grab bottles of Gatorade. Whenever Melanie heard them coming, she would fade silently into the recessed doorway that led into the stockroom, hoping desperately that they would come and go without noticing her. Usually, she escaped their attention. But this day was different. This was the day that Sam Kelly spoke to her.

"Hey," he said as he passed by the doorway where she stood in the shadows. "You're Melanie, right?"

Melanie kept her eyes downcast, studiously examining her shoes. She nodded. "Yeah."

"I thought so. You're in my Communications class. I'm Sam."

"I know," she said quietly. Her heart galloped in her chest. Of course she knew him. She sat right behind him in the lecture hall, positioned at the perfect angle to stare at him for the whole hour without being noticed. She had practically memorized the laugh lines in the corners of his eyes, the sharp angle of his jaw, the soft fade of his haircut. They had never spoken, but she knew him intimately.

"Sam!" an obnoxious voice called from across the store. "Stop hitting on that poor girl and let's go!"

"I'm being nice!" he shouted back. He lowered his voice as he turned back to Melanie. "I'm not hitting on you."

"I know."

"Did you get her number?" another voice taunted.

"Guys, what the fuck?" he complained. He shook his head. "So rude."

His friends laughed, then filed out of the store, their purchases already paid for.

"Sorry," he said to Melanie. "I better go."

"Okay."

"Nice meeting you."

"You too."

He began to walk away, paused, then turned back to Melanie.

"Hey," he said.

"Hey."

"I lied."

"Okay."

"I *am* hitting on you."

Melanie's breath tapered off to nothing. She kept her eyes glued to the floor. She couldn't bring herself to look up at him. He was making fun of her. He had to be. Guys like him always did.

"Sorry, I'm really bad at this," he continued. "But…maybe I could text you sometime?"

Melanie raised her head. Her brow was furrowed in confusion. Was he serious? How could she even tell? She had no frame of reference. Nothing like this had ever happened to her before.

"You look…concerned," he said. He started to back away. "You know what, never mind. It was a stupid—"

"Yes," she said quickly.

"Yes, it was stupid, or yes, I can text you?"

"Both."

Sam belted out a surprised laugh. "Holy shit." He laughed again. "Holy shit, you're funny. I never knew you were funny."

Melanie's face flushed. She shrugged. "I'm not."

"No, you are. You totally are." Sam dug into his pocket and pulled out his phone. "All right. We're doing this. What's your number?"

ANASTASIA LEANED AGAINST the door frame, watching Juliet get used to her new form. The black apron and gloves were gone. She sipped a glass of red wine.

Juliet stared at her naked body in the mirror as if seeing herself for the first time. In fact, she was.

She was extraordinarily beautiful, tall and lean, with an exquisite face that seemed torn from the pages of a fashion magazine: full lips, high cheekbones, and light brown eyes that seemed almost golden in contrast to her dark brown skin.

"Good?" Anastasia asked.

Juliet laughed. Tears spilled down her face. "Sorry," she said, wiping them away. "I just…" She trailed off. "My skin." She turned around, looking over her shoulder at the mirror. She laughed again, in disbelief. "My ass."

Anastasia smiled. "It *is* a great ass."

"I don't know what to say," Juliet replied. "Thank you."

Anastasia acknowledged the thanks with a toast and a sip of her wine. Her heart swelled. Although she didn't have any kids of her own, she felt a sort of maternal love—equal parts pride and protectiveness—for the people she helped transform. They were her children. All of them.

MELANIE STOOD IN front of the full-length bedroom mirror in a pair of plain cotton panties and a simple white bra. She hated the way she looked. She hated her thin, limp hair. Her mud-brown eyes. Her weak chin. She hated her dimpled thighs and her pigeon toes. She hated her rolls.

Most of all, she hated the wine-colored birthmark that stained the right side of her face. It was an inescapable daily reminder that she would always be different. That she would never fit in.

She glanced down at the phone in her hand and re-read the last text message from Sam.

just one pic, it read.

She held the phone in both hands and typed with her thumbs.

why?

cause ur beautiful

Melanie looked at herself in the mirror again. She poked at the soft bulge of fat around her midsection, running her fingers over the rows of thin pink scars she had carved into her flesh. She didn't feel beautiful. She felt disgusting.

She lifted the phone and typed a response.

i cant

As her finger hovered over the Send button, another message came in from Sam.

i wont show anyone. i promise

Then another.

pleeeeeease

Melanie stared at the screen. She chewed her lip for a moment, then deleted the message she was about to send. Instead, she sent a different response.

ok

Before she could second-guess herself, she quickly tapped the phone's camera icon. Then she reached behind her back and began to unhook her bra.

"YOU COST ME fifty bucks."

Melanie looked up from her salad. She was sitting alone in the crowded university food court, studying for her Comparative Biology class. One of Sam's baseball teammates—Tyler? Taylor?—was emptying his lunch tray into the trash can next to her table.

"Excuse me?" she said.

"Nothing," he replied. He added his dirty tray to a stack of others. As he exited, he called back to her, loud enough for everyone to hear. "Nice tits, though!" Then he joined his teammates outside, exchanging laughter and high fives as they headed off across campus.

Melanie glanced around the food court. It seemed like everyone had stopped what they were doing to gawk at her. She looked blankly at the book in front of her, trying to ignore the stares. The full weight of the guy's words hit her. Her stomach rolled. She felt sick.

Sam said he wouldn't show anyone the photos. He promised.

He lied.

Melanie buried her face in her hands. Her skin felt hot. Her eyes burned. She wanted to disappear.

"Is anyone sitting here?" a female voice asked.

"No," Melanie said, her voice muffled behind her hands. "You can take it."

The chair scraped on the tile floor. It squeaked as someone's weight settled into it. A hand touched her arm.

"You okay?"

Melanie raised her face to see who had touched her. Sitting in the chair beside her was a beautiful black girl in her early twenties, with flawless dark skin framed by tight, caramel-colored ringlets. Her citrine eyes sparkled in the sunlight.

"Yeah," Melanie said. She wiped her cheeks self-consciously. "Sorry."

"Don't apologize." The girl handed Melanie a clean napkin. "Here."

Melanie took the napkin. "Thanks."

"I'm Juliet."

"Melanie," she said as she blotted the tears from her eyes.

Juliet looked at her sympathetically. "They got you too, huh?"

"Too?"

Juliet snorted a short laugh. "Girl, fifty bucks is nothing. I cost him twice that."

"I don't understand. What was he talking about?"

"The team takes bets on who can get the most homely girl to send them nudes. They call it 'dog catching.' Apparently, I was quite the catch."

"Oh God," Melanie moaned. She clutched handfuls of hair on the sides of her head. "I'm so stupid."

Juliet put her hand on Melanie's arm and spoke gently. "No, you're not. You're human. And they're monsters. They took advantage of you. Which one was it? Was it Sam?"

"How'd you know?"

"Because he got me too."

"But you're not...you're gorgeous."

"Ha. Yeah, no..."

Juliet dug her iPhone out of her back pocket, tapped and swiped a few times, then handed the phone to Melanie.

Melanie furrowed her brow, puzzled. On the screen was a photo of a morbidly obese black girl with raging acne and crooked teeth.

"Who's this?"

"That's me."

Melanie looked up at Juliet. Her skin was unblemished, without a trace of discoloration. Her teeth were perfect. She was two hundred pounds lighter.

There was no way she was the same girl as in the photo. It was impossible.

"Come on," Melanie said.

"Swear to God."

"When was this taken?"

"August, I think?"

Melanie looked down at the photo, then up at Juliet again. August was two months ago. Nobody could change so much in such a short time. It wasn't just an extreme makeover—the girl in the photo was a completely different person.

"How is that possible?" Melanie asked.

A small smile curled the corners of Juliet's mouth. "Can you blow off class for the rest of the day?"

"I don't know...why?"

"There's someone you should meet."

MELANIE'S SHOES CRUNCHED on the gravel as Juliet led her along the side of a cinderblock warehouse in an industrial part of town. A freight train loaded with coal rumbled past on the other side of the dirt parking lot. Its horn let out a deafening blast as it approached an intersection.

"Where are we?" Melanie shouted over the din.

They arrived at a wooden door with a frosted window. Painted on the glass was a stylized logo resembling a chrysalis hanging from a leaf, under the words *Imaginal Studios*. Juliet opened the door.

"After you," she said as she ushered Melanie through.

Melanie entered the warehouse. Juliet followed her in, closing the door behind her. It was dark inside, especially in contrast to the brightness of the clear October sky.

"Anastasia," Juliet called. "You here?"

Anastasia's voice shouted from somewhere. "Be out in a sec!"

As Melanie's eyes adjusted to the darkness, some of the details of the warehouse began to emerge. It was a huge space with high, beamed ceilings and a polished concrete floor. Near the center, several life-sized sculptures stood on solid-looking bases. Each was a human form, exquisitely crafted from what looked like marble. A wide black curtain spanned the warehouse from front to back, concealing the other half of the room from view.

Melanie approached one of the sculptures, gazing at it in awe. Every muscle and tendon of the figure was perfectly detailed. The artistry was extraordinary.

"Wow," Melanie whispered.

"Amazing, right?" Juliet said. "Anastasia's great." She motioned Melanie over toward a small kitchenette in the corner of the warehouse. "Come on. We can wait over here."

The kitchenette had a battered refrigerator and an electric stove, along with a table and chairs that looked like they were stolen from the 1970s. The yellowed Formica countertop was cluttered with a variety of glass canisters and earthenware jars. Each was labeled with black wax pencil on what looked like medical tape.

Melanie browsed the labels as she passed. One jar was labeled *TURTLE BEAKS*. Another read *PEREGRINE TALONS*. There was a wicker basket of what looked like desiccated mice, their eye sockets empty and sunken. A small brown bottle with a rubber eyedropper was simply labeled *VENOM*.

"You want something to drink?" Juliet asked. Glass bottles clinked together on the refrigerator door as she opened it.

Inside the fridge, Melanie glimpsed a jar labeled with the word *UMBIL-ICAL*. A tangle of purple-white tubules sagged wetly against the slime-streaked glass.

"No, thanks," Melanie managed to say. She began to back out of the kitchenette. "You know what? I should probably go," she said.

"Everything okay?" Juliet asked.

"Yeah, fine. It's just...I just remembered I've got this big test—"

"Sorry to keep you waiting," a voice said from behind her. "You must be Melanie."

Melanie turned. Walking into the kitchenette was a tall, slim Asian woman. Stylish cat-eye glasses with dark-rimmed frames complemented her high cheekbones. Her ink-black hair was pulled up in a messy bun. She wore torn jeans and a simple white t-shirt loosely tucked in on one side. An unusual pendant on a thin black cord hung around her neck. It looked like some kind of sigil or rune.

"So," Anastasia said as she took a seat at the kitchenette's table. "How can I help?"

ANASTASIA WATCHED MELANIE closely as the girl talked about her life. An abusive stepfather. A mother who labeled her defective. Merciless bullying, from kids and teachers alike. The callousness of Sam Kelly and his enablers. Depression. Bulimia. Self-mutilation.

Anastasia's heart ached for the girl. She had heard similar stories so many times before.

Every year, a fresh crop of students poured into town from around the country to attend the local university. Many of them were away from home for the first time. They were alone, scared, depressed. College was supposed to be a new beginning, but for some of them, it was just a continuation of the cruelty, the stares, and the insults they had experienced their whole lives. Those were the ones Anastasia sought to help. College couldn't give them a new beginning. But *she* could.

As a fleshcrafter, she had the unique ability to remake individuals into their best selves, from the outside in. It wasn't just about how they looked; it was about how the way they looked affected the way they felt. She knew some might say she was just reinforcing the worst tendencies of a society that prized superficial appearance above all else, but she was a realist. She had to play by the rules of the game she was in. If the game was rigged in favor of the young and beautiful—and it was—then she wanted to give her clients every advantage that she could. Besides, her work wasn't just about physical beauty. It was about freeing the beauty trapped within.

That's what she liked to tell herself, anyway.

The reality was that, for some, the ugliness was more than skin deep. Some had been injured so profoundly by others' cruelty that the psychological wounds had festered, poisoning them with resentment, hatred, and rage. Anastasia did her best to heal their spirits as well as their bodies, but it wasn't always possible. Some were just too far gone. They would choose to use their newfound beauty as a weapon to exact revenge on their tormentors, to inflict the same sort of pain on others that had once been inflicted upon them. It wasn't an ideal outcome, but Anastasia felt like it was worth the risk. If the worst that happened was some bullies got their comeuppance, she wouldn't lose any sleep over it.

Once Melanie finished her story, Anastasia carefully explained who she was and what she did. Melanie was understandably skeptical. They always were.

"This can't be real," Melanie said. She looked back and forth between Anastasia and Juliet, searching for a sign that they were messing with her. "It's crazy."

"It's real," Juliet insisted. "You see what she did for me."

"But how?" Melanie said to Anastasia. "You're not a doctor."

"No, not quite," Anastasia said. She gestured at the sculptured figures in her workshop. "I'm more of an artist."

"So, you're, like…magic?"

Anastasia laughed. "It's a little more complicated than that," she explained. "But the details aren't important. Let's just say, I have a gift."

"And you really think you can help me? Like you helped her?" Melanie looked at Juliet.

"If that's what you want," Anastasia said.

Melanie was quiet for a moment. She stood up and walked over to the kitchen window. The glass was covered with dark paint on the outside, making the window dimly reflective on the inside, like a large black mirror. Melanie looked at her reflection. She touched the birthmark on her face. Her hand fell away.

"Will it hurt?" she asked.

"Not at all," Anastasia answered. "It's just like falling asleep."

"And then what?"

Anastasia looked to Juliet for her reply.

"And then you wake up," Juliet said.

"And I'll be…pretty?"

Anastasia smiled. "You'll be stunning."

"Okay." Melanie nodded. She exhaled a deep breath. "Let's do it."

A FEW DAYS later, Sam and four of his friends were seated in a corner booth in the back of Shooters, the campus sports bar. A football game played on the widescreen TV mounted on the wall. The crowd let out a collective groan as the Eagles intercepted a pass and ran it back for a touchdown. A waitress approached the table. She placed a fresh bottle of beer in front of Sam.

"From the ladies," she said, nodding her chin over her shoulder toward the bar.

Sam looked past the waitress. At the bar, a stunning brunette with crystal blue eyes was looking in his direction. She cocked an eyebrow, then sipped her drink. Sam toasted the beer in her direction. She smiled, then whispered something in the ear of the equally stunning black girl sitting next to her. The black girl peeked over her shoulder at Sam, then whispered something back to the brunette.

Sam slid out of the booth and made his way over to the girls. In their new forms, Melanie and Juliet were unrecognizable to him. But they recognized *him.*

"Usually I'm the one buying the drinks around here," he shouted over the din.

"What can I say?" Melanie shouted back. "When I see something I want, I like to jump on it." Her eyes dipped toward his belt for a second. She sipped her drink. Juliet elbowed her and laughed, embarrassed.

"I'm Sam." He extended his hand to Melanie.

"Alexis." She squeezed his hand. Their eyes locked.

"Good grip," he said.

"Yep."

Juliet cleared her throat. "I'm Sasha."

Sam ignored her. He seemed transfixed by Melanie's gaze. "Do I know you?"

"Not yet," Melanie replied.

MELANIE LED SAM by the hand down a short hallway at the back of the bar, then pulled him through a door marked *Employees Only.* The small break room was empty except for a table and chairs in the middle and a ratty old couch along one wall. A neon Budweiser sign flickered on the wall, bathing the room in an eerie red glow. Melanie locked the door, then turned and kissed Sam passionately. Their tongues intertwined. She walked him backward to the couch. He sat down hard.

"Take off your pants," she breathed.

"What?"

"You heard me," Melanie said as she straddled him. "I said take…" She grabbed his belt and began unbuckling it. She licked at his lips. "Off." She unbuttoned his jeans and unzipped the fly. "Your pants." She kissed him deeply as he raised his butt off the couch and tugged his jeans past his hips to his knees. They slipped down around his ankles.

Melanie's hands dug into his boxer shorts. He moaned.

Then, suddenly, she began to laugh. She pulled her hands from his boxers, backed off his lap, and stood, still laughing.

"What's wrong?" he asked, confused. "What happened?"

She laughed even harder when she saw the look on his face. "I'm sorry," she said, tears streaming down her cheeks. "It's just…I knew it. I could tell just by looking at you."

"What?"

"You *do* have a pencil dick."

Sam's face turned red. "Fuck you."

"I was telling my girl out there, 'He's just got that tiny-dick energy, you know?'"

"And you're a cunt."

"That's a big word from a guy who's hung like a toddler."

Sam growled and lunged at her. Unfortunately, his jeans were still down around his ankles. He stumbled and crashed into the table, tumbling awkwardly to the floor. That caused Melanie to break into fresh peals of laughter.

"No, don't get up," she said. "I'll see myself out."

As she turned and unlocked the door, a folding chair flew through the air and crashed into the back of her skull. Stunned, Melanie slumped against the door and slid to the ground. Her head felt heavy, full of sand. The ceiling lights doubled in front of her eyes.

Sam loomed over her. He buttoned his jeans, then slipped off his belt and wrapped it around his fist, leaving the buckle end dangling.

He locked the door.

THE DOOR TO Anastasia's studio burst open. Juliet stumbled in, supporting Melanie's limp body. Melanie's shoes dragged on the floor. Her chin hung down to her chest, her hair obscuring her face. Her dress was torn down one side. Blood trickled down the inside of her thighs. Ugly purple bruises bloomed across her ribs, her shoulders, her arms, her neck. Everywhere.

"Anastasia!" Juliet yelled. Her voice was strained.

Anastasia rushed from the back room. "Oh my god!" she gasped. She ran to help Juliet, positioning herself under Melanie's other arm. "What happened?"

"He beat the shit out of her!"

"Over here." Anastasia steered Juliet toward the kitchenette. They dragged Melanie to the table, then tipped her backward and laid her down. Her head lolled limply to the side.

Anastasia wiped the hair away from Melanie's face. She was almost unrecognizable: eyes swollen shut, lips mashed, teeth broken. Blood poured from her hairline and trickled from her ears.

"Oh no," Anastasia whispered. She leaned down and tapped her fingertips against Melanie's cheek. "Melanie? Sweetie? Can you hear me?" She peeled back one of Melanie's eyelids with her thumb. "Melanie?" Melanie's pupil was dilated. Unseeing. Anastasia pressed her fingers into the girl's neck, feeling for a pulse. Nothing. She lowered her ear to Melanie's chest and listened. Still nothing.

"Is she gonna be okay?" Juliet asked.

"I don't know."

Anastasia stepped away from Melanie's body and began to move quickly around the kitchenette. She removed a black ceramic bowl from a cabinet, then began scooping ingredients from various canisters into it.

"What are you going to do?" Juliet asked. "Can you help her?"

"I'm going to try."

Juliet watched as Anastasia removed the jar labeled *UMBILICAL* from the refrigerator and opened it. She plucked out a thick purple umbilical cord, sliced it open lengthwise with a scalpel, then scraped a spoonful of black blood from the inside and dropped it in the bowl. Next, she reached into a canister and pulled out a handful of squirming caterpillars. She squeezed them in her fist, crushing them. Greenish liquid dripped from her hand into the bowl. She flung the remains of the caterpillars into the trash, then wiped her hand on a towel.

"You should go," Anastasia said. "In case..." She didn't finish her sentence.

"In case what?"

Anastasia didn't know how to answer. There were so many things that could go wrong. She had never worked on anyone who had died before. Physically, she might be able to repair the girl. But she didn't know what would happen to Melanie's soul. Was it even still in there? Was there anything left? Or was she just an empty vessel? If it was still intact, would it remember what had happened? Would it remember the violence? The terror? The pain? Could that kind of psychological damage be repaired? Or would the scars be indelible, etched forever in the girl's memory? Anastasia didn't have any answers. But she knew she had to try.

Finally, she said, "Just go."

Juliet headed for the door. As she opened it, Anastasia called out to her.

"Juliet! One more thing."

Juliet stopped. Anastasia looked down at Melanie's destroyed face, then back at Juliet. Her eyes were ablaze with anger.

"Who did this?"

"CAN I HELP you?" Sam asked.

Anastasia stood in the aisle at Home Depot, looking up at a display of interior doors for sale. She glanced at the associate's name tag. It read *Sam Kelly.*

"I sure hope so," Anastasia said. She indicated the doors. "Are these things heavy?"

"Depends who's lifting them," Sam said with a smile.

"Just me, unfortunately."

"You're gonna try to install one yourself?"

"Is that a bad idea?" Anastasia put on her best *I'm-just-a-dumb-girl-in-a-man's-world* face.

Sam sucked air through his teeth. "Yeesh. I wouldn't, if I were you. It can be tricky."

"Hmm. That's a problem."

"You don't have anyone to help you out? A boyfriend or something?"

It took every ounce of strength for Anastasia not to roll her eyes. The guy thought he was being so smooth. "Nope," she said. She patted her biceps. "Guess I gotta put these bad boys to work."

Sam laughed. "Tell you what..." He lowered his voice conspiratorially. "We're not supposed to, but...I can probably stop by after work to help you out if you want."

"Really?" Anastasia said, beaming. "You'd do that?"

"For that smile?" Sam replied. "Anything."

ANASTASIA ENTERED THE warehouse. Sam followed her in.

"Can I get you something to drink?" she offered. "Beer?"

"Can't," Sam said. "Gotta head to baseball practice after this."

"How about a Coke?"

"That'll work."

"Coming right up."

As Anastasia headed to the kitchenette, Sam wandered over to admire her sculptures.

"These are yours?" he asked.

"Yep."

Sam whistled, impressed. Anastasia opened the fridge, retrieved a bottle of Coke, and pried off the lid with a bottle opener. She glanced over her shoulder at Sam. He was facing away from her, inspecting one of the marble figures. Turning back to the counter, she slipped her fingers into the pocket of her jeans and removed a small square of folded paper. She deftly opened it, revealing a fine orange powder inside. With the paper creased into a V, she dumped the powder into the mouth of the bottle, then swirled the soda to mix it in.

She turned and held the bottle up for Sam to see. "As requested." She sat down at the kitchen table and pushed a chair out with her bare foot. "Have a seat."

Sam walked over and sat down. Anastasia slid the drink across the table to him. He grabbed it and took a long swig in one smooth motion, then wiped his lips with the back of his hand. "Thanks." He looked around the warehouse. "So, you've got this whole big place to yourself?" He took another sip of Coke.

"Just me and my thoughts," Anastasia replied.

"Wow. Kinda lonely, no?"

"Sometimes."

"You should stop by one of our games some night. We usually head over to Shooters after. I'll buy you a drink."

Anastasia smiled. "I'd like that."

Sam took another swallow of his Coke, then offered the bottle to Anastasia. "Sip?"

"I'm good."

Sam yawned. "Sorry. Long day." He rubbed his eyes with his fingers, then slapped his cheek as if to wake himself up. "Didn't realize I was so tired."

"I'll bet," Anastasia said, watching him closely. "What time did you start this morning?"

Sam's eyelids sagged. "Around ssss…" His head bobbed. He blinked his eyes, then rubbed them again. "Ssseven…" His voice trailed off. His eyes closed. His chin slumped to his chest.

Anastasia was impressed. The drugs had worked even faster than she had expected. She took the bottle out of his limp hand. "Sweet dreams, asshole," she whispered.

Anastasia walked quietly over to the counter and drew open one of the drawers. Inside was a black folded cloth. She took it out, put it on the counter, then unfolded it to reveal an exquisite Yanagi sushi knife. The white carbon steel blade was honed to a razored edge, as sharp as a scalpel. It would slice through Sam's throat with surgical precision. He wouldn't feel a thing.

Anastasia turned and opened another drawer, pulling out a folded plastic tablecloth. She would spread it on the floor under Sam's chair—it would be easier to clean up the mess when she was done with him.

"What's that for?" Sam's voice said.

Anastasia gasped in surprise. She spun around. Sam was right behind her, fully conscious. Before she realized what was happening, he picked up the knife off the counter and weighed it in his hand.

"Ooh, nice. This is solid." He pressed his thumb against the tip. "Sharp, too." He looked her in the eyes. "Someone could really get hurt with this." His words dripped with menace.

"How—" Anastasia started to ask. Sam cut her off.

"What, did you think I was gonna drink that Coke after what you slipped into it?"

"I don't know what you're talking about," she said, trying to remain calm.

"Come on, now. I practically invented that move. What did you use? Roofies? GHB?"

Anastasia started to back away. "Look, let's just forget it, okay? I can find someone else to hang the door."

Sam laughed. "Oh, right! The *door!* That was good, how you got me out here." He laughed again. "Do you think I'm stupid? You think I don't know what you are?" With the tip of the knife, he pointed at the sigil pendant hanging around Anastasia's neck. "Sorry, but that's a dead giveaway. You might as well be wearing a black pointy hat and riding a broom."

Anastasia's eyes darted to the counter, trying to think of some way to free herself from the situation. She spotted a canister with the words *GHOST PEPPER* on the label.

"So, what was your plan, exactly?" Sam continued. He took a menacing step forward. "Were you gonna knock me out? Cut me up?" He slashed the knife through the air. "Use me in one of your twisted rituals?"

Anastasia grabbed the canister of ghost pepper and flung an arc of the fiery red powder toward Sam's face. Sam ducked. The powder sailed over his head and sprayed across the floor behind him. Although he had avoided the brunt of the attack, a fine dust of searing chili powder still ended up in his lungs when he inhaled. He began to cough and heave.

With Sam momentarily incapacitated, Anastasia sprinted across the warehouse and through a curtained doorway in the back.

"Hey!" Sam choked. "Bitch! Get back here!" Still gasping for air, he ran after her, the knife clutched in his hand. He pushed through the curtain, then came to a sudden stop. The sight was unlike anything he had ever seen before.

Hanging from the rafters was a circle of huge, white, teardrop-shaped sacs, six of them in all. Each one glowed with soft white luminescence. Shadowy figures of different sizes and shapes seemed to float inside. Some were in the fetal position. Others drifted weightlessly, their limbs seemingly suspended in mid-air. A Polaroid photo was taped to the side of each sac, each with a name written on the bottom in thick black marker.

"What the hell?" Sam muttered. He approached the nearest sac, with a Polaroid labeled *Nora.* The girl in the photo had a gaunt face with hollow cheeks and a beak-like nose. She looked vaguely familiar. He was pretty sure his buddy Tyler had nailed her at some point. She was the one Tyler had called Icky-Bod, partly because of her resemblance to Ichabod Crane from the *Sleepy Hollow* story, and partly because of the cystic acne that dotted her skeletal frame.

The shadow inside the sac shifted, twisting in Sam's direction as if aware of his presence. Sam lifted the knife and poked it into the side of the sac, creating a fingernail-sized slit. A grayish-white liquid leaked from the hole and dribbled down the outside. Curious, Sam dabbed a finger into the effluence, then rubbed it between his fingertips. It had a slimy texture, almost like an egg white.

He lifted his fingers toward his face, examining them more closely. The flesh itself seemed gummy, as if his fingertips were made from soft wax. As if they were…melting. Disgusted, Sam tried to wipe his hand on his jacket. The skin sloughed off bloodlessly, degloving his fingertips to the bone. The flesh fell to the floor and into a puddle of fluid, where it rapidly disintegrated into colorless goo.

Sam stared at his hand in numb horror. Steam began to rise from the bones protruding from his mutilated fingers. Pits and divots appeared in the bones as they liquified like melting ice. A terrified groan escaped from Sam's lips.

Suddenly, a gush of the viscous fluid spewed from the sac and splattered on the floor. Sam jumped backward. The tiny slit he had made in the sac had widened into a foot-long gash. An arm poked through the breach in the membrane. The limb was grossly deformed. It was bone-thin and far too long, more like the arm of a primate than a human—a gibbon, or some sort of sloth. Two bony, elongated fingers protruded from the end like pincers. The arm grabbed for Sam, clutching at his jacket.

"Gah! What the fuck?" Repulsed, he reflexively batted the appendage away. The knife flew from his hand and clattered to the floor, out of reach. "Shit!" He dropped to his hands and knees and bent down close to the floor, searching for the weapon. Instead, he saw a pair of feet.

Anastasia's feet.

Before Sam could react, Anastasia lashed out and kicked him in the face. He shouted in pain and surprise. Blood erupted from his nose.

"Oh, you're so *fucked*," he growled as he climbed to his feet. He wiped his arm across his face, then spat a wad of gore onto the ground. The blood smeared on his teeth made him look like a crazed animal. "Come here."

He lunged for Anastasia. She tried to dodge away, but he managed to snag a handful of her shirt as she moved. Wrapping his arms around her torso, he lifted her off the ground and body-slammed her to the cold concrete floor, his full weight crushing down on her as he took her down. The wind whooshed from her lungs. Temporarily stunned, she stopped struggling and rolled onto her back, gasping for air.

She looked to the side. The knife was on the floor, just out of reach. She extended her arm to reach for it. Sam saw what she was trying to do. He grabbed her wrist and smashed it against the ground, causing Anastasia to cry out in pain.

An inhuman wail echoed through the room, merging with Anastasia's anguished scream. Sam turned his head toward the sound. Behind him, the sac he had violated moments earlier split fully open, dumping its lifeform onto the floor in a torrent of milky white fluid. The thing flopped onto its belly. It raised its head and glared at Sam through bluish, cataract-covered eyes.

It was an abomination.

It had human-like limbs and a human-like form, but it was far from human. It was as if a human body had been liquified, then had re-congealed into something comprised of the same parts, but in all the wrong places. The head was a misshapen, oversized mass. The eyes were too far apart, with one at least two inches higher than the other. The mouth was in the middle of the face, between the eyes. It had no lips, just an irregular black hole with an obscene tongue rooting around inside.

The oversized head tottered on a thin neck connected to a pair of narrow shoulders. The rib cage was flared wide open, with only a thin layer of pale flesh holding its organs inside its body. Intestines swelled and pulsed just under the skin. There were no legs to speak of, just boneless protrusions of flesh that looked more like flippers than anything you'd see on a human.

"Jesus!" Sam exclaimed. "What the fuck is that?"

With a gurgling moan, the monstrosity began to haul itself upright, reaching up with its claw-like hand and grabbing the sac next to it for leverage. As the creature dug its fingers into the membrane and pulled, the second sac began to tear. The Polaroid, a photo of a round-faced girl labeled *Elaine*, fluttered to the ground. More grayish-white fluid sloshed to the floor, partially coating the thing's limbs. Steam began to rise from its mottled flesh.

The second sac ruptured, spilling another mutant form onto the floor in a flood of liquid. It sprawled on top of the first creature, knocking it to the ground. Fluid from the torn sac rained down on the pair.

The second creature was as equally deformed as the first, but in entirely different ways. It had no face at all, save for a wide, Cheshire Cat mouth full of tiny, sharp teeth that spanned the entire width of its skull. Doughy rolls of soft fat pooled on the floor around its corpulent torso.

As the two creatures struggled and squirmed, their flesh began to bond together. Translucent webs of skin formed between their limbs. One of the first creature's arms was subsumed between rolls of fat on the second creature's belly. Their heads fused at the temples like a pair of conjoined twins. It was as if they were two plastic figures, melting together under a blowtorch.

Anastasia watched with a mixture of disgust and awe. As incomprehensible as it appeared, she knew exactly why it was happening.

As a fleshcrafter, she was able to reduce a human to its most basic elements, the functional equivalent of stem cells. Once disintegrated, the cells could be manipulated to regrow anew into a new, more ideal form. However, like the metamorphosis of a caterpillar into a butterfly, the process took time. In the interim, the smallest disturbance could cause the transmutation to go horribly wrong. That's why Anastasia protected her progeny, keeping each in separate cocoons until their transformation was complete.

But now, the cells had been commingled. They were amalgamating into a single organism, a nightmare chimera fueled by its most elemental animal instincts. Fear. Rage. Hunger.

And it was coming for them.

The creature began to propel itself toward where Sam had pinned Anastasia, dragging itself along the floor with its elongated arms, its fleshy, legless body oozing behind it on a slug-like trail of slime. A shriek resonated from its dual mouths as it churned in their direction.

"No! Get away!" Sam yelled. He fell sideways off of Anastasia and backed away from the thing, his face twisted with revulsion.

Free from Sam's grasp, Anastasia scrambled in the direction of the fallen knife, snatched up the weapon, and climbed to her feet. She looked at the remaining cocoons hanging from the ceiling, then down at the blade in her hand. A painful realization hit her. She knew what she needed to do.

As the creature continued to advance in Sam's direction, Anastasia moved along the circle of cocoons and sliced the blade down the side of each sac. One after another, the membranes burst, dumping their inchoate lifeforms onto the floor.

Rebecca...Laura...Christine...

Melanie.

The figures squirmed in a vile stew of liquefying flesh and imaginal fluid, climbing over and across one another like newborn puppies in a litter. Steam erupted violently into the air. The fog came alive with the shadows of flailing limbs and twisting bodies. Anastasia lost sight of Sam as visibility in the room dropped to zero. The air began to reverberate with ear-splitting shrieks and gut-churning moans. Noises like soaking bath towels sloshing and slapping in a tub of water issued from the writhing mounds of agglutinating flesh hidden in the steam. Bones cracked. Tissues fused. Organs spilled.

Suddenly, a scream ripped through the air. A man's scream.

The fog began to dissipate. What remained was a monstrosity that defied imagination. It was a behemoth of flesh and bone, of hair and teeth, of eyes and mouths. In some places, its flesh was stretched tightly over protrusions of muscle and bone. In others, its skin was flaccid and blubbery. Easily ten feet tall, it towered over Anastasia on a crab-like arrangement of legs. Pairs of multi-jointed arms protruded from its distended torso. A tight cluster of eyes was pressed into a singular, malformed face. Rows of teeth erupted through bleeding gums inside a seething, drooling maw.

The creature had Sam. It held him aloft above the warehouse floor.

"Let...me...go!" he yelled, his body bucking and twisting as he tried to break away from the hands that gripped him. In desperation, he swung his one free arm, pounding the thing repeatedly in the face. His fist squelched into one of the creature's eyes. The monster wailed in pain.

Then it tore Sam to pieces.

His body came apart in the middle, ripping in half just under his rib cage. Blood burst out in a hot rush and pattered to the floor. Gore spilled down the front of the creature, slicking its skin with a crimson sheen.

The thing flung Sam's remains into the shadows, then turned toward Anastasia. She stared at the monster in mute horror. She could feel it glowering at her, evaluating her. It began to move in her direction. She remained motionless, closing her eyes as the creature drew within inches of her face. She could feel the moist heat radiating off its skin. Its odor was revolting, like rancid oatmeal made with spoiled milk, burnt and left to rot.

One of the creature's hands reached for her...and touched her cheek. It was gentle, almost a caress. Anastasia held her breath and prepared to die.

Instead, there was a massive crash, followed by a cold rush of wind. Anastasia slowly opened her eyes. The giant roll-top door in the back of the warehouse was destroyed, its metal bent outward in great jagged tears. The creature was gone.

Trees rattled and branches snapped as the thing fled into the forest behind the warehouse and back in the direction of the university campus. A flock of birds erupted from the trees to escape the stampeding beast. Still numb with shock, Anastasia watched the birds soar through the night sky, silhouetted across the orange-hued light of the autumn moon. Her gaze drifted downward, moving past the university bell tower to the blazing lights overlooking the college's sports field. On the baseball diamond, Sam's teammates were warming up for their evening practice.

Anastasia wasn't sure if the monster was headed in that direction. But part of her hoped it was.

THE KIND PEOPLE OF DENARY

Daniel O'Connor

"**W**HAT IS ALL OF THIS shit and where does it come from?" He sat on his couch, mumbling to himself. The "shit" to which he referred was basically everything in his view: books, records, the lamp, his phone, the couch, and his nearly empty whiskey bottle.

These thoughts would pester him whenever he washed down his marijuana edibles with a 92-proof chaser. He'd tell himself that the earth was rock, water, plant life, oxygen, some other crap, but yet all of this random stuff was made from it. Plastics, fabric, whatever. Did we need any of it?

Then, most of the man-made objects would orbit his head—if his THC/booze concoction was potent enough. It had previously possessed enough potency to get his ass bounced from the NYPD, and to transform his wife, Kathleen, into his ex-wife, Kathleen. She, free from his shackles, remained back in Staten Island with their house, while he, (former) Officer Bladen Dieci, relocated to a shithole apartment in a shithole town in northern Arizona.

He'd been filling out job applications with a plastic pen that he deemed to be a worthless creation of man when his phone rang. The chewed-cap Bic float-circled his head as he scanned the caller ID. He raised his right hand and watched the pen, along with a tattered paperback copy of *Ten Little Indians*, pass cleanly through his forearm, like Casper the Friendly Ghost. He was sure it was all hallucinatory. Pretty sure, at least.

Bladen envisioned the radio waves, the base station and the cell tower, as he stared at the phone in his left hand. The caller was Uncle Arlo. Sheriff Arlo.

"Hello?"

"Bladen! It's your old uncle! Hey, boy!"

"Hi, Uncle Arlo."

"You doin' better since you came out west? Nothin' like the desert. Should be a good restart for a kid like you."

"I'm thirty-one."

"Still a kid. I'm pushin' seventy now, Blade."

The paper job application floated up to join the pen, the book, and all of the other objects in orbit. If Bladen owned a laptop, there'd be little need for the pen or the paper, but his current finances didn't permit such an extravagance.

"So kid, you wanna be a deputy?"

The orbiting ceased.

"A deputy? For you?"

"Yup. Down here in Denary."

"Um, Uncle Arlo, you do know that I was shit-canned from NYPD, right? Harold and Kumar would have a better chance of passing a drug test for your department…"

"Who? Are they like a Cheech and Chong? I get it! Anyway, we can work on all that. I basically *am* the department. We have me and my three deputies. We don't even really need that many, yet we do need one more. Long story. Come on down to Denary and we'll talk. Decent pay, benefits, and you can stay with me 'til you get on your feet."

Bladen's next call was cross-country. He reached voicemail.

"Hey, it's Kath. Leave a message. Fake IRS and fake Dell Computer can fuck off."

THE NEXT MORNING, Bladen Dieci rolled south, deeper into Arizona, in a Ford that had rolled off the assembly line while he was in high school detention. It was blue, apart from one black door. Denary was a little more than an hour's drive, as the vulture flies.

He was just finishing an Egg McMuffin when he saw the road sign.

Welcome to Denary
Where our kind are the kind kind

All Bladen knew about the place was that there had been some strange and brutal murders there ten years prior, and not long after, his father—Uncle Arlo's twin—ventured there to visit his brother and was promptly diagnosed with an aggressive brain tumor. He was never again whole enough even to return to New York to die. Bladen never went to see his dad as the end neared. He'd meant to, but it all happened so quickly. At least that's how he rationalized it.

He saw his father's body at the Staten Island funeral home, after it had arrived there like some fucking Amazon Prime delivery.

BLADEN WALKED INTO the Denary Diner, greeted by the sound of Dwight Yoakam and the sight of his uncle sitting in a booth, eyes down under his Stratton straw hat, tying and untying some kind of rope knot. Uncle Arlo sure looked every bit the cowboy. That he came from the Big Apple thirty-some years before and that his actual first name was Nick mattered little. This was who he'd become: the wrangler with the rope and the big sheriff's hat.

"Blade! Hell, you got skinny."

Arlo stood, dropping his piece of rope to the table. His smile was broad, uncomfortably so. Bladen noticed that the years were catching up with his uncle; he was still tall and broad, but now a tad hunched over and maybe a bit wobbly. The men embraced.

"Good to see you, Uncle Arlo. I can't thank you enough…"

"See that? A Buntline Hitch," said Arlo, pointing to the length of rope. "Was hooking my key ring to it. Killin' time. Easy knot."

As Bladen sat in the booth across the table from Arlo, the waitress approached. Her smile might have been broader than the sheriff's. Her middle-aged choppers screamed tobacco and gum disease, but she presented them proudly.

"Hello, handsome! I'm Maggie, I'm a Taurus, I love lake fishin', and we make the best omelets in Arizona! Your uncle told me all about you, big city policeman. Good for you. Can I get you some coffee?"

"Uh, yes. Black, please. No food, thank you. I just had a couple of McMuffins on the drive," he said, smiling.

"Mc whats?"

Bladen laughed, politely. "I'm sure your eggs are better, but I was starving."

"But really, Mc whats?" she pressed, eyes and mouth wide.

"McMuffins. Egg McMuffins?"

"That's a new one, I guess." She chuckled before heading to the coffee station.

Bladen looked over at Arlo. Same giant smile.

"You do know what Egg McMuffins are, right, Uncle Arlo?"

"Yes. Hey, you ever tie a Knute Hitch?"

With the coffee cups near empty and the small-talk dwindling, Uncle Arlo got down to business.

"I know you have questions, Bladen, and I know that one of them is about why we are meeting here rather than at my house—I'll get to all that." Arlo was still smiling, as were the older couple who had just come through the door, nodded, and headed to a booth toward the back.

"That did cross my mind."

"I know. Well, first off, we need to have at least four law officers in the town. Not that we have any crime, but it's just how it is with shifts and all. I'm gonna be stepping down soon. I'm not in the best of health, and I need to find someone I can trust. Not that you're gonna be sheriff. Not right off, anyway. That wouldn't be right for the deputies who've been in the department for years. Not that they'd even complain. One of them'll get promoted, you'll become a deputy, but your rank won't matter for the job I have for you." Arlo grasped his nephew's hand and stared into his eyes, smiling all the while. "It's a very important job."

"Sounds weird."

"Finish your coffee, Bladen. I'll have to tell you the rest in private. Get in your car, follow me to my house, and we'll talk out front of it."

BLADEN SHOVED THE key into the ignition, popped a THC lozenge, and followed his uncle's sheriff's SUV through backstreets and brush until they came upon a neat Mediterranean-style single-story home. It featured a small, gated courtyard with a detached casita. Thick dark clouds gathered as Uncle Arlo exited his vehicle and loaded himself into the passenger seat of his nephew's old Ford. The first thing Bladen noticed was that for the first time since he'd arrived in Denary, there was no smile. Arlo's withered scowl looked like something on Rushmore as he turned toward his nephew.

"What do you know about the mass murder that took place here back then?"

"Well, it was strange as fuck, as far as I know."

"That it was."

"Wasn't it the old mayor?" asked Bladen.

"Was the mayor, the sheriff, the school principal, and a local preacher. They just all got together and went through the town shootin' up anyone they seen: kids, the elderly, didn't matter. Then best the FBI could figure was that the mayor, when they was done, killed his accomplices and then himself, as they had probably all agreed on beforehand."

"Sick."

"And that school principal was a woman. You don't usually see females involved in this kinda thing. Anyway, the nagging piece was that a couple of very young children—witnesses who hid and escaped death—wouldn't stop sayin' that they saw more than just the four murderers. They said there was maybe six or eight of 'em and more than just one female killer. Problem was they couldn't identify them. They were terrified and never got a clear look at faces. But they never changed their story. Not once."

"But, even if there were more accomplices, nothing further has happened in like ten years, and it looks like everyone in this town is pig-in-shit happy all the time."

"Almost everyone," replied Arlo, his face steady as an Easter Island Moai.

The rain began to pepper Bladen's Ford.

"Not long after the murders," continued Arlo, "a young girl came. She arrived with her mother, off of a freight train, they said. Now Bladen, this is where things take a strange turn. In the course of this story, I'm going to tell you something that I have never uttered to anyone. If you don't want to hear it, please tell me now. You are family, and I couldn't imagine telling this to anyone who isn't. But if you don't want to know, I'll be forced to trust some-one else."

"Can I vape while you tell me?"

"Vape? Christ, kid, either smoke or don't smoke, but what's with that electric shit?"

"Just tell me your story, Uncle Arlo."

Sheriff Arlo studied the rain as it pelted the windshield.

TEN YEARS EARLIER

ON ARLO'S SECOND day as sheriff of Denary, they stepped through the front entrance of the tiny police station, each toting one small, weathered piece of luggage. They presented huge smiles, the only such grins in a town burdened with fresh grief. The girl appeared to be about fourteen; the mother looked more like a grandmother. They donned sprightly attire, mother in blue, child in pink. The youngster possessed the most dazzling blond locks and eyes like select drops of tropical ocean. Unlike the girl, the mother's features were unremarkable, even drab. But again, the dress was a nice shade of blue. They managed to get themselves seated across a desk from Sheriff Arlo as he, though swamped, made time for his two visitors. The station secretary, a sweet dark-skinned go-getter in her late twenties, who everyone affection-ately called Miss Nini, bustled around the office, from desk to desk.

"We were saddened to learn of the horror that has befallen your town, Sheriff," offered the mother. "I am Ludovica, and this is my daughter, Giada. We have traveled a long way to see you."

"Oh. Where from?"

"East. By train."

"Train? The nearest train station is almost…"

"Freight train, sir. It didn't actually stop."

Both ladies continued to smile.

"Okay," sighed Arlo, feeling pressed for time, "what can I do for you?"

"With respect, sir, it is what we can do for you," replied Ludovica. She glanced over at her sunny-faced daughter, at which time the girl spoke, high-pitched, Disney princess-style.

"Mister Sheriff, I can take away all of your sadness and bad thoughts! If there are naughty people in your town who are pretending to be nice, I can make them nice for real!"

Arlo began to stand, ready to show them the door, when, for whatever reason, he decided to ask, "How would you go about doing all that, young lady?"

Giada's smile grew even wider. "All I do is hold your head in my hands!"

Ludovica nodded, but Arlo had lost patience. "Miss Nini here will show you ladies out," he bellowed, loud enough for the secretary to hear. As she approached, the sheriff added, "If you folks need a ride somewhere, I'll have a deputy take you. Good day now."

Their smiles remained as Miss Nini led them to the outer office. Arlo sat back down, slipped on his reading glasses, and directed his attention to the paperwork on his desk. He was going to find out if any other townspeople took part in the mass murder. No matter that the FBI had taken over the case. Toward the bottom of the pile were the grisly crime scene photos. One of them—a shot of two dead children—filled his frame of vision when Miss Nini hurriedly came through the door. Arlo looked up to see her shaking, tears pouring from her captivatingly cocoa eyes.

"It works," she cried.

"What?"

"I let the little girl take my head into her hands. I... I feel beautiful. Sheriff, I feel so free."

A smile took hold of Nini's face. It was not unlike those of Ludovica and Giada.

PRESENT DAY

RAIN WAS SEEPING into the Ford. It invaded via the cracked window that provided an escape for Bladen's blueberry-scented vapor. Uncle Arlo continued his decade-old story.

"That smile that day on Miss Nini's face was the first one in our town. Now everyone has one and has had one since the day that little girl grabbed their heads."

"You mean the whole town did that shit, Uncle Arlo?"

"All but one of us."

Arlo stared through the vape cloud, sans any trace of a smile.

"You didn't do it? How is it that you're the only one?"

"It was all voluntary, from the mayor on down, but everyone did it. Call it peer pressure or the desire to belong, or maybe they all just wanted to feel as good as it was advertised to be, but they did it. Stood in line to be touched by Giada, with Ludovica grinnin' beside her. They all shook, they all cried, and they all became so *motherfucking* nice."

"They have no idea that you didn't get…baptized, or whatever," stated Bladen. "That's why you keep that goofy grin on in public."

"That's right. Try smiling for ten minutes straight. Then think about doing it for ten years."

"How did you get away with not participating?"

"This is hard, Blade. Your father helped me. Of course, I couldn't have known, but I think…Bladen, I think that's what killed him."

The vaping ceased. The window rode back up. The rain intensified.

"What do you mean? How did it kill my dad?"

"The short answer? He was my twin. He liked the idea of being happy and carefree for life. He knew I didn't want to do it. As sheriff, I needed a clear mind, a neutral thought process. I needed an analytical brain."

"Get the fuck…"

"Yeah, he volunteered to dress as me and go kneel before Giada. No one knew any better. Well, no one except Giada, I suspect."

"But how did—?"

"He got headaches almost immediately. His vision started to go, along with his equilibrium. Got the brain tumor. Died looking up at me."

"The touch of the girl gave him the brain tumor?"

"I'm sure of it. She sensed our deception and made him pay for it."

"But the girl and her mother came to help the people…"

"Seemed that way at first. I'm still the only one who thinks otherwise."

"Where are they now, Uncle Arlo?"

"The grateful mayor had set them up in a little trailer near the tracks. It was clean and modern. Hell, I'd live there. One night, a few years back, Ludovica, the mother, well, she was just gone. The girl said she went back east and that they'd reunite one day."

"She just left the girl here alone?"

"Blade, let's say that little Giada is, um…beyond her years."

"By now she's, what, like twenty-four? Does she still live in that trailer?"

"How about we go in the house now?"

Bladen held his piece of luggage over his head to shelter himself from the downpour. Arlo walked in front of him, oblivious to the weather. They passed the casita, the courtyard, and approached the front door. Arlo turned the knob and opened it.

"You didn't lock your door?" asked Bladen.

"No crime in Denary, boy."

WITH BLADEN SEATED comfortably in a living room chair, Arlo walked over carrying two full shot glasses and handed one to his nephew.

"Here's to my new deputy. We gotta go make it official at the mayor's office, but that'll just be a formality."

Bladen slid his head back and downed the whiskey. "Will I have to put that bullshit smile on all day?"

The sheriff put his hand out for the empty glass. "No, because they'll understand that you were never touched by Giada. Kid, you will be the first person to move into Denary since that, er, girl, and her mother, got here."

"What? In all those years?"

"Yeah. No one has moved in. Or out for that matter, 'cept for Ludovica, I guess."

"How is that possible?"

"Beats me. Above my pay grade. No kids been born here, either."

"Can you pour me another shot? This tale is fucking with my vibe. The rain seems to have slowed. I'm gonna go to the car and grab my other bags."

"Need a hand?"

"I'm good."

Bladen stood and strode toward the door. He walked into the courtyard, toward the gate that led to the street. Something made him stop in his tracks by the casita. He glanced back at the front door of Arlo's house, then stepped to his right, not toward the gate but toward the door to the casita. He turned the knob.

Locked.

THE OFFICE OF the Mayor was smaller than Bladen had anticipated, but the furniture was pretty sweet. Mayor McComb was adored by the townspeople. He didn't exactly have a hard act to follow, since the previous occupant of his office checked out of life as a mass murderer. Arlo referred to him as Mayor McComb-over, but only when complaining aloud to himself. He made a mental note to share the joke with his nephew.

"Soon as we get you sworn in, we'll get you fitted for your uniform," said the smiling rotund leader, four strands of hair across the top of his head, looking like the Finger Lakes. "This here is Deputy Gonzalez. We call him Alamo. He's gonna be the new sheriff once Arlo signs off."

The deputy reached out and shook Bladen's hand.

"So they call you Alamo?" stuttered Bladen. "Guessing you're from Texas?"

"Arizona, born and bred," answered the deputy, with a grin as wide as the Lone Star State. "I used to work for the car rental company. Alamo."

"Oh."

"Hey, is that a touch of booze on your breath?" quizzed Alamo, still smiling, of course.

"I...I..."

"Yup. I gave him a shot for nerves," interrupted Sheriff Arlo, fake grin eating his face.

McComb and Alamo burst out in laughter. In walked Miss Nini, bible in hand, already guffawing.

"I told you about our lovely Miss Nini," said Arlo to Bladen, forcing his own awkward laughter.

"Yes. So nice to meet you, Miss Nini."

"Oh, but she is Deputy Mayor Nini now, for the past three years," responded Arlo.

"Ready to get that hand on the bible?" she asked, eyes still lovely, teeth still prominent.

TWO HOURS LATER, Deputy Bladen Dieci had a pair of temporary and slightly baggy uniforms, a bag full of equipment, and a Smith & Wesson pistol. The first thing he did after signing for his supplies was to place a call to Staten Island. To Kathleen.

"Hey, this is Kath. Leave a message. Fake IRS and fake Dell Computer can fuck off."

THAT EVENING, HE sat in his uncle's living room again, plopped on the sofa, half-scrolling through his phone while Arlo mastered some complicated knot tying from his recliner.

"Why no TV, Uncle Arlo?"

"I was never one for the television. I'd rather read a book or tie some knots. I got games, if you wanna play."

"Games?"

Arlo stood. He strolled over to a closet and opened the door. There they were, stacked high. Monopoly. Risk. Clue. Maybe twenty board games in all. Still in plastic.

"Holy hell," said Bladen. "I never pictured you…"

"Did you say 'Pictionary'? I got that, I think."

"I did not. Why all the games?"

"That's what they do around here. Every goddamned house is filled with these. I don't play unless I have to—you know, if I'm a guest. I bought these to blend in, but I never have anyone over so I ain't never opened 'em. I'll play if you wanna."

"POP A SIX and you move twice!" exclaimed Bladen. "You don't know that rule?"

"Whatever."

Bladen danced his little blue game piece around the Trouble board. Arlo then placed his palm on the clear plastic dome, pressed down, and set to motion the single die imprisoned within. As it landed on the number one, he spoke.

"I have her, Bladen."

"What's that?"

"Giada. I have her. Or I have *it*."

"Hmmmm. Okay. Uncle Arlo, I am going to ingest some marijuana cookies before you go any further."

Bladen walked to his bag, removed a cookie, and bit. Arlo moved his red game piece one space.

As crumbs tumbled from his lips, Bladen spoke. "I never made detective in NYPD, but it wouldn't take Sherlock Holmes to conclude that she is in that locked casita."

"*It*. Not *she*. Not for a long time."

"Maybe that's a tad harsh, Uncle Arlo?"

The sheriff laughed. "Your move."

Bladen pressed the plastic bubble. Another one.

"Fuck me," he mumbled. "Uncle Arlo, you do realize that you are committing a felony by holding someone against her will."

"I've learned—the hard way—that evil can't be eradicated. It can only be relocated," answered Arlo. "If I ate your THC cookie, maybe I'd get a little high, but if I ate a THC cookie from every person in this town tonight, well...you tell me."

"You'd be screwed. Also, are you saying that everyone in town has edibles?"

"No, jackass. I am saying that this here, at the time, young girl took the bad out of a whole town, and that might include some major league bad from a couple of folks who might have been murderers. It seems, after what has transpired since, that all of that evil didn't just vanish. It went into her. Changed her to a...a...thing."

"I'm having another cookie, Uncle Arlo. Want one?"

"Not for me. Listen, I'll be right back. Don't cheat."

Arlo stood, grabbed some keys, and stepped into the kitchen. Bladen heard the fridge door open followed by the sound of containers being moved about. The refrigerator door closed and Arlo walked back in, past his nephew, and to the front door. He was wearing big headphones and carried a decent-sized piece of rectangular Tupperware. The door to the courtyard slammed behind him. Bladen sat staring at the Trouble board. The game pieces began to rise from their slots and float.

"No!"

They stopped and returned to the board. He grabbed his phone and tapped, expecting to get Kathleen's voicemail once again. A man answered.

"Listen," said the deep voice, "enough of this shit. Do you even know what time it is, you fucking loser? She wants nothing to do with you. Go away."

"W-What?" stammered Bladen. "Who is this?"

"This is Kathleen's husband. Her real husband, in the here and now." Click.

Bladen started to call the number back but decided against it. *Husband?* This needed to be processed. His hands went cold, his throat tight. He gazed at the game on the table and reached for his vape pen. By his first puff, Arlo was back.

"Did I give you permission to fill my house with that vape shit?" he said through the initial cloud. He spoke more loudly than normal, as his headphones were still on.

"Sorry. I wasn't thinking straight. I'll go outside."

"Never mind, kid. Just do it. Who cares?"

"Uncle Arlo, were you just in the casita?"

"Yeah. I fed it. It eats once a day. Raw meat."

"Why the headphones?"

"It tries to trick me. I don't listen no more. Also, it has a toilet in there, but I think it eats its own shit."

"Here's the deal, Sheriff—Uncle Arlo—you are gonna take me into that casita, because I sometimes have trouble with reality. Maybe you do too. So I need to know right fucking now if you are crazy, if I am crazy, if we are both crazy, or if neither of us is crazy. That last possibility is the scariest of all."

"I am going to show you, Bladen. I'll give you the headphones and I'll shove some other shit in my own ears."

He presented his nephew with the huge ear cups and the attached Sony Walkman cassette player.

"Cassettes? I don't know if you're old school or cutting edge, other than the fact that I actually do know. Let me see what's in that player…"

"It's the only tape I got. I bought the machine at a flea market and the tape was already inside."

"Hmmm," uttered Bladen as he popped open the player and removed the cartridge, "Let's see, *Once, Even Flow, Alive…* hell, the print is worn to shit, but that's Pearl Jam! You like them?"

"I dunno. I hear it every day, so I guess maybe a little. I ain't never flipped it to the other side, though."

"Okay, let's do that. Tomorrow, you'll hear all new songs."

"Don't bother."

"Hey, it's done. It'll be 'Oceans' for you tomorrow!"

"Well, you're wearing it first."

"I'll be kind—rewind. Now take me to see the girl."

"Listen, uh, did you move your piece ahead while I was out?"

"Excuse me?"

"Bladen, your Trouble game piece. Did you cheat?"

"Of course not."

Arlo looked down, studying the board, for a full minute.

"All right," he finally said. "I will take you out there, but promise me that you'll understand. I've had it locked in that casita for years, since I noticed the changes beginning. I'm the only bastard in Denary that isn't brainwashed, so it was all up to me. I drugged it while it slept in its trailer, then brought it here. Took me weeks to get that brig set up. The town thinks that Giada up and left to go find her mother. They wouldn't understand why I have *her* here, even if they saw for themselves. They are that batshit, Bladen. I don't know if I have the power, or the will, to kill it. That's my curse. I keep it alive. It eats once a day."

"You said that part already—about the eating."

"Oh, and it don't wash or nothing, but there is a shower in there too, near the toilet. It eats its own…"

"Shit. I know. You said that already as well."

AS ARLO SLID the key into the door of the casita, he hummed to himself—not a tune, but a steady drone, designed to assist the cotton balls in his ears with blocking out extraneous noise. Bladen stood behind him in the darkness of the courtyard, the sounds of Pearl Jam glutting his skull. Behind the heavy front door was a second one. Gated. Steel. Arlo unlocked that as well. He turned to his nephew.

"The vape?"

"What?" asked Bladen, lifting a cup from his ear.

"That vape thing. Ditch it."

"Sorry." He blew out the last cloud and set the vaporizer pen on the ground.

Stepping into the dimly lit casita, Bladen coughed, then gagged. The first thing he saw was the enormous cage. A jail cell. There was also a sign:

WARNING! HIGH VOLTAGE!

Hanging from above, covering the top half of the cell, were several altar cloths, embroidered crosses facing inward toward the bars. The walls were covered in crucifixes, which were affixed to the soundproof tiles. Bladen could see shadowy movement within, but the deepest part of the cell was dark as night, due in part to the boarded and barred windows, and the altar cloths were no help. Pearl Jam filled his head as fear filled his heart. Arlo motioned Bladen to look in. He knelt below the hanging cloths, peering.

Too dark.

Arlo went to the corner of the room and retrieved a heavy flashlight. He handed it to his nephew. Nineties grunge blasted in Bladen's ears. He turned on the light and trained it on the back of the large cell. Almost before the light hit, a figure retreated into the shower area, which couldn't be seen from in front of the bars.

Bladen's left ear was on the far side of his uncle and out of his view. The new deputy, using one finger, slid the earphone off, hoping to hear anything.

"Can you help me, sir?" came the voice, pixie-like and soft. "He keeps me here and does things to me. Terrible things."

Arlo, cotton-eared and humming, slowly stepped to the other side of his nephew, and Bladen re-positioned the headphone cup. Pearl Jam again. The sheriff stomped his foot in frustration, realizing that Bladen would not be able to see into the shower area. He interrupted his humming to utter a single word.

"Cunt."

ARLO AND BLADEN were back in the main house. The new deputy took off his headphones.

"You could have given me some of those cotton balls to stuff in my nostrils, Uncle Arlo. What the fuck was that? Godzilla's colonoscopy?"

"It eats its own shit."

"Yeah, yeah—I got that. You just could've...never mind."

"That goddamned shower," sighed Arlo. "Used it as a hiding spot. My faulty design. I can't think of everything. It don't hide from me. Guess it don't want you getting a look at it. Slick bastard knew you were with me. Explain that one. Tomorrow you can draw it out with food."

"Uncle Arlo," began Bladen, placing his hands on the taller man's shoulders…"Uncle Nick—remember when you were Uncle Nick?"

"Yeah," he responded with a trace of an actual smile.

"Uncle Nick, is there a terrified and sickly young blond woman imprisoned in your casita?"

Arlo stood silently. His smile died. He removed Bladen's hands from his shoulders.

"No," was all he said.

The sheriff turned and walked toward his bedroom. With his back to his nephew, he said, "I'm tired. If I ain't awake by ten tomorrow, come and get me. Don't bother tryin' to get in that casita without me; it's locked tight, and I have the only key. You're a kind-hearted kid, Bladen, but the thing in that cage killed your father. Remember that."

One more vape, one more edible, and Bladen was ready for bed.

THE MORNING SUN shoved past the overmatched window shade. Bladen Dieci hadn't slept much. The image of a girl held hostage tortured him as the coyotes prowled the night. A girl in an Arizona cage; a girl in a New York relationship. He ambled to the bathroom, then the kitchen. As the coffee brewed, he saw the Trouble game still atop the living room table, he saw the Blood Knot draped on Arlo's chair, and he saw the clock on the wall—a wooden cat with moving eyes and tail. He surely had taken something, but before he knew it, it felt like he had stared at that cat for two hours.

Ten a.m.

He turned the corner toward his uncle's bedroom. Sticking halfway out of the crack below the door was a thick envelope. It contained something, but Bladen first spotted the handwritten scrawl on the face of it.

I tied my last knot, kid. Don't come in my room. Just read the contents within. God be with you.

He blasted through the door. Sheriff Arlo was adorned in full uniform.

167

He swayed slowly below his final knot. The rope had been tied to an attic beam, which had been exposed by the removal of a ceiling fan, which sat neatly in the corner of the bedroom, a few feet from a toppled folding chair. Bladen ran to Arlo, but it was obviously too late. He knew not to disturb the scene, because an investigation would soon come. The keys to the casita hung from the late sheriff's belt.

BLADEN SAT IN the living room, eyes on the Trouble board, holding a cassette he'd found in the envelope, along with a suicide note. His mind raced, trying to find an order for what his next actions should be.

Call it in? Read the note? Listen to the cassette? Enter the casita?

He decided the order would be: 1) Read note. 2) Enter casita. 3) Play cassette. 4) Call it in. He then added: 2) Ingest marijuana. The others were pushed to 3, 4 and 5.

It was more than a note. Arlo had left to Bladen his mortgage-free house, his life savings, his truck, and a detailed account of the inhabitant of his casita. He explained why he performed a drop-hanging on himself: for forensic reasons that would clear Bladen of any suspicion. He also noted that there would not be much of an investigation because all of the law enforcement officers in Denary were oblivious to anything but kindness. He concluded that they would not consider the detached casita a part of any potential crime scene, so he needn't worry. He also wrote that he hoped Bladen had more resolve than he and might consider slaughtering the "thing" that had given his father a brain tumor. The note concluded with a reminder to play the tape and an apology regarding the future chore of reattaching the ceiling fan.

Bladen devoured a pair of laced cookies, took the key ring that dangled from the belt of the man who dangled from the ceiling, dropped a raw steak into a bowl, removed the Pearl Jam tape from the Walkman, replaced it with the suicide cassette, and walked out the front door. The headphones dangled at his side.

THE HOT SUN warmed his neck as he unlocked the casita door. Blood oozed from the cold steak. He opened the second door, the steel one. He thought he heard a man's voice within, a deep one. Gravelly. It ceased immediately. He blamed it on the cookies.

"Hello?" said Bladen, hesitantly. "I don't know if you really like raw steak, but I…"

"I'm used to it," came the cheerful response. Sounded like a twelve-year-old girl.

"I can…I can get you something else," he stammered.

"It's okay."

"I want to help you," replied Bladen.

"Where is that man? The sheriff."

"He was my uncle," answered Bladen, ducking to see beneath the altar cloths. He saw the flashlight in the corner.

"*Was?*"

"How do I give you the steak?"

"There are two very little, locked openings, side by side. You need to turn off the electricity, open them both…"

"Oh yeah, I read that," said the deputy. He placed everything on the floor, retrieved the flashlight, took Arlo's instructions from his pocket, and shone the light on them, reading.

FEEDING: *Turn off electric on wall switch, open ONLY ONE of the pair of side-by-side food slot doors. The monster can't fit both hands through just one slot opening. It needs BOTH hands on you to fuck with your brain…*

Bladen went to the wall. There were two labeled switches, one larger than the other.

LIGHT

CAGE

First he hit the light. A single dim bulb on the ceiling turned on. Didn't do much. Then he pulled the larger switch. A low buzz that he hadn't even noticed, stopped.

"Good," said the childlike voice. "Now just come and open *both* slot doors. Or you could just open this whole cage and get me the heck out of here."

Bladen walked to the slots. The prisoner was again hiding in the shower stall.

"I'm just opening one slot for now," he said as he unlocked it. He kept an eye on the shower as he placed the bloody bowl of steak on the small shelf. "If you come out of there so I can see you, I might open both slots, or probably even the whole cell."

"I'm shy."

"What? I'm talking about getting you out of here!"

"Okay, maybe not *shy*, but I…I'm so ugly now. I've been here for so long. Mistreated, malnourished. It all hurts so much, Bladen."

He had his hand on the second slot door.

"I never told you my name," he said, taking his hand away.

"Silly, the sheriff told me about you when he fed me yesterday. Why did you say he *was* your uncle? Did something happen to him? He is not a good man, but still, I wouldn't wish harm on him."

"He was a good man! I…I think so, anyway."

"Has he passed away?"

"He has. He's gone."

"Oh, no. I am probably too silly for even offering this," said the juvenile voice, "but, though I am a good girl, I do have special powers."

"You do?"

"Yes. Have you seen the kind people of Denary? I made them that way! I help people."

"My uncle said you're evil."

"No way. He was evil, Bladen. I don't know why my touch never helped him. He was the only one."

"He said you killed my father."

"Who?"

"My dad. Uncle Arlo said you gave him the brain tumor."

"I'm not sure what any of that means. I don't believe I ever met your father."

"Your hands touched my father."

"When?"

"When he stood in for my uncle. My uncle never received your touch."

"None of that is true, Bladen. My hands only help. Do you have access to your uncle's body? If you can bring his remains to me, I might—no promises—be able to bring him back. But only if we hurry."

"Bring him back?"

"Yes. Hurry!"

THC RACED THROUGH his bloodstream as Bladen raced out of the casita. In the cage, hurried footsteps bolted toward the raw meat.

Minutes later, Bladen Dieci was dragging Arlo's body through the courtyard and into the darkened casita.

"Hurry!" said the girly voice. "Either let me out or bring his head by the food slots."

Bladen, winded and sweaty, peered into the cell. Giada was still hiding in the shower stall. He lugged Arlo's body near the food slots.

"I will come to help your uncle, but only if you don't look at me. Okay?" asked the prisoner.

"Whatever," huffed Bladen. "Just do it. Bring him back."

"You'll need to open the other slot, too."

Bladen heard the footsteps within the cage and pondered if he should open the second slot door. Arlo's head was just in front of it.

That was when the hand came through the slot.

It grabbed Bladen by his throat. When he was six years old, Bladen had seen something billed as the World's Largest Pipe Wrench. His dad took him to see it. Now it felt like that wrench was crushing his windpipe.

This was not the appendage of a girl. It was calloused and thick. It stank. Bladen grew dizzy as he heard the command again. It was delivered in a deep growl.

"Open it."

The key ring was in his hand. Bladen decided he'd rather die than unleash whatever was in that cage. At that instant, something else slid through the open food slot. Losing vision and sense, Bladen couldn't tell what the snake-like entity was, but it looped through the key ring, like one of Arlo's ropes, ripped it from his grasp, pulled it toward the second slot, operated the key, unlocked the other opening, and enabled the second hand to slide through the cage. The hands then went, not to Arlo's head, but to Bladen's. Though his throat was now free, the grip on his skull was overpowering, and he couldn't move. He felt the tears coming. His body shook violently. As, just seconds before, he felt the cold sting of death approaching, he now enjoyed a rush of the greatest happiness and peace he would ever experience. Light years beyond any drug.

The hands released him.

When he finally stood, wearing the largest smile ever to grace his face, night had fallen. The daylight hours had passed, as if he'd been anesthetized. He stepped over his uncle's body and pulled down the altar cloths. The light was dim, the shadows full, but he could see Giada behind those bars.

To almost anyone, the sight could be described as "grotesque," but not to Bladen. He wiped his most recent tears as he studied the figure before him. It was large and naked. Shaped more like something from a cave drawing than a human. Its body was a combination of patches of matted hair and oozing blisters, but muscled. Atop its voluminous head were small, scattered remnants of the blond hair that had adorned Giada upon her smiling arrival in Denary. Foam dripped from its mouth, like a rabid dog.

In a voice like an ancient Roman earthquake, came the command:

"Open the cage."

Bladen complied, and the creature rose. Its dark yellow eyes stared into his as it emerged. It pointed at a corner of the room.

"Wait," was all it said. Bladen walked over and sat on the floor. The Walkman was already there. The creature stalked out into the night, to prowl amongst the coyotes.

Still grinning, Bladen put the headphones on and pressed *play.*

The first voice belonged to Arlo. "Talk into this, you fucker. If you ever want to eat again, you will explain what you are. Otherwise, you can rot in there and starve."

The tape rolled on, with the deep gravelly voice taking command.

"I am <u>Sorbera</u>. We are Sorbera. We are the beginning of time. We are the end of time."

THE CREATURE, LIT only by the moon, came upon the first house in its path. The home of Miss Nini. She stood alone in the kitchen as it came through the front door and into the living room. It strode past a table with Chutes and Ladders, Scrabble, and Sorry stacked upon it.

IN ARLO'S CASITA, the cassette continued to roll. "Your people, many of them, were no longer pure," said the creature. "They were taken by <u>Haagabus</u>. Haagabus is what you call a demon. A powerful mutator of souls. Your world, for all generations, has fallen to Haagabus. I, we, the Sorbera, consume Haagabus. We absorb them, and all evil."

WHEN MISS NINI saw the beast before her, right beside her double oven, her smile grew wider. It took her head in its hands and opened its jaws. Stinking foam dripped onto Nini's face as the Sorbera's mouth covered hers.

"WE LIVE FOR what you'd call a thousand years," said the Sorbera on the tape. "We absorb the evil, but then, as we must do, we return to retrieve the rest. We consume the entire soul."

Bladen absorbed these words through the headphones, never altering his smile.

MISS NINI'S REMAINS rested on her tiled floor. She was unrecognizable, a mass of dry, shriveled skin and pulverized bone.

THE SORBERA HAD visited eleven more homes before it entered Alamo's. The former car rental agent had just packed up his game of Chinese Checkers when his front door caved in.

"Giada?" he asked, as if seeing a human figure. His bliss remained as it grabbed his head. The creature's dripping mouth cranked wide on Alamo's. As they touched, the snake-like appendage that Bladen had seen slithered its way out of the demon's wretched mouth, down the deputy's throat, and through to his stomach.

AFTER CONSUMING THE souls of Alamo and his sleeping wife, the Sorbera visited every home in Denary, like Santa Claus on Christmas. The final house belonged to the mayor. The monster claimed the souls of McComb's wife and elderly mother as they played Jenga, then took to the staircase. Mayor McComb awoke as it came through his bedroom door. His smile was on before he could reach for his eyeglasses. It took him before he could stand. The awful fetor of the sticky tongue filled his nostrils as it burrowed into his intestines. From the rear of the Sorbera emerged another appendage, not unlike the tongue, but more of a tail. A slim, serpentine rapier, thorny spikes covering it like porcupine quills.

The splintery tail tore through McComb's silk pajamas and shredded its way into his rectum, and up through his intestines, until it met the tongue deep inside his abdomen. As it had done, in this exact manner, to virtually every citizen of Denary, the Sorbera consumed the mayor's soul. It sucked all liquids from his body, crushed every bone, and filled itself, satiating a decade of hunger.

IN THE CASITA, the cassette had long stopped. Bladen Dieci remained on the floor, grinning, four feet from his uncle's body. The light of the moon, which had shone in through the open door, became eclipsed by a figure. The Sorbera stood at the entrance.

WHEN GIADA AND Ludovica had arrived in Denary, they came as stowaways on a freight train lugged by a steam locomotive. Technology and environmental awareness have nearly done away with the image of the smoking, chugging train, yet here was Giada, admittedly looking quite different, sitting again in an open-doored boxcar. The Sorbera, now strong and full, was going home to its mother. Beside it sat a new companion.

"Where are we going?" asked Bladen, beaming.

"East."

The one-hundred-and-eighty-car train rattled slowly through the night, with the classic image of locomotive steam replaced by floating clouds of blueberry vapor.

"East?" he asked. "Ever been to Staten Island?"

BAD MOON RISING

Steven Pajak

F REDERICK HARRISON LAZILY STOKED THE fire and listened
as the old woman, Anya, spun her yarn. Her husband, Milo, the mayor
of Karavostasi, one of three villages of the Folegandros Islands, sat nearby,
embarrassed by his wife's archaic tales of beasts who slaughtered children in
the night, though he'd seen the small, dismembered bodies hidden beneath
stained sheets in the basement of the hospital.

The night was dark, and the frigid wind that tore at the eaves made
melancholy sounds that reminded Harrison of his haunted past. It was a perfect night for such nightmarish tales. The fire was warm and the food good,
so Harrison listened, sitting beside the hearth, his piercing green eyes staring
out from beneath half-closed lids, though he wasn't tired. In fact, he did not
sleep, but he feigned weariness as the hour grew late. He'd spent the last six
months at sea; firm ground beneath his feet, food that had not recently swum
in briny water, and good company awoke within him long-forgotten emotions.

Harrison had debarked the fishing vessel, *The Vassago*, at Karavostasi's
docking port just hours ago, under cover of darkness. The tiny island—twelve
square miles—was a juxtaposition of cerulean waters against rocky cliffs, with
narrow streets paved with stone, dotted by whitewashed homes overlooking
the Aegean Sea. Harrison's reputation as a beast hunter was known across the

land, and rumors of mysterious, brutal slayings at the full moon carried him to this village. He was no stranger to death; in fact, Harrison had murdered men, had even drained them of their blood, though he no longer thirsted for the blood of men.

"You will help us?" Milo asked, after his wife recounted the horrors that had befallen the village the last six months. He held out a canvas sack which contained a modest sum of money collected by the villagers—payment for Harrison's services. "You will kill the beast?"

Harrison nodded and accepted the sack; it disappeared into the interior pocket of his well-worn peacoat. "Tell me again of the first murder."

Anya's eyes shifted to her husband, as if seeking permission to respond. After brief hesitation, she spoke, her voice low and hushed, so as not to be heard by her young ones. The mayor's teenaged son and eight-year-old daughter listened from the shadows of the loft, unbeknownst to their parents, but Harrison was acutely aware of their presence. He caught wind of their scent the moment he entered the home. He could hear the steady beat of their hearts and hear their shallow breathing.

At one point, as Anya recounted the horrible slaying of the first victim, Harrison looked directly up at the young ones—they couldn't be seen in the shadows from the room below, yet Harrison saw them clearly, as if they were backlit by candlelight. The young girl, Adonia, became quickly unnerved by the stranger's attention and hastened to her bed. Bastion, the older of the two who turned thirteen six months ago, stared back at the man with dark black hair and green eyes for a moment longer before finally slinking away in the darkness.

Something about the boy—an intuition, a supernatural feeling he long ago learned to trust—seemed off to Harrison, as did the boy's scent. He dismissed his intuition for the moment, as the hour grew late. Harrison realized Anya had fallen silent, and she and her husband gazed at him, as though mesmerized by his appearance.

"I'll need to speak to witnesses in the morning. Can you arrange that?"

Milo nodded. "Yes, of course. But we must make haste, for tomorrow the moon is full and the cycle begins."

Harrison nodded. "May I bed in your barn?"

"You may rest here, near the fire," Anya offered.

Again, Harrison nodded. While he retrieved his bedroll and made his place near the hearth, Milo and Anya retreated to the loft, leaving him alone.

He lay on his side, his head propped on his hand, his eyes staring into the fire. He could hear the soft whispers of their conversations from their bedroom, even above the crack and spit of the fire. He quickly tuned them out, mindful of their privacy. He shifted to his back after a while and lay awake the remainder of the night, waiting for dawn.

AT SUNRISE, MILO emerged from the loft, his ample belly preceding him as he descended the stairs. He scratched at his unruly hair and then shrugged his suspenders over his shoulders. He regarded Harrison with red, tired eyes. "Did you sleep well?"

Harrison paused slipping his bedroll into his pack. "I did, thank you."

Milo continued to stare as Harrison finished gathering his things and shouldered his pack. Harrison could sense the other man's unease around him. Milo was quite aware of Harrison's reputation as a beast hunter and had no doubt heard the gory details—some true, many embellished—about his journeys and the creatures he'd slayed. To ease the man, Harrison said he would wait outside and excused himself.

Less than ten minutes later, Milo appeared dressed in an old suit and stuffed a battered fedora down on his balding dome. He squinted against the bright sun, then motioned for Harrison to follow, as he started down the stone road toward the center of the village. As they walked through the village, Milo's unease lifted and he grew comfortable enough to ask Harrison questions, trying to learn more about the mysterious beast hunter, while Harrison gave vague responses, so as not to seem rude.

"How is it you come by your...trade, Mr. Harrison?"

"It's my family's work. It was expected of me."

"How many creatures have you slain?"

"Too many to count."

"Have you ever been injured by such foul beasts?"

"Yes."

Milo waited a moment for Harrison to elaborate, but he did not. They continued in silence before stopping a few minutes later outside a small dwelling. Milo removed his hat and knocked on the door. He fidgeted and wiped sweat from his brow with the sleeve of his jacket. After a moment, a woman in her early twenties peered out from the gap between door and jamb.

"Excuse me, Mrs. Stamopolous, we are sorry to intrude on your morning. May I present to you Mr. Harrison. He has come to help us...with our situation. May we come in and speak with you and your husband?"

She stepped back and opened the door fully to allow both men inside. She escorted them to the kitchen and offered tea, which they both refused.

"My husband is at market. He won't be back until midday."

Milo looked at Harrison, unsure if they should speak to the woman without her husband present, but Harrison focused on the woman. He moved past Milo and stood before her, towering more than half a foot above her. He bent slightly at the waist and offered his hand. She hesitated, but only a moment, and accepted it. His grip was gentle, but his skin cold. She looked up into his crisp green eyes and when he spoke, his voice was soft and monotonous.

"May I question you about your son, Adrian, Mrs. Stamopolous?"

She fixated on his eyes, locked in, oblivious to her surroundings. She couldn't look away as the stranger's eyes seemed to glow like radioactive lanterns.

"Yes."

"Very good. How old was your Adrian?"

"Ten."

It saddened Harrison that a boy was taken so soon, and in such a violent manner. "Why was he out alone during the night?"

"I don't know."

"Was he lured out?"

She hesitated. "I don't know."

"What do you mean, lured out?" Milo asked.

Harrison ignored him. "Did Adrian speak of anyone following him in the days before?"

"No."

"Are you certain?"

She hesitated again. "I don't know."

"Was Adrian with anyone unfamiliar that day? A stranger?"

"No."

"Can you account for his whereabouts the entire day?"

"He went to school. He returned home, did his studies. We had dinner. He played with Bastion in the yard until dark."

"Bastion? Milo's son?"

"Yes."

This gave Harrison pause. Then he asked, "When did you notice Adrian missing during the night?"

"We did not…until the constable…" She trailed off. Her face wretched and her hands came up and clutched her apron, pulling and fouling the material.

"I think that is enough," Milo said, stepping forward and putting a hand on Harrison's elbow. "You're upsetting her. We should go."

Harrison held the woman in his gaze and nodded.

"Mrs. Stamopolous, you will not fret."

The woman's face suddenly relaxed. "I will not fret."

"No, you shall not."

"I shall not."

"You will be strong for your family."

"Strong for…my family."

"You will trust that I will avenge Adrian."

"Avenge Adrian…"

"You will not let our visit spoil this lovely morning."

Harrison stood erect, and Mrs. Stamopolous blinked rapidly for a moment when he broke eye contact. She looked around, as though she were unaware of her surroundings, then she looked at Milo and smiled shyly.

"Thank you for coming by on such a lovely morning, Mr. Mayor." She bowed her head slightly. "Mr. Harrison."

Harrison nodded. "Thank you for your time. We will see ourselves out."

As soon as they stepped outside, Milo took Harrison's arm. "What was that in there? You did something to her."

"Time is wasting. Take me to the family of another victim."

MILO ESCORTED HIM to three more homes in the center of town. Harrison asked Milo to remain outside while he interviewed the grieving families. Suspicious of the request, Milo hesitantly agreed and waited anxiously with his hat in his hand for the young man to emerge before moving on to the next family. With three more houses to visit, Harrison surprised Milo when he asked instead to be taken to the body.

"You don't want to speak to all the parents?"

"No. I learned what I needed."

"What have you learned?"

Harrison only looked at Milo and said, "Take me to see the body, please."

The basement of the hospital was dark and smelled of mildew and death beneath the astringent malodor of disinfectant. They followed the mortician through a maze of hallways before he stopped outside a grimy door. The man was thin and frail, and his back hunched by age. His eyes were quick and nervous and shifted between Milo and Harrison. He frowned and was hesitant to honor Harrison's request, but Milo nodded his approval.

"You can go in, if that is your wish, but I won't cross that threshold again," the mortician said. "I've never seen such carnage in all my years..." He trailed off, no doubt conjuring the images of the torn and rendered corpse in his mind.

"I'll only be a moment," Harrison said. He went to the door, turned the knob, then stopped and spoke over his shoulder. "I'd like to do this on my own."

Milo did not plan to enter that room again, either. He saw the body in the woods after the constable woke him and informed him of the tragedy. The sight of the torn limbs and dismembered head plagued his dreams each night since. He was grateful Harrison spared him the embarrassment of having to look away.

"I'll wait for you outside. I cannot stomach the smell of this place."

OUTSIDE, THE AIR was fresh and carried the cold tang of the sea. Milo stuffed his hat over his head, snorted the putrid stench from his nose, and spat. He pulled a handkerchief from his pocket and daubed his mouth. It wasn't long before Harrison was beside him, moving so silently Milo didn't notice his presence until he spoke.

"Tell me how to get to where the body was discovered."

Milo looked at the taller man whose back was to him as he looked toward the docks. "I can take you there."

Harrison turned and faced the nervous man. "Thank you, but I need to be alone for this part. Just point me in the direction and I'll be on my way."

Milo, although hesitant, agreed. The foul scene of the carnage was another place he did not care to revisit. He retrieved a small field pad from his coat pocket and drew a crude map and then gave verbal directions and landmarks.

"When you return, you will tell me what you learned? You know something, yes?"

"I have my suspicions, but I must be certain."

"Of course, of course."

After Milo left him, Harrison started off in the direction of the woods near the coast. When he left the road and angled across the rocky field, he sensed he was being trailed. He picked up his pace slightly, though he gave no indication to his followers that he was aware of their presence. He entered the woods moments later, where the slain bodies of the children were found over half a year, spread out but all within a quarter-mile stretch along the eastern shore.

The woods provided cover from his followers, and Harrison moved quickly through the trees, faster than the human eye could track, and hid among a thick copse of wild fern. He peered through the foliage, his calm eyes tracking the sound of their steps. After a few moments, Milo's children emerged from the tree line and stopped after several paces.

"Where did he go?" Adonia whispered. Her blue eyes were wide, and she wrung her small hands in front of her, while Bastion stood silent, his eyes darting, scanning the wood for movement. "Has he disappeared?"

"Don't be stupid. A man can't disappear."

Adonia's lips pouted, but she said nothing. Bastion could often be cruel with his words, and she didn't want to anger him when he was already clearly frustrated.

"He's out there. He has to be."

"Maybe he knew we were following."

Bastion glared at his sister. "Heard you trampling around like a bull probably."

"I heard you both, long before the woods," Harrison spoke from behind them.

Adonia yelped, and Bastion spun and took two quick steps back in surprise. He recovered well, and the panicked look upon his face fell away quickly, replaced by a scowl.

"You are cruel for scaring my sister like that," Bastion snarled.

"Why are you following me?"

The boy looked away and gave no answer. Adonia came forward now, no longer pouty. Instead, her eyes lit up at the sight of Harrison, and he could tell by the way she looked him over that she was smitten with him. He was tall and handsome, and looked like a man of twenty, though he was centuries old. Women were often smitten with him, though the way the girl of but eight looked at him made him uncomfortable.

"Why have you come to this foul place?" Adonia asked and wrinkled her nose.

"That is my business and none of yours."

"Have you found something?"

"You two must go. Now. This is no place for children."

"Let's go," Bastion said, taking his sister's hand. "He is right. We shouldn't be in the wood. This place is dangerous."

"But we're with Mr. Harrison. He won't allow harm to come to us."

The boy fell silent as his gaze drifted to the woods beyond, his attention drawn to something. When he noticed Harrison looking at him, he quickly became anxious.

"We must leave now, Adonia, and let this man do his work."

Adonia stood her ground for a moment but relented when she saw Bastion's brow furrow and lips purse. She allowed her brother to lead her from the offensive place. Harrison watched them with careful eyes until they exited the tree line, and the boy looked back over his shoulder one last time.

Harrison remained rooted until he was certain they'd reached the road. He breathed deeply of the woods and caught the faint scent of blood, of decaying death. He moved with purpose, following his senses deeper into the woods where he quickly located a massive dead tree, at least three foot in circumference. At the base, a hole two feet high and one foot wide opened into the hollowed heartwood. Death was within, he was certain of it. On his knees, he peered inside, his green eyes seeing what no mortal man could in the dark. A hole within the earth beneath the tree. A burrow? A nest?

No, a lair.

He removed his coat, folded it, and set it beside the tree before placing his hat atop the waxed canvas garment. Without hesitation, Harrison entered the hollow. His broad shoulders made it a struggle for him to squeeze inside, but he managed to muscle through. The hole was slightly larger within, but still a tight fit for his frame. If the burrow narrowed further as it sloped into the earth, he would be unable to turn around, might even become trapped. The idea did not frighten him, though—he feared nothing and had not for a long time.

He forged ahead, using his powerful hands and arms to pull himself downward, and within minutes, he was within the beast's lair. The den was about six feet deep, wide, and high. A nest of some sort lay nearby, made from torn clothing, grass, and leaves. There were also bones, stripped of their flesh—they may have been human, but could be animal. The walls and ground were scarred by claw slashes. Harrison saw them, even though no light from the surface reached this place. He understood immediately this was where the beast retreated after it killed. Where it…recovered.

Harrison detected another scent—faint, and he almost missed it—but it was familiar, a scent from last night. He breathed in the aroma more deeply to be sure, but he was not mistaken. He sighed, saddened by what he discovered, but more by what he must do.

LATE AFTERNOON CAME, and Harrison waited until after lunch to excuse himself to take a smoke. He paused at the door long enough to make eye contact with Milo and beckoned him to follow with the motion of his head. He waited only a few moments in the yard before the mayor joined him, clutching nervously at his hands.

"What is it? What have you discovered?"

"You must impose a strict curfew this night. Everyone must remain indoors when the sun sets. It is imperative that no one must venture out, or they will risk certain death. Is that clear?"

Milo nodded, his frightened eyes never leaving Harrison's.

"You have found the beast?"

Harrison's eyes shifted down and to the left for a second, then he locked eyes with Milo. "Yes."

Milo's eyes narrowed, and he leaned in slightly. His lips pursed as though he wanted to say more, but before he could speak, Harrison said, "Go now with haste. Spread the word while light is still upon us. Make them understand the graveness of this…situation."

"Yes, of course." Milo took several steps before he stopped and turned. "What will you do now?"

"I must prepare. Go now, Milo."

THE SUN BEGAN to fade, hanging a fiery yellow-orange-red hue over the horizon. In a few hours, Harrison would find the beast that preyed upon this town, and he would put an end to the horror. Of this he had no doubt. The apprehension he felt gnawing at his belly was…what? Guilt? Melancholy? No. He was heartless and cold and incapable of feeling human emotions. He had learned to emulate emotion, yes, as camouflage among men and women with beating hearts and warm blood in their veins.

But that was not entirely true. Not any longer. Not since he'd met a man name Morris Meridian in France during the war. Morris had shown Harrison true compassion in the face of hatred. Meeting Morris had changed Harrison at his very core, igniting the short wick of humanity buried deep within, which had been snuffed out by centuries of mindless bloodlust and the loneliness of immortality. It was because of Morris' compassionate plea that Harrison allowed the German soldiers dignity in death, even after they shot his body full of holes just moments before. Those pleas now warmed Harrison's belly and restored his faith in man, setting him upon the path of protecting them against the evil supernatural beings bent on rendering human flesh.

After setting Milo off to declare strict curfew on this night of the full moon, Harrison stalked the woods where the beast dug its lair within the cool earth. Soon, he found himself clawing down into the cavity and sitting in the dark silence, hoping to set his mind at peace with what he knew must be done this night. A night where the moon was full and high in the sky, and the beast exuviated its human form and set out in search of flesh and warm blood to satisfy its primal compulsion. But peace eluded him, and thoughts of violence overtook him, as in his mind he slayed the beast over and over in a ruthless and bloody fashion.

Taking the creature's life would be easy—physically, though not mentally. Harrison had the advantage of centuries of experience born in battles across many lands and against many enemies, both natural and supernatural. He possessed combat skills learned from many people and cultures at his employ. He had the benefit of strength, agility, and immortality that the fledgling beast lacked. He would defeat the young creature with little effort...which made him feel this was but for sport, the thrill of the hunt. He knew in his heart, though, that was false. He would take a life to save lives. Even so, the truth would not quell the conflict that filled him.

BASTION SAT UPON his bed, a book opened on his lap, though he was not reading. His thoughts were distracted by the arrival of the stranger the previous night. He knew why his father had called upon such a man, and he expected a man who fought beasts to instill fear in any with whom he crossed paths. But the sense of blind urgency to flee that overcame Bastion whenever he was near the beast hunter unnerved him, because he didn't understand those heightened emotions.

The sound of the rope swing groaning against the tree bough ceased. Though he hadn't noticed the sound when he was deep in thought, the sudden cessation of the monotonous resonance registered. He closed the book and set it on his bed before crossing the room to the window where he spied the beast hunter engaging Adonia in deep conversation. The way his sister looked at the man with such adoration made his belly churn with bitter jealousy, which ignited quickly to molten rage.

Bastion did not know why he felt as he did, but he understood that if he allowed the fury to overwhelm him, he would lose control of himself. He didn't think that he would harm anyone, but the thought that he might in a fit of blind wrath enact violence terrified him. He had always been a kind and caring boy. . .

He returned to his bed and picked up the book. It trembled in his hands—whether from rage or terror he could not decide—and he dropped the tome as though it were hot. He clasped his hands tightly, trying to control them before finally burying them under his thighs. He closed his eyes and focused on his breathing to control his emotions. Several minutes passed before he heard Adonia's soft steps on the risers before moving across the floor to her room.

Bastion smothered the immediate desire to race to her room and confront her for fear his tenuous grasp over his emotions would loosen and the rage would again overwhelm and spill forth. He willed himself to remain on the bed with his eyes closed until his breathing evened out and his hands no longer trembled. A moment later, he stood at the entrance to her room. She sat by her window, unaware of his presence until he cleared his throat.

"Bastion, you startled me."

He remained at the threshold, afraid to get close to her. "What did he want with you?"

Adonia stares at him blankly. "What did who want with me?"

Bastion took two quick steps into the room, then stopped abruptly. He clenched his fists at his sides, nails digging into his palms. He swallowed hard.

"The stranger. He spoke with you. I saw from my window."

"He's not a stranger," Adonia quipped. "His name is Harrison."

"What did he want with you?"

"Nothing."

Bastion stomped his foot. "Tell me."

Adonia's eyes widened at her brother's anger. "He…"

"Out with it."

The girl's eyes shifted back and forth as though trying to remember. Finally, she said, "He said my dolly was pretty and I asked him to play tea party."

Bastion's eyes slitted with suspicion. "He told you something…something…important. What did he tell you?"

Adonia shook her head and her face wrinkled with confusion. "He didn't say anything except that my dolly was pretty."

"You're lying!"

"I am not!" Adonia stood and stomped past her brother.

He gripped her arm, halting her. "Did he tell you something about me?"

"Get your hand off me or I'll tell Mother!"

Bastion held his grip for a few seconds before finally releasing his sister. She stormed out of the room, her feet rapidly carting her down the risers. A moment later, he heard the door slam when she exited the house. Bastion remained rooted, concern and suspicion in his eyes. Unconsciously he stroked the Saint Christopher pendant he wore around his neck as he wondered what the stranger wanted with Adonia.

LONG AFTER EVERYONE was asleep, Harrison went to the barn and found what he'd asked the girl to leave for him. He'd used his glamour—the first time he'd used the hypnotic ability on a child, thought he felt it as necessary—and wiped any remnant of their true conversation in the yard from memory. He hesitated before locking eyes with her and only proceeded when he sensed the boy watching them from his room. He suspected the boy would question her. If Bastion did interrogate her, Adonia would only remember Harrison complementing her doll and politely declining to play tea party.

He made his way casually into town, carrying with him the blanket with Adonia's scent. He allowed the blanket to drag along the cobblestone roads while he worked his way through the center of town. The houses were dark and the streets empty. After a while, he crossed over the barren land and trekked his way to the woods where the torn and mangled bodies were previously discovered.

Harrison worked his way through the brush and trees and after only several yards, he sat cross-legged on the ground and wrapped the girl's blanket over his shoulders and head, so that the girl's scent was upon him. The full moon hung high above the canopy, keeping the shadows at bay, but no doubt beaconing forth the changeling like the pied piper of Hamelin, leading the beast to him and certain death.

He closed his eyes and slowed his breathing to ten breaths per minute. He opened his senses fully, his nostrils flaring with each inhale, waiting to catch the scent of the beast on the light breeze. He listened intently for any sound that would betray the creature as it honed in on Adonia's essence. He didn't wait long. He picked up the smell first, both familiar and yet not, and he instantly knew that his suspicions had been realized. Accompanied by the quick snapping of twigs and crunch of dead leaves, the beast abandoned stealth and came fast and hard.

Harrison held his ground, though the hair on the back of his neck stood on end like antennae receiving and processing information, screaming that danger was fast upon him. He remained motionless until the last second, when he knew the Lycan was in mid-attack, rolled to his left, and in the blink of an eye was on his feet. The young werewolf slammed against the cold ground, its claws flailing and gouging earth with awkward fury. Before the creature even understood its prey had disappeared, Harrison struck, moving so quickly he was but a blur. The were-beast noticed something at his peripheral and started to turn its muzzle, but Harrison's fist hammered the beast, fracturing its jaw and sending it sprawling several yards through the air.

The Lycan made a pitiful yelp as its body came to a jolting halt against a gnarled and twisted olive tree. The werewolf struggled to get on its feet but staggered and went down, favoring its left shoulder. The creature tried again as Harrison walked toward it, and was successful. It reared up slowly to its full height of six feet, raised its muzzle skyward, and howled, a rageful sound that no doubt struck fear into the hearts of the Karavostasi citizens who woke in terror but had no effect on Harrison.

The beast fell silent and fixed its yellow eyes on the vampire. Its lips curled back tightly against its teeth, a warning to its foe. Harrison only sensed deep fear in the creature, for it had never faced an enemy more powerful in its young life. It growled deeply as Harrison continued to approach, and when it realized the vampire could not be backed down, it fell back on its haunches and sprung from its powerful hindquarters, launching at the enemy.

The wolf's attack was aggressive and instinctual but completely thoughtless. The changeling was young and inexperienced, and Harrison would soon teach it a deadly lesson. The creature arced through the air, its claws and teeth bared, its belly exposed. Harrison launched himself into the air with both arms and fists extended, driving them like hammers into the wolf's chest. He felt bone crunch and flesh tear and his fists cut like knifes through the thick fur and hide, collapsing one of the wretch's lungs when he slammed the limp canid to the ground.

The young changeling whined and whimpered, the pain of the severe wounds no doubt horrific. Harrison kneeled beside the werewolf—his emotions suddenly overwhelming him—wanting to comfort the wretch. He touched the coarse fur of its head and stroked the suffering creature. With great effort, it turned its frightened face to look away, as though it could not bear the sight of the vampire.

"You shall not suffer long, little one," Harrison said as he stroked the beast.

It lay whimpering and shivering for a few moments before, without warning, the creature suddenly slashed at Harrison, ripping its claws across his chest, then kicking him backward with its powerful haunches. Harrison pushed himself up slowly, first to one knee and then to his feet. As he watched, the changeling struggled onto all fours and loped off lamely into the brush, moving deeper into the woods.

Harrison did not immediately give chase, though he could have easily run the changeling down. He knew where the dying Lycan was headed. He walked slowly after it, hoping it would succumb to its wounds before he found it, to spare him from having to look into its pathetic eyes when he delivered the final deathblow.

He tracked it through the brush to its lair and followed it deep into the earth where he found it curled among the rags and bones. Its yellow eyes watched him in terror, and it panted fast and heavy, its shattered ribs rising and falling as it laid dying.

"Sorry little one. This was not your fault."

One of the creature's eyes rolled toward Harrison. It reached out to him with a clawed hand, and Harrison took it, holding it between his hands.

"You're not alone. Go in peace now, young friend."

The young wolf hitched one last breath, and its mangled chest rose, fell and was still. As Harrison watched, the Lycan morphed to its young human form. Harrison gently crossed the boy's arms across his naked body. After a moment, he closed both of Bastion's eyes. He sat with the corpse for several minutes before he inspected the boy's body. Gently, he rolled the boy over and found the puckered scar of four ragged claw slashes that started at the top of the clavicle and angled down to the center of his back.

The alpha that turned this boy into a beast must have left the island after siring the boy, for Harrison detected no scent of another. And the carnage left behind had an alpha remained would have been tenfold.

Why the alpha wolf had come here, why he had chosen the boy, and why he'd abandoned his progeny were mysteries that would never be answered.

As dawn approached, Harrison drug the boy from his lair, then carried him to a clearing near the rocky shoreline, where he built a pyre from fallen olive branches. He laid Bastion's body upon it and set it ablaze, watching in silence as the boy turned to ash and was returned to nature.

Later, before the sun rose, Harrison quietly snuck into Adonia's room. He watched her sleep for a few moments. Within hours, she would learn that her bother was missing and he would be assumed to be the victim of the beast of Karavostasi. Harrison became melancholy, longing for his own death but knowing he was cursed to walk the world for ages. From his pocket he retrieved what dangled from the wolf-boy's neck. He placed the St. Christopher medal upon the girl's pillow and then slipped away into what remained of the darkness.

As morning dawned, Harrison boarded the first fishing vessel he came to. Soon, he was again at sea, future destination unknown.

Author's Note

Frederick Harrison first appeared in my novella, *The Mortality of Morris Meridian* (fear not, no spoilers here). Harrison quickly became a favorite of readers, and I was asked by many to continue his saga in future works.

This story, "Bad Moon Rising," is the first in what will hopefully become a series of stories and/or novellas that will focus on Harrison's adventures between 1944 (when Harrison first meets Morris Meridian) and the present time (when he last meets his old friend.) There are a lot of tales to tell over the nearly eighty-year timespan.

If you've read *The Mortality of Morris Meridian*, you understand the profound impact that Morris had on Harrison and why Harrison chose the path implied in this short work. If you haven't already read the novella, I encourage you to do so. It appears in the anthology *If I Die Before I Wake Volume 4 – Tales of Nightmare Creatures* by Sinister Smile Press. Although "Bad Moon Rising" stands on its own as a short story, *The Mortality of Morris Meridian* provides you with deeper insight into Harrison's backstory and reveals how his faith in humanity was restored after centuries of distrust and hate for man.

I don't know when we will next read about the exploits of Frederick Harrison, or where his next story will take us, but I do know that I have some glorious journeys planned for him, and I hope you will all come along for the ride.

JOHNNY'S GOT A GUN

Curtis A. Bass

T HE RATTLE STARTLED ME AS I walked past the open door to Mom and Dad's bedroom. It was the sound of a phone vibrating on a wooden surface. A faint glow across the room, on top of Dad's bureau caught my attention. A cell phone was receiving a text. My cell phone. The one they confiscated, along with grounding me, for staying out too late one night last week. One night. What's the big deal about that?

Seeing the coast was clear, I ducked in the room to check the message.

Benjie: Prowl 2nite

I knew the message wasn't from Benjie, but from Digges, using Benjie's phone. He can't afford his own. I tapped in a quick "I'm in" and erased the message. No sense in snooping adults reading my personal messages. I was so ready for a prowl. We usually reserved them for weekends, but today was special. It was Halloween, and I expected Digges had something cool in mind. No matter that it was Wednesday. It wasn't like I had to worry about school tomorrow, given what had happened.

Digges and Benjie were my "hoodlum" friends, as Dad called them, and the reason I was grounded. Yeah, Digges had a record and Benjie is just a doofus hanger on, but they treated me nice. Better than anyone else in my stuck-up school. Except Tyler, but that's done. I tried not to think about that. Dad says fifteen-year-old boys don't cry.

MOM AND DAD went to bed at ten thirty and the house settled into the quiet of night. About eleven, I eased out the window of my bedroom. God bless ranch houses. I had on my long johns, a thermal T-shirt, sweater, thick leather jacket, and knit cap. It was cold as a bitch out, but that's October in Massachusetts for ya. I met up with Digges and Benjie at the all-night 7-11 a quarter mile from my house. I spotted them a block away, two figures loitering in the parking lot under the streetlight. Benjie was taller but slighter than Digges, who was wiry but solid, earned from his hard-scrabble life. Benjie was gangly and fidgeted constantly, reminding me of junkies I'd seen. I bumped fists with Digges and then Benjie when I got there. Digges had on a knit cap like me. Benjie was without a hat, his colorless, lank hair hanging around his face.

Our "prowls" were mostly roaming around. We'd sometimes break into abandoned buildings or factories. Nothing major, but it relieved the monotony.

"It's the witching hour, boys," Digges said. "Midnight on Halloween, restless spirits and ghosts can move back and forth between Hell and earth."

Benjie giggled, but there was a nervous edge to it.

"Let's go," Digges ordered.

"Where we going?" I asked.

"You'll see." That was all I could get out of him. As we continued, I began to get a sinking feeling. There was a hollowness in the pit of my stomach. We were nearing the school.

"We're not supposed to go to the school, Digges. They said it's a crime scene. It's got police tape all around it. We might get arrested or something."

"Don't get your panties in a wad. The CSI guys have been all over this place since Monday. If there were any clues, I'm sure they found 'em. It ain't like they don't know who did it. And there ain't nobody standing guard over it at night. I just want to take a look-see. If there's any restless spirits out tonight, that'll be the place. Don't you want to see all the bloody floors and walls? All the bullet holes in the blackboards? I know I do."

"Me, too." Benjie giggled in a higher pitch, now tinged with fear.

"I know you do, you fuckin' psycho," Digges said to him, derision in his voice. Benjie was unrepentant and giggled some more. I looked down, not wanting to be singled out as scared.

"How are we getting in?" I asked.

"I know a window where the lock's been busted for a few years. I guess you just can't get decent maintenance men no more." Digges growled out a soft laugh.

WE FOUND DIGGES' malfunctioning window behind the school in a dark bend in the architecture. With practiced ease, as if he'd done this a thousand times, Digges pulled an unused old crate over to give himself a boost. He hoisted himself up to the window ledge and balanced while pushing the window open. Then he was in. He had barely cleared the sill when Benjie scrambled up after him. I didn't like the idea at all. I was afraid we'd get in trouble. But I didn't want to look like a pussy. So I climbed up and struggled through the window. I overbalanced going in and landed on my ass. Digges and Benjie howled with laughter at me.

It was much warmer inside since they keep the heat turned on all winter. It was dim, though. The soft glow of the emergency exit lamps and the ambient glow coming in the windows from outside was the only light. It was an overcast night with no star or moonlight. The school was in a residential section with no overnight business lighting, only a few lampposts on the school grounds. There was a coppery smell in the air, with a hint of dead things beneath it.

"What's that fucking stink?" asked Benjie.

"You idiot. That's the smell of blood, shit, and piss decomposing. They ain't got around to cleaning it up yet. This is just like it was a minute after Jenkins stopped shooting," Digges told us. He looked about as if he was fascinated.

"You were in school Monday, weren't you?" I asked Digges. I'd been home with a fever. It probably saved my life.

"Yeah. Come on. I'll show ya."

We exited the classroom. It was darker in the hallways without windows, just the reddish cast of the emergency exit lights. We crept down a hallway toward the north end.

"He began up here. Classes were changing so the halls were full of people. Yeah, the bastard was goin' for the maximum kill. I wasn't but about twenty, thirty feet from him when he started. You always hear people say they thought it was firecrackers or a backfiring car. Where I come from, I knew in a flash it was gunfire. Bam! Bam!" Benjie and I jumped at Digges' outburst.

"I spun around and made eye contact with Johnny. We ain't never been friends, but he ain't never crossed me, either. He just looked at me for a second. He had a big grin on his face, but his eyes were wide and it looked like wasn't nobody home. Johnny was gone. I dived behind a trashcan, but I think I was safe anyway. He coulda killed me, but he didn't. I been thinking about it ever since. He coulda shot me right then. But he stopped, looked at me, and moved on. Why? I really wish I knew." Benjie's mouth dropped open as he hung on Digges' every word.

"Whoa," he murmured. I was kinda creeped out by his story. We knew Johnny. He was an ass, but to do something like this? And to be standing there while Digges narrated what happened just seemed wrong. I looked around the hall, wondering if evil was a physical thing or left a stain. That thought made the hairs stand up on the back of my neck, and I sidled a little closer to Benjie.

"He came on down this way," Digges continued, walking down the hall. "Most of the people had cleared the halls by then. I was watching from behind my trashcan. He shot some of the wounded who were still in the hall. I seen this one girl, Misty, who was on the floor wounded. She turned her head and looked at him. He put the gun right in her face and pulled the trigger. Her head busted like a cantaloupe." I shuddered at that thought. Misty was a sweet girl who never said anything bad about people. She had said she'd save a dance for me at the Halloween dance. The one that was supposed to be tonight, but now cancelled. Why would he do something like that to her? How did he become such a monster?

"Most of the classrooms have locking doors," Digges said. "That's what saved people's asses. Before he could blow the lock off, they'd busted out the windows and were gone. He found a few more people, but after the big start, he mostly just shot up the place. I bet it pissed him off. He was loaded for bear but only killed ten people. I saw him go in and out of several classrooms. I don't know if he killed anybody there or was just shooting off. There was wounded kids all over the place, and now the shock of what happened wore off, they started screaming and moaning and shit. I think that was scarier than him shooting."

I imagined the awful moment when the initial shock wore off and the screaming began, and I shivered involuntarily. God, that was so sick. Benjie was just eating it up with that stupid grin still on his face. Our friends were dead, and Digges was making it into a side show.

"Once he was done with the classrooms, he came back to finish off the wounded. But instead, he suddenly come running down the hall back toward me, turning and firing behind him every couple a steps. I seen some guys coming through the gun smoke with rifles with laser aims. One of 'em took him down with a head shot. Then everybody got in on it. I bet that guy had a dozen bullets in him by the time they stopped." Digges paused, his breath coming quicker. I could see in the dim light that he was lost in the past, reliving the moment. Maybe even enjoying it. I was afraid I was going to throw up.

"Dude," Benjie said reverently, clearly impressed. "I didn't see nothing. I was outside when it started."

We had been making our way slowly down the hallway as Digges talked.

"There were several students dead right here," he said, stopping. In the dim light I could just make out the floor was discolored, and I suddenly did a little dance step trying to get out of it.

"It's dried now. Ain't gonna mess up your sneaks," Digges told us.

I still didn't want to be standing in folks' blood, dried or not. A fly buzzed my ear, and I slapped it away.

As we walked farther along the hall, I detected more and more discolored places on the floor and even the walls. The stench was worse in some places, and I was closer than ever to hurling.

"Folks ain't nothing but a bag of blood. Poke a hole and blood goes everywhere," Digges said, as if he were philosophizing. I swiped at another fly buzzing my ear. A drop of sweat ran down my forehead, so I pulled off my knit cap and stuck it in my pocket. As I reached up to smooth down my short hair, I felt a faint breeze lift the hair at the nape of my neck. Someone whispered something behind me. I spun around but only saw the dim hallway. Something touched my ear. I swatted again.

"What's wrong with you?" Digges looked at me, annoyed.

"A fly keeps landing on me."

"It's freaking October. Ain't no flies."

"Well, something touched me, and I thought I heard something."

Digges laughed with delight. "Yeah, the ghosts of all the dead students have come to get ya, Chad. It's the witching hour."

"Don't, Digges. I'm scared of ghosts," Benjie murmured, as if embarrassed to admit it.

"You pussies. I show you some of the coolest crap in town and you're scared of ghosts? I gotta find me some new friends."

"I ain't scared, Digges. Not really. It's just Chad's trying to spook me and it's dark." Benjie placed the blame on me, and I didn't even want to be here.

Johnny's got a gun. I heard the whisper behind me. At least I thought I did. But when I looked, wasn't anybody there.

"Digges, was that you?" I asked.

"Me, what?"

"I thought I heard you say, 'Johnny's got a gun.'"

"I heard it was a big freakin' gun, but I didn't say nothing. Why would I do that?" Something crawled over my ear. I jumped, swatting at it. *Johnnyjohnnyjohnny.*

"Something's on me! And there it is again. Can't you hear it?" I was dancing a jig trying to get the insect or whatever it was off me.

"I don't hear nothing," Digges said, but he did a quick glance in both directions.

"I don't like this, Digges," Benjie said, nervousness growing in his voice. "Let's go."

"Pussies," Digges spat at us. "Let me show you this." We walked on toward the south end. He stopped at a large stain.

"I figured it out from the video on TV. This is where Jennifer Kellar bled out. Fuckin' shame. She had one fine ass." I remembered that from the news report. She was one of the prettiest girls in school. Her boyfriend was on top of her trying to protect her, and the bullets went right through him. I always choked up when I thought about that.

Somebody help me!

Benjie jumped as if touched by an electric wire. "I heard somebody whispering in my ear!" He backed violently into a locker, making a loud *clang* that echoed down the empty hall. "Which one of you is fucking with me?"

"Cut the crap, Ben," Digges warned. I stumbled into Digges.

"What the fuck, Chad?"

"I got pushed."

"Ain't nobody there to push you. You trying to cop a feel?"

"We need to get outta here," Benjie gasped, totally spooked. "Shit, something touched me."

"You're scaring yourselves like a bunch of old women."

Hn, hn, hnnn. I couldn't tell if that snickering was in my head or not. Benjie must have heard it, because he yelped and bolted. The first classroom door he tried was locked. He dashed toward a second door, but Digges caught up and grabbed him.

"Don't freak out on me," he commanded. Benjie yanked open the door.

"I can't stand this dark. Lemme turn on a light." He palmed the classroom light switch. There was a brilliant flash during which I got a momentary sight of every blood vessel in my eye. Benjie's yelp was cut short, and we were plunged into a deeper darkness. Within the dark I saw a pulsing purple blob in front of my eyes.

"What the hell?" I shouted.

"We must have blown a fuse," Digges said. At least one of us was still calm. The purple blob slowly faded. It was totally black now in the classroom. The windows, mostly boarded up, were only fainter black against funereal black.

"Benjie. You okay?" No answer. "Hey, Benj. Can you answer?" Still nothing. "The shock mighta knocked him out." Digges sounded worried.

"He fell right here," I said, fumbling for the doorjamb in the dark. I couldn't see Digges. He bumped into me, then grabbed my arm. I was glad for the human contact. It was eerie in the darkened school. I felt more and more that evil might be an actual thing, lurking in this hallway.

"We need light. Ain't you got your cell phone?" he asked.

"No. Dad took it. Benjie's probably got his. If we can find him."

"We need to stick together," he breathed in my ear. "Benjie must be on the floor near here. You feel around the left, I'll take right." We both got on our knees and started sweeping motions with our hands. After a few minutes, Digges called from several feet away. "Anything?"

"Nothing."

"Okay, turn and start toward me." After a few minutes, my sweeping hand found Digges' sweeping hand.

"Well, hell. Where is he?" Holding my wrist, he stood up. I joined him, and we crept forward. The doorway was just a bit darker black than the surrounding black. We stepped into the hall.

"Benjie-jie-jie!" he yelled, the sound echoing down the eerie black void of the hall.

"That's weird. Why's it echoing so much?" I asked.

"Empty places in the dark? I don't know."

Hn, hn, hnnn.

"Digges, did you do that?"

"Nah. I bet it was Benjie makin' voices to scare us." I wasn't so sure. It didn't sound like Benjie. In fact, it didn't sound like a voice at all. If Digges hadn't said he heard it, I would have sworn it was inside my head.

Hn, hn, hnnn, kill you all.

That was totally inside my head. Until Digges yelled.

"Stop fuckin' around, Benjie. Come on, Chad. We're leaving." A sudden burst of gunfire rent the air. Digges dropped, pulling me with him.

"Jesus Christ! Who's shooting?" I squeaked. Then there was a deadly quiet.

Johnny's got a gun.

Somebody help us.

Hn, hn, hnnn. Kill you all.

"We need to get outta here, fast," Digges hissed into my ear.

"We can't leave Benjie."

"We don't know where he is. He probably hightailed it outta here when the lights went."

We got up and fast walked down the hall, our hands on the lockers, looking for the first open classroom. Another burst of gunfire sounded, accompanied by frantic screaming.

"Oh, shit. It sounded just like that," Digges groaned. We had stopped, pressed up against the lockers. A light breeze slipped by. I could smell gunpowder. And a thicker coppery odor that must be blood. What the hell was happening? We slipped along, our backs to the lockers, until we found a door, but it was locked. We moved across the hall to check the opposing classroom. Digges' feet went out from under him. He pulled me down as he fell. The floor was slick with wet slime. What the hell? I raised my hand to my nose. It smelled of blood.

"Shit, there's wet blood all over the place," Digges yelled. His composure was failing. Mine was pretty much gone. My brain kept screaming over and over "I gotta get out a here." That frantic mantra was nearly drowned by the thundering of blood in my ears. I felt my heart might burst as it jackhammered in my chest. We scrambled to the wall and found another door, but again, it was locked. I jiggled it frantically as if extra tugging might magically make it open.

Johnny's got a gun.

Somebody help us!

Helphelphelp!

Ohgod ohgod ohgod!

Gonna kill you all!

I'm scared. Somebody help me!

I'm afraid. Don't leave me!

I clamped my wet hands over my ears, but the sound was in my head. I could smell the fresh blood as it smeared my face. I wanted to scream but could barely catch my breath. Digges grabbed one of my hands, and we went running down the center of the hall, slipping and sliding. Just as we began, an awful pain slammed into my back. I went crashing face first to the ground, skidding forward in the slime. Was that how it felt getting shot in the back?

Hn, hn, hnnn. Kill you all.

You need to die. I hate you all.

I pushed myself up realizing I'd lost Digges' hand.

"Digges," I called. "Digges, where are you?" The blackness was pressing in on me, and I was hyperventilating in full panic. I pressed up against a locker, not knowing what to do other than keep moving. My teeth were chattering even though it wasn't cold in the school, and my speeding breath was causing shallow moans. I edged down the hallway, seeking the next classroom. Looking back up from where I'd come, I saw faint, ethereal images: people lying on the floor, a boy on a girl as if shielding her, a girl whose head was a shapeless mess. The moans and screams were coming from them. Tears flooded my eyes. Then, closest to me, I saw a boy on the floor. A boy whose feet had outgrown his body and with long, floppy black hair and wide, sightless eyes. It was Tyler, my best friend.

"Oh no. Oh, Tyler. No, no. If I'd been here, I would have been standing right beside you when this happened. I'm sorry." I wasn't sure what I was sorry about, but it felt wrong that he died alone. The image faded into nothingness. With a short scream, I turned to run and bumped into someone hard enough to make them grunt.

"Thank goodness, Digges." He didn't answer.

"Digges?" I felt up his arm to his head. Digges had short wiry hair. I felt longer, oily hair. Benjie.

"Oh, Benjie. We didn't know what happened to you."

"Johnny's got a gun, Chad. He hates you. You need to die." He clamped both hands around my throat, squeezing. I broke his hold and shoved him hard, skittering away, hoping he couldn't find me in the dark.

"Hn, hn, hnnn. Chad. You're going to die. Johnny's got a gun. Gonna kill us all," Benjie crooned like it was a psychotic nursery rhyme. I continued to put as much distance between me and him as I could.

I was nearing another door when I felt an explosion of pain in my abdomen. I went down, again. I felt a body on top of me. I wanted to struggle, slip away, but I couldn't move. I heard, as if in an echo chamber, *"Come on, buddy, we gotta hide. Gotta get away. Come on."* Then it was gone. There was no one on me.

Hide!

We gotta hide!

Johnny's got a gun gotta gun gotta gun gotta gun. JohnnyJohnnyJohnny.

Kill you all.

I scrambled up and immediately felt an explosion in my head, followed by piercing pains all over my body. I went down screaming.

Gotta gun gotta gun.

Help help help!

I'm scared! Don't leave me!

I scrambled to the doorway beside me, using the knob to pull myself up. It was unlocked, thank God. I stumbled in and looked at the far wall. The black was interrupted by faint glimmers of gray slipping through boarded-up windows.

"Shit!" I muttered.

"Gonna kill you, Chad." That wasn't Benjie's voice, but it was probably him, coming from very nearby. I slammed the classroom door and locked it. I immediately heard him throw his weight against it.

"Let me in, Chad. Johnny's gotta gun. He's gonna kill us all. Let me in!"

"Nothin' doin'. Go away," I yelled, knowing it would do no good. I ran toward the windows, falling over desks. Damn, I was gonna be bruised tomorrow. If there was a tomorrow. Once at the windows, I tried to pull off the plywood cover. It wouldn't budge. A loud crash against the door and the breaking of glass came from behind me. Benjie must have used something like a fire extinguisher to break the window in the door. I renewed my efforts to pull off the plywood. One strip started to give. With a squeal like nails on a chalkboard, it gave way. I looked over my shoulder. With the small amount of light provided by removing the board from the window, I could see Benjie crawling through the door's window. I yanked frantically at the next board. It stubbornly refused to give. Benjie stood up in front of the door. In a frenzy of terror, I grabbed a nearby waste can and threw it at him. He batted it away.

"Hn, hn, hnnn. Gonna kill you all," he murmured, menace in his voice. Gunfire started up in the hallway again; people screamed.

Johnny's got a gun!

Help! Help! Hide!

Somebody help! I'm so afraid.

Don't leave me!

Johnny's gotta gungungungungungun.

Kill you allallallallallall.

"I hate you all," Benjie said. "Kill you all." With his eyes vacant, he lurched toward me. I jumped right, picked up a chair, and heaved it at him. He caught it but stumbled backward. I tried to dash around him, but there were too many desks in the way. I noticed a supply closet at the back of the room. I ran for it, snatching up a chair as I went. Benjie was quick. As he neared me, I swung the chair at him. Since he was already moving, the blow knocked him to the ground. I reversed direction and dashed out into the pitch-black hallway. I knew the south entrance had to be directly down the hall to my left.

Johnny's got a gun, Chad. Johnny's got a gun!

Gonna kill you all.

I put my left hand on the lockers and began running toward the door. I knew it would be locked, but I was out of options. After a few yards, some-thing grabbed me around my neck, yanking me to a stop. I screamed. Yeah, I screamed like a baby and tried to swat whatever was holding me.

"Jesus, Chad. Stop! It's me, Digges," the dark shadow said.

"Digges?"

"Yeah, damn, man. You fight like a girl."

"I found Benjie," I told him. "I think he's possessed or something." Digges didn't respond, but a chill crawled over me as his grip tightened.

"Yeah. It's what Johnny wants." His voice was flat, as if reading a card. "Johnny's got a gun, Chad. Gonna kill us all." I stood dumbfounded. In the moment before I could react, he slid his arm around my neck and began squeezing. I scratched at his arm, trying to break free, but it was like a steel band.

"Gonna kill us all," he whispered in my ear, as if it were an endearment.

We both went flying sideways when another body crashed into us.

"Kill you all! Kill you all!" Benjie screeched. In the momentary pile up, I gasped in some much-needed air and bit down on Digges' arm. His salty blood flowed in my mouth a moment before he yanked his arm away. I scrambled away on my hands and knees, trying to get to my feet, but the floor was slick with blood. Tears and snot were running down my face mixing with the blood. So much blood. It was all over me. I stank of death. Stumbling to my feet, I ran a few yards before they went out from under me again and I slid along the slimy floor.

Johnny's got a gun. Gonna kill you all.

"You can't get out, Chad. Johnny's got a gun," Digges yelled.

"Oh, crap." I was crying harder now. "I just want to go home!" I whimpered. I ran again. A faint glimmer of light rose up before me and coalesced into the grinning face of Johnny Jenkins. "You're gonna die, Chad. You're all gonna die. Hn, hn, hnnn." He pointed his large handgun at me.

I skidded to a stop.

"Fuck you, Johnny! Fuck you. You're not even real. You're dead," I screamed at the apparition. I charged at him, determined to end this one way or another. He was as insubstantial as a patch of fog. When I passed through him, I only detected coldness and a sulfurous odor, like rotten eggs.

A loud rattling in front of me made me stop, but my feet slid out from under me, and I landed on my ass, in the stinking mess of blood.

A sudden flash, like a million suns going on at once, blinded me.

"What in hell do you kids think you're doing?" More lights. I froze. A group of men entered the hallway with flashlights. Policemen, guns drawn. The lead one was silhouetted by the lights of the men behind him. I could see he had one hand on his taser. I had never in my life been so glad to see policemen. I raised my hands and didn't move. There was a blur of action beside me.

"Kill you all!" Benjie shouted as he charged. The policeman fired his taser, and Benjie went down in a quivering mass. I didn't dare move.

"Come on over here, kid. I'm not gonna hurt you," one of the men said to me. I slowly lowered my hands and stood. I could see in the beam of his flashlight that my hands were no longer bloody, that my clothes had no bloodstains on them.

I told them that we were just looking around when the lights went out and we got spooked. Benjie was panicked and that was why he rushed them. What was I supposed to say? I didn't know what had happened.

"There's another one of us somewhere in the building. Digges."

"Vito Digges? Shoulda known that bad seed was involved. Kid's always in trouble." With a gentle whoosh, the emergency lights flashed on.

"We got that transformer fixed a half hour ago. Wonder why the power's just now going on?" the cop said, looking up at the lights. "A frozen limb fell on it. Knocked out lights all over this side of town. Once we got it back on, we got the alarm of intruders here in the school. If we hadn't been able to fix it, you could have had the whole night to roam around." I shuddered at the thought. We probably wouldn't have survived till morning.

"Let's get you and this guy down to the station for a checkup. We'll find your friend and bring him, too."

DAD AND MOM were none too happy to be called down to the police station in the middle of the night. I'm grounded "until further notice." Probably for the rest of my life.

After that night, I began having nightmares. Awful nightmares, every night. Mom took me to a counselor, and I eventually spilled my guts about what happened at the school that night. So I've been on Zoloft for a few weeks. Doctor Savage gave Mom some psychobabble. Let's see, it says on my official papers "depression, commonly known as survivor's guilt, stemming from a schizo-affective disorder manifesting in paranoia, feelings of guilt, auditory and visual hallucinations." I'm so drugged up all the time I feel like I'm underwater.

I've talked to Benjie. He doesn't remember hardly anything. He says we met up for a prowl and he woke up in a cot down at the police station.

So, nothing happened. That's the official story. I'm just a crazy, mixed-up kid. It was all in my head, right? Yeah, I call bullshit. Something totally messed up went down that night. I snuck out just after eleven and we slipped into school before midnight. We were in the school no more than thirty, maybe forty minutes. Then how come when the cops got us it was freaking three a.m.?

And if nothing happened, how come Digges is still in the state nut house rocking back and forth chanting "Johnny's got a gun"?

THE ROCK-HARD PLACE

David Rider

January 20

W E'RE STRANDED ON THIS DESOLATE, godforsaken rock. Half of our group are trying their best to deal with this situation and survive. The others are frightened and upset. And there's something here with us.

I was the one who discovered the corpses of its previous victims. I sensed the entity's noxious presence in the air. It materialized from the darkness and pursued me, amorphous and unknowable.

Some of the others refuse to believe me. They don't accept there *are* dead bodies. They're outright denying them—even though I told them where to see the evidence.

The only way we're going to survive is to pull together, but it hasn't been one day into this miserable mess and that seems an unachievable challenge.

The sun is setting. The group is afraid of what nightfall will bring. Considering our dire circumstances, it's difficult not to be scared. I intend to maintain reason and document what happens here. I'm making it my responsibility to warn others if we don't make it.

MY NAME IS Fiona Alva.

I'm one of the survivors of a boat crash on the reef surrounding this uncharted island.

We crashed because, as old as he is, the captain had little to no experience at his job, although he did a good job selling himself. The brochures looked professional. His motivation was money—collect the cash and take the tourists to explore the new island. To him we were suckers, rubes at his carnival. He came off as ignorant but didn't care, spouting nonsense over the P.A. system to make it appear like he knew what he was doing. He kept contradicting himself. "I've been bringing folks out here for four, five years..." Except everything I'd researched—and his own literature—said the island had only appeared three years ago. It's possible this was his first time at the helm of a boat this size.

I was standing near him in the cockpit when he announced, "I'm going to swing around from the east, so get your cameras ready."

I had literally *just* started to tell him, "You better slow down...volcanic islands are surrounded by dangerous reefs," when he drove into one.

The entire craft was jolted to starboard with a sickening crunch. Instant chaos ensued. My face was slammed into the bimini's support frame. Two passengers were thrown overboard to land on jagged coral inches below the water's surface, shrieking as their skin was punctured. Those of us still on the listing boat found ourselves dazed and bloodied, on our knees, having difficulty compensating for the angle at which the deck now slanted. My glasses had snapped at the bridge and the halves hung askew from my ears, the left lens irreparably shattered.

For the record, if anyone is responsible for putting us in this situation, it's the charter boat's captain. The entity I later encountered lurking in the cave may be more dangerous, but Captain Denault is the person who all but delivered us into its clutches.

HAVING SWUM THROUGH choppy waters alive with shark fins, the eight of us staggered onto the foreboding black beach.

Aside from sparse patches of vegetation here and there, this is a hard, rocky place. We knew beforehand this young island was a geological oddity. Exploring it was the whole reason I traveled to this region. The first lesson I learned was you can't prepare your mind for the bleakness of a beach composed of obsidian volcanic gravel. A few of my fellow tourists had lost their footwear in the crash. They cut their bare feet on sharp rocks reaching the beach. Having read the NASA study of Hunga Tonga-Hunga Ha'apai in the South Pacific—and that field team's experience getting such shards in their sandals—I'd worn jogging shoes.

Captain Denault surveyed the small beach. His demeanor alternated between bewilderment upon finding himself here and, conversely, thinking of himself as its conqueror. In the hours since the crash, he hasn't apologized or accepted blame for landing us in this predicament. Rather, the look in his dim eyes says, "I meant to do that...didn't I?"

Several individuals required medical attention. I'd completed advanced first-aid training courses during college, and set to work suturing and bandaging open wounds. As I went from one patient to the next, Denault paced around, observing me like an authority figure, saying, "Yes, very good, continue doing that." He wanted the others to believe he had assigned me emergency triage duties.

Not everyone was having it. A handful of people glared at Denault, openly resenting his assumption of leadership. Arguments ensued. He stood his ground, doubling down. The pompous man provoked ire and seemed to thrive on name-calling and belittling his opponents.

Disharmony isn't going to solve any of our problems, so I resolved to get away from the escalating hostilities. I washed my hands in the water, slid my first-aid kit in my pack, then wandered inland to assess our status.

The uphill trek was treacherous. Without laser-focus on your next step, spraining an ankle is a given. The volcanic cone is uneven and grooved with deep gullies carved by the lava flows responsible for birthing the island. I'm of medium height, and the ashen walls around me are taller than I am.

I wasn't alone. Scores of sooty terns nested in the rocks. Most scampered or fluttered away at my approach; some didn't. I made mental note of this— if a rescue isn't imminent, we'll need a food source. A major problem with that, of course, is there's no wood to build a fire. If eating raw chicken is unwise, I'll have to assume the same goes for seabirds. Catching fish is a smarter move.

I crested the dome and surveyed the comma-shaped island in its entirety. It was less than a mile long. We had come ashore in the inner curve, but on the other side I spotted the partially submerged wreckage of another yacht embedded in the surrounding reef. Someone else had been recently shipwrecked here.

I began my descent toward that side of the island, but the going was much steeper—leading to a sheer drop into the ocean. I walked diagonally to the far end where the slope was more gradual, and the area in which the other potential survivors would likely have come ashore.

That's when I came upon the cave.

If I thought the rocky terrain was black, it was nothing compared to the beckoning darkness inside the cavern's open, craggy maw. I stood before it, frozen with curiosity. Theoretically, I could take three paces and enter—but the connection between my brain and legs had short-circuited. I can't label it fear, per se, because I *wanted* to move closer. However, the entrance was so void of light that it looked like a naturally occurring Vantablack effect. This seemed an impossibility, as the sun's rays were angled directly inside. My arrested muscle memory convinced me I would walk face-first into a solid surface like a Road Runner cartoon.

After an indeterminate amount of time, my feet finally shuffled forward. I reached out with one hand, fingers outstretched, expecting to touch rock. They passed into shadow. Even more curious: the shadowy zone was not cool as one might expect—it was hot. Was this caused by the undersea volcano?

I stepped backward and removed my pack. It seemed a prudent move to leave my belongings behind so others in our party could surmise where I'd gone. I set my phone to airplane mode—no sense running down the batteries searching for a nonexistent signal—and stuck it inside the waterproof pouch with my field journal and other essentials. I fished out my penlight and clenched it between my teeth as I stripped off my outer shirt and tucked it into the backpack. Even in a one-piece and shorts, the heat might be intolerable. Since there was no telling what gases I might encounter, I took the extra precaution of removing the paisley bandanna from my hair and tying it over my nose and mouth.

The moment I stepped into the cavern, the intense heat engulfed me like a cocoon. Perspiration soaked through my suit within the first minute.

When (or if) I emerged, it wouldn't be as a butterfly—although I *would* likely lose several pounds of water weight.

I swiveled the light along the curved ground and tight walls as I ventured forward. It wasn't long before the ceiling dipped lower. Soon, I was crouching. And when I had to crawl under an overhang on my hands and knees, stinging sweat running into my eyes, I almost turned back. But despite the scrapes on my palms and kneecaps, I forged ahead, following the swirling ridges carved into the black tunnel.

The shaft opened into what might as well have been another realm. Although the air was still thin—and I wasn't getting much of it through the fabric—the temperature grew cooler. It made no sense. If anything, I had journeyed closer to the dormant volcano's central chamber.

I shined the beam around the pit's high ceiling, panned it across a far wall, then down to the ground. A foul odor assaulted my nostrils moments before the light revealed a horrific tableau: a carpet of desiccated human corpses lay strewn from one end to the other.

My heart leapt into my throat, forcing a gasp from my lips. It echoed through the cavern.

Something among the bodies heard me.

A presence reacted to the sound of my breath. It rose from its nest of cadavers and wheeled in my direction. Darker than its surroundings, it was a shape without features or form. Using the bodies as scale, it appeared to be larger than a grizzly bear. I sensed it studying me, registering me as an intruder in its lair.

What it was, I can't say. My glasses had broken when the boat crashed. Though I'm presently able to see through one lens in order to log this journal entry, I wasn't wearing it inside the cave.

The entity launched itself forward, almost gliding rather than striding, and closed the twelve-foot distance between us by half. I didn't want to let it get closer than that.

With no room to turn around, I pushed myself backward through the shaft, facing my attacker barreling toward me. As I frantically backpedaled, the penlight's jittery beam illuminated a shocking development: the behemoth was squeezing into the small opening to give chase. It moved closer in fits and starts, gaining on me. I know this because the ground in my wake was swallowed by its inky blackness. Moreover, the light revealed little of its nature. When my rear end bumped against the lowest part of the overhang

I'd first shimmied under, I knew I was almost free and clear. It also meant I'd have to sacrifice speed by flattening myself to get through this last obstacle. That's when my pursuer caught up to me.

Its roar—if it could be called that—blasted into my face like silent, icy wind. Having held my breath, I can't speak to its odor, but it *felt* toxic.

I cleared the tight space, got to my feet, and sprinted toward daylight. The thing unfolded itself from the fissure and loomed so large it filled the tunnel. In the moment before I exited the cave, I risked a final glimpse back and saw the dark entity had ceased its pursuit.

I dashed outside into the sun, pulled down my bandanna, and gulped the cool air like it was a refreshing beverage. I grabbed my pack on the fly and hurried back the way I'd come to tell the others.

A nagging thought occurred to me: if the thing in the cave was avoiding sunlight, what would stop it from coming out at night?

I'M STILL PONDERING that question now, as the pink sun sinks into the ocean.

When I returned to the group, Denault was waiting and pulled me aside. He saw my agitated state and listened to my account. He objected when I said the others needed to be warned. I told him we could be its next casualties if we didn't prepare. He said I had no proof and would only cause panic. It became clear he wasn't concerned about our well-being in the slightest. He cared about staying in control. There was no room in his narrative for a larger-than-life threat that he was ill-equipped to handle.

Fortunately, a few of the others overheard our discussion. They wanted to know everything. I stepped away from Denault—much to his obvious consternation—and reported every detail I recalled about the first victims in the cave. I said that they appeared Asian and had been turned into breathless husks. I explained my theory about the entity staying away from daylight. At that, their eyes flicked to the sun as they came to the same realization I had.

Three of us have set up camp around a large, circular pool located in the island's tail. We've passed around bottles of water and shared bites of energy bars. Denault and four others have hunkered down in the nearby twisted canyons of hardened magma. They are an anxious, fearful group, looking to their de facto leader for direction or affirmation yet receiving neither.

It's too dark to write more tonight.

January 21

AT DAWN, SOMEONE brought an unattended backpack to Captain Denault.

A man had gone missing.

No one saw him leave. His name is unknown. The others thought he was from Washington state. They suggested organizing a search party.

Denault proclaimed it a good idea and, while rummaging through the man's pack, added, "Let's do that."

I stepped forward to point out there's only one place he could be, and I knew the way.

His eyes narrowed when he asked, "What's your name, anyway?"

I told him.

He said, "Where are you from, Alva?"

I asked why it mattered. He didn't answer. Instead, he appraised the group and said, "Okay, we have a guide. Now I need a man to lead this expedition."

I scoffed at him, shouldered my bag, and began hiking uphill. Two volunteers from the pool group, a man and a woman, came after me. When I glanced back at Denault, he was studying us as he bit into an apple from the missing man's pack.

WHEN WE REACHED the cave, I recommended that one of them stay outside and the other come with me. That way, we could leave a witness behind if anything happened.

They agreed with my plan. Patel said he would accompany me. Duran said she would keep watch from just inside the opening and be ready to bolt.

Before we went in, I brought my companions up to speed on the gases associated with volcanic eruptions: sulfur dioxide and hydrogen halides. I told them the tunnel was on a slight upslope, so there weren't likely any carbon dioxide traps. I put on my bandanna and advised they do the same. As they tied their shirts over their mouths and noses, Duran asked if I was a geologist.

I said I wasn't and led the way into the cave.

IT WASN'T MY imagination.

I saw the look on Patel's face as the cave's darkness engulfed us. He was just as confused as I'd been at how it trapped light—and the manner in which my penlight's beam barely penetrated the gloom. He tapped his phone's screen, brightening the flashlight to maximum.

Duran poked her head in, pulled it quickly back out, and peeked back inside. She said, "What the hell?"

"I know, right?" I said.

We could only see a few yards ahead. Yesterday I'd walked fifty feet to reach the overhang I needed to crawl under. In this pitch blackness, knowing we were heading toward danger, every step felt too far.

Patel had started to remark about the oppressive heat, when we heard a sound that stopped us in our tracks: a low, raspy breathing. It filled our ears, amplified by the cavern's acoustics. We couldn't locate the source. There was only that noise from the dark—weak lungs pushing and pulling air, in and out, in a tortured, hellish struggle for life.

I overrode my instincts and crept forward, presently hearing another sound in tandem with the first...that of a body being dragged.

Patel saw it first but, upon witnessing an unexpected sight, would not walk closer. I continued forward several steps until my nearsightedness approximated Patel's better vision and could see what he had.

The missing person was lying on his back, fighting for oxygen, while being yanked backward across the ground the way one pulls a heavy garbage bag. Although the thing itself blended into shadows, its physical points of contact with the man appeared semi-transparent. The entity's fierce hold around the lower half of its victim's face and throat revealed his twisted lips fighting for air under its thick, smoky hand. He reached out for me, wide eyes pleading.

I scrambled forward without thinking, locking my fingers around his forearms as he seized mine. I found my footing and tried to haul him backward. The entity was inhumanly strong. Patel rushed to my side, grabbed the man's ankles, and pulled—while avoiding looking at the thing that held him fast. I didn't look, either; to do so would invite madness.

We lost ground. The entity wouldn't relinquish its prize. Upon reaching the overhang, it collapsed its size and backed into the crevasse, pulling the man after. Duran appeared next to me, having left her station, and snagged one of the man's arms in a vigorous grip. The three of us braced our feet against the rock in desperation, straining with all our strength.

In the end, the entity was too strong. It wrenched the man from our collective grasp. His imploring, frantic eyes were the last we saw of him before he was consumed by the darkness.

ONCE OUTSIDE THE cave, Duran and Patel collapsed on their backs, chests heaving as they took in fresh air. Their eyes were wide with confusion. I knew exactly what they were going through. They had questions no one could answer. They were frustrated. They wept for the man whose life we failed to save.

As we hiked downhill to report what we'd encountered, Patel, for the tenth time, asked aloud, "What the hell is that thing?" But this time, he met my gaze like his very sanity depended on an answer. I felt obliged to offer a theory, however sketchy it might sound.

"We're all here because we wanted to experience life. A new island has been born. Where years before there was open ocean, now there's land. We wanted to explore, and be among the first to walk its beaches and ponder its origins. Visiting seabirds are excreting seeds that bring flora, and soon, relatively speaking, a vibrant jungle. But we're here before all that happens, not long after a volcano erupted and conjured this miracle from the earth's core."

"Yeah, we get that," Duran said. "But what the hell *is* that thing?"

I eyed them. "Something that was born *with* the island. And now we're here to feed it."

No one spoke after that.

IF THERE'S A tactful way of explaining to already-frightened people that their doom is imminent, I'd like to know it. Not that we were putting it in those terms. We started by focusing on plain facts.

Denault didn't let us get far. He read our expressions, saw the dire direction in which our story was headed, and stopped us as we described the entity. "You're not making any sense. Are you listening to what you're saying? You should be ashamed of yourselves." He addressed the frightened faces behind him. "Can you believe these three? I mean, *look* at them."

The group's dynamic shifted. In that moment, two things happened in immediate succession.

The first was that Patel, Duran, and I became something other than fellow survivors of a crash. We were shunted into a different category, literally *the* **Different** category. This had been happening before the crash—of course it had—but now it became overt. Now I felt scrutinizing judgment from Denault's committee as surely as I felt the sun on my skin.

The second thing happened as a result of the first: their minds closed. I've read books on how men like Jim Jones or Marshall Applewhite substituted their version of reality for actual reality in the minds of their followers. Denault did it in less time, with less effort. Facts can be ignored if one's neural pathways are rerouted to reject objective truth. The problem with an avoidance of deeper analysis is that one becomes reactive without understanding. And when negative emotions fuel that state of being, ties to social mores become tenuous at best.

There wasn't a monster. It hadn't dragged a man into its cave. Had there ever even been a man?

Duran didn't like where this was headed. She pointed at Denault and said, "Hey, motherfucker, I'm from San Diego. I'm of Filipino descent, but I went to the same high school as my grandparents. Don't pull that shit!"

Denault turned to the others, raising his eyebrows in a "Gee, what did I say?" expression. But he didn't acknowledge her statement. He only smirked.

I put a hand on Duran's shoulder and stepped forward to face Denault. I told him we needed to stay united because the threat is real. I explained that the entity comes at night, and we have to assume it will be back. Its most direct path is down through the canyons where he and his group made camp.

He didn't accept that, therefore his people didn't.

It's approaching sundown again, and they're returning to their chosen nooks with fear tarnishing their faces.

Duran, Patel, and I have reconvened around the pool. It feels good to strategize. We've agreed to huddle together for warmth during the night. One of us will stay awake and keep watch while the others sleep. We've rationed our food, but there wasn't much in the first place. It will be gone by tomorrow. But Duran thought she saw fish in the water, meaning they're coming through underwater channels. We've decided to do some fishing in the morning. Our spirits are high. Constructive thought amongst allies fosters hope.

I'm writing this while staring across the open waters toward the eastern horizon. Last night at this time, I saw a light from a ship in the far distance. I wonder if we're near shipping lanes.

January 22

PATEL NUDGED US awake around midnight.

I disengaged from Duran's warmth, and the two of us looked in a direction Patel was pointing. I retrieved my spectacle-half from my breast pocket and settled it on my nose, squinting through the right lens.

Roughly one hundred and fifty yards away, silhouetted against the starry backdrop atop the volcanic dome, a woman was being dragged away by the bulky dark entity. It held her by the mouth and neck, pulling her uphill—kicking but not screaming—with the ease of a tall man tugging a small dog on a leash. The number of stars it blocked, compared to the woman's size, indicated it had grown larger. Its form seemed to constantly vary, one second appearing blob-shaped, then morphing into a tripedal beast with its next step.

A white shape stood up from a gulley. Denault. He was at the base of the hill, twice as close as we were. Given his proximity, it was likely he'd heard the woman struggling as the entity took her. Yet he did nothing. I'm not saying there was anything he *could* have done—he was an out-of-shape man in his mid-seventies, and the terrain was perilous even in broad daylight. But if all he had to do was ascend a ramp to reach her, he appeared too frightened.

I know this because he turned toward us, seeking witnesses to his cowardice.

Two more white faces poked up from hidey-holes, their heads swiveling this way and that like dimwitted gophers. They saw one of their own being taken and looked toward their leader.

"Yo," Duran shouted in a challenging tone to them, "do something!"

Denault offered no sign of having heard. He refused to allow the words of others to affect him.

For the next minute, we all watched and listened as the entity yanked its prey over the top of the dome and vanished from sight.

Silence returned to the island. Only the sounds of the waves lapping against the rocky beach could be heard.

Denault dropped back down into his shelter.

His two remaining minions did the same.

Patel's fists and jaw tightened.

Duran began to sob.

I held her.

I needed to figure something out.

WHEN DAWN BROKE, our stomachs grumbled back and forth. We joked that they were communicating with each other. Patel's was the loudest. When it "spoke," he translated aloud in his stomach's baritone voice: "I'm so hungry."

Duran's tummy gurgled in answer. She added, "Me too."

When mine chimed in next, I said in a high squeak, "When will Mamá bring us chorizo and eggs?"

We laughed ourselves into hysterics, culminating in sobbing that only fueled our nagging headaches. We desperately needed protein.

And so at noon, having spotted a small school of fish swimming in its depths, Patel splashed into the clear pool. He reported a moderately strong current around his feet. After perhaps an hour, he wrestled a small reef shark out of the water.

I had a Swiss Army knife and Duran knew how to skin a fish. She set to work on a flat rock preparing our shark sushi breakfast. It was no California or spider roll, but it did give our gastric juices something to attack.

When I approached Denault's people to offer our leftover meat, I was told to fuck off. They had already captured and killed sooty terns and were figuring out how to de-feather the tiny bodies. I advised against eating them. Not only is seagull meat oily and gamey in texture, but they carry parasites like trichinella and are known to have *E. Coli*.

They looked to Denault for counsel. He ignored me completely and gestured for them to proceed.

I turned to Duran and shrugged. We walked back to the pool together. She plucked another strip of fish meat from my hands and popped it in her mouth. As she chewed, she asked, "Are you an ornithologist?"

I told her no, I wasn't.

THE THREE OF us sat on the beach at sunset, staring at the ocean beyond Denault's crashed boat. I pointed in a direction where I'd seen lights the last two evenings. "I think we're near shipping lanes. We could swim for it."

"I'm terrified of sharks," Duran said.

"I'm more afraid of that *thing*," Patel said, glancing over his shoulder. "It's getting dark."

We turned to look in the direction of the volcano.

At its base, Denault's two followers were studying us. They had been puking up tern meat and wildly, explosively defecating for the past hour. They looked miserable. They also looked hostile. I didn't doubt they were somehow blaming us for their choices. It's a truism of human nature that we resent others who are better off.

As night falls, Denault is nowhere to be seen. Patel speculated he'd pilfered supplies from the bags of the two people who had been killed. He isn't sharing what he has.

Dark clouds are lining the horizon. If there are ships out there, we aren't going to see them tonight.

January 23

THE ENTITY DESCENDED the volcano in a darkness so total I didn't see its arrival until the last second.

With no stars or moonlight thanks to the cloud covering, all I had to go by were variations of ebony, the obsidian entity's light-sucking non-shape against the gray-black of the surrounding igneous landscape. One moment it wasn't there, the next it loomed over us like a sudden, massive wall.

My lungs seized and a scream died in my chest. With no frame of reference for its proximity, I spun and grabbed Duran's and Patel's collars—literally pulling them awake—and yanked them in the opposite direction. Duran shook off sleep quicker than Patel and recognized the threat's immediacy. She and I scrambled around the circumference of the pool, tugging him by his arm and shirt while he reacted to the rude awakening and gathered his wits. When he saw what was coming, he cried out and propelled himself backward.

The entity shambled after us in eerie silence. Its size had multiplied, but by how much was impossible to calculate. It didn't help matters that my half-glasses had fallen off during our frantic scramble. The only certainty was the thing's steady stride showed it was gaining on us. When it got within two yards, it stretched out a giant hand and reached for Patel.

Duran saved his life by clamping her own hand over Patel's lips and nostrils. She would later tell me the idea came to her when we saw how the entity always grabbed victims by the mouth—perhaps to prevent its prey from screaming. She also described how its toxic coldness sought purchase between her fingers.

Failing that, the entity reacted as if enraged. It reared back and swung its arms in a tantrum over its head, then lurched forward. In another second, it would be close enough to grab Duran's face.

With a strength I didn't know I had, I heaved the three of us into the pool. The drop-off was severe—like falling through ice over a lake—and the frigid waters swallowed us. Completely blind, I gripped their hands and swam in a direction toward the middle.

We surfaced beyond the entity's reach…and saw it wasn't stepping into the water. Yet it still tried to reach us. Its many limbs flailed in our direction, slicing the air with swishing sounds, coming close enough to prompt us to swim farther away.

So there we stayed, the three of us facing each other—arms intertwined, treading water in the black pool, watching each other's backs—while the monster paced around the shore.

It seemed to go on for an hour. At some point, I felt the current swirling around our feet. Patel saw that I felt it and gave me a slight nod. I looked at Duran and saw she was shivering in terror. We had eaten a shark caught in this same pool. There was no denying it had come through an underwater channel linked to the ocean. The reef teemed with the same predators of which Duran had a severe phobia.

Her teeth chattering, Duran stared at me and asked, "For Christ's sake, how are you not afraid?"

I replied, "There's no reason to fear what can be understood, and we're learning even now."

In an incredulous voice, she stammered, "What are we learning?!"

I told her we had learned the entity's limitations. We knew the conditions that precipitated its arrival. We knew it was lethal within six feet, but keeping our distance and denying it access to our faces helped. I added, "Fear is for individuals who can't or won't act smart enough to avoid the threat. Compared to them, we're relatively safe."

"How is this 'relatively safe,' Alva?" she cried. "If that thing doesn't get us, what's swimming under our feet will!"

"I have less fear about the known world than the unknown."

That answer silenced her. She kept her eyes locked on mine. After a while, she nodded, accepting this. Her trembling lessened as she drew strength from an inner reserve.

Patel threw his glance toward the shore and said, "Look."

One of Denault's people had emerged from his rocky nook. Either the wind had carried our conversation in his direction or he had awoken to evacuate his bowels. His head popped up like a Whac-A-Mole game, but unlike the game, his face uttered an audible taunt: "Shut the fuck up over there!"

The entity whirled and advanced in his direction.

The man didn't see or react to it.

Patel yelled, "Dude! Run!"

He didn't. He continued shouting. He called us names and remarked about the color of our skins. Then his voice was choked off and he was lifted skyward, hands scrabbling at the thing's grip over his face. And just as abruptly, he was slammed headfirst into a rocky ledge—a move aimed at stunning rather than killing. It took the fight out of him.

The entity dragged him into darkness.

We stared after it in shock. There was no relief or joy at being spared for one more day. None of us would make a move to get out of the water for another hour.

Before we did, Duran's eyes tracked a movement behind us, and she whispered, "Check that."

Patel and I craned our necks to follow her gaze, toward the tail of the island, as far away as one could get from the volcano.

Denault crouched behind a rock, having observed the whole thing. He had moved to a different spot, saving himself without alerting his own people.

THE SUN ROSE behind gunmetal-gray clouds, and the ocean breeze smelled of rain that hadn't yet begun to fall.

We planned our day, with item one being "Stay away from Captain Denault and First Mate Mongo." We had nicknamed the remaining minion that because he was large and muscular and acted more witless than the others.

Denault had crept back to his original shelter when it grew bright enough to see. He and his musclebound goon were huddled together hatching schemes of their own. That they occasionally stole glances in our direction made us uneasy.

I told my friends I planned to swim out to the boat for useful supplies. Not that it seemed like Denault was smart enough to prepare for anything, accidents or otherwise. But if there was a chance he was—and if we needed to spend another night in the water—having a wetsuit or two would be an asset.

Patel agreed to monitor my progress from shore. He would have come with me if I'd asked, but there was no way I wanted to leave Duran alone. I had a bad feeling.

We caught and shared a fish for brunch, and I'm taking some time to jot these notes and steel my nerve before I get in the water.

PATEL IS DEAD.

We wanted to eulogize him, but we never learned his first name.

Duran didn't stop crying for the rest of the day.

She said, "Marisol. My first name is Marisol. It means 'of the sea and sun.' I want you to know that in case I'm next. I was born in San Diego in 1993, and I play the oboe, and I see the Padres whenever there's a home game. You can say that about me after I go."

I shushed her and told her she wasn't going to die. We were going to survive this. I cleaned the dried blood from her face and held her until she fell asleep.

IT ALL HAPPENED while I was scavenging Denault's boat.

My short swim to the reef was uneventful, aside from being prodded from below, twice, by curious sharks. I expected that and crawled aboard the tilted vessel without being bitten.

I went below deck and emerged with nothing of use except a cooler bag containing four bottles of water. I had slung it over my shoulder when I heard a commotion from the shore.

I could only see sparse details from that distance. Mongo yanked Duran by the arm toward him, delivered a savage haymaker to her face, and she went down. Denault had a pistol trained on Patel, who was shouting and gesturing in anger. Then rain began to fall as a jagged branch of lightning exploded from the clouds, illuminating the world, and thunder boomed at the same time I saw Denault fire his weapon.

I dove off the reef and knifed through the water as hard and as fast as I could. This time the sharks left me alone. Between strokes, I caught glimpses of what happened next: Mongo was trekking uphill with Duran slung over his shoulder, unconscious. Patel was laying on his back on the black gravel. Denault sat motionless on a boulder.

I stumbled onto the beach and knelt next to Patel. His eyes were open, rain pattering into them, and a red, burning flare spat strontium nitrate from deep in the center of his chest. He was gone. I closed his eyelids and water streamed out.

I went to Denault, whose face was slack. He was studying the flare pistol.

He didn't look at me and didn't resist when I took it from his hands and slid it in my waistband.

I grabbed my backpack, stuffed the water bottles inside, and hurried uphill as fast as I dared.

The clouds had deepened to a purplish black as I neared the summit and circled around toward the cave. Lightning lanced and thunder clapped loud enough to make me jump.

When I found Mongo, he had Duran face down, blood streaming from a gash in her forehead. She was awake but gagged and grunting in anger. He started to hog-tie her ankles to her wrists.

I came from around the cave's entrance behind him. He didn't notice me until I entered his peripheral vision. When he saw I was aiming the pistol at him, he raised his hands. I screamed for him to back off. He took his knee from her spine. I told Duran to come to me. She scrambled to my side and freed herself from her bindings.

Mongo shouted, "He said to tie her up. We buy ourselves time if we offer her to it. Don't you see? It's her or us!"

Upon hearing these words, a crushing sadness filled my heart. Until that moment, I hadn't fully grasped how far we had slipped, how much we had forgotten ourselves. This is where we were. This is what we'd become. In an age of technological wonder and achievement, there are some of us willing to surrender themselves to the whims of nihilistic would-be dictators because it's easier than facing hard truths and trying harder to be better people. We're still only several steps removed from sacrificing girls to appease angry volcano gods on a madman's orders.

"Hey, wait," Mongo said, squinting at the pistol. "Flare guns only have one shot." He stood and came toward us.

I backpedaled into Duran. We lost our footing.

The entity lunged out of the cave at the same time. It was the middle of the day, but thanks to the storm, it was also black as night. The thing seized Mongo by the mouth and throat and raised him high as he kicked. Lightning streaked behind them, offering a brief silhouette that burned itself into our retinas before the world went dark again and we tumbled downhill and fell off the cliff.

By some miracle, we missed hitting the jagged rocks below. We plunged into the angry waves, hands linked and not letting go. When we surfaced, another flash from the heavens illuminated the foreign yacht on the reef. I kicked toward it, tugging Duran in that direction.

We reached it, and I boosted her up, passed her my pack, and we boarded *The Butterscotch Princess*. Below deck, water had breached her hull and flooded most of the main cabin, but a smaller cabin was unaffected.

Once Duran fell asleep, I explored the boat. I found some encouraging items and formulated a plan. I'd tell her about it in the morning.

January 24

WHEN I AWOKE, she said the rain was still falling. I told her that was a good thing. I showed her the emergency inflatable raft and the two flare cartridges I'd found. I told her if we leave now, if we paddle toward the shipping lanes—and if the current is with us—we might stand a chance. She said she was afraid and apologized for that. She wanted to be strong. I told her what she needed to hear: that the sharks will leave us alone because reef sharks stay near the reef.

She asked, "Are you a marine biologist, Alva?"

"No," I told her. "I'm a science nerd. I spend my time reading and learning because the only thing I fear is ignorance. And I wish you'd call me by my first name."

She said, "Tell me your plan, Fiona."

I told her we'd let rain collect in the raft and drink that first. We'd ration the bottled water. We'd catch and eat fish. And we would only shoot the flares if a boat was heading toward us. If we kept our wits, we'd be fine.

What I didn't tell her is we'd likely feel other sharks brushing their fins against the bottom of the raft. Or that the makos we'd encounter in open waters have been known to bite boats. I also didn't tell her if our water runs out and we're not picked up by a passing ship, we're likely to die from exposure and dehydration.

She said, "What about Denault?"

"What about him?"

"Do we just leave him?"

I put my hand to her cheek. The fact that she even asked, after all this, told me everything I needed to know about her. "He made his choices. Now he has to face the consequences."

"And what about our choices?"

"Our choices have been limited as a direct result of his actions. He put us all between a rock and a hard place. People died. Now he's got to live on that rock, however short his life may be. But as for me, I'll take the hard place every time."

She nodded.

I said, "We're going to make it, Marisol. Do you trust me?"

She nodded again.

"Then let's go."

WE ARE MARISOL Duran and Fiona Alva.

We won't let fear control us.

We're going to be smart.

We're going to survive.

And when we pass Captain Denault watching from the shore as we paddle away together, we're going to flip him off. Because fuck that guy.

INTERIOR LIGHT

Gary Robbe

THE 1963 FORD GALAXY 500 XL was magic. That's what Dewey, the car salesman, told Frank the first time he saw the car. That day, the white Galaxy gleamed in the sun, captivating.

Frank was like a moth spiraling toward a flame. The car was beyond big. The bright red interior screamed. Frank checked the engine, a spotless 260 V8, not exactly a monster but at least a V8.

Strands of blond hair rattled across Frank's forehead as he leaned into the engine. Dewey stood over him and jangled the keys.

"I can picture you driving through Frisch's on Friday nights, the radio cranked up, all the pretty girls gawking and dreaming of being inside this baby."

Yeah, he was able to picture that.

What the Galaxy 500 lacked in sportiness and cool, it made up for in size. It was a behemoth.

It was noticed. It's what Frank Glyn needed.

"And drive-ins. You can fit eight girls easy in this beauty."

"I just need one."

Frank took the Galaxy for a test drive. Dewey was right. He felt the magic as soon as his hands touched the steering wheel. When he turned the column-mounted shift selector to drive, a wave of pleasure, just short of an orgasm, jingled up his arms to the rest of his body, and he gasped before he pressed his foot to the gas pedal. Frank knew then the car was in control, not him.

"Bench seats. I'd buy the car myself, but I'm married." Dewey laughed. "Ain't got need for bench seats like this anymore!"

Frank didn't need to be convinced. The car was just what he needed, even with the sense that he wasn't alone in his head, that something else was calling the shots now. Crazy.

He bought the Galaxy 500XL, paid in cash with money he earned working part-time at Holzhauser's Department Store the past two years. He was seventeen. Dewey asked him what he was going to do, now that he was the owner of such a fine car. Frank said, "Leave. I'm just going to leave."

This was what he had been dreaming about for years. Get away from his asshole parents, who really weren't parents at all, but poor imitations, pod people that saw Frank as the freak, not themselves. Get away from all the bad memories of school, the rejections and anger that marked his time there. Get away from all the losers who identified and were drawn to him like a knife to the belly—so called friends who did nothing but serve as a reminder that he was a loner and an outcast, regardless of the seaweed clinging to his ankles.

The Galaxy was perfect. He loved it. And somehow, in a way he couldn't explain at the time, the 1963 Ford Galaxy 500XL two-door fastback with a 260V8 engine loved him back.

After he pulled the car into his driveway, he touched and caressed the smooth paint finish and the miles of stainless like the skin of a lover. If he ever had one. Jeanine came to mind.

Jeanine was one of the prettiest girls at Colerain High, rough around the edges, which he liked, but the girlfriend of one of the toughest greasers in school. She talked to Frank sometimes.

He didn't know why, except maybe because he was an oddball and she felt sorry for him. Frank didn't care. She was his fantasy girl. He pictured her next to him in the Galaxy, driving away from everything they used to know, driving toward adventure. He was caressing her inner thigh when someone called out.

Roger, his next door neighbor, and loser friend. "Nice. We can fit a gadzillion people in this motherfucker!"

"I'm not going to be a taxi service," Frank said.

"Hell, we can have orgies in this thing."

"This *thing* has a name. Galaxy."

"You're funny, dude!"

They drove to Frisch's that night. Frank, Roger, and another loser friend, Bill, drank a few beers along the way, smashed the empty bottles against road signs, mailboxes, and one unfortunate Corvair parked in the street. Roger and Bill, excited to be in someone's car, were oblivious to Frank's constant reminders to not spill a fucking drop of anything in his car.

They pulled into Frisch's and parked in the first available spot beneath the wavy, corrugated awning, checked out the mounted menu, then ordered Big Boy sandwiches, fries, and cherry Cokes. The three of them conspicuous nobodies in a monster-sized car.

A continuous line of souped-up and flashy cars rumbled through the parking lot, each balancing carefully on the speed bumps, most filled to bursting with teens and twenty-somethings. A cacophony of horns, some with obnoxious tunes, like Dixie, or La Cucaracha, a Plymouth Road Runner's high-pitched beep-beep, a Volkswagon Beetle yapping like a Chihuahua. Kids milled about and hassled the smart-dressed carhops delivering trays of food and removing trays piled with garbage. Banter, cat calls, shouts, and elbows out opened windows, greased heads and lipstick laughter. And loud music—rock and roll, blaring from all directions. Multiple radio stations playing different songs that blended into an unintelligible composite of white noise.

The interior lights of the Galaxy flickered on and off incessantly. Frank was annoyed about that. Shouldn't the lights be off when the doors were closed and the overhead light switch turned off? Also, the radio only picked up AM static, and Frank was annoyed with that too.

"Can't you find any stations?" Bill asked from the back seat.

"Shut the fuck up," Frank replied. The only fucking car without music. The static played to his ears, turned up loud the way it was, and Frank was sure he heard voices saying his name, *Frank*, over and over. Pretty fucking weird. He turned the radio off. He needed to talk to Dewey about that.

"Hey, Frankie, where'd you get that tank? You join the army?" Warren's GTO's rear wheels were poised on the yellow speed bump behind the Galaxy, ready to tear it off the asphalt, four or five of the top-tier greasers with their heads out the windows, cackling and jeering at Frank and his new wheels.

"Ain't it your bedtime, boys? Time to get Grandpa's car back to the nursing home where it belongs!"

The 1963 Ford Galaxy 500 XL, brilliant white in the bent lights beneath the awning, was a car that was too big for Frank, Roger, and Bill to hide in. Betsy, oldest woman on the carhop crew, stood by Frank at his window and laughed at all the comments coming their way. Frank shushed Roger from yelling back. Bill wolfed down his sandwich.

"Fuck them," Frank said. He wanted to jump out and kick the door of the GTO, especially where Will Connick was sitting. Will had embarrassed him in study hall a few days ago, smacked his chest and busted an ink pen in his front pocket. Frank had to go through the whole day advertising a Rorschach inkblot design on his shirt. He hated Will with all his guts but was afraid of him as much. "Damn it, Bill, you're getting sauce on the seat!"

The GTO must have driven through the parking lot twenty times before Frank decided he had had enough. The girls that were there that night were as invisible as they wanted to be. No one said anything nice about his new car, except Betsy, who only said it would be the perfect car for her and her three children. She made sure they got the joke—two children and an imbecile husband.

The Galaxy seemed to grow bigger by the second as he backed out of the stall and Frank nearly clipped a Mustang at one point and a menu bar at another. A steady stream of cars rolled through, and Frank found it almost impossible to squeeze into the queue. His hands nearly slid off the steering wheel. But the car took over, it seemed like, managed to surf cool like a pro over the speed bumps on their way out. "Thank you, car," he said to himself.

Jeanine Flower, prettier than ever, appeared out of nowhere and waved to Frank as they passed the last cars in the lot. She looked directly at him. *Him.* And smiled. Frank smiled smugly and waved back. *Fuck you, Will Connick.*

Frank perked up, then, the night not being a total waste. He dropped Roger and Bill off at their homes, even though they protested that the night was young. He told them he wanted to drive alone for a while. "Tired of just hanging out," he said.

As he drove, he felt strong, invincible. Like someone else for a change. Everything outside the car was fuzzy as if whatever was out there didn't matter. Frank turned the radio on. A voice in static rain and a clanking noise coming through, like a metal ball dropping down stairs, one step at a time; *trunk, trunk, trunk, trunk. Trunk.* The voice repeating the word "trunk" over and over. The car *talking* to him.

Headlights coming his way chopped the night in pieces and scrambled them about the road, the Galaxy's headlights kicking the pieces aside as it moved through them. Frank had no idea where he was. The voice in the static continued to say *trunk, trunk, trunk…*

The windshield melted before his eyes, the steering wheel smoked. An urge to panic, like that of a swimmer caught by a vicious undertow, came over him, but before Frank could work his useless legs to hit the brakes, or flail his arms for anything solid, he found himself outside looking at the open, mouth-gaping trunk of the Galaxy.

He knew what it wanted. What it needed. The Galaxy was a god, and he was its servant. He would be rewarded well. This came to Frank not in words, but more like implanted thoughts, as if the seeds of his mission were just revealed.

You will have to sacrifice. You will eventually have it all.

But I am always hungry.

Frank was one with everything. All the colors of the night swept into him, as well as countless lesser souls of flying things caught in the brilliant cloud of this god's light. Was he dead? Was this what happened when the lights went out? Was this what it felt like to be a ghost, stuck between worlds in the body of a god?

Frank snapped out of the trippy daze with his head against the steering wheel, the Galaxy in park, engine running, pinging like it wanted something, pebbles in the valves. The headlights were off but the interior light on. Sort of. It pulsed on and off as if there were a loose connection. Frank breathed out slow and long, relieved he was still alive. He must have been dreaming. Or someone, somehow, slipped some acid in his food or drink. Roger or Bill?

He thought of the still vivid image of the open trunk. The gaping mouth of God. The Galaxy. It was so clear.

Even gods must eat.

The Aztec priests made sacrifices to their gods, cutting out the hearts of their victims. The Mayans threw children into sinkhole caves, for their gods. Biblical stuff.

The windshield was splattered with the gooey remains of flying bugs. Frank had no idea where he was, and turning on the headlights didn't help. No lights from houses or streetlights, only trees and stars and something of a moon somewhere.

He put the car in drive and moved forward, slow, the headlights off a bit, nervous like he was. In no time the car was going faster, curving this way and that, almost too fast. Frank tapped the brakes, but the car seemed to be driving itself. It knew where it was going. This way and that. The road everywhere but in front of him. Lots of trees. Shadows jumping about from the sides of the road. The headlights, not quite aligned, bounced from the black asphalt to the tree-tops, up and down, side to side, as if the Galaxy were cross-eyed and couldn't focus on a damn thing. He was okay now, everything normal. Whatever happened was over, the trippy dream message tucked away neat. Frank never felt more relaxed. Jeanine had waved at him. Frank pictured her beside him (bench seats), her hand scratching the inside of his thigh, then...

Bang.

Something smacked the front side of the Galaxy. Something big. The steering wheel almost left his hands, the car rolling to the left and right, and then a bump, bump, lifting Frank's ass off the seat a couple inches.

The headlights did their own thing, one on the road but the right one wobbling across the trees and bushes before settling on the road like its brother—two beams meandering straight ahead into black nothingness.

The Galaxy screeched to a stop. Frank gripped the wheel with everything he had. He didn't remember pressing so hard on the brake. All he remembered was the bang and the bump.

What the fuck?

Frank stumbled out of the car, engine running, lights crisscrossed, and went to the side of the road. A dark form lay in the weeds, a deer perhaps, or a large dog. He got in the car and backed it up. The rogue right headlight skimmed the top of the dark form.

A body. The legs stretched in a one hundred eighty degree angle on the asphalt, the rest of the body swallowed by the weeds and flickering shadows.

Frank dropped his head onto the steering wheel. His eyes clouded with tears and he squeezed them shut until the pain rolled to the back of his head. "No, no, no..." When he opened his eyes, the body was still there. Still hadn't moved, either. The engine rumbled softly with the occasional tick, tick. His breaths and heartbeats were trying to outpace each other. Frank was surprised to find himself already outside, walking to the body, thinking, *Who is this?* Not the body on the ground, but the person moving toward it.

He came to the body. Will Connick. The prick who ruined his shirt. The prick who laughed at him. The prick who dated Jeanine. He was bent in impossible places. He was dead.

The prick.

What the fuck was he doing out here in the middle of nowhere? How the hell did this happen? He must have been walking home. Drunk. He stumbled into my car. What am I gonna do?

It was an accident, clear and simple. No, not so clear. Not so simple. He had been drinking himself earlier. And how could he explain why he was out this way when he didn't even know where the fuck he was? Also, everyone knew he and Will disliked each other.

Trouble. Big trouble.

Frank stared at the body. His thoughts ran rampant. *Find the nearest house. Call the police.* He turned and looked at the rear of the Galaxy. *The trunk.* The dream. God. The mouth of God.

He turned the Galaxy off and used the trunk key to open it. No way he could explain this urge, the calling, to move the body into it. *Call the police? No way.* The road was deserted and dark, no houses around. He was the last person on earth, and he had to tidy things up.

Will was a broken ragdoll. He wasn't as big as Frank always thought he was. When he touched the limp body, a rage flash-burned inside him, a rage toward Will and all those who were like him. And oddly enough, at the same time, a love for this vehicle that was more than a vehicle, more than metal and plastic, rubber and glass, something that needed more than gasoline, oil, antifreeze, and water to keep it running.

Frank lifted Will from beneath the arms and dragged him to the car. Frank felt stronger than he had ever felt. Will weighed nothing at all. He didn't look at the dead kid's face—no way he could do that. He pulled, then pushed, and slid Will into the trunk, using Will's jacket to help.

There wasn't much blood, but some did get on his hands and forearm; he wiped it off with Will's jacket before slamming the trunk lid shut.

Frank started the car and turned the headlights on. He wished he had a flashlight. He looked up and down the road, surprised no one had driven past, then walked around the car checking for anything that could have come off Will. The body of the car and the bumper seemed okay, even though it was hard to see anything. He felt good. No fear. No remorse. He walked on a cushion of air. The interior light flickered on and off.

He hesitated by the trunk. Felt the cool metal. A breeze carrying with it the scent of pine and something sweet with decay. He closed his eyes, reopened them, and lifted the trunk lid. It was black-hole dark, but the crescent moon was over the trees now and there were stars, and he saw…nothing. The trunk was empty. Empty.

Frank felt along the felt liner and the sides of the trunk. His eyes could have been deceiving him, and if they weren't, he at least expected to find sticky traces of blood or who knew what that might have seeped from the body. From Will. There was no trace. Nothing.

Will was nobody now.

Frank threw up.

When he had nothing left inside him, he sat behind the wheel and closed the door. The interior light went out, then pulsed and flashed over his head, across the roof like the northern lights, not just a dull yellow tinted light, but shades of green, pink, orange, and blue. It mesmerized him, held him, even though somewhere deep in his mind he thought the top of the car might be on fire, an electrical fire of some sort.

Frank touched the steering wheel, and as soon as he did so, his whole body spasmed, emptied, as if he was ejaculating to an electric current orgasm, the current jolting a pressure release unlike anything he had ever experienced before. It went on and on, wave after wave. He screamed in pleasure and bit his tongue. His mouth filled with blood.

Then the car was moving. The headlights realigned and dug into the road. Frank's breaths swallowed and digested the air easier, and now he knew where he was and where he needed to go. And he knew what his purpose was.

The 1963 Ford Galaxy 500 XL was a hungry god.

THE NEXT DAY, he washed and waxed the Galaxy. There was no sign of the impact with Will Connick, no dent, scrape, drops of blood, or tufts of hair. The trunk was spotless.

"What should I call you?" Nothing came to him, so he thought that was what the car was saying to him. No name. "So, I guess I'll refer to you as Galaxy, or the car." Frank stared at his reflection in the driver's side window. The image was smiling. When the image walked away, Frank was still smiling.

His parents were pissed at him because he told them he was leaving, going on a journey.

"Going where?" they asked in unison.

"Who the fuck knows?" Frank said.

"What about college?"

"This is something I need to do. Fuck college for now."

"What will you do for money? We aren't giving you a dime."

"I don't need your money."

"We should never have let you get that damn car."

Fuck you, he thought.

Frank wiped down the dashboard. He wiped the red seats. He wiped the interior lights. He stole his dad's G.I. angle-head flashlight and put it in the glove compartment. He stole a handful of knives from the kitchen and put them under the bench seat. He figured his mom would never notice.

Now, to feed the car. See what worked, what didn't. He drove to the country. Frank enticed a stray cat with a can of tuna. The cat hopped into the open truck of the Galaxy, a move Frank hoped for but didn't really expect. He slammed the trunk lid shut. The cat squealed as if all the air was let out at once. Frank said a prayer, a simple prayer he made up on the spot, a prayer of hope that the Galaxy was satisfied with the humble sacrifice.

When he opened the trunk five minutes later, the cat, and any sign of a cat, was gone. The can of tuna, untouched, remained. It was holy tuna. Frank buried it in the soft dirt along the edge of the woods. Ten feet from the two-lane road, way out in bug-fuck country.

HE DIDN'T GET the same response with the cat that he got from Will, but he noticed the car seemed stronger, peppier, and he did too. Like he was one with the god that embodied the Galaxy, like he was a god himself. Even Jeanine noticed him, came to him the next day in school, asked him what he was doing that weekend. He almost fell into a locker, but he played it cool. He *was* cool. And he had no doubt he was being rewarded by the Galaxy.

The cat was not enough. Nor were the stray dogs he fed the trunk later that week. The god was demanding and exact in its tastes. He would have to move on to bigger things.

"Damn," Roger said. "How the hell did you get Jeanine to go to the drive-in with you?"

"She likes me," Frank said. "It's that simple."

Bill said, "Fuck, you know she's just pissed about Will disappearing on her. You're going to be nothing more than a rebound fuck. If you get that far."

"Better a rebound fuck than no fuck at all." They all laughed.

"What's playing?"

"Does it matter?" Frank nodded to the spacious bench seats. "I think *Werewolves on Wheels*. Don't know what else." Frank eyed both of his friends. The only friends he really ever had. They were annoying. "Hey, you guys want to come? I can sneak you both in the trunk. Once we get in, though, you can't stick around."

"Cool. You are going to let us out, though, right?" Bill snickered.

They stopped at a convenience store a few blocks from the Mt. Healthy Drive-In, Frank and Jeanine in the front seat, Roger and Bill in the back. Jeanine looked sexy as ever, long brown hair that didn't end and a T-shirt and shorts a size too small, showcasing her killer body. Frank was beside himself.

"Okay, guys, in you go. When we get to the back of the drive-in, I'll let you out."

"Maybe I should get in the trunk too. It's fucking big enough. Save a little money."

Jeanine turned and stared past Bill and Roger to the trunk that seemed to meet the horizon and the setting sun.

"No!" Frank panicked at the thought. "It'll look too suspicious just one driver going to the drive-in in a big car. Really."

It was obvious Jeanine wanted the adventure of sneaking in, and she started to say she could switch with one of the idiots, but Frank cut her off even before the words formed in her mouth. "These two know the drill. Maybe next time, okay?"

"Sure." She edged closer to Frank. He had no doubt the Galaxy was urging her to do so. Frank got out and opened the trunk. It looked innocent enough. "C'mon," he said.

"Let us out now, you hear?" Bill and Roger laughed as they crawled in. Frank slammed the trunk lid. Jeanine was watching him through the rear window. He lingered a minute, waiting to see if any sound came from within (the cat screech, the dog yelps), but there was nothing. He patted the trunk and got back in the car.

When they made it past the ticket booth, Frank drove to the back of the drive-in lot, stopping several times like he was deciding where to let them out. "I want them to sweat a bit," he told Jeanine. The look in her eyes said everything. She was already hot, almost sweating herself. Fuck, the car was an aphrodisiac.

He picked a clear spot where no one would notice a couple of clowns escaping from a trunk. He hopped out and flipped the trunk open. Clean. Empty. "Ha! Those sons of bitches already jumped the fuck out!" Jeanine got out too and scanned the rapidly filling drive-in lot.

"How?"

"Probably sneaked out one of the times I stopped—I think there's a latch that will open the trunk from the inside. Those fuckers. That's a good one on me."

"But where'd they go?"

"The goal is to disappear, blend in. They'll find someone we know, or they'll sit up front somewhere in the grassy area. They'll find us when it's time to leave."

She put her arms around him and kissed him full on the lips, tongue teasing. "Let's stay back here," she said. "I don't want any neighbors around."

IT WAS BIG news: three teens missing in one week, all from the same high school. Theories abounded, that they met with foul play, possibly drugs, or that they simply ran off somewhere, joined a carnival, or a commune in some distant place. The police questioned Frank and Jeanine, who were the last to see Roger and Bill, and especially Jeanine, because she had been Will's girlfriend at the time of his disappearance.

Frank explained that his two friends had been fine, they must have had something cooked up when they went to the drive-in, because he and Jeanine never saw them again after he snuck them in. Jeanine said they looked everywhere for them when the drive-in closed, and they simply assumed the boys caught another ride home. As for Will, she didn't know where he went on the night he went missing—they had had a fight at Frisch's and he stalked off to who knew where. He liked to hitchhike, she told them. The police checked Frank's Galaxy, the trunk, but there was nothing to cast any suspicion on him. They shrugged their shoulders.

Frank and Jeanine became a thing; they met every chance they could, had sex everywhere they could, but most often in the spacious front or back bench seats of the Galaxy. Jeanine had incredible orgasms when they did it in the car. She couldn't explain it.

Sometimes, Frank wondered where they really went. Roger and Bill were alive when they went into the trunk. So were the animals. Were they still alive, somewhere? And Will was pretty much dead. Was he still? He had read enough science-fiction stories to know of such things as portals. Was the trunk of his car a portal to some magical place?

Or was his car simply hungry for flesh?

He was convinced the Galaxy was a god, that it had picked him (not the other way around) to be a part of this. And Jeanine. She suspected something, *felt* something even if she couldn't understand, couldn't possibly understand.

"My dad has a car like this," she said. She was sitting next to Frank in the Galaxy, the motor off and the windows down, because it was hot, even at this dusk hour. They were at Mount Airy Park, in one of the out of the way picnic areas, seven or eight other cars nearby. A party in the woods and only the coolest people could be here, drinking beer, Boone's Farm apple wine and MD 20/20. "Only it's a Pontiac. He said Fords are pieces of shit. I told him he might know what shit looks like and feels like, but he's wrong about this car." She put her hand between his legs. "Every time I'm with you, I just want to do naughty things."

"Yeah? How naughty can you get?" Frank was thinking of raising the game. Thoughts had been racing through his mind the past couple days. He didn't feel any guilt for tricking his friends into the trunk. Killing them. No, sending them someplace. And Will, he was dead already, even if Frank had been the one to turn him into a ragdoll. No guilt there. If anything, there was a bit of a thrill, a high, that he was wanting to repeat. Maybe take the car that night, Jeanine and him, drive cross country, do whatever the fuck they wanted. The Galaxy knew what it wanted; it wanted to move on. It wanted to make Frank happy. It wanted to serve Frank the way he served it. Feeding the belly of the beast.

Was Jeanine part of the plan? She had to be. No one at the park paid him any attention, but Jeanine was popular, and everyone wanted to be near her. A constant stream of the coolest coming to her window, sometimes passing a joint or a bottle. Frank was sure they couldn't understand why she was with a dweeb like him, but no one said anything. Jeanine, on the other hand, was all over Frank, couldn't get enough of him, made sure everyone who came to her window knew it.

"Let's go for a ride," she whispered in his ear. Her eyes were like blue chestnuts, her rear swaying and brushing the wax on the passenger door. Yeah, Jeanine was a part of all this. The plan.

Frank thought it was a good idea. The car speaking through Jeanine, wanting to move on, not stay static.

He put the key in the ignition.

HOME. HE WAS home, the Galaxy in the driveway in front of the house, engine off. Night. The interior light flickered. His hands on the wheel, wet, bloody. Like a hook being ripped from the inside of his throat, he shrieked and bolted upright, turned, and there was Jeanine, fine, breathing regular and hard, head leaning against the passenger door. Asleep.

"Fuck!"

She stirred. She was out deep but alive.

He stared at his hands. The blood was gone; his hands were dry. *I was fucking dreaming*, he thought. He didn't remember a thing about driving here or where they had gone, what they did. How much time had passed since they left the park? He didn't even remember leaving the park.

He shook Jeanine.

"Come on, wake up."

She opened one eye, which caught the interior light just beneath the rearview mirror, the other eye searching for something else to focus on. After a minute, it found Frank, and like the headlights after hitting Will, her eyes realigned and came awake, saying in the language of eyeballs, *What the fuck is going on? Where are we?*

"We're at my house. I don't remember driving here. Do you?"

She smiled.

"Do you remember anything?"

"Don't you?"

Frank closed his eyes, tried to think hard. See if any kind of image came by. One did. Mom. Empty eyes looking at him from the inside of the trunk.

The rest of her face looked like it had been scratched off. "No. No. No."

He bolted from the car and ran into the house, the door already ajar, no lights on, the furniture everywhere but where it should be. He tripped into the ottoman and fell against a big sloppy chair that somehow blocked the way to the kitchen. "Mom? Dad?" He heard water running in the sink. It sounded like a massive waterfall in the silence.

"They're in the trunk," Jeanine said behind him, in the dark.

"What?"

"God, it's so perfect. You can do anything, and the car will take care of it. But it's a two-way street. That's why we came here. Remember? You were so *into* it then."

Frank turned and faced her, traces of night sliding off just enough to see part of her face, the eyes part. It was Jeanine. But it wasn't.

This was someone else. Someone who only vaguely looked like Jeanine, only vaguely sounded like her. It was the eyes. They were too large for Jeanine, and they seemed to glow green in the dark room. The pupils stood out oval. A cat's eyes.

Jeanine grinned ear to ear. That stood out in the dark, too.

"My parents?" Even as he asked it, there was an emptiness behind the words, as if losing his parents barely rippled the void in the pit of his stomach. Like they had been somebody else's parents, not his, like they were only remotely connected to him in any way.

Wasn't that the way it had always been?

"Who are you?" he asked the shadow with cat eyes and grinning teeth. He stepped back.

"I understand, now. I can see."

It was the car, of course. The Galaxy had reached out to her, touched her the way it had him. Did he have eyes like that? Was the magic changing? Was this what the Galaxy wanted, a sacrifice before they moved on?

They.

It wasn't just him now, was it?

In the gray dark, Frank made out that there had been a struggle. What happened? The blood on his hands had seemed real, and he was sure it was. Before it had been so easy, so detached. He put a dead body in the trunk. He lured unsuspecting animals into the trunk. He lured his friends. Gave them up.

They went willingly.

He wanted to up the game. Well.

FRANK AND JEANINE packed some clothes and some food in a picnic basket, took a small cooler that Frank loaded with a bottle of juice and four of his dad's Hudepohl beers. Frank found his dad's loaded Smith & Wesson revolver and put it in the glove box. Everything else went into the backseat. There had been a lot of blood in his parents' bedroom and the hallway, but they didn't bother to clean it up. Frank closed the blinds and locked the door. They never found the weapon that made the mess. He was sure the trunk took care of that.

Then they were on the road, driving west, taking the smaller roads instead of the interstate. Jeanine said she wanted to see the country. And, she said, they would certainly come across hitchhikers. The world was open to them. "Nothing can stop us," she said. "We can do anything."

Frank sped past a motorcycle cop hiding behind a billboard. He glanced at the rearview mirror to see if the cop was following. "I guess we're invisible on the road," he said. He swerved and leveled a mailbox by the side of the road, the pieces flying over and into the car like feathers.

How could anything harm something that was a god?

He swerved across the center line, forcing a pickup truck off the road and into a mailbox and yard. "This is fun."

"Do you miss your parents?" Jeanine asked.

"Who?"

"I kind of wish we would've stopped by my house. Give me a clean slate as well."

"What's it matter? We're in the here and now." He looked at Jeanine, still with those cat eyes, which he was sure was only a hallucination, the god playing tricks on him. "They are probably gone now anyway. I have a theory. I think my Galaxy here can jump around time when it wants to. I mean, what's time to a god? Right now, we are probably ten years in the future, or four years back from where we started. That's why that cop couldn't see us. Why things disappear in the trunk."

"Can we get back?"

"Who the fuck wants to get back?" Frank smiled for the first time since they left his house. Was that days ago? "It's like, once you start feeding this machine, I know it's a god, or *the* God, somehow, you want to do more. And the more exciting it is, the more—what's the word—terrified, traumatized, tortured the sacrifice is, the stronger this god gets. And that's good for us."

"I didn't know you were a philosopher-poet." She yawned. "Where the fuck *are* we, anyway?" Both sides of the road were lined with wavering blue trees. Occasionally a driveway cut in, but they were well in the country, well away from telephone poles, houses, and mailboxes.

"Somewhere in southern Indiana, I think." He watched the road unwind before him, the car speeding up to an impossible speed, over a hundred miles per hour, but the wheels were glued tight to the road, like the car owned it. He wasn't worried at all. They could go supersonic on the curviest roads and this car would be fine.

"Oh look!"

He saw it, a young man and a young girl, both with floppy hats and as hippie as could be, both with exaggerated well practiced thumb swipes.

The car braked. Jeanine got out and pulled her seat forward so they could get in.

The girl was talkative and California all the way, the guy more laid back, stoned.

Frank drove for about an hour, then pulled off the road. It seemed like a desolate stretch, no homes, nothing. Perfect.

"May I?" Jeanine asked. Frank smiled and nodded. She took the revolver out of the glove box, and it took the couple in the backseat a good slow-motion minute to realize what was being pointed at them by the friendly girl up front.

The girl and her boyfriend, both crying and freaked, were directed to the rear of the car. Frank opened the trunk. The guy shook his head. The girl sobbed hysterically until Jeanine smacked her on the side of her head to shut her up.

"Nothing's going to happen to you. Climb in. If you don't, my trigger-happy friend will blow your friend's skull cap clean off."

The man, shaking, climbed into the trunk and curled into a fetal position.

"I'm going to show you a magic trick," Frank said. "Well, actually, I'm going to show your friend here a magic trick. You're part of the act." He closed the trunk lid. Jeanine giggled while she held onto California girl, forcing her to look at the closed trunk.

Frank lifted the trunk. "Ta-dah!" Empty. The girl screamed. Jeanine hit her hard on the side of the face, knocking the girl down, and she whimpered, face wet with drool and blood. Frank tossed Jeanine a knife. "Gut her," he said. "Then we'll feed her to the car like her boyfriend."

IT WAS LATE afternoon, and the sun was in their eyes. The visors didn't help much, and even with the windows rolled down, it was broiling hot. Neither of them had any idea how much time had passed since putting the couple in the trunk; their brains seemed to have shut off for a while leaving only a vague memory of ecstatic bliss from making love in a daytime aurora borealis. They were spent, coming to with the car moving at a steady speed on a two-lane road. Somewhere in farm country.

"Do you believe we each have a soul?" she asked.

"I don't know. I guess."

"I think it's possible a soul can inhabit anything. A shell of metal as easily as a shell of flesh. I think a car like this can hold a lot of souls."

"You think too much."

"I'm hungry. Can we stop somewhere?"

"Why not?" That said, the car slowed down and then abruptly turned into a driveway on the right, hidden by trees, one that Frank hadn't even seen. The Galaxy churned up the dirt road, spewing a cloud of dust behind it.

Frank could tell by the way Jeanine was looking at him that the hunger wasn't all about food. And it wasn't all about sex, either. She needed more than the hitchhikers provided. She wanted blood. She wanted that *rush*.

They stopped by a run-down once-white house with a peeling roof and a collapsed front porch. A rocking chair was still rocking, as if someone had abruptly left it. Moments later, before Frank could get out of the car, an old man, heavyset with pig-like jowls, wearing overalls and a John Deere cap, stepped out from a busted screen door. Frank noticed these details before he saw what the man was holding—a double-barreled shotgun.

"Whoa," Frank said to Jeanine, "get a load of Elmer Fudd here." He rolled the window down, put his hands up, and said to the man who was waiting on the porch silently, "We're lost. We don't want no trouble, man."

The man nodded. His white hair puffed out from his cap. He didn't say anything but motioned with the shotgun. *Turn around. Get out.*

"Sure." Frank backed the Galaxy up off the dirt drive into some high grass and turned the car around, making it look like it was a lot of effort. He made sure he rutted some of the old man's weedy yard. With one hand on the wheel, he leaned across Jeanine and opened the glove box. "Roll your window down, honey."

He pulled the car forward, Jeanine now facing the crazy old man who was now holding the shotgun in the crook of his arm, relaxed. His eyes, though, were anything but, squinting like he was trying to move such a big vehicle out of there with will alone.

Frank's hand was still in the glove box. He fumbled beneath some papers, pulled his hand out, and through the open window, he fired one, two, three shots before the old man could even flinch.

"Damn!" Jeanine screamed, holding her ears. "What the fuck!"

Frank laughed, hopped out of the car, and stepped on the porch. The old man was half in, half out of the doorway. Frank stood over the man, leaning into the house. "Anybody home?"

"Are you still hungry?" he said to Jeanine, now standing next to the man. "Check the kitchen and see if the old guy has anything good to eat. He looks pretty well fed." This was a new Frank. Impulsive. In control. A take-charge kind of rebel.

Jeanine stepped around him and over the body, three neat red holes in it, a puddle seeping out beneath it. "Can barely hear you with all these bells going off in my ears, motherfucker."

She came back a minute later and handed Frank an ice cream drumstick. "That's all the motherfucker had, that and who knows how many jugs of lemonade."

Frank studied the body while he nibbled at the cone. "Okay, help me move him to the trunk. Car's gotta eat you know, or our fun times'll be over. This should make the god happy, this great big fat pig."

"Old meat," she said.

It took twenty minutes to drag the dead man over to the rear of the car, then lift and drop him into the trunk. Frank and Jeanine panted with the effort, and both were drenched in sweat.

"Look at this, my hands are bloody," Jeanine said, disgusted but smiling at the same time. "I'm going inside to wash up."

"No need, the car will take care of it. Like with my, uh, parents." Funny, how the words seemed to dig a little inside him, struggling to get out. Parents. Then a new slide came before him, like one of those round slide projectors the teachers used in school, a new slide that took his attention from the previous one. "We've got to get moving. The body's fresh. Car's happy."

Jeanine went ahead and opened the passenger door. She looked at the woods across from the house. Not so blue now. "Maybe we can fuck right here, outside the car for a change—we're close enough."

Frank closed the lid to the trunk, picked up the shotgun, and walked to the driver's side door. "We need—" An explosion slammed him into the door, the glass shattering, the shotgun flying out of his hand. Jeanine screamed.

His arm. It felt as if he jammed it into a hornet's nest. White-hot fire erupted from the dozens of new craters up and down his arm. Frank dropped to one knee while ducking his head down, to catch a sideways view of where the blast came from, all the while pulling the door open with his one good hand.

A thin old lady—she had to be a hundred—stood on the porch, a shotgun leveled at Frank and the huge target of an automobile. Smoke poured from her head. *No,* Frank thought in a millisecond, it was her frizzy white hair. She was crazy eyed and shaking, but the shotgun somehow remained steady. As Frank slammed the door, another blast rocked and rattled the side of the Galaxy. Jeanine was already inside, ducking down.

"Damn!" Frank screamed from the pain. His eyes clouded with tears, and while he fumbled for the keys, the old woman wailed outside, the sound reaching them through the shattered driver's side window.

"Shoot her!" Jeanine shouted.

"I don't have my fucking gun!" He started the car, almost started to black out, then started to cry, before he threw the gearshift in reverse. The Galaxy screeched and spun in the dirt, just as the woman miraculously had another gun, a pistol, the biggest pistol Frank had ever seen in his life. He held onto the wheel for dear life and pulled it down as hard as he could, the car arcing around to face toward the road. He stepped on the gas while the heavens cracked open, unleashing blast after blast of merciless thunder and lightning.

The Galaxy was all over the road, Frank barely able to hold the steering wheel, blood now rolling into his eyes from who knew where. Jeanine was back in the seat, telling him to turn here, turn there, don't panic, and for god's sake stop whimpering.

"You're getting blood on the seat," Jeanine said.

"Fuck that. It hurts." He turned right onto a street that looked like it was buried in the trees, pulled over, put the car in park. He closed his eyes and took deep breaths as if he were about to go underwater. When he reopened them, Jeanine was still there, quiet, staring straight ahead. He groaned while he turned to check out the damage. Two holes in the rear window, spidering cracks from each. The driver's side window was gone except for a few shards that promised to cut him deep if he didn't knock them out. Frank was sure the side of the car was punctured and dented good.

"Here." Jeanine tossed him a greasy rag she had retrieved from the back seat. "I think she got you with rock salt."

"Burns like Hell."

"You're lucky. If she had real shells, you'd be out of an arm. I can't believe she fucked this car up so much. I mean, this car is a god, right? Invincible and everything? Well, not so much." She watched as Frank applied pressure to his arm, thinking it would stop the pain.

Frank leaned back into the seat. "Why isn't *He* making this go away?"

"Maybe it's a *She*. Maybe the magic has run out."

He burned a hole through her chest with his eyes, started to say something, then shook his head. *What the fuck's wrong with her? Why isn't she doing more to help me out?*

"So. Will wound up in the trunk, right?" Jeanine was dead serious, calm, but he noticed how her breathing picked up. She was seething inside.

Frank struggled with the words. "Didn't mean to. It was an accident. He stepped in front of me, killed him on the spot. There was nothing I could do."

"And your friends, the ones I used to see you with?"

"I didn't know about the trunk then," he lied.

"That was the first time I was part of it," she said. She was calling him on it. She opened the door and got out, went back to the trunk, flipped it open.

Frank jumped out too. "What are you doing?"

He stood by her as she checked; the old man was gone.

"You're going to have to drive," Frank said.

NIGHT. THE HEADLIGHTS blazed ahead on the country road, somewhere deep in Illinois. They had been driving for four or five, or ten hours, neither of them sure. Especially Frank, who mumbled and groaned as he lay balled up in the corner against the door, like he was a sack of tiny gnomes crushed together, each one complaining about every bump in the road.

It was hot and humid, and it bugged Jeanine immensely that there was no window to roll up, no way to stop the wind rush that blasted and eroded the side of her face. "Can't you do something?" she asked. "Maybe say a prayer, talk to the car, see if it can heal itself. I mean, the old guy disappeared, right? That means something's working."

Frank mumbled, "Something isn't right." He wanted to be careful. Maybe Jeanine was all wrong. Maybe this was the Galaxy's way of saying, *You should not have let a girl come between us.* Maybe the Galaxy was jealous about the attention he was giving her. A true servant owed all his attention to God. He knew what he had to do—when he got some of his strength back.

It would have to be the right time. If they came across a late-night hitchhiker, he could simply push her into the trunk along with the dead body and slam the lid shut before she could do anything about it. She would go to the happy place. Be with Will again.

But he had so much pain up and down his fucking arm, and his forehead, which felt like a brick had hit it. And his left eye was clouded and almost glued shut from the gooey substance seeping out of it.

No way he wanted Jeanine driving all the time. No way could he let the car go on without somehow fixing up the damage to it. Maybe that would make things right. That, and putting Jeanine where she deserved to be.

And now, watching her drive, he felt she was a dark thing with no sympathy for him, only contempt. He wanted to hurt her. Do it right. Hurt her bad.

There were knives under the seat. And huddled like he was, it would be easy to slip his good arm under and select a good-sized one and hide it until the right time, like when she stopped in some out-of-the-way place. He could ask her to turn on the interior light, so he could see what he was doing, then get her quick-like in the abdomen or chest. If he caught her by surprise, he might be able to stab her several times, slice the fight out of her.

Blood. There would be blood, lots of it. But the car likes that. And the car cleans itself. Blood would likely be just the thing to bring the Galaxy around, give it the strength it needed to heal itself.

"You know," Jeanine said, "I don't mind that you got rid of Will. He was a royal jerk. A fuckhead. But you did in your only friends? That's pretty fucking cold."

Frank still huddled up, feeling the car on the road, a bumpier road than before, rocks kicking underneath the wheel wells and undercarriage. "Where are we?"

"I need to rest. Wasn't planning on being the driver the rest of the fucking trip, wherever we're *tripping* to. Looks like some gravel pits here, figured it would be a good place to stop for a little while." The car came to a stop, and she shifted into park. Then she turned the ignition off.

Frank lifted his head up. "Gravel pits? We should be outside St. Louis by now."

"I think we've been going in circles."

She opened her door and slid out, stretched, walked out of his line of vision. The interior light came on, blinking like a mad chameleon zeroing in on lunch. Frank opened his side too. He had to be strong. He hoped he was strong. "What do you mean, circles?"

"I think the car is taking us in a roundabout way. Like you said, it drives itself. Don't know what it has in mind."

"We'll find out, I'm sure."

"Let's look at your arm." She stood by the driver's side, the door open, the interior light bright and steady now.

"I want to take a look at the trunk first," he said. They were in the middle of nowhere, and it was wicked dark, oil dark, only a few stars poking between clouds. He heard what was probably an owl, or hawk, screech from not too far away, and something splash in water that he couldn't see. Maybe if he put the headlights on.

He limped to the rear of the Galaxy and popped the trunk. She came around as he expected she would, curious to see why he wanted to look in the trunk. Curiosity killed the cat. He kept the knife he had taken from beneath the seat hidden in his good hand, away from any ambient light sneaking out from the car interior. The trunk was forever deep black.

She stood behind him though, out of reach from his good arm. Like she knew. "There's nothing there."

"The light's not working." He stepped to the side, but she didn't move closer, didn't take his bait. He leaned into the trunk. Knife ready if she came next to him and leaned in too. An electric current of pain shot up his side and he lifted his head up and away from Jeanine, so that she couldn't see him wince. That was all it took.

The blow from behind knocked him in the opposite direction he had been looking, threw him against the back bumper and to his knees. He crumbled into the gravel along with all his senses. A bright light burst inside his head. His own interior light, seeping out from cracks newly opened, then the panic arm flail and mouth gulp of being under water.

He wasn't under water. He was wet, face down in what tasted like blood. And in a fetal position that he couldn't quite unwind from. *If I'm tasting blood, I'm not dead*, he thought. Frank twisted his head, numb and heavy, and focused on a light hovering above him. An angel?

The light fell and a shadow form moved over him like a great dark cloud, and he blinked and blinked to chase it away, or to see what it was, and everything went black, to nowhere, then light again, then black. And so on.

The ocean waves were so loud they nearly drowned out the voice trying to reach him. But when he became aware his eyes were open and Jeanine was saying something, he tried to lift himself. He was too heavy. His eyes tracked to Jeanine, her imperfect, unfocused self, right there over him, her breath holding him down. *He was in the trunk.*

"It wants *me*, Frank, not you. Not anymore. I'm sorry it had to turn out this way." She held onto the trunk lid, letting it drop and rise as if she wasn't sure about closing it all the way.

"Please…"

"It has plans for me, Frank. It has plans for you." She lowered the trunk lid, slow, giving him a last glimpse of the few stars and clouds behind her. Jeanine's face was illuminated by the interior lights shining through the rear window.

"Don't close it, Jean." This couldn't be happening. What happens when the trunk lid closes? The terror of that thought exploded from every cell in his body. He was falling down a bottomless hole with nothing to grip or latch onto, nothing to slow the fall into the unknown.

"Don't close it, Jean. Please."

Jeanine turned the flashlight on. All he could see was her torso and an arm directing the beam of light off to the side, the trunk lid poised to close all the way. Frank struggled to move, but something was holding him, as if he were tied down by thousands of steel-strength threads. Gulliver tied on the beach by the miniature Lilliputians. He was paralyzed from the neck down.

"This is my car," he said.

"Not anymore," Jeanine whispered.

He was sinking. "I worshipped you," he said to the car. The Galaxy was God. He was part of God.

Part of God. He really was now.

"Say hello to Will for me," Jeanine said. She closed the trunk.

CREVICE

Scotty Milder

T HE KID CAME UP THE road at sunset.
Henry sat on his porch, sucking his pipe and watching the sky go from
blue to gold to red. This was what he did most evenings, ever since Emma
was gone. He'd sit out there, smoking and thinking, as the sun dipped behind
the smooth white tooth of Mount Belknap. He'd listen to the wind tickle the
pines. He'd wait for the screaming.

The footsteps came long before he saw the kid. Hard soles on gravel:
scrape-crunch, scrape-crunch, unhurried but steady. An old table sat next to
the porch swing. Henry felt along the lower shelf to where he kept his Ruger
Blackhawk. He didn't get a lot of visitors out at the cabin, which was tucked
off Beaver Creek Road on the dangling ass-hairs of Fishlake National Forest.
Nobody lived inside twenty miles. The closest town was Marysvale, which he
supposed you could call a town if you didn't want to call it what it actually
was: a shitsplat with a couple hundred surly Mormons and not even a working
laundromat.

So, anyway, who the fuck was this coming up his road?

The kid materialized a couple minutes later. He was tall and thin, with
long hair looped up into a ragged topknot. Dusty jeans and a denim shirt. He
carried a walking stick, swinging it lazily. An enormous campers' pack
bounced on his shoulders.

He saw the cabin and stopped. His shoulders slumped. He looked for a moment like he wanted to turn around. Then he lifted his hand and waved.

College kid, Henry thought as he raised his own hand. Not from BYU, not with that hair. Probably down from UT or up from Southern. That's where all the art farts seemed to end up.

Apparently deciding Henry was harmless (Henry thumbed back the Ruger's safety), the kid started walking again.

"Heya," he said. He stopped twenty feet away from the porch, keeping a respectful distance. Henry appreciated that. He took his hand from the revolver but left it within reach. Just in case the kid decided to get hinky.

"'Lo," Henry said.

"Is, uh...?" The kid made a show of looking around. "Am I anywhere near the Mount Baldy trailhead?"

Henry laughed. The kid stood there, smiling indulgently.

"Son, you're miles off," Henry said. He flapped his hand back the other way. "You gotta go back down to the road, then down *that* way another ten miles." He gestured to the South. "The trail ain't marked, but walking like you are, you oughta see it."

The kid gazed down the road. "Shit," he said, then: "Sorry, sir, I don't mean to curse."

Henry laughed again. "I don't give a fuck."

The kid grinned. "We're in Utah, so you never know." He sighed. "I suspected for the last couple miles I was in the wrong place. I didn't remember the trail being so wide."

"'Cause it ain't a trail at all," Henry said gently. He didn't want to hurt the kid's feelings, but he couldn't stop himself from pointing out the obvious. "It's a goddamned road."

The kid smiled and nodded. *Touché.*

"Yeah, my Spidey sense was pinging the moment I took the turn. But I was *certain* the trail was here. Classic confirmation bias, I suppose. Knew for sure I was in the wrong place when I saw your cabin."

Henry eyed the kid's backpack. "You been camping up this way before? It's late September in Utah, son. You're liable to freeze your dumb ass to death."

The kid patted the sleeping bag tied to the backpack's rails.

"Rated for subzero temperatures. And I've got one of those space blankets just in case."

Henry harrumphed and sucked on his pipe.

"I went up Mount Baldy with my ex-girlfriend a couple years ago, and it was frig…it was *fucking* gorgeous," the kid went on. "But we drove that time, and I guess I didn't remember the way as well as I thought I did."

In spite of himself, Henry was intrigued. The kid looked like one of those scruffy tree-huggers you saw loafing around Moab. But all those dip-shits spoke in that *woah…peace, bro* drawl they got from the movies. This kid sounded like a lawyer. Or, at least, like he hadn't left all his brains at the bottom of his roommate's bong. He spoke in complete sentences, for one thing.

"How the hell'd you get all the way out here if you didn't drive?" Henry asked.

The kid shrugged. "Hitchhiked."

"Up *Beaver Creek*? That's hardly more'n an old Jeep trail."

The kid shrugged again. "I hooked my way to Sulphurdale and wandered across the road to the nearest bait shop," he said, grinning. "I found this husband and wife down from Kanosh who were headed out to fish Trapper's Creek. Offered them forty bucks if they'd take me as far as the turnoff."

Henry nodded, impressed. "Well, you best get on walking if you want to make it," he said. "We're a cunt's hair from sundown. Hope you brought a lantern."

The kid laughed, enjoying Henry's profanity. Then he looked up at the rapidly descending sun, and the laugh died in his throat. "What's it, five miles back to Beaver Creek Road?"

"Seven and a half," Henry said. "Almost to the foot."

"Shit," the kid said again, then looked at Henry hopefully. "I don't suppose…you'd let me bunk down out here for the night? I've got my tent and my own food. I could just find a flat spot over there in those trees. You'd hardly know I was here."

Henry thought about it. The kid seemed harmless enough. And even if he wasn't, Henry had the Ruger.

But the kid wasn't the problem.

The problem was what he might hear.

Send him on down the road. It's for his own damn good.

But it was seven-and-a-half miles to the highway, another ten down to the trailhead, fifteen yet again up Baldy. The kid had clearly been hiking all day, and he looked wrung out. Fact was, he'd get just out of view of the cabin and set up in the woods anyway. Not anything Henry could do about that; he didn't own the land past the bend.

And if the screaming started, the kid would still hear it.

Maybe up here you can keep your eye on him.

"No skin off my ass," Henry said finally, and to his eternal regret. "Make yourself at home."

THE KID'S NAME was Payton Williston. He'd recently gotten back from nine months overseas, he said. He didn't explain, but Henry thought that probably meant military. *Got back and found out my apartment and my girlfriend were both gone*, he said with a papery laugh. *Hard old world, I guess.* Henry found himself liking Payton, in spite of himself.

Henry sat on the porch, sucking his pipe and watching Payton raise the tent. The kid worked with clean efficiency. The tent was red and gold, one of those expensive domelike deals with a mesh skylight and a fancy rainfly. It was easily big enough to sleep four; how the kid shoved it all down into his pack Henry didn't know.

The sun was almost gone by the time he finished. Thin, purplish light haloed Belknap's summit, which jabbed the sky like a dagger. Cold, indifferent stars sprayed out of the sky, surrounding a thin crescent of moon.

Once he was done, Payton settled into the tent for a while. Henry lit his own lantern and listened to Payton rustling around in there, watched the bob and sway of a bright white light through the fabric. After maybe twenty minutes, the kid squirmed out and ambled back across the road. One of those LED headlamps was strapped to his head. He switched it off before he got to the porch, so as not to blind Henry.

"I just wanted to say thank you again," he said. "I really appreciate you not running me off."

Henry sucked on his pipe, then surprised himself by gesturing to a folding lawn chair leaning against the rail. "Why don't you sit a minute and catch your breath?"

Payton smiled. "I guess I wouldn't mind that," he said and clomped up onto the porch.

His eyes snapped past Henry to the dirty window behind him. He froze.

"Someone else here?" Payton asked. His tone remained light, but there was a pinched quality to it and, without even realizing it, he shifted his body to the side. *Military for sure*, Henry thought, amused. He already knew what Payton had focused on; the hulking, slope-shouldered figure was impossible to miss even in the gloom beyond the window.

"Nawp," Henry said. "Just us. That right there's a beekeeper's suit. Got it hanging on an old department store mannequin. Found it in a dumpster down in Cedar City. The mannequin, I mean, not the suit."

"You keep bees out here?"

Henry sucked on his pipe. "Sure don't," he said.

Payton eyed him for a second, waiting to see if he'd elaborate. When Henry didn't, the kid opened the lawn chair and settled his lithe frame into it. It *twanged* under his weight.

"I gotta ask you something, sir," Payton said. "You've already been so generous, and I don't want to offend you. But my head is pounding and my back's killing me. I could really use a joint right now. Do you mind?"

"Don't mind a goddamned bit, so long as you share it."

Payton grinned and reached into his breast pocket. He produced an expertly rolled joint and a book of matches. The flame flared all across his face as he lit up, making him look momentarily ghastly. Then he shook out the match, took a drag, and passed the joint to Henry.

"So you're out here all by yourself?" Payton asked through a cloud of smoke.

Henry inhaled. It had been a long time since he'd partook the reefer, and his lungs—accustomed to the smooth oiliness of his tobacco—tried to fight it. He held his breath, wrestling them into submission. The taste was warm and rich. His mind filled with a sudden and pleasant fog.

"Yep," he said and passed the joint back. "Last five years. Used to live over in Beaver. My wife and I ran a garage, right there on Center Street. I worked on the cars and she kept the books. When she passed on, I just packed it all up."

"Oh, I'm sorry to hear that," Payton said.

"I'm not," Henry said. "I mean, I'm sorry about Emma. Sure I am. She was a goddamned peach. Prettiest girl you ever saw, back in her day. And smart as a whip. I woulda run the garage into the ground if it weren't for her. She kept us in the black. Five trips around the sun since, and I still miss her like she went yesterday. Wasn't sorry to let the business go, though. That kinda work ain't for an old man, and without Emma there to josh me about my ass crack hanging outta my jeans, it just…I guess it just felt sad. Haunted, like."

Payton nodded. "So what brought you out here?"

"This cabin used to belong to my daddy, and his daddy before him, and back and back and back. Old Mormon story. My great-granddad—or maybe my great-great-granddad, can't remember which—came on over from England and bought into the Prophet's patter hook, line, and sinker. Was one of the originals to come down from Salt Lake and settle Beaver. Then they run his ass out because he wouldn't take a wife or three and couldn't give up on the drinking and the whoring. So he come up here and built this cabin and kept himself to himself. At some point he married a Paiute, and I guess that lady was my great-great-grandma. My daddy and my brother used to use the place as a hunting lodge. Then, when my brother…when he passed, I was the only one left. So I guess it's mine now."

"And after you?"

Henry shrugged. "Emma couldn't have kids, and I don't think my nephew even remembers it exists. He's up in Oregon making computer chips and being the all-around human equivalent of the backdoor trots. I'll probably go in my sleep one night and ten years later some hunter will decide to poke around inside and find my bones. National Forest'll take it then, I reckon."

Payton made a face. "That's grim," he said.

Henry chuckled. "Is it? Don't strike me that way."

The kid offered the joint. Henry waved him off. His mind already felt sluggish. He didn't want to get so high he couldn't wake up. In case…

As if on cue, a coyote yapped. Payton glanced in the direction of the sound. Henry squinted, trying to decide if it actually *was* a coyote. It probably was.

"What about you?" Henry asked. "You got that old pioneer stock running through those veins?"

Payton nodded. "I suppose so. My mom's people didn't come out this way until the fifties. From Connecticut, originally, solid Presbyterian stock. But my dad's family was part of Brigham Young's original wagon train out of Missouri."

Henry eyed the joint in the kid's hand, which had burned down to a roach. "I'm guessing that old-time religion didn't take," he said.

Payton grinned. He licked his fingers and pinched off the joint. "Did for everyone else," he said.

"You down from Salt Lake?"

"Wrong direction," Payton said. "Up from St. George. I teach high school English. Well, student teach, actually. Close enough."

"I'll be damned," Henry said. "You struck me more like a snow bum than a desert rat."

Payton grinned. "It's the man-bun, right? Look like I should be running the chair lifts up in Park City?"

Henry laughed. "I suppose that's exactly what I thought."

"Desert rat through and through. Grew up outside Vegas, went right over to St. George for college. Did a two-year stretch there before, uh, before I went overseas." He held up a fist and offered a wry little smile. "Go 'Blazers. Anyway, I'm finishing up my final year now."

"I'll be damned," Henry said again. English teacher. Explained his smart way of talking.

Payton stood. "Well, I think I'm gonna turn in. Thanks again. Maybe I'll see you in the morning before I move on."

He started down the porch.

"Hey, kid."

Payton stopped and looked back. The flickering light from Henry's lantern made him look watery and insubstantial.

"You hear anything weird in the night, you just stay put," Henry said. "Don't go stomping around those woods looking for it. Okay?"

Payton cocked his head. Henry couldn't see the kid's face, but he could imagine the quizzical expression. "Weird? Like how?"

"Like anything," Henry said. "Sound is funny out here. Just…"

He licked his lips. They were suddenly very dry. His mind groped for the right words for what he was trying to say. They danced out of reach. It was the kid's marijuana. Henry cursed himself.

"Just stay in your tent," he managed finally.

He could barely see Payton nodding. "Okay," the kid said. "Sure thing." He switched the lamp back on and trudged across the road.

HENRY WATCHED PAYTON climb into his tent. The white light from his headlamp bounced around in there for a little bit and then snapped off. A few minutes later, the burbling sound of the kid's snores drifted across the road.

Henry looked up at the sky. Stars gazed pitilessly back. For a second it seemed like they were moving, but he figured that was just his eyes. They felt like they'd come untethered and were just bobbing around in their sockets like discarded pool toys. He extinguished the lantern, got to his feet, and stumbled toward the cabin's front door. The porch felt like the deck of a ship caught in a squall. Blood roared in his ears. His mouth felt like it was filled with cotton. *Fucking idiot,* he thought.

The cabin was a single room, all dark wood and a low ceiling. Shadows crawled up into the exposed rafters and crouched there, waiting. A double bed rested against the back wall, the once milk-white sheets yellow with age. A card table with a bent leg sat awkwardly in the other corner, next to an old wood stove that he never used. He did all his cooking on an old propane camp stove out on the porch.

The beekeeper's suit stood at the foot of the bed, standing watch like a sentry.

Henry lurched over to the bed and sat. Ancient springs protested. He stripped off the sweater and dropped it into the pile of dirty clothes next to the rusted wire milk crate he used as a bedside table. A smell wafted up at him: putrid, almost alive. It was getting time for his monthly trip down to the Wash House in Parowan.

He kicked off his boots and, after a few confused seconds of trying to remember how to work his belt buckle, managed to strip down to his skivvies. He flopped back onto the mattress, letting the squeal of the springs sink into his head like a drill. All those familiar lumps and coils kneaded his muscles. He pulled the old wool blanket over his body and rolled onto his side.

Give it a minute, he thought. *Don't drift off just yet. Just in case.*

Maybe it won't happen tonight.

Still. Just in case.

Right before sleep consumed him, he remembered that he'd left the Ruger out on the porch.

HENRY FLOATED ALONG on a warm, lymphatic haze. His head was a balloon and his body was a string, *lift-lift-lifting* into a sky the color of old tobacco. His heart *thud-thud-thudded* in the paper cavern of his chest. The sound of rushing blood was the surf slamming against a rocky black beach.

Emma was out on that beach. He saw her at a distance, wetted by sea spray, obscured by the brownish mist. She lurched along damp stones. Her mouth hung open, the jaw distended like the maw of some deep-ocean shark. She might have been smiling, or laughing, or maybe just screaming. He couldn't hear her because the surf had become a howl, and the howl filled the world.

Pinpricking that howl came the tremulous cry of an infant.

(*Oh no*)

The tiny voice rose and fell like a gently ebbing tide.

Vines wriggled like snakes through old pine needles. Pink flowers opened to a rust-colored sun.

"*Henry!*"

(*Wake up*)

"*Henry, help me!*"

Behind the flowers, a blackness.

A blackness that moved.

HENRY CLAWED DESPERATELY out of sleep. It clung to him like tar, tried to drag him back down. He pushed it roughly away.

Silence.

Then:

The cry was far off and plaintive, trickling out of the mountains like a brook.

"Shit," he said.

It was a baby's cry for sure. Not a coyote or an owl. The terror and anguish was unmistakable.

Outside, on the road: *scrape-thud, scrape-thud...*

Henry pushed himself up onto his elbows and shook his head, trying to clear the fog that still gripped at him with wet, slippery hands.

Footsteps clomped up onto the porch, and then the kid was banging on the door.

"Hold on!" Henry tried to shout. It came out a croak.

He managed to get to his feet and stumbled across the room. The floor pitched and yawed, and the door seemed like it was moving farther away rather than getting closer. *The fuck was in that reefer?*

Payton's fist thundered the door.

"Hold on I said!"

Henry swung it open. Payton stood there, shirtless but still in his jeans and boots. He clutched arms as white as fish bellies.

"You hear that?" he asked and looked up the road toward the mountains.

For a moment there was nothing. Then the cry rose again, ghostly and wrong.

"Yeah, I hear it," Henry said flatly.

"It's...is that a *kid*?"

Henry shook his head. "It's nothing. I told you, sound's funny out—"

"That's a fucking baby," Payton said. "Do you think there are other campers out here? It's pretty far to bring an infant."

"Could be," Henry said. "I don't know."

"It's—"

A scream split the night, and Henry closed his eyes. He knew this scream well and knew exactly what the kid would make of it.

"*Henry!*" Emma cried. "*Henry, help me!*"

Payton stepped back. His eyes were like saucers.

"No," Henry said, licking his lips. He took an unsteady step out onto the porch.

"The fuck is that?" Payton hissed, taking another step.

Henry tried to talk past the cotton that filled his mouth. His head felt swimmy and weird.

"It's not..."

"*Henry! Help meeee!*"

Henry took another step.

"It's not..."

The kid stepped back again. He was almost to the edge of the porch now. His eyes darted like he was a scared dog, itching to bite.

"I don't..." Henry said and realized there was no finish to that sentence.

"What the fuck did you do, old man?"

"I don't..."

Somehow Henry was on his knees. The blood roared in his ears, waves slamming a black beach, and Emma was out there, and she needed him.

That bitch is doing something to me, he thought. *She wants him and She won't let me stop him from coming.*

"*Henry! Help meeeeeee!*"

Payton scurried down the steps. Henry tried to call out, but the blackness rose up and took him.

HENRY WOKE TO sunlight and the piercing shriek of a faraway falcon.

It took him a moment to realize he was still on the porch, his cheek mashed into the rough wood. His neck hurt, his back screamed bloody murder, and his head pounded with the surly thud of a clamoring hangover.

He grunted and pushed himself up. The sun was high in the sky. That meant it was approaching noon. He'd been laying there, ass-up and face-down, for at least ten hours. Whatever happened to him, it wasn't the kid's marijuana.

Get off it, he told himself angrily. *You know exactly what happened.*

Henry blinked the sleep out of his eyes and gazed across the road. He saw, without any surprise, that Payton's tent was still there. If Payton had come back, he surely would have packed up and headed down the mountain by now. Henry also liked to think the kid wouldn't have just left him lying there on the porch.

She got him, he thought. *Sure as shit, She got him.*

But he had to be sure.

The fog had left his mind, at least. Evaporated under the heavy blast of sunlight. Henry gathered his legs beneath him. He put his hand on the table next to the swing and prepared to lever himself up. His eyes landed on the lower shelf.

The Ruger was gone.

He supposed he could figure what happened. When he'd been jawing with Payton on the porch, the kid must've seen it. Then, when the screaming started and the nice old man started acting like a goddamned lunatic, the kid must've decided to grab it. For protection from Henry, maybe, or from whatever was going on up the mountain.

Maybe he *did* come back. Maybe he was crouched over there in the tent, revolver cocked and waiting for Henry to approach.

Henry glanced at the tent again. It looked forlorn. Abandoned, like one of those ghost ships drifting for decades all around the Arctic Sea. The rainfly flapped drowsily in the light autumn breeze.

She got him, he thought again. A wave of unexpected sadness crashed down. Like a wave against a black beach.

Henry pushed himself to his feet and went inside.

IT TOOK HIM almost twenty minutes to put on the beekeeper's suit. He used to be able to get into it in less than five, but his old joints and arthritic fingers were working against him now. For a moment, he tried to recall how long it had been since he'd had a reason to wear it, then shook his head angrily. *Five years, you dumbshit. You haven't put it on since Emma.*

By the time he got outside, the day was sweltering. The inside of the beekeeper's suit was a wet oven. The mesh trapped his breath, and it slithered—mucosal and foul—up his nostrils.

He shuffled across the road toward the tent. The falcon screamed again, diving for a kill. Muffled by the suit, it sounded like a far-off train whistle.

"Hey!" Henry yelled. "Hey, kid, if you're in there with my gun, don't shoot, okay?"

No response. He hadn't really expected one.

He pushed back the tent flap and peered inside. It was dark in there, and the mesh obscured his vision even further. But it was clear Payton hadn't come back. That expensive sleeping bag gaped like something flayed. The silvery insides caught the dim light and glimmered.

Henry let the flap drop back into place. It waggled obscenely, like a tongue.

He'd have to come back and torch all the kid's shit. There was a bare patch behind the cabin, near where he parked his pickup. He had some gas cans in the bed; the fuel in there was old, but he thought it would catch. He'd just toss it all into a pile, soak it, and hope to hell he didn't burn down half the goddamned forest. If Payton told anyone where he was headed, they'd all think he got lost somewhere on the Mount Baldy trail. Henry's cabin was far enough up the road he didn't think anyone would come this way.

And if they do, what'll they find? An old man as clueless as they are.

Henry stepped out onto the road. He gazed down the way Payton had come, toward Beaver Creek Road, thinking he must have been more lonely than he realized to not send the kid away. He knew better. But it was sure nice to have someone to talk to, if only for a little bit.

He turned and looked the other way. Pine trees swallowed the road like a constricting throat. He could just see where the ground started to rise and the road became a trail.

You know what happened, he thought. *Ain't any mystery to it. So why go up there?*

Because he had to. He'd stayed out here for five years, and at first he told himself it was because hearing Emma's screams every night made him feel like she was still there with him. Even if he knew it wasn't really her at all. But that was just a lie he told himself; this was the real reason. He knew someone would come along someday, and he knew what would happen. It was Henry's job to clean it up. Like it had been his dad's. And his brother's.

He'd take some of the gasoline, for all the good it would do him.

A QUARTER OF the way up the trail, the heat fell suddenly out of the day. Even inside the suit Henry felt the sweat dry to a crust on his skin.

The ground steepened. He plodded on, the gas can banging against his shin. His breath came in ragged, choking gasps. Black spots exploded in front of his eyes, and he forced himself to stop and catch his breath.

He heard the falcon again, closer this time. Except this time it didn't sound so much like a falcon. There was a buzzy undertone to it.

"Hold on, you whore," he muttered. "I'm coming."

He continued on, slower this time. There wasn't any rush; it's not like She was going anywhere.

Eventually he came to a dead pine tree, split right down the middle from a lightning strike. The trail—hardly visible at all now—veered off to the right and looped through a toss of pinkish-white boulders before continuing into the foothills. Henry got to the tree and turned left. The packed dirt crumbled into loose shale. He picked his way carefully.

He hadn't been entirely honest with Payton. It wasn't that Emma *couldn't* have kids. It's that when she had one—more than forty years ago, now—the poor thing came out all wrong. Cyclopia, the doctors called it. Henry's only son had been born with one enormous and unseeing eye, a bony growth in the place of a nose, and a brain as scrambled as a bowl of mashed potatoes. He'd lived three hours and squalled the entire time.

They hadn't even given the child a name, simply had him cremated and scattered his ashes over in Bryce Canyon. And after that, Emma refused to try again, even though the doctors told her the next one would probably be different. She'd insisted Henry get a vasectomy, and he did so without complaint. Emma had never seen their son, but Henry had, and as thoroughly as his heart broke for the boy, the sight also stirred a terror in him that he never quite let go of.

After his brother disappeared (he could guess what happened), Emma and Henry began coming up to the cabin maybe two or three times a year. Looking back, he didn't quite understand why; it wasn't like this was anyone's idea of a vacation spot. The two of them would sit on the porch, never speaking as they listened to the screams and yaps from up the trail. Henry knew what was up there—everyone in the family did, except maybe for the idiot nephew in Oregon—but Henry had never seen it himself. Never had any desire to.

Then, one night five years ago, the screaming stopped. It was replaced by the plaintive cry of an infant.

For three days that went on. He knew he should've gotten Emma off the mountain. The hollowness creeping into her eyes told him what that sound was doing to her. But, for reasons unknowable, he didn't.

Emma knew better. But on the third night she waited for him to go to sleep and went up the trail anyway.

That morning—after he woke to find her gone—was the first and last time Henry put on the beekeeper's suit. It was old and yellowed even then; he thought his dad got it up in Salt Lake, or maybe even his granddad. Didn't matter. It wasn't a Hazmat suit, but it seemed to do the trick.

He went looking for Emma. Stepped off the trail at the split tree, which was where his father and brother said to turn.

And, eventually, he found *Her*. Like he knew he would.

The way was precarious, steep, and treeless, with treacherous ground.

He pushed on. He edged his way around the mountain until he came to a scatter of boulders and a copse of dead pine trees. They had no business growing this high up the mountain. Their fire-blackened trunks were twisted and bent like his own fingers.

An almost sheer granite wall rose just beyond the trees. A jagged crevice ran down the center of it.

Bulbous plants shaped like malformed pitchers sat scattered amongst the rocks and along the base of the trees. The skins were mottled green and brown. The wide, conical flowers sprouting from their rubbery lips were dazzling: neon pinks, reds, greens, yellows. It was a spray of color that—like the trees—didn't belong in the arid brown crags of Southern Utah. They were as alien to this place as an undersea jellyfish.

Henry's feet crunched over shale. He stood at the edge of the trees and set the gas can between his feet. The liquid sloshed inside.

The flowers turned to him. The leaves flattened into sun shapes, revealing red stigma that opened like proboscides. They began to whine.

Henry ignored them and scanned the ground. Green vines snaked out of the crack in the wall and splayed all around like cables. He could see parts of Payton here and there. Near one of the arciform trees lay a length of wetly glistening flesh that he thought was probably the meaty part of a thigh. Tangled in the vines between two of the pitcher plants was an arm worried down to the bone. The still-untouched hand curled up toward the sky.

Payton's torso hung across the crevice. The skin was mostly gone, and the wet ropes of muscle shimmered in the sun. Vines snaked in through gashes in the stomach, through the holes where the legs used to be, into the crimson patch that had been his groin. They twisted out of the arm holes, slithering across the chest and abdomen like tentacles feeling their way across the black depths of the ocean.

Payton's head hung limp on the neck. The rawhide was gone. Long hair fanned his face.

The Ruger lay beneath the torso, gleaming like new. *At least She had the consideration to polish it*, Henry thought acidly. It didn't matter. There was no way he was traipsing all the way over there to get it.

Payton's head tilted up slowly. The mouth fell open as a vine pushed out between the teeth. It fell across the chest like a tongue. The eyes were gone, and Henry saw tiny pink flowers growing in the sockets.

The flowers screamed.

Payton screamed.

A hundred different voices needled Henry's ears: all pleading for help, all threaded with startled agony. The infant's cry was buried in there, so light as to be almost indistinguishable. Henry shuddered to think about where She'd learned that sound.

Emma's voice was the loudest, of course. Or maybe it only seemed that way to Henry. "*Help me!*" she cried, the approximation so close to perfect that he wanted to go to her. Perfect but for the insectile rasp underneath it. Like if a wasp's nest figured out how to mimic a human voice.

His eyes went to the crevice. He felt *Her* moving in there: ancient and tumorous, blacker than the darkness that surrounded Her. And *knowing.* That was the worst part of it. She knew exactly what She was.

The vines began to crawl over his ankles, probing at the suit, looking for entry. Their caress was sensual, and Henry felt his balls shrivel at their touch.

He picked up the gas can and upended it, sloshing the liquid as far as he could reach without stepping into the nest. He'd done this the last time, too. It didn't matter. The plants and the flowers would shrivel to blackened husks. The vines would curl back into the crevice. And within days it would all begin sprouting again.

Henry supposed if the searchers made it up this far they might find what was left of Payton. Burned meat and shards of broken bone. Then maybe there'd be questions. Henry discovered he didn't care.

At least it would stop the screaming for a while.

The flowers sang as he set the now-empty gas can down and fumbled for the ancient Zippo tucked into the top of his boot. He touched the flame to the closest vine and scrabbled backwards. Fire roped up the vine, exploding through the pitcher plants. The screaming lost all human character, became the blat of a jet engine.

Maybe this time it'll work, he thought. *Maybe the fire will get in there and send Her back to that black beach She came from.*

But he could feel Her in there watching him. The bitch who took Payton. Who took his brother. Took his Emma. Took God knew how many thousands of others through the centuries. He didn't know if She had a face, but he knew She was smiling.

Flames licked at the sky, sooted the already blackened trunks of the pines.

He grabbed the empty gas can and trudged back the way he came.

Behind him, underneath the crackling, came the tittering, happy giggle of a baby.

ABOUT THE AUTHORS

NICK ROBERTS is a resident of St. Albans, West Virginia, and a graduate of Marshall University. He is an active member of the Horror Writers Association and the Horror Authors Guild. His short works have been published in *The Blue Mountain Review, Stonecrop Magazine, The Fiction Pool, Haunted MTL, The Indiana Horror Review*, and anthologies by publishers, such as J. Ellington Ashton Press and Sinister Smile Press. His novel, *Anathema*, won Debut Novel of the Year at the 2020-2021 Horror Authors Guild Awards. His second novel, *The Exorcist's House*, will be released in 2022 by Crystal Lake Publishing. Follow him at www.nickrobertsauthor.com, www.facebook.com/spookywv, www.twitter.com/nroberts9859, and www.instagram.com/spookywv.

MATTHEW R. DAVIS is an author and musician based in Adelaide, South Australia, with over sixty short stories published around the world. His novelette "Heritage Hill" was shortlisted for a 2020 Shirley Jackson Award and the WSFA Small Press Award, he won two 2019 Australian Shadows Awards, and he's been nominated numerous times for other honors. He's published a collection of horror stories, *If Only Tonight We Could Sleep* (Things in the Well, 2020), and one novel, *Midnight in the Chapel of Love* (JournalStone, 2021), with plenty of projects lined up for 2022. He's worked extensively on short films, video clips, and independent features, most recently as an extra on the splatterpunk movie *Ribspreader*; he plays bass and sings in heavy, progressive bands such as Blood Red Renaissance and icecocoon. When not working at various jobs or creative endeavors, he likes to spend time with his photographer partner and her lovely pest of a cat. Find out more about Matthew at www.matthewrdavisfiction.wordpress.com

ALEXANDR BOND has been writing since he was nine years old and has a love for the supernatural and cosmic horror ever since he first was introduced to H. P. Lovecraft. His work has been published in *Cosmic Horror Monthly* as well as a number of NaNoWriMo anthologies, and more can be found on his blog alexandrbond.wordpress.com. When not writing, he spends his time reading and learning; most recently, he is learning how to speak Deutsch. He currently resides in North Carolina with his family.

SCOTT HARPER has been drawn toward the fantastic since childhood. He endlessly read the terrifying tales of Dracula and the Zombie in the 1970s Marvel horror magazines, preferring them to the tepid books he read at school. Influenced by these works and authors such as Bram Stoker and John Steakley, Scott's writing combines horror and dark fantasy elements with comic book action. He enjoys training at the gym, lunches with his wife, and walking his two dogs when not writing. Find out more about Scott at www.scottharpermacabremaestro.com.

R.E. SARGENT is the author of three novels, four novelettes, and many short stories in the genres of suspense, supernatural, and horror. He is an active member of the Horror Writers Association, the Alliance of Independent Authors, and the Community of Literary Magazines and Presses. His short story, "Lucy," was featured in the 2021 Splatterpunk Award–nominated anthology *If I Die Before I Wake Volume 3 – Tales of Deadly Women and Retribution.*

R.E. lives in the Pacific Northwest with his wife and their Chocolate Lab. And the rain. Lots and lots of rain. He is thankful that writing is an indoor activity. Find out more about R.E. at

RICHARD CLIVE is a horror and science fiction writer who lives in the medieval town of Conwy, North Wales, with his wife, daughter, and pet Labrador. When not writing fiction, Richard works as a journalist but originally studied film and scriptwriting in Manchester. His stories can be found in several horror anthologies, including Sinister Smile Press' *If I Die Before I Wake - The Better Off Dead Series: Volume 5*, as well as the upcoming *Institutionalized*. Richard's short story collection, *Strange Frequencies*, will be published by Sinister Smile Press in mid-2022.

RENEE M.P.T. KRAY grew up in Michigan with eight siblings and a small army of cats. Her love of reading and writing went into maximum overdrive when she read *The Lord of the Rings* at age ten, and since then, she's spent her time obsessively scribbling story ideas into notebooks. After being homeschooled all through elementary and high school, she earned her BA in Literature from Ave Maria University and her MFA in English and Creative Writing from Southern New Hampshire University. She has self-published two collections of short stories: *Think Again: A Captivating Compendium* and *Restless: A Year of Ghost Stories*. However, none of these pursuits have been as challenging as trying to get her pug, Potato, to stop eating dirt. Find out more about Renee at www.reneemptkray.com.

WARREN BENEDETTO writes short fiction about horrible people doing horrible things. His stories can be found in anthologies from Scare Street, Black Hare Press, Devil's Rock Publishing, Black Ink Fiction, Ghost Orchid Press, Eerie River Publishing, Dark Lane Books, Sinister Smile Press, and Dragon Soul Press; in publications such as *Dark Matter Magazine*, *Sanitarium Magazine*, and *365Tomorrows*; and on podcasts such as *The NoSleep Podcast*, *Tales to Terrify*, and *The Creepy Podcast*. He studied Evolutionary Biology at Cornell University and has a Master's degree in Film/TV Writing from the University of Southern California. When he's not writing, he works as Director of Global Product Strategy at PlayStation, where he holds 20+ patents for various types of gaming technology. He is also the developer of StayFocusd, the world's most popular anti-procrastination app for writers. He built it while procrastinating. For more information, visit www.warrenbenedetto.com and follow @warrenbenedetto on Twitter.

DANIEL O'CONNOR was born in Brooklyn, NY. He lost both of his parents, and all grandparents, before he was eleven years of age. Reading played a major role in his being able to navigate through those challenges, while moving from family to family.

Daniel's recent novel, *Canni*, won the Independent Press Award and the NYC Big Book Award for Horror Novel of the Year. It was a finalist for same with Top Shelf Magazine. *Canni* was also the #1 requested horror title at Netgalley and has made the Amazon Horror bestseller list.

His previous novel, *Sons of the Pope*, reached #1 in four Amazon sales charts and has been praised in writing by writers and directors behind works such as *Dexter*, *True Blood*, *The Devil's Advocate*, *Only Son*, and the V.C. Andrews novels. An interview with Daniel can be found at www.booklife.com/oconnor.

STEVEN PAJAK is the author of novels such as the U.S. Marshal Jack Monroe series and the Mad Swine trilogy, as well as short stories and novellas. When not writing, Steven works as an administrator at a university. He continues to be an avid reader of Stephen King and Dean Koontz, John Saul, Richard Matheson, and many other favorite authors in the horror, suspense, thriller, and general fiction genres. Steven lives in the Chicagoland area with his wife and two teens. Find out more about

Steven at www.stevenpajak.com.

CURTIS A. BASS, from the American South, writes short stories in a variety of genres including science fiction, horror, mystery, and young adult. He's had stories published in online and print journals such as *Youth Imagination, Fabula Argentea, Page & Spine,* a *Scars Best of 2020* anthology, and an upcoming young adult anthology. When not writing he prefers to stay active ballroom dancing or downhill skiing. He is currently working on his second novel while his first remains hidden in a desk drawer. Find out more about Curtis at www.curtisstories.blog.

DAVID RIDER is the author of "Tweakers, Crane Girl and the Semi-pocalypse" on Kindle, as well as the novel series We Are Van Helsing.

As a teenager, he once visited Mackinac Island in Michigan, and the only monster he encountered was his own stupidity—somehow getting lost on an island eight miles around yet walking its interior footpaths for a full eighteen miles.

He lives with his wife and kids in a rural Midwestern town that also has confusing footpaths that he has recently gotten lost on while walking the dog. He clearly needs a compass.

GARY ROBBE is an educator and writer currently living in Colorado. He has numerous stories published in e-zines, magazines, and anthologies, and is an associate editor with Bewildering Stories. He is a member of the Horror Writers Association, the Rocky Mountain Fiction Writers, and is a founding member of the Denver Horror Collective.

SCOTTY MILDER is a writer, filmmaker, and film educator living in Albuquerque, New Mexico. He received his MFA in Screenwriting from Boston University, and his award-winning short films have screened at festivals all over the world, including Cinequest, the Dead By Dawn Festival of Horror, HollyShorts, and the H.P. Lovecraft Film Festival and CthulhuCon. His independent feature film *Dead Billy* is available to stream on Amazon.com and Google Play.

His short fiction has appeared or will appear in *Dark Moon Digest, KZine, Lovecraftiana Magazine,* as well as anthologies from HellBound Books, Dark Moon Books, Dark Peninsula Press, Dark Ink Books, and others.

He teaches screenwriting and film production at Santa Fe Community College and the Seattle Film Institute. He is also the co-host of *The Weirdest Thing* history podcast with actor/theatre artist Amelia Ampuero. You can find him online at scottymilder.com or www.facebook.com/scottymilderwrites.

MORE FROM SINISTER SMILE PRESS

THE BETTER OFF DEAD SERIES

Do you love IF I DIE BEFORE I WAKE – The Better Off Dead Series? The Better Off Dead Series delves into the farthest corners of your mind, where your deepest, darkest fears lurk. These masters of horror will haunt your dreams and stalk your nightmares, taking you to the edge of sanity before pushing you to the brink of madness! Read the series now!

If I Die Before I Wake Volume 1: Tales of Karma and Fear
If I Die Before I Wake Volume 2: Tales of Supernatural Horror
If I Die Before I Wake Volume 3: Tales of Deadly Women and Retribution
If I Die Before I Wake Volume 4: Tales of Nightmare Creatures
If I Die Before I Wake Volume 5: Tales of the Otherworldly and Undead
If I Die Before I Wake Volume 6: Tales of the Dark Deep
If I Die Before I Wake Volume 7: Tales of Savagery and Slaughter (6/6/2022)

THE LET THE BODIES HIT THE FLOOR SERIES

Let the Bodies Hit the Floor is the latest series from Sinister Smile Press, the creators of The Better Off Dead series. These volumes bring you the very best in horror/slasher/stalker/serial killer crime fiction. The more vicious and bloodier, the better. So, put on your pee-pee pants, because you're in for one hell of a dark, sinister journey.

A Pile of Bodies, A Pile of Heads Volume 1
A Pile of Bodies, A Pile of Heads Volume 2
A Pile of Bodies, A Pile of Heads Volume 3 (12/5/2022)

THE SINISTER SUPERNATURAL STORIES SERIES

The Sinister Supernatural Stories series brings you delicious horror that focuses on elements of the supernatural. Pull up a chair and dig in, but never after dark—everyone knows bad things always happen after dark.

Screaming in the Night: Sinister Supernatural Stories Volume 1

INSTITUTIONALIZED

Institutionalized is an upcoming anthology from the creators of The Better Off Dead series. This installment brings you stories of the mentally unbalanced, the damaged and disturbed, and the criminally insane. Some are locked up. Some are not. We recommend you sleep with one eye open.

Institutionalized (9/5/2022)

NOVELS/NOVELLAS/COLLECTIONS

Devil's Gulch: A Collaborative Horror Experience
Partum by EV Knight
Them by James Watts
Beast of Sorrows by James Watts
Shadows of the Damned by James Watts

Sinister Smile Press
Horror Themed Anthologies
and Collaborative Novels
Creating Nightmares is our Passion,
and business is good